x 19/12. 3/13
x 3/16. 2/17
x. 2/14. 8/20

The
Immorality
Engine

NEWBURY & HOBBES INVESTIGATIONS BY GEORGE MANN

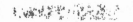

The
Immorality
Engine

A NEWBURY & HOBBES
INVESTIGATION

GEORGE MANN

A TOM DOHERTY ASSOCIATES BOOK
NEW YORK

This is a work of fiction. All of the characters, organizations, and events portrayed in this novel are either products of the author's imagination or are used fictitiously.

THE IMMORALITY ENGINE: A NEWBURY & HOBBES INVESTIGATION

A Tor Book
Published by Tom Doherty Associates, LLC
175 Fifth Avenue
New York, NY 10010

www.tor-forge.com

Tor® is a registered trademark of Tom Doherty Associates, LLC.

Library of Congress Cataloging-in-Publication Data

Mann, George.
    The immorality engine / George Mann.—1st ed.
        p. cm.
    "A Tom Doherty Associates book."
    ISBN 978-0-7653-2775-8
    1. Intelligence service—England—Fiction.   2. Murder—
Investigation—England—Fiction.   I. Title.
    PR6113.A546I66 2011
    823'.92—dc22

                                                        2011021548

First Edition: October 2011

Printed in the United States of America

0   9   8   7   6   5   4   3   2   1

For Fiona Jenny Mann. That completes the trilogy!

The
Immorality
Engine

CHAPTER

1

The soft loam sucked at his boots, thick and oozing, as if trying to pull him down into its slick, waterlogged depths, down amongst the corpses and the coffins and the dead. Newbury shifted, looking for somewhere even remotely dry to stand. All around him the ground was clotted with mud, made worse by the incessant rain that pattered like a drumbeat upon the brim of his hat. Mist, rising from the warm earth, curled around the forest of listing headstones, clinging to the trees and shrubs and casting the entire scene in an eerie, ethereal shroud. Figures moved like shadows, all dressed in black, their pale faces hidden behind veils or hands.

Nearby, crows were picking at the stringy flesh of a dead fox beneath the shelter of an ancient oak tree. Newbury watched them with a grim fascination.

Around the huddled group of mourners, a

perimeter of uniformed bobbies stood like ghostly sentries, half-visible in the vaporous morning, there to ward off roaming Revenants and other unsavoury things that loomed unseen in the shadows.

Graveyards such as this one had become the hunting ground of the soon-to-be-dead. Newbury wondered if perhaps the Revenants felt a kinship with the recently interred, or whether it was simply the lure of warm bodies that drew them in; people gathered in a quiet place, unsuspecting and too lost in their mourning to notice the shambling approach of the plague-ridden flesh eaters. He supposed it didn't really matter. Either way, he wasn't convinced a handful of bobbies would be able to stop the creatures if they decided to attack.

He looked around at the faces in the small crowd. There were six people attending the funeral. He couldn't help thinking there should have been more. He watched their unmoving shapes, hulked low against the torrential rain. They were there to bury Amelia Hobbes.

Newbury tried to listen to the words of the vicar, who conducted his sermon in a solemn, monotonous voice at the side of the grave. Beside him, a small altar boy clutched an umbrella as shelter for the holy man, but was bearing the brunt of the weather himself, soaked to the bone, his once-white robes now splashed with mud and dirt. A large pile of earth was heaped neatly beside the coffin-shaped hole, ready to be replaced once the ceremony was over. The scent of it filled Newbury's nostrils, fresh and damp.

Across from Newbury stood Mr. and Mrs. Hobbes, the parents of both the dead girl and her older sister, Miss Veronica Hobbes, Newbury's assistant, who stood beside him, unwilling to lift her face to meet their judgemental glares. Currently, the faces of the two middle-aged socialites were obscured, wreathed in drifting mist, but Newbury had spoken to them earlier and had seen only relief in their eyes. Relief to be free of the burden of their strange, tortured daughter: the girl who could see into the future.

Newbury had shaken their hands and offered his condolences, and had tried not to judge them too harshly. But having seen the manner in which they behaved towards Veronica, he had not been able to suppress a feeling of righteous indignation. It was clear to him that they were interested only in themselves, their fortune, and their reputation, and that their children were nothing but ornaments to be seen and admired. Amelia, broken, had been hidden away from prying society, moved from asylum to asylum, hospital to hospital, until only recently when Newbury himself had intervened, calling on the mercy of Her Majesty the Queen to have the unfortunate girl taken into the private care of Dr. Lucien Fabian, the Queen's personal physician.

Fabian's efforts had been an abject failure, but Newbury knew there was far more to it than that. The whole matter had been a terrible travesty, a betrayal of the worst kind. And of course Fabian wasn't here to see his charge put in the ground.

On the other hand, Dr. Mason, the man who had looked after Amelia during much of her decline, in the period preceding her transfer to Fabian's Grayling Institute, was in attendance. He seemed more concerned for Veronica than he did for himself, his eyes trained on her throughout the service. Newbury decided this was an admirable trait, although he couldn't help feeling a spark of annoyance at the other man's attention.

To Newbury's right was Sir Charles Bainbridge, Chief Inspector of Scotland Yard, fellow agent to the Queen, and his dear friend. Bainbridge was older than Newbury by a decade, approaching his late forties, and he walked with a cane, his left foot damaged during some long-ago adventure. He wore a bushy grey moustache and a stiff top hat and looked bedraggled by the weather, even huddled beneath a heavy winter overcoat. He was staring into the hazy distance, lost in his own thoughts.

Newbury glanced at Veronica, who stood to the left of him. She was clearly distraught, sobbing openly, her head bowed. Her dark hair was lank and wet, clinging to her pale cheeks, but she seemed oblivious to the weather. The rain could do little to disguise the tears that streamed freely down her face.

Newbury looked up at the sound of footsteps. The pallbearers were approaching with the coffin.

Newbury moved closer to Veronica as they watched the men lower the coffin into the slick, waterlogged hole in the ground. Veronica stifled a single sob. The vicar continued to drone on, talking now of birth and resurrection. Newbury sighed. *Birth and resurrection.* That was what this was all about, one way or another.

The six pallbearers retreated slowly from the sides of the grave, their boots squelching in the sticky mud. Veronica stepped forwards, grabbed a handful of soil from the muddy bank, and cast it into the hole. "Good-bye," she said solemnly, then turned her back on the grave to face Newbury, a defiant gleam in her eyes.

Newbury watched her parents over her shoulder as they mumbled disapprovingly to each other. He smiled at Veronica, trying not to let her see his disdain. "Come on. Let's get you out of this dreadful rain, Miss Hobbes."

Veronica nodded silently. Her eyes were rimmed with red, her face forlorn. Abandoning all sense of propriety, Newbury stepped forwards and wrapped his arms around her shoulders, pulling her close. "Veronica. Come now, before you catch a chill." He whispered quietly in her ear. "This place will do you no good."

She leaned in closer to him, resting her head on his shoulder. He felt her body shaking with tears. For a moment, it seemed to Newbury as if they were alone in that sad, misty place; the other figures, all dressed in black, became nothing but inky smudges, hazy and out of focus. At that moment, only Veronica mattered.

Newbury led Veronica gently away from the congregation and towards the row of waiting carriages, nodding once at Bainbridge, whose face was creased with concern and infinite sadness.

Newbury did not look back again as he helped Veronica step up into the carriage and climbed in after her, dripping rainwater over the seats. He sat beside her, taking her hand in his own. "Lead on, Driver."

The drumming of the raindrops on the roof drowned out any response from the man hunched on the dickey box outside, but the horses juddered suddenly into motion, knocking Newbury and Veronica back into their seats. The wheels creaked as the carriage eased away into the foggy morning.

CHAPTER

2

There was a definite aroma about the place. Not unpleasant, Veronica thought, but distinctive, unusual. The mingling scents of herbal teas, tinged with the sweet stink of opium. She peered in through the open door.

Chinese men lounged about, carousing and laughing, or engaging in serious conversations at the many scattered tables while drinking tea and smoking cigarettes. Amongst them, waiters dressed in white smocks hurtled about, slinging armfuls of crockery about them with a practised ease.

Veronica looked up at Bainbridge, who was regarding the place with a wary eye. "It looks innocuous enough," she said. "Are you sure this is the place?"

Bainbridge nodded. "Indeed so. This is the place."

"Then where is he?"

Bainbridge shrugged. "I suspect they have another room out the back. A . . . lounge area."

Veronica smoothed the front of her dress. "I shall go inside and make enquiries."

Bainbridge puffed out his chest and turned towards Veronica with a stern expression. "You, Miss Hobbes, will kindly wait out here. This is no place for a lady."

"Poppycock!" she exclaimed loudly, causing one of the waiters to look round in surprise. "I'll have none of it." She led the way through the small doorway, not looking back at Bainbridge, in case he tried to stop her.

She looked incongruous in such tawdry surroundings. Dressed in an immaculate grey suit, her long skirt swishing about her ankles, her dark hair pinned back expertly from her pretty face, she was the very picture of a professional woman. Only the lively pink of her blouse and the set of her jaw betrayed her determination to be different from the other women of her age, who she thought spent their time sewing or mewling over men and had very little that was exciting in their lives.

Veronica had decided long ago that she would not embrace that life, and had subtly guided herself towards one that had her visiting unsavoury establishments such as the one in which she was now, or worse, indulging in adventurous undertakings that could in no way be considered proper pursuits for a woman of station. And that was exactly the way she liked it.

This particular establishment was known as Johnny Chang's Tearooms, renowned as a den of thieves, pickpockets, and newly arrived sailors from the East. The place had another reputation, too: a haven for fallen gentlemen, a place where one might go to dabble in the mystical arts or freely imbibe that dreadful oriental weed, opium. The drug had become known as the scourge of the East, but—Veronica thought wryly—it had become the scourge of the British upper classes, too. So many good men had been lost to its poison. In its way, the opium curse was as foul a disease as cholera or the Revenant plague, only it affected the rich and poor alike, and was a thousand times more insidious.

Veronica stared at the blank faces all around her. She could barely believe that Newbury would choose to patronise a place such as this.

She stood motionless as a Chinese waiter shuffled past, his arms laden with teacups and dirty bowls. A hush had fallen over the patrons as they stared openly at her, a mix of puzzlement, lechery, and suspicion on their faces.

One of the waiters approached her. He was a small man with clipped black hair and a broad, toothy grin. "May I help you, madam, sir?" He gave a swift bow of his head to both Veronica and Bainbridge in turn, making sure to keep his eyes on them at all times.

Veronica was about to speak when Bainbridge bustled forwards and raised his cane in a threatening fashion. Veronica noticed the people around the edges of the room bristle in anticipation. "You can stop with all that *politeness* and smiling straightaway. I know what sort of place this is," he barked, full of bluster and unnecessary confrontation. His moustache twitched, as if in disgust. "My name is Sir Charles Bainbridge of Scotland Yard and I'm making enquiries after a gentleman. I have reason to believe he . . . frequents this establishment."

The waiter smiled, then shrugged in a placatory fashion. "I am sorry, sir. I do not understand of what you speak." He motioned to the tables around them, to the vagabonds and thieves who were still eyeing the two interlopers warily. "As you can see, your friend is not here." The waiter took a step back from Bainbridge and bowed his head again. "I am sorry I cannot be of service to you today." It was clear this was intended as a dismissal.

Bainbridge practically snorted in fury. "Now, look here! This is wholly unsatisfactory. I demand to know where I may find Sir Maurice Newbury!"

The waiter's face was impassive.

Veronica put her hand on Bainbridge's arm. "Sir Charles. Please stop."

Bainbridge gave her a scornful look, but seemed to visibly draw back from the smaller man, expelling a long sigh.

Taking matters into her own hands and refusing to let go of Bainbridge's sleeve, Veronica pulled him on towards the rear of the premises, pushing past the waiter, and refusing to make eye contact with the three men who sat at a small table against the back wall, playing cards and smoking. One of them watched her with a wry smile, clearly enjoying the show. She saw him call off the two men beside him: larger, bulkier men—bodyguards, she presumed—who were both preparing to rise from their seats to challenge her. She wondered if this were the eponymous Johnny Chang. Whatever the case, he appeared to be granting her passage, but for what reason, she could only guess.

The waiter called out loudly behind them, but Veronica ignored him and stormed on. A heavy red curtain was draped over an open doorway in the rear wall. She supposed this was what separated the main tearoom from the less salubrious establishment in the back.

"Through here." She led the Scotland Yard inspector through the curtain into the shadowy room beyond, still ignoring the effervescent protests of the waiter. The man seemed reluctant to give chase beyond the threshold of the tearoom, as if doing so would somehow take him from the safety of his own domain to somewhere much more danger-ous and terrifying. A realm beyond the bustling world of tea-cups and cigarette smoke that he usually inhabited. A world filled with the ghosts of the living.

At least, that was how it seemed to Veronica as she passed beneath the velvet curtain and into the large, sumptuously decorated room beyond.

The lighting was dim, and it took her eyes a moment to adjust. Heavy fabric drapes hung on the walls in reds and greens, and the windows had been covered with thick cur-tains. Little clusters of divans and chaises longues, each piled with colourful silk cushions, were placed carefully to form discrete, distinct areas for the patrons. The supine forms of innumerable men lay draped upon the furniture, drowning amongst the puddles of soft fabric. The air was thick with the sickly sweet aroma of the opium, but aside from the sounds spilling through from the tearoom, the place was shrouded in silence.

A Chinese man in red silk drifted amongst his vacuous-looking clientele, tending to their needs, refilling their pipes, and rearranging their cushions. The skirts of his cheongsam whispered across the tiled floor, giving Veronica the strange impression he was floating, a spirit made flesh. The notion was exaggerated by the curls of oily smoke that hung in the air like wraiths, rising from the still bodies like souls evacuating the dead.

Veronica coughed and put a hand to her mouth, choking on the thick vapours.

Bainbridge was looking around, his eyes wide. "The excess!" he exclaimed. "The decadence!" He shifted his weight onto his cane, as if weighed down by the simple fact of being in such a hedonistic place. "Can you see him?"

Veronica shook her head. She moved slowly into the room, finally releasing her grip on Bainbridge's arm, and wandering between the low divans and heaps of cushions in search of Newbury. She stepped over the splayed legs of a semiconscious Chinese man whose eyelids fluttered briefly but without interest as she passed by. She heard Bainbridge's footsteps fall in behind her.

The attendant paid the two of them little heed as they went about their search, glancing up only once before continuing to drift between his patrons, unconcerned by their sudden appearance or the commotion they had caused at the front of the house. Veronica wondered absently whether he, too, was operating under the influence of the soporific drug.

They moved methodically from divan to divan, from chaise longue to chaise longue. The clientele formed a rich mix of cultures and classes. More than once Veronica thought she'd found Newbury, only to realise upon closer inspection that it was just another fallen gentleman, still trussed up in his formal attire, lounging decadently without a care in the world. She hated to think of Newbury in those terms, to identify him with these layabouts. She knew he was different, that he used the drug for other reasons, to open his mind, to allow himself to think. At least, that's what he insisted, and what she wanted to believe. She knew Bainbridge was far less forgiving of Newbury's vice, and suspected she was deceiving herself. But it was a little lie, and it enabled her to carry on.

Veronica finally found him stretched out on the floor amongst a heap of cushions, near the back of the large room, apparently unconscious. He was wearing his usual dark suit, but the collar was open, his necktie loose around his throat. A spent pipe was discarded by his left hand, and his flesh had assumed a deathly pallor. He looked thin and uncared for, with pursed lips and bruised eyes. His raven-coloured hair was unkempt and plastered to his forehead with perspiration, and his breathing was short and shallow. His right hand lay limp upon his chest.

Veronica suddenly couldn't breathe. Her hands felt cold and clammy. She couldn't bear to see him this way. She wanted to rush to his side, but she knew it would do neither of them any good. He looked ill. He looked . . . close to death.

Veronica took a moment to gather herself. Just as she was about to say something, Newbury licked his lips and spoke. "Go away, Charles." He hadn't opened his eyes, and his voice was a dry, rasping croak.

Bainbridge looked momentarily flustered. "How did you—?"

Newbury slowly peeled open his eyelids. His pupils were

pinpricks in the semidarkness. "The cane, Charles. I knew it was you the moment you entered the room."

Bainbridge glanced down at his cane, perplexed.

Newbury turned his head to regard Veronica. "And Miss Hobbes, too." He closed his eyes again. "What the devil are you doing bringing a lady to a place like this?"

Bainbridge flushed. "Well, I . . ." He slammed the end of his cane down hard against the tiled floor. "Get up, you damn wastrel! Do you hear me? Get up! I have no time for your foolish games."

Newbury grinned. His fingers twitched, but otherwise he didn't move.

Veronica dropped to one knee beside him. She put her hand to his face. His cheek was damp and unshaven. "Maurice. We need your help."

Newbury sighed. He turned towards her and opened his eyes. There was a gleam there that had been missing before. "Then, I suppose, Miss Hobbes, that's a different matter altogether." He shifted, pushing himself up into a sitting position. He glanced warily at Bainbridge, who was peering down at him with a disdainful expression. "What is it that's so pressing, you had to come and find me here?"

Bainbridge reached down, cupped Newbury beneath the arm, and helped him to his feet. "If your brain's not too addled to understand me, Newbury, I'll tell you on the way."

CHAPTER

3

Contrary to Bainbridge's assertion, the journey from Johnny Chang's passed in awkward, embarrassed silence.

Bainbridge stared out of the carriage window, his face creased in a deep frown, watching the city roll by as the steam-powered hansom clattered noisily over the cobbled roads. He refused to look at Newbury, who was slumped on the opposite seat, his eyes lost in shadow, his chin resting forlornly on his chest. His hair was lank and he looked haggard. He smelled of stale sweat and tobacco smoke.

Veronica tried not to stare, instead shooting furtive glances in his direction. She found herself wishing she could hear his thoughts. It pained her to see him in such a sorry state. She wanted nothing more than to grab him, shake him, and slap him hard across the face, then hold him and tell him that everything was going to be well. But she couldn't, for a thousand reasons.

She could not promise him that. She did not know with any conviction that everything *was* going to be well.

Newbury's addiction to the oriental weed had grown steadily more acute over recent months. It had begun with the occasional absence from the office. This in itself was not unusual for Newbury, who was often called away at short notice by the Queen, or found himself tied up in a case with Sir Charles and unable to meet his more prosaic commitments.

But the absences had grown more frequent, more erratic, and more keenly felt by others further abroad than the museum. Veronica had even been hauled before Her Majesty to give account of herself, to explain why Newbury had not attended the Court's summons and why Veronica was failing in her duty to keep him from straying. The monarch had admonished her gravely and ordered her to bring the errant Newbury to heel.

Sir Charles, too, had called on her on more than one occasion, partly to express his concern for his absent friend and partly to solicit her input on certain cases, which was only too welcome a distraction. Veronica suspected that Sir Charles also felt some measure of responsibility for her in Newbury's absence, as if she somehow needed protecting and it fell on him to take the place of his friend during this "temporary period of illness," as he had begun to call it.

She supposed it *was* a form of illness: a malaise of the spirit, perhaps, and a sickness of the body. Newbury had come to rely on a drug he once told her was a tool, the means by which he achieved the clarity of thought that helped him to solve his cases. But his need had become a physical one, and his body craved the weed. It became so integral to his process—to his daily life—that he now found it impossible to operate without it. And if he knew what a detrimental effect it was having on his health, he refused to acknowledge it.

Sir Charles was wrong: this wasn't a phase that was going to blow over. And no matter what she told herself, Newbury could not continue in such a fashion. She would have to intervene. But not for the reasons Her Majesty had impressed upon her: for Queen and country and the safety of the realm. She would do it for Newbury, because she loved him, and because she refused to stand by and watch him commit a slow and degrading suicide. He would have to learn to live without the drug. There was no other choice. The only problem, she admitted to herself, was the fact that she hadn't the slightest idea how to begin.

So instead she joined the two men in their silence, each of them avoiding the only subject that was playing on their minds.

Soon enough, the hansom sputtered to a stop outside the police morgue, and the driver rapped loudly on the roof to inform them that they had reached their destination.

Bainbridge was up and out of the cab before Veronica had even had a chance to gather her thoughts. She heard him barking commands at the driver, which did little to dispel the sense of tension between them. She looked over at Newbury, who was still slouched over in his rumpled suit. "Sir Maurice. We have arrived."

Slowly, groggily, Newbury raised his head. He glanced out of the window with bleary eyes. "Yes, indeed, Miss Hobbes." His voice was little more than a dry croak. Veronica was beginning to wonder whether dragging him out of the opium den hadn't been a huge mistake.

Then, as if digging deep into the reserves of his strength, Newbury pulled himself upright, groaning in protest, before beckoning for Veronica to exit the carriage ahead of him.

Outside, Charles was tapping his cane impatiently on the pavement. Veronica stepped down and took her place beside him, hoping that his simmering temper would soon abate. She didn't want to find herself in the middle of another row.

Newbury emerged into the searing daylight a moment later, squinting up at the austere building behind her. A smile played momentarily on his lips. "The morgue?"

"Well, of course it's the bloody morgue!" said Bainbridge, barely containing his frustration.

This appeared to pique Newbury's interest. He raised one eyebrow, and Veronica caught another glimpse of the old gleam in his eyes. "What brings us to this most dreadful of places, dear Charles?"

"A body. What else would it be?" snapped Bainbridge in a condescending tone.

Veronica rolled her eyes. "I'm not sure this is helping, Sir Charles. . . ." It was clear to her that he was deeply concerned for his friend, but was far too reserved to be able to express it by any means other than frustration. Newbury would understand this, of course, but had always enjoyed baiting the older man. Recently, this combination had proved rather more explosive than was healthy for either of them.

Bainbridge sighed, relenting. "Yes. I need you to see this body, Newbury."

Newbury grinned. The colour seemed to be returning to his cheeks. "To establish a cause of death?"

"No. To identify the victim."

Newbury ran a hand over his bristly chin. "Very well. Lead on, then!"

Veronica couldn't help feeling relieved at the enthusiasm evident in his voice—even if it *was* enthusiasm for a corpse.

The morgue was cold and unwelcoming. Veronica felt a chill pass down her spine as she stepped over the threshold and through the double doors. Or perhaps it was something more. Trepidation? Fear? Unease? She'd never felt comfortable around corpses and she hoped she never would. She'd seen plenty of them in her time—even taken a life in the course of duty—but something about seeing a human body laid out in such a way filled her with a terrible sense of dread. She hated how a person—a living, breathing, intelligent person—could be reduced to this, to nothing but an unmoving mass of flesh; how all that potential could so easily be invalidated. It was as if everything they stood for, everything they'd experienced or seen or had yet to see were suddenly worth nothing. All their deeds and loves and foibles: all of them amounting to this. A slab of meat on a slab of stone, ready to be butchered. Sometimes, seeing a corpse like that made her wish she hadn't lost her faith in God. Living in a Godless universe could be bleak and dark, and the reality of death was a black cloud that scared her more than anything else in the world. Fear, however, could not distract her from what she saw as an ultimate truism: that God did not, and never had, existed.

Other times she wished she could be more like Newbury, able to disassociate himself from his emotions, to examine a corpse and see a puzzle there, to look past the dead person to the mystery beneath. But, truthfully, she was glad she was still shocked by such sights, and glad that she had not become so cynical or worn down by her experiences that they were now merely commonplace to her.

This, she mused, was one of those days. She wanted dearly to be anywhere but in the morgue, anywhere away from the stench of death and decay and the sight of bloated, festering corpses and the remains of people who had met untimely ends.

So when the tall, thin mortuary attendant ushered the three of them inside, giving Veronica the most disdainful of looks, she almost wished she could find an excuse to wait outside. But she knew that was out of the question and refused to bow to stereotypes. She would steel herself and press on. It was, after all, only flesh and blood. The dead people themselves had no further need of it.

The mortuary attendant—so pale himself that he could quite easily have passed for one of the corpses—looked down his nose at Newbury, then turned towards Bainbridge, raising a disapproving eyebrow. "Sir Charles. Another most irregular visit. How can I be of assistance to you and your . . . associates?" His voice was reedy and nasal. He held his hands out before him, his fingertips pressed together to form a spire before his chest.

Bainbridge pursed his lips and Veronica saw his knuckles whiten on the handle of his cane. For a minute she thought the chief inspector might strike the insolent fellow, but he managed to restrain himself. "You can help, *my dear fellow*"—he exaggerated those last three words to indicate his impatience with the man—"by taking me and my *associates* to see the unidentified body that was brought in by my men two nights ago." He twitched his moustache testily.

"The young man in the suit? The suspected criminal?" The mortuary attendant seemed incredulous, as if he couldn't quite understand how the three people before him could want to sully themselves with such distasteful business.

Bainbridge glowered but did not respond.

After a moment, the mortuary attendant shrugged. "If you'd care to follow me." He turned, holding his head high, and strode off into the labyrinthine warren of corridors that sprang from the reception area, his footsteps echoing loudly off the tiled walls.

Bainbridge set out after the attendant, and Veronica followed with Newbury, sliding her arm under his, supporting him as they walked. It was as much for her own comfort as for his, of course—as they wound their way deeper into the building, beneath the acid glow of the lamps and the gleaming, tiled archways, she felt a knot tightening in her stomach.

The place was filled with the stink of blood and faeces, the tang of iron. As they walked, Veronica became aware of the atrocious sounds of the surgeon's art: the rasp of a bone saw, cutting through the voiceless dead. The sound of fluid spattering on tiles. A man coughing and spitting. The wet thump of an amputated limb dropping to the floor.

She clutched Newbury's arm a little tighter. For the first time that day, he turned towards her and she actually felt that he was seeing her. He patted her hand, took a deep breath, and seemed to grow in stature. It was as if being needed was somehow enough to rejuvenate him, to refresh him. As if it were the lifeblood that sustained him, imbued him with vigour. Was it neglect, then, that had driven him to such terrible depths? Was it loneliness?

It seemed Bainbridge had been right, whatever the reasons. What Newbury needed was a good mystery, some solid work. She wondered what he would make of the chief inspector's little puzzle.

The mortuary attendant led them to a quiet corner of the morgue, where the body they had come to examine was laid out on a marble slab and covered in a thin white shroud. It was cool in the morgue, but the cadaver had already started to smell. Veronica wrinkled her nose in disgust. She hoped that Newbury wouldn't want to do anything more invasive or prolonged than take a quick look.

"If you have no further need of me . . . ?" said the mortuary attendant in his snide, reedy voice. Bainbridge offered him a curt nod in reply, and, with a haughty expression, he turned about and left the room.

Newbury turned to smile at Veronica, then extracted his arm and approached the slab. He hovered for a few seconds by the side of the body. "So, Charles. What's the story?"

Bainbridge frowned, as if unsure where to begin. "He was found on Shaftesbury Avenue, the night before last. Lying in the gutter. No obvious cause of death." He shrugged. "There are some . . . confusing circumstances. Take a look—see if you recognise the poor beggar."

Newbury wiped his brow with his shirtsleeve. He was sweating despite the chill. Veronica wondered if that had something to do with the opium he'd imbibed this morning, or if his body was already beginning to crave more.

Gently, Newbury took hold of the shroud and peeled it back, slowly revealing the body beneath. Veronica blanched at the sight of the waxy, bloated face, its eyes still open and staring, but now milky and sunken. The corpse had been stripped by the police surgeons and looked pale in the harsh yellow glow of the lamplight.

Newbury walked slowly around the slab, poking and prodding the body, spending a minute or two examining the face, rolling the corpse onto its side so that he could take a look at the dead man's back. His expression gave very little away.

After a minute or two more, he stepped back from the slab and looked directly at Bainbridge. "Clearly, Charles, this is Edwin Sykes. I'm sure there are a hundred men who could have corroborated that for you. Why drag me halfway across London to see his corpse?"

Bainbridge smiled. "What do you suppose killed him?"

"Confound you, Charles, for dodging my question. I can't see any obvious cause of death. Probably a heart attack, but there'd need to be a full autopsy to be sure. He's clearly been dead for a couple of days." Newbury rubbed a hand thoughtfully over his chin. "I should have thought you'd be pleased, Charles, to know that one of the most notorious burglars in London is on a slab?"

Bainbridge chuckled. "And there's the rub, Newbury. There's the rub. You see—as you've confirmed—Sykes has been dead for at least a couple of days. We've had his corpse in the morgue for two nights, guarded and locked in this room. But last night a burglary was committed on Regent Street that has all the hallmarks—down to the very last detail—of Sykes's work. So either something very unusual is going on, or Sykes was never our burglar in the first place."

Newbury looked thoughtful for a moment, before his expression broke into a wide grin. He glanced at Veronica. "Very well. It seems the two of you have my attention. So what next? Regent Street and the scene of the burglary?"

Veronica shook her head. "No, Sir Maurice. Chelsea, and the scene of a bath."

Newbury looked down at his rumpled suit, clearly embarrassed. He smiled sheepishly. "As you command, my dear Miss Hobbes. But first, answer me this: What of Sykes's personal effects? Had he been robbed?"

Veronica gestured towards Bainbridge, who pulled a small rectangular object from his trouser pocket and held it out to Newbury. It was a crumpled address card. Newbury took it and turned it over in his palm. It was emblazoned with the legend, PACKWORTH HOUSE.

"That's all we found on him. No wallet, no jewellery, no papers. Just that card, stuck in the lining of his jacket pocket. Whoever stripped him of his personal effects must have missed it."

Veronica nodded. "It seems as if it was more than just an opportunistic robbery. I find it hard to believe that someone happening across his body in the street would take such care as to remove *all* the contents of his pockets. What purpose could it serve them? The valuable items, yes. But his papers? To do so, they must have spent some considerable time beside the body, risking being seen all the while. It seems somehow . . . unlikely."

Newbury frowned and handed the card back to Bainbridge, who tucked it away in his pocket once more. "Packworth House. Isn't that the home of the Bastion Society?"

"Yes," Bainbridge said. "It seems he was a member of that illustrious set. No doubt bought his way in with all that plundered money."

"Or not," Newbury countered, "if, as you say, he wasn't your burglar after all. The circumstantial evidence certainly suggests not. And you never *were* able to pin anything on him."

"Hmmm," was Bainbridge's only response.

Veronica approached the slab and picked up a corner of the shroud. She tried not to look too closely at the grisly, staring face of the dead man or breathe in his ghastly scent. "Sir Maurice?"

Newbury took the other side of the shroud. Together they covered the body once again—the body of Edwin Sykes, or someone who looked *very* much like him.

CHAPTER

4

"For God's *sake*, Newbury! Look at the state of this place."

Bainbridge thumped into Newbury's drawing room with a thunderous roar, like a bear with a proverbial sore head. He strode first towards the sideboard, which was heaped with dirty wineglasses and plates, then to the fireplace and Newbury's favourite armchair, around which thirty or forty newspapers had been discarded haphazardly on the floor. He knocked a heap of tobacco ash off the arm of the chair with his cane.

Veronica sighed. Just when she thought he'd finally begun to calm down.

"Mrs. Bradshaw!" Bainbridge continued to bellow at the top of his lungs. He charged towards the door, flung it open, and shouted down the stairs, calling for Newbury's housekeeper. "Mrs. Bradshaw! Get up here at once!" He turned to Newbury. His voice lowered a fraction, but his tone was still harsh, critical. "I know you're no disciplinarian, Newbury, but this really is unforgivable. What happened here?"

Veronica tried to take in the situation. Bainbridge was right: The place was in a miserable state. The curtains were still drawn, even though it was now midafternoon, and the room smelled of stale tobacco smoke and sweat. It clearly hadn't been aired for days. Worse were the stacks of dirty plates and unwashed glasses and the smaller piles of tobacco ash from Newbury's pipe, left spotted around the room in various bizarre locations: the windowsill, the coffee table, the arm of his chesterfield. It was as if Mrs. Bradshaw had given up trying.

"Mrs. Bradshaw!" Bainbridge was beginning to grow red in the face.

Newbury crossed the room and put a placating hand on his friend's shoulder. "She's gone, Charles."

Bainbridge looked flustered and confused. "Gone? Where? Have you granted her leave?"

Newbury shook his head, and Veronica felt a pang of sadness as the gravity of his situation sank in. She really had gone. He'd chased her away. "She gave up on me, Charles," Newbury continued, "and I can't say I blame her. I kept unsociable hours. I had the most irregular habits. . . ." He trailed off. Veronica knew that he wouldn't be able to give voice to the real reason Mrs. Bradshaw had left his service, but they were all very much aware of it. She could not watch his descent into addiction, or what it had made of him.

Something seemed to break, then, inside Bainbridge. His expression softened. All the rage, all the disdain seemed to pass out of him, and all that was left was the deepest concern for his dear old friend. Veronica watched as he placed his arm around Newbury's shoulders. "Buck up, old chap. We'll put it right. We'll get things back on track."

Newbury sighed. "Pop the kettle on, Charles. I haven't had a good pot of Earl Grey for some time."

Bainbridge gave him a hearty slap on the back. "I'll get to it, Newbury. Right away. I'm sure Miss Hobbes here will run you a bath in the meanwhile."

Newbury smiled thankfully. "And Charles?"

"Yes, Newbury?"

"I fear you may have to wash a few cups and saucers."

Bainbridge chuckled, but Veronica could hear the undercurrent of sadness in the laughter. "Good God, it's a few years since I've had the pleasure." He set off in the direction of the kitchen.

Veronica stared at Newbury, and he looked back, his eyes filled with the apology he couldn't offer. "He'll be alright, you know," she said. "He just doesn't understand."

"Do you?" Newbury looked away, staring into the cold, open grate of the fireplace.

"No. But I'm trying to." She became aware that she was bunching her hands into fists by her side. She inhaled deeply to steady herself. "Right. A bath. And then Regent Street."

Newbury nodded. "Quite so, Miss Hobbes. Quite so."

Veronica eyed the object on the table and tried unsuccessfully to suppress a shudder. She wished she hadn't seen it, and now that she had, she wished she could simply ignore it. But things were never that simple where Newbury was concerned.

She hadn't known where to start. The drawing room was an intolerable mess, but she didn't have the time—or, if she were truly honest with herself, the will—to clean it up. Instead, she had resolved to discuss the matter with Bainbridge and plot a means by which to recover Mrs. Bradshaw—or, if that proved too difficult—to make alternative arrangements on Newbury's behalf. But then she had realised that there wasn't even a place to sit, her sense of duty got the better of her, and she began to tidy up regardless. She'd started with the landslide of discarded newspapers beside Newbury's favourite armchair, collecting them up into a tidy stack. And that's when she saw it: the *thing* resting on the coffee table, as if it had always been there. A human hand, dismembered at the wrist, fingers in the air like the legs of a dead spider. It had been carefully dressed and arranged, the pale flesh inked or tattooed with a variety of arcane symbols.

Now Veronica was perched on the edge of the chair, staring at the object with a growing sense of unease. What was Newbury up to? Where had he gotten such a thing? She knew she shouldn't be surprised: Newbury had a study full of bizarre objects, the trophies of many years. But this was different. Strange words had been written on the fingertips in Newbury's own handwriting.

Veronica reached over and tentatively picked it up. The flesh was cold and pliable; the hand had been treated with some sort of chemical preservative. A pentagram had been neatly drawn on the palm in black ink. Various objects had been wedged between the fingers: a penny, a holly leaf, a sprig of parsley, a rolled-up fragment of parchment. She was careful not to dislodge any of them. Where the wrist had once been, the stump was carefully wrapped in waxed paper and bound with rough string. She was thankful for that.

Veronica carefully turned the hand over. More strange symbols had been drawn on the back of it, and again she recognised Newbury's handwriting. The symbols meant nothing to her; she had no way of discerning meaning from what she saw, no frame of reference against which to judge them. But they worried her nonetheless. They signified that Newbury was once again dabbling in the occult, and the implications of that were too dreadful to even contemplate. Her duty to the Queen was to keep a discreet eye on Newbury, to ensure he didn't stray too far from what Her Majesty deemed to be an acceptable path. Veronica had already failed in that duty by neglecting to report Newbury's recent escalation of opium abuse. Discovering this grotesque, dismembered hand meant that she now either had to report to the Queen or pretend that she hadn't seen it. She knew that she should tell the monarch, but also that she wasn't very likely to. Nevertheless, that still left her with a question. Should she tackle Newbury on the issue and try to put a stop to it herself?

In the end, the decision was made for her when she heard a polite cough. She looked up to see Newbury framed in the doorway, grinning and dressed in a smart black suit, hair swept back from his face. "I see you've found Angus," he said, his voice now filled with the confidence it had been lacking since they'd pulled him out of Johnny Chang's earlier that morning.

"Don't be so morbid," she scolded in reply.

"You're the one holding the body part," he reminded her, laughing.

She placed it hastily back on the table. "What is it? What's it for?"

Newbury crossed the room, coming to perch on the arm of the chair beside her. He looked suddenly serious, all sign of his recent levity gone. He searched her face as if looking for a sign in the way she returned his gaze. "I have the notion that something dreadful is going to come to pass, Veronica. This—" He gestured towards the mummified hand on the occasional table. "—this *experiment* was an attempt to divine some meaning from all that, to give substance to my instincts."

Veronica frowned. She measured her next words very carefully, in a level tone. "Forgive me, Sir Maurice, if I speak frankly . . . but couldn't this simply be the effects of the Chinese weed? Lucid dreams, hallucinations, that sort of thing? You have to admit, you've not exactly been yourself of late. Couldn't the drug have inspired a kind of paranoid delusion?"

Newbury looked pained. "On the contrary, my dear Veronica. I believe the weed has helped me obtain a certain measure of clarity in the matter. The skein between this world and the supernatural world is thin, and sometimes, under the influence of the drug, I feel that veil lifting. I see . . . other things, glimpses of the spirit world, of the future and the past. It's beguiling, like a siren song. The weed is a medium for that. Nothing more."

"And did it work, this experiment of yours? Did you come to any conclusions?" Veronica didn't know what to make of his words. She couldn't easily discount them. She, who had a clairvoyant sister locked away in an institution, channelling visions of the future through her seizures. She, who had fought Newbury's predecessor, Aubrey Knox, the rogue agent who had lost himself to the mysteries of the occult and become obsessed with the pursuit of power through ancient pathways.

The Queen would not have appointed her to monitor Newbury's interest in the dark arts if she was not concerned that there was real power to be gained from its exploitation. A siren song, as Newbury had called it, luring him towards the rocks, full of promises of enlightenment. That was exactly what the Queen feared.

But this? It sounded more like the delusions of a man who had given himself over to the vagaries of the poppy than anything rational.

As if hearing her thoughts, Newbury put his hand on her arm. "The only conclusion I could draw was that we need to pay a visit to your sister at the Grayling Institute. She is perhaps the one person who could shed some light on the matter—the only one who can tell me if I'm going mad, or if we really are on the precipice of something disastrous." He smiled. "Assuming you have no objections, of course."

Veronica tensed. She hadn't expected this. And of course, she trusted Newbury implicitly. But Amelia was ill, terribly, terribly ill, and Dr. Fabian had insisted that she stay away. More than that, in fact: he had insisted on her complete and total isolation from Amelia while she underwent her treatment. The notion did not sit easily with Veronica, but she had observed the doctor's wishes, hoping to do the right thing for her sister's recovery. And now Newbury, the man who had done so much for Amelia, needed something from her in return.

Veronica didn't know how to respond. She would do anything for Newbury, of course. But was he thinking straight?

To jeopardise her sister's treatment on a whim, a simple search for validation . . .

"I—" She turned at the sound of clinking china, thankful for the interruption. Sir Charles shouldered open the door, carrying a silver tray filled with teacups, saucers, milk jugs, and sugar bowls. His cane was dangling from the crook of his arm. He glanced over at the two of them and saw Newbury sitting on the arm of her chair, freshly dressed and shaved. "Ah, Newbury. Much better, old chap. Come and give me a hand."

Newbury smiled at her, a twinkle in his eye, and went to rescue his old friend from the embarrassment of having anything more to do with making the tea.

Veronica gave a sigh of relief. She would consider her next move carefully. If Newbury was right—if something awful *was* going to happen—surely Amelia would be able to help, to offer them an insight of some kind. But she feared that any instincts of Newbury's might be compromised by his growing addiction to the opium poppy. And that left her with a horrible quandary. For if she couldn't trust Newbury, whom on earth could she trust?

She watched the two men bustling around each other as they poured the tea, just like old times. It was a case of taking things a day at a time. That was all she could do. Newbury was there, and he was more like himself than she had seen him in months. They had a mystery to solve. That was enough for now. The rest could wait.

At least until after tea.

CHAPTER

5

The garden was alive with activity. A red squirrel scrambled up the side of a nearby bush that had been elaborately shaped to represent an ancient god: Poseidon, thrusting his trident triumphantly towards the sky. Other gods surrounded him, looking on with austere, unwavering gazes: Ares, Zeus, Hades, Aphrodite. The entire pantheon was there, silent in their evergreen vigil.

Elsewhere, birds described wide, concentric circles in the sky, or dived elegantly towards the lake, skimming the surface of the water as they attempted to plunder its murky depths for small silvery fish.

Amelia Hobbes pressed her fingertips against the cold glass of the windowpane, as if trying, unconsciously, to touch the world outside. She'd been locked in her room for days, cooped up like a bird, wings clipped and useless. She longed to inhale the fresh spring air, to walk about on her own two feet—anything but being perpetually confined to this uncomfortable wheelchair.

She sighed, pushing herself away from the window. The wheels of the chair creaked and groaned in protest. She was only torturing herself. Soon she would be able to walk outside again, to see other people. That's what she had to focus on. *Soon*. At least, that's what Dr. Fabian had told her.

Amelia turned the wheels of her chair, rolling slowly back into the gloom of her small room. She felt better than she had in months—years, even—and Dr. Fabian finally appeared to have found a means of suppressing her episodic fits, those brief, harrowing spasms in which she was able to see, momentarily, into the future. The last episode had been over two weeks ago, the end of a horrendous period of almost constant seizing, from which she recalled only the briefest moments of lucidity. That was when the doctor was experimenting with the dosage of the new drug he had prescribed for her—an anticonvulsant, he had explained, to put an end to her nightmares.

While his methods were clearly extreme—keeping her locked in her room with no visitors, for a start—Amelia had no real reason to fault the doctor's regime. She *was* showing signs of improvement. She felt her strength returning. She'd gained weight. She'd taken a few tentative steps on her own, when she knew she wasn't being observed. And most important, the seizures had stopped.

All of this, she knew, should have left her feeling revitalised, uplifted. But she couldn't shake the persistent sense of melancholy that had stolen over her. Melancholy and ... fear. Fear of the future, of the things she had borne witness to in her dreams. Fear of the unknown, too: the things she hadn't seen. And more acutely, more urgently, fear of Mr. Calverton, that deranged, frightful assistant of Dr. Fabian's, that *thing* with all the qualities about him of a creature from a nightmare and none of anything right and sane.

From what she had managed to glean from snatches of conversation with the doctor, Mr. Calverton had once been a normal man, but lost his legs "in the course of duty." Dr. Fabian had personally crafted machine replacements for him, steam-powered pistons that operated in a bizarre parody of their biological counterparts, enabling him to walk with a juddering, almost comical gait. His face was hidden behind a smooth porcelain mask, leaving only his vacant, watery eyes on display. And he always wore a black velvet evening jacket, a cravat, and white gloves. He seemed unable to speak, for in the few months she had been at the Grayling Institute, Amelia never heard him utter a sound. She wondered what terrible fate had befallen him to reduce him to such a state.

Amelia turned her head, glancing toward the door. She was expecting him at any moment: the *click-clack* of his metal feet on the tiled floor, the scraping of the key in the lock, and then those strange eyes, boring into her from across the room.

She shivered. In other circumstances, she might have been differently disposed towards the man, but she had had glimpsed his future and knew his story was still unfolding. The truth of Mr. Calverton had yet to be uncovered.

Well, it wouldn't do for him to know of her fear. She should look busy when he arrived. Amelia leaned back in her wheelchair and reached for a book that she had left, upturned, upon a side table. It was a romance of sorts, the tale of a rich landowner who had fallen in love with a girl from the village. She knew it was nonsense, of course, that it was a reflection of desire rather than reality, but nevertheless she'd been enthralled by the tale. It was her one source of contact with the outside world, the means by which she could reach out and touch something other than the drab, day-to-day existence of her life inside the Grayling Institute.

Amelia parked her chair beside the fireplace and turned the pages of her book, drinking in the colourful fictional world, imagining the garden of the manor house in the story to be filled with the same topiary and scampering animals she had seen from her own window that morning. Imagining herself in that place.

A short while later, Amelia became aware of the clanking steps of Mr. Calverton in the passageway outside her room. She stirred, realising she'd been dozing in her chair. Hurriedly, she reclaimed her book from where she'd let it fall on her lap and flicked the pages, trying to find her place. The key scraped in the lock and slowly the mechanism turned with a metallic *click*.

Amelia didn't look up as she heard the hinges creak open. Instead, she kept her eyes on the book, scanning the same line over and over, never actually taking it in. Her mind was racing. The sheer presence of the half-mechanical man made her skin crawl. Something about his blank, featureless face, his rasping breath, his perpetual silence. And those eyes: always watching, gazing down at her, drinking her in. She couldn't help but imagine a lascivious sneer hidden away behind that porcelain mask. She attributed all manner of deplorable thoughts to him, murderous thoughts, deranged, deviant thoughts. But she had no way of knowing the truth. She could only put her faith in Dr. Fabian and the knowledge that he was doing his best to make her better.

It didn't mean that she had to trust the mechanical porter, however. She'd just have to keep her wits about her in his presence.

Amelia pretended to finish the paragraph she had been reading and looked up, placing her book facedown on the coffee table. "Is it that time already, Mr. Calverton?" She said this brightly, without a waver in her voice, as if the idea of being escorted by the strange man-machine into the bowels of the great house were not at all a terrifying prospect.

Mr. Calverton cocked his head to the left. His eyes remained fixed on her face. No sound was forthcoming other than his wheezing breath and the hissing release of steam from the pistons in his thighs. But she had learned to take this movement of the head as an affirmative.

"Right, then. Time for my treatment." She folded her hands on her lap and sat back in her chair. "Come along, then, Mr. Calverton. We don't want to keep Dr. Fabian waiting."

The man's head remained cocked for a minute, entirely still. Then sharply, decisively, he changed his position, his head snapping back into place. He entered the room, the pistons in his thighs hissing and venting, and maneuvered himself around to stand behind her, gripping the handles of her wheelchair with his gloved fists. Gently, he moved the chair around so that Amelia was facing the door, and then they began the ponderous decent to the treatment room.

The walk would take them fifteen minutes, weaving through the corridors and passageways of the old house, down through dank, dimly lit tunnels that seemed to descend forever, until finally they arrived at the treatment room. It was a stark, fearsome place, filled with the great machine that was somehow curing her of her seizures. And of course, Dr. Fabian, who would be waiting for them with an expectant grin.

They had made the same short journey once a day for the past few months, and Amelia could have followed the route with her eyes closed. But she did not have the strength to make the journey alone, and suspected that even if she did, Dr. Fabian would not allow her the run of the house. Whilst he assured her that it was only to aid in her recuperation that she was kept locked in her room—and judging by his successes, she had no reason to doubt him—she still could not help wondering if Mr. Calverton was as much a minder as he was a porter, assigned to keep a watchful eye on her and report back to his master. Perhaps she was being too fanciful. Nevertheless, the doubt continued to gnaw at her. She wondered what she might find if she were ever able to explore one of the side passages that branched off from the tunnels she took with Mr. Calverton, see what lay in the darkness beyond. And she wondered when Mr. Calverton's time would come, and how long it would take before her vision of him became a reality.

Today, however, she was grateful for an uneventful journey to the treatment room. It was a vast underground space, a cavern carved out of the bedrock and filled with the strange mechanisms of the Queen's physician. It smelled of oil and soot. And just as she had anticipated, Dr. Fabian was already there, waiting for them, glancing pointedly at his pocket watch to signify his displeasure at their late arrival. She wondered if Mr. Calverton would be berated for that later.

"Good morning, Amelia. How are we today?" The doctor poked his wire-rimmed spectacles back up his nose with his index finger—a nervous tic that she had noticed him enact a thousand times before. He was a short man, balding, with only a few trailing wisps of dark hair around the temples. She'd placed him in his early fifties, but she could have been wrong—she found it very difficult to be sure.

She offered him her best beaming smile. "I feel well today, Dr. Fabian. Better than I have in months. I think if only I was able to go into the gardens for some fresh air, then I'd—"

"Amelia, Amelia." He cut her off with a sad expression that suggested he was tired of going over the same ground with her, day after day, week after week. "I know Dr. Mason had very different ideas about your physical well-being, but I assure you, it would set you back enormously if you were to catch a chill. It's simply not worth the risk." He approached the wheelchair, his hands held out in a placatory fashion. She noticed a series of tiny puncture marks on his left wrist, where she assumed he'd been self-medicating. He dropped into a crouch before the chair. "Soon, my dear. Soon we shall have you up and about. You're doing so well. Let's not spoil it now by getting ahead of ourselves, hmm."

Amelia nodded, biting back her frustration. She knew he was wrong, about this at least. She longed for the cool breeze on her skin, the fresh air in her lungs. She could take precautions not to catch a chill. She knew there was another reason why he would not let her out, but she couldn't even begin to fathom what it was.

It was pointless arguing with him, though. She had tried that before, and it had got her nowhere, and at least he had her best interests at heart. She believed that much.

Dr. Fabian stood, clapping his hands together to signify they had reached the end of their discussion. "Well, then. If you are ready, Miss Hobbes, we shall begin."

"I'm ready," she said, although in truth she was never ready for what came next. She looked up at the huge brass sphere that dominated the entirety of the treatment room. It was the size of a small house and looked more like a furnace than like anything medical. It was fed by an array of pipes and shafts that gleamed in the bright electric lights, like a spider at the centre of a shining web. In its belly was a small brass door, the door through which Amelia would be taken for her daily treatment. She felt a knot tighten in her gut. If only there was another way . . .

Dr. Fabian turned to Mr. Calverton, who was loitering in the shadows of the great machine. "Mr. Calverton, could you please escort Miss Hobbes to the treatment bay?"

Mr. Calverton stomped forwards, his metal feet tapping out a harsh rhythm on the stone floor. He took the handles of her wheelchair once again and slowly rolled her towards the gaping mouth of the brass door.

Amelia fought the urge to leap out of the chair and flee. She knew it would be over with soon, and she would feel better again in a couple of hours. The pain didn't last. Not for long.

Mr. Calverton parked her wheelchair before the threshold of the sphere and stooped over her, gently placing one arm beneath her knees and the other around her shoulders. Carefully he lifted her out of the seat, all the while keeping his strange and unblinking eyes on her face. She smiled weakly as she wrapped her hands around his neck, and together the two of them entered the bizarre treatment machine.

Dr. Fabian, in his more whimsical moments, was prone to referring to the sphere as his "engine of life." Amelia always thought that sounded like self-aggrandizing nonsense, and had asked him on more than one occasion to explain the actual purpose of the machine. But, full of his usual bluff and pomposity, the doctor simply told her not to concern herself with it—that his miraculous contraption would make her better, and that she needn't worry herself with the details. She should simply lie back and accept her treatment like a good patient, and then revel in the results.

At first she'd found this patronising and troubling, but she'd grown accustomed to the doctor's offhand manner, and she had, indeed, found herself able to revel in the results of his ministrations. She was alive, for a start, and that was something she had never expected. Dr. Mason had warned her that she was unlikely to see the summer. Yet, thanks to Dr. Fabian, here she was.

Inside the brass sphere, Mr. Calverton's metallic footsteps echoed like miniature detonations. Amelia tried not to look up. She didn't want to see the cluster of apparatuses that hung from the ceiling on long multijointed arms, the needles and the masks and the blades and the throbbing lights. Nor did she want to look up into Mr. Calverton's burrowing eyes.

Instead, she focused on the chair. It was mounted on a platform at the centre of the sphere, up a short flight of steps. Mr. Calverton took them slowly, careful not to jolt her with his sudden, jarring movements. The chair itself was similar to a dentist's: black leather, with a footrest and a deep angle that meant lying almost horizontally. Only, unlike any dentists' chairs she'd encountered, this one came with arm and leg restraints.

Mr. Calverton approached the chair and laid her, almost reverentially, upon it. He was labouring for breath.

"Thank you, Mr. Calverton."

The faceless man cocked his head in acknowledgement and then turned his back on her, descending the short stairway and exiting the sphere the way they had come. The door slammed shut behind him with a loud *clang*, and Amelia heard dead bolts sliding into place.

Dr. Fabian's monotonous voice echoed around the interior of the sphere, piped in through the brass speaking tube that connected the contraption to his workstation outside. "Try to relax now, Amelia. It's time for you to undress."

Amelia sighed. She hated this bit. She sat up and unbuttoned the back of her nightgown, slipping it over her head so that her modesty was protected only by her undergarments. She knew that no one except Dr. Fabian could see inside the sphere—through a sequence of adjustable mirrored panels that allowed him to observe the progress of the treatment—but she couldn't help imagining Mr. Calverton lurking in the shadows, watching her undress. She shivered, and it was only partly because of the cold. She draped the nightgown over the stand beside the chair.

"Very good, Amelia. Now, lie back and try to remain calm."

She did as she was told, placing her wrists and ankles in the metal brackets. They snapped shut, seemingly of their own volition, to hold her in place. She felt her heart thudding against her ribs.

There was a grating sound from above as the mechanical arms swung into motion, creaking in their sockets. Amelia flinched involuntarily in anticipation of what was to come. She looked up and saw the pod of needles descending.

"This won't hurt, Amelia. Just lie back, close your eyes, and think of something else."

She tried to think again of the gardens at the rear of the institute, the topiary sculptures, the darting animals, the sunshine reflecting on the lake. But as the machine descended, she couldn't repress her scream. She bucked against the restraints. Her voice was raw, as if the sounds were being ripped from her throat. She wanted only to be away from there, from the chair and the sphere and the pain.

Above her, the pod of needles opened like a cluster of fingers, and then they were upon her, stinging as they punctured her flesh, pricking holes in her face, arms, chest, thighs, feet. Her body was alive with pain. Crawling with it, as if all her nerves were suddenly, simultaneously on fire. She screamed again, her body racked by the violence of her torment. Miniature pistons fired as the needles continued to sink into her flesh. She heard them, hissing with escaping air. Dr. Fabian was talking again in the same monotonous voice, disembodied and echoing throughout the room, but she could not discern his words. All she could think about was the pain, her screaming, and the intense white light that was blinding her, preventing her from seeing what was happening.

Another needle slid into her throat. Something warm flushed through her body. She bucked again in the treatment chair, and then, after a moment, she was still.

CHAPTER

6

It was late morning before they arrived at Piccadilly. The sun was high in the sky and Piccadilly Circus was bustling with people.

Bainbridge, Newbury, and Veronica abandoned their hansom—one of those dreadful steam-powered affairs that Veronica despised so much—on Shaftesbury Avenue with the intention of making their way to Regent Street on foot.

Almost as soon as they stepped down from the cab, however, Veronica realised their error. She found herself being jostled by the press of tourists, workers, shoppers, and beggars. The place was overflowing with people. She held on to her handbag, cautious of the pickpockets that she knew to be active in the area.

Newbury fought through the milling people until he reached her side, taking her arm in his own and maneuvering her away from the tide of bodies. Bainbridge followed close behind, using his cane to part the throng before him like Moses commanding the Red Sea. Veronica couldn't help but laugh at this vision of the chief inspector, stomping through the busy morning crowds with a stony expression, people shuffling out of his way to let him pass.

She realised Newbury was trying to get her attention. He leaned over, speaking loudly so she could hear him over the noise of the crowd. "Have you seen it yet?"

"What?"

"The crime scene. The place where the burglary was committed last night."

Veronica shook her head. Bainbridge had called for her at her rooms in Kensington that morning and they'd set out to find Newbury directly. She knew only as much as he did—that the evidence at the scene suggested Sykes had been involved. "No. I haven't seen it yet. Why?"

Newbury shrugged but didn't elaborate. She wondered if it were some sort of test, and whether or not she'd passed, but Newbury wasn't giving anything away. Did he suspect that she and Bainbridge had already been to visit the crime scene without him? Were the drugs now inspiring paranoia in Newbury, too? She considered pressing him on the matter but he'd already turned his attention back to the crowd, weaving down the busy street and pulling her along behind him.

The mob in the Circus was unusually dense, people packed in with little or no room to move. Veronica strained to see what was holding their attention, but was granted nothing but the rear view of people's heads and the briefest glimpse of something bright and brassy, shining in the midday sun.

There was a sudden cheer from the front few rows of spectators, and she felt Newbury start at the noise. He still had his arm looped through hers, and she clung to him so as not to lose him amongst the multitudes. At least, that was what she told herself as she leaned into him a little closer.

Newbury craned his neck, trying to see over the people in front. "It's some sort of demonstration," he said, pushing his way through.

More cheering. Veronica tried to dodge a man who was waving his arms above his head with wild abandon and received an elbow in the ribs for the effort. The guilty little urchin—a girl of no more than ten—charged off, ducking between people's legs. Veronica checked her bag. Thankfully, nothing appeared to be missing.

She glanced over her shoulder to see Bainbridge behind her, resolutely forging a path through the crowd, keeping pace with her and Newbury, his face like thunder. She was jostled roughly left to right, and clung to Newbury for dear life until, a moment later, they burst through to the front of the crowd to be confronted by one of the most bizarre spectacles she had ever seen.

Two men, dressed in full plate armour, sat astride identical brass warhorses, and appeared to be attempting to club each other to death.

Wooden barriers had been erected in a large oval to form a sort of arena, around which a crowd had gathered to watch the spectacle that was unfolding within.

The two men—dressed, Veronica gathered, as mediaeval knights—were locked in fiery combat, swinging flaming braziers at each other as their strange, mechanical mounts bucked and weaved and circled. The horses were clearly automata, of some sort: iron skeletons clad with shining brass plates, powered by tiny steam engines hidden somewhere in their workings and evidenced only by the jets of hissing vapour that issued from their nostrils. Each was bigger than a normal horse, with glowing, demonic eyes and sculpted manes. As they danced around each other with jarring but surprisingly rapid movements, Veronica caught glimpses of their internal workings, exposed as the overlapping plates of their bodies parted at the seams. Cogs whirred inside them like hidden clockwork nervous systems.

The two men were knocking each other about with tremendous vigour. Veronica flinched as one of them struck the other hard in the chest with his brazier, denting the steel plating of his opponent's armour and sending hot coals spinning into the audience. The crowd parted to avoid the fiery missiles with a loud roar, but it was a roar of approval.

Veronica beckoned for Newbury to lean closer and spoke loudly into his ear. "What are they doing?" She turned her head to catch Newbury's response.

"Fighting," he said with a broad grin.

She gave him a playful slap on his chest. "I realise that. But why?"

"I have no idea. But it's keeping this lot entertained."

Veronica looked back, searching for Charles in the sea of faces. He was right behind her, and offered a resigned shrug. Then, spotting something, he pointed to a wooden board propped up against one of the barriers. It had been painted white, with words neatly stencilled onto it in red paint. Veronica tried to read around the people who stood in front of her, but they seemed intent on not staying still for even a mo-

ment. Eventually she managed to decipher the words FOR
CHIVALRY! FOR ENGLAND!

Veronica frowned. Saint George's Day had passed months
earlier. She wondered what it all meant. A demonstration by
an Arthurian society, perhaps?

She had little time to wonder further as Newbury, clearly
growing tired of the entertainment, dragged her away, towards Regent Street and the scene of the previous night's
crime.

Regent Street was almost as busy as Piccadilly Circus itself,
with shoppers milling before impressive window displays
filled with all manner of luxury goods, from exotic food ham-
pers to oil-powered shaving kits, antique books to imported
automata.

One store appeared to be selling Revenant Repellent Kits
hand over fist. Veronica smiled at the hopeful faces of the
customers as they emerged from the shop clutching their
talismans and holly sprigs, still attributing supernatural causes
to the plague that had infested the slums the prior year. People needed an enemy, something palpable to hide from. They
would rather see devils than pox—at least devils could be
kept at bay.

Veronica wanted to feel scornful towards these people for
their naïvety, but she could not. They were only doing what
they thought would protect their families from the Revenant
curse, and surely it was better than nothing. Even hanging a
talisman on the door was *something*, regardless of how little

effect it had. And if it made them feel better . . . well, she couldn't judge them for that.

She turned to see Bainbridge pointing towards the front of a nearby jeweller's store with the end of his cane. The legend on the sign read FLITCROFT & SONS, FINE JEWELLERS. There were wooden shutters over the windows and the door was shut. There were no lights on inside the premises.

Veronica had heard of them by reputation, of course, but she'd never had reason to pay a visit to the store. Indeed, she suspected most of the items for sale inside to be well beyond her means. Shops like this one catered to the lords and ladies of high society, and whilst she could never be considered poor—she had a small allowance from her parents that she supplemented with her income from the Crown—neither could she afford to squander her money on elaborate and unnecessary trinkets.

"This is the place." Bainbridge approached the door and tried the handle. It was locked.

Veronica studied Newbury. He was shielding his eyes from the glare of the sun, staring down the street. He looked slightly more himself following their visit to his Chelsea home, but the dark bruises beneath his eyes and the pallor of his skin said a great deal about the general condition of his health. This was not the Newbury she had come to know. Even now. Even with the fire of a case in his belly. There was something else at play, and she had yet to discover what it was.

Bainbridge rejoined them. "Right, when you're ready."

Newbury searched the other man's face, puzzled. "Are we not going inside?"

"Round the back. I want to show you how he got in."

Newbury nodded and trailed after Bainbridge.

The rear of the shop was as featureless and nondescript as the rest of the buildings in the long row, save for the two uniformed bobbies who were loitering outside, kicking their heels, deep in conversation. One of them was smoking a cigarette. He swiftly cast it away when he saw Bainbridge coming, but was unable to hide the riffles of smoke that still curled from his nostrils. He quickly adjusted his posture and stood to attention, wearing a guilty expression. His companion fought to contain a wide grin.

"Hardly surreptitious, Peters," Bainbridge said as he approached the pair, clearly attempting to hide a chuckle at the uniformed man's expense.

"No, sir, not surreptitious at all, sir." The man looked utterly crestfallen.

Bainbridge leaned in close to him, lowering his voice. "A little tip for you, Peters. If you're going to have a sneaky smoke while on duty, try not to get caught."

The man, Peters, looked visibly relieved at Bainbridge's leniency. Veronica thought he might even grab the chief inspector by the hand. "Yes, sir. Sound advice, sir. I'll remember it well."

"See that you do, Constable." Bainbridge patted the man firmly on the shoulder, then motioned the two of them aside with a wave of his cane. He pointed it at the rear door of the shop, which was down a short flight of stone steps and across a small yard. "So here we are, Newbury. Take a look at that.

See if you can't spot anything the rest of us might have missed."

Newbury nodded politely at the two bobbies then crossed the street, taking the steps two at a time, and dropped to his knees in the yard, examining the flagstones along the approach to the door. Veronica followed him at a reasonable distance, keen to see what was going on without disrupting his train of thought.

From his pocket, Newbury withdrew a small magnifying lens, about the size of a penny piece. He held it up to his right eye, clutching it between his thumb and forefinger. From where Veronica was standing, it made his eye look suddenly enormous. She stifled a laugh.

She sensed Bainbridge moving to stand beside her and looked over at him. He stood watching Newbury with interest. "Remarkable," he said without the slightest hint of irony.

Veronica grinned. Bainbridge was a traditionalist. He did things the old way. That wasn't to say that he was outmoded—far from it—but simply that his thought processes had been worn into familiar grooves over many years of policing. In most instances, this read like a shorthand that could sometimes seem like arrogance to those who didn't know him better: He would arrive at the scene of a burglary or murder and immediately suggest the means by which the crime had been committed. It was a kind of insight, Veronica mused, a way of seeing the world through the criminal's eyes gleaned from years of experience and many hours spent cogitating on the motives of the men he sent to the gallows, prisons, or asylums. He could walk into nine out of ten crime scenes and immediately put his finger on the solution. It was the reason he had risen so swiftly through the ranks at Scotland Yard, and the reason he was such a trusted agent to the Queen. But sometimes, on those rare occasions when his intuition failed him, when he found himself flummoxed by circumstances outside his realm of experience, he called on Newbury.

Newbury had a knack for turning things on their head, of being able to take any situation and see it in a different light. He offered a perspective that often seemed obvious with hindsight, but represented a logical leap that many people would find unimaginable. And that made him a truly remark-able detective. He was able to glean insight from the slightest fragment of a clue. And his experience reached beyond that of the traditional detective: Newbury was an anthropologist and an expert in the occult. His work for the Queen had tended to centre on this latter trait: Newbury was the man she called in when something unusual or otherworldly was suspected, or when all of her other agents were confounded.

Veronica watched as he scrambled around the yard on his knees, ruining his fresh suit, bowing his head so low that his nose was nearly touching the ground. He continued in this manner for some time, moving from the foot of the steps right up to the shop door and then back again. Then, suddenly imbued with energy, he leapt to his feet, pocketed his magnifying glass, and ran over to the two bobbies, who were watching all of this with growing confusion.

"Show me the soles of your left feet," he said, the urgency in his voice enough to cause them to both turn around and do just as he said. Newbury ran a hand through his hair, bent low to examine the proffered shoes, and then proclaimed "Ha!" before bounding back over to stand before Bainbridge.

Veronica was taken aback by this sudden alteration in his behaviour, but was gladdened by it; it was more energetic a display than she had seen from him for many, many months.

"A man, Charles. He was here late last night, after the light rain. His stride was confident and purposeful, and his shoes were flat-soled size nines." He eyed the chief inspector triumphantly. "What size shoes did the dead man wear? Sykes?"

Bainbridge smiled. It was clear he was relieved by Newbury's sudden outburst of enthusiasm. Vindicated, too, she suspected, since it had been his idea to involve Newbury in the case. Although Veronica knew there was more to it than a simple desire to help Newbury find a reason to drag himself away from the opium dens, she also believed he was utterly perplexed by the mystery and in need of his friend's assistance.

"Size nine," Bainbridge conceded. There was a glint in his eye. "Take a look at the rear door, Newbury."

Newbury was like a bloodhound that had suddenly got hold of a scent. He turned and made a beeline for the door. Veronica followed him, curious to see what he would do next.

The door itself was a heavy wooden affair, unmarked and unremarkable, and clearly designed to keep people out. It was at least an inch thick—she could see this because it was now standing ajar—and was lockable from the inside by virtue of a large dead lock and two thick iron bolts. It had been crafted from a dark hardwood, possibly mahogany.

Newbury was on his knees again. Veronica crouched low to see what he was looking at. He was running his hand around the inside edge of a large circular hole in the door, admiring the smooth, clean edges of the cut. The hole was about the size of a dinner plate and had been punched clear through the door. Through it she could make out a grille of iron bars—another lockable barrier between the rear yard and the shop beyond.

"Have you seen this, Charles?" Newbury beckoned the other man over without averting his gaze from the door. "Around the hole, here." He traced his finger around the rim of the aperture. The door sported a series of eight smaller marks, nothing but faint indentations in the wood. They were evenly spaced around the outside of the larger, central hole.

Veronica looked at Bainbridge, who was standing over them, grinning. "Yes, I've seen it, Newbury. Perplexing, isn't it?"

Newbury stood. "Perplexing, indeed!"

Veronica sighed. "Can someone please explain what the devil it is you're talking about?"

Bainbridge laughed. "Yes, I'm sorry, my dear. Allow me to explain." He leaned on his cane. "Edwin Sykes, whom we—until now—presumed to be responsible for a series of daring and elaborate burglaries all over the city, had a most ingenious method of entering a property."

"Go on," Veronica urged him.

"Well, he'd somehow managed to lay his hands on a mechanical device. We have only secondhand reports of what it looks like, but we've seen the results of its work."

"The holes in the door?" Veronica suggested.

"Yes, but you'll soon see there's more to it than that."

"So what is this thing, this device?"

Newbury stood, turning to smile at her. "It's a spider," he said.

"A spider?"

"Exactly that," he continued. "A large mechanical spider. See those eight small markings in the wood around the central hole? We believe that's how it fixes itself into place while it burrows out the main entry point. It's a dead giveaway. I've never seen anything else like it."

"But there's a full-height metal grille behind that door. And what use is a hole like that? Are you saying that Sykes—or whoever was responsible—reached through that opening to pick the lock on the other side? And what about the dead bolts?" Veronica gave them both a dubious look.

"No, Miss Hobbes, that's the clever part." Bainbridge tugged at one corner of his moustache. "As we understand it, the spider does the lion's share of the work. It's a sort of automaton device, with limited intelligence. Once it's cut the entry hole, it crawls inside and picks the locks. As many of them as are necessary to clear a path. All Sykes had to do was stand back and wait for his miraculous toy to grant him access, then stroll right in to the treasure inside."

Veronica looked at the hole in the door with some admiration. "A remarkable device indeed." She searched Bainbridge's face. "Why did you never put Sykes away for his crimes?"

Bainbridge sighed. "There was always too much doubt. A watertight alibi. No evidence. We all suspected he was guilty, but had no way of proving it. We tried laying traps to catch him, but he was always wise to them. We investigated his financial situation, but the paper trail appeared authentic. Even searched his property once, but found nothing incriminating whatsoever."

"So how did you know it was him?"

"Oh, he was guilty. I'm sure of it. Intuition, whatever. He was our man."

Veronica smiled. She had come to trust Bainbridge's instinct almost as if it were her own. "We're all guilty of something, Sir Charles. Are you sure that Sykes was guilty of exactly what you'd pinned on him?"

Bainbridge glanced uneasily at Newbury. "I was . . . I was *certain* of it. But now . . . Well, you've both seen the body in the morgue. And then this—" He gestured to the door. "—well, it throws everything out of the window. Wait until you see inside."

Newbury stepped forwards and grabbed the edge of the wooden door, swinging it open towards them and revealing the full extent of the metal grille inside. It was forged from heavy iron bars and filled the doorway completely, and it was also hanging open, the lock picked. "Well," he said, still clearly riveted by the unfolding mystery, "After you."

Bainbridge stepped up and pushed the grille aside. "If you'll forgive me, Miss Hobbes—in this instance, I should rather observe safety than etiquette."

Veronica strode forwards and bustled past him into the dark interior of the shop. "In that case, Sir Charles, I should absolutely go first."

Bainbridge raised an eyebrow at Newbury, who patted his friend on the arm as he followed her inside. "No point arguing when she's made up her mind, old man."

"Less of the 'old,' you darn fool," he said, with mock offense, but Veronica could hear the relief in his voice. They were working together again, just like old times.

Veronica heard the grille clang shut behind them. Bainbridge's voice was disembodied in the darkness. "Just a moment . . . Ah, there!" The dull glow of a lantern filled the room, casting everything in a warm orange glow. It took her eyes a minute to adjust after the harsh sunlight.

"Open those shutters, will you, Charles? It's awfully dark in here," said Newbury.

"Sorry, Newbury. We'll have to make do with lantern light. The shutters are locked and the darn keys are missing," replied Bainbridge gruffly.

Veronica glanced around. The place seemed to be opulently furnished: polished glass display cases of various shapes and sizes made a maze of the layout, and large gilt-framed mirrors adorned the walls. A fine mahogany counter stood in one corner, out of the way, as if the owner was embarrassed to remind his customers that the establishment was, in fact, a shop, and that the items within were for sale. She wondered where the owner was. Probably down at the station filling out reams of paperwork.

Her first impression was that nothing appeared to be out of order. Unlike many of the other crime scenes she'd attended in her time, the place seemed untouched. None of the glass cases had been shattered for easy access to the jewels, no paperwork was scattered over the floor, no safe hanging open on the far wall.

Newbury had crossed to a low rectangular cabinet and was stooped over it, examining something on its surface. She went over to join him. The cabinet was entirely devoid of jewellery. All the display trays were still in situ, but there was not a precious stone or a gold band to be seen.

"Look." Newbury pointed to a spot on the surface of the

cabinet. A large disc had been cut out of the glass, identical in size to the hole in the door. The removed panel had been neatly placed to one side, right beside the hole. The rest of the glass pane was entirely unblemished.

Veronica gasped in awe.

"Exactly," said Newbury. "There are very few tools that could cut a hole like that through a glass case, especially so quickly."

Bainbridge strolled over and placed his lantern on the cabinet. "And the other cases are all the same. Whoever did this worked the entire place over in the space of a couple of hours last night."

Newbury frowned. "It had to be Sykes. No one else could have pulled this off. It bears every hallmark—"

"But Sykes is dead. You saw his corpse this morning, with your own eyes! We must have gotten it wrong, Newbury. We must have had the wrong man all along."

Newbury shook his head. "No. I can't believe we'd be that off the mark. We've had him in our sights for months, if not longer. There has to be more to it!"

Veronica watched the two men as they tried to fathom their next move. "Have you been to visit Sykes's apartments, Sir Charles?"

He nodded. "Yes, yesterday, before all of this happened, when we discovered he was dead."

"And . . . ?"

"And there was nothing out of sorts. Clean as a whistle. His housekeeper was still there, frantic that something might have happened to him. We found no evidence of any crimes, nothing that linked him to any of the previous burglaries. No sign of any mechanical spider, no hidden chambers on the premises."

Newbury shook his head in dismay. "Just like the last time you searched his rooms."

Veronica rapped her fingernails on the glass surface. "But we still have a mysterious death on our hands. And a burglary. Do we have any leads whatsoever?"

"No! That's what's so damn infuriating. Nothing makes sense. It seems like too much of a coincidence for the death and the robbery not to be linked, but there's no sign of any evidence, and no leads to show us where to even begin looking!" The frustration was evident in Bainbridge's voice.

"We do have one possible lead." Newbury's words were delivered quietly, contemplatively. "I admit it's not much, but the address card you found on the body, Charles. What of the Bastion Society?"

Bainbridge leaned forward so that his face was lit by the glow of the lantern. Veronica saw he was grinning. "Yes. By Jove, Newbury, yes! It's not much, you're right, but it's something! Let's pay them a visit this afternoon. What do you say?"

Newbury reached for the lantern. "I've always wondered what that lot gets up to in that big house of theirs. I say we go poking around."

Veronica smiled. "Isn't that, Sir Maurice, exactly what we do best?"

He laughed, then scooped up the lantern and disappeared into the darkness near the door, leaving the others to find their way behind him.

CHAPTER

7

Dr. Lucien Fabian hated rushing. And today, he felt nothing but rushed.

He had arisen early, taken rounds with his patients, and then administered another battery of treatments to the Hobbes girl, all before lunch. Then Mr. Calverton had appeared with a note card from the palace, and all of a sudden he had to abandon his half-eaten beef Wellington and his half-drunk glass of merlot, get in his carriage, and head off at a phenomenal speed to see the Queen. He clutched the seat, fearful that the driver was going to lose control of the vehicle at any moment—or, perhaps worse, plough directly into the path of an oncoming ground train. They bounced over the cobbles, almost dislodging the glasses that perched precariously on the end of his nose. The engine was raging, and black smoke billowed around the carriage like a dark smear across the windows. He wondered if the driver could even see where they were going. The day had not exactly worked out as he'd anticipated.

Then there was the Queen herself to contend with. What could she possibly want? What was more important than his work? The message had been clear—this was no medical emergency. The life-giving equipment he had cocooned her in was still in perfect working order, breathing on her behalf, pumping the blood around her veins, feeding her. So what was it? Why had he been so rudely torn away from the Grayling Institute? He hated the notion that he was permanently available for her every whim, on call like a lapdog. Was it like this for her other agents?

Of course, Victoria refused to acknowledge his true standing at her Court. She acted as if he weren't important in the least, like she could operate perfectly well without him. At first he'd wondered if this was a sign of her embarrassment, her way of disguising the fact that he was, perhaps, the man who now knew her most intimately of all, at least medically speaking. But he had come to alter this opinion, realising that she was simply a heartless witch.

He chuckled at his own joke, quite literal in this case. Victoria's heart was now nothing but a series of brass cogs and elaborate timing mechanisms, ticking beneath her rib cage like a secret, buried clock. He had constructed it for her, and placed it in her chest with his own hands. That heart was, perhaps, the finest piece of work he had ever crafted. It was a shame he hadn't given it to someone more deserving.

Fabian sighed and stared out the carriage window. He supposed that her attitude towards him was to be expected. She was, after all, the ruler of the biggest empire in the world. She was bound to feel the need to assert her will. But it did nothing to alter his mood as they charged on towards Buckingham Palace for an interview that he neither needed nor desired.

Sandford, the agent's butler, had proved his usual accommodating self. He'd ushered Fabian in through the private entrance, taking his cloak and offering him a stiff drink. From the look on the old man's liver-spotted face, Fabian had gathered he might need it, so he accepted it with grace and downed it quickly, thankful for the fortification.

Now he was standing before Queen Victoria herself, resplendent in her mechanical glory.

The audience chamber was kept shrouded in a permanent gloom, the heavy drapes pulled shut over the curtains. The reasons for this were twofold: both to keep prying eyes from seeing in—the world outside the palace knew little or nothing about the Queen's current condition—and to protect her from the sunlight, as light sensitivity was an unexpected side effect of his treatment regime. Anything stronger than a dull glow would cause her to recoil in agony, so she mainly inhabited this one room at the palace, wired into her life-support system, hidden away in the darkness.

The Queen rolled forward in her wheelchair to greet him. She looked old and tired. Fabian moved to inspect the machinery that encased her. She was lashed into the chair, held in place by two large tubes that jutted from her chest, feeding her collapsed lungs with oxygen from the tanks that were strapped to the rear of her device. Humming machines pumped fluid around her body, a pinkish substance created by the Fixer, distilled from the essence of rare plants he had obtained in the jungles of South America.

"How are we today, Majesty?" Fabian bustled around her as he checked the connections and levels of the machines.

"We no longer sleep, Doctor. We pass the nights alone in the darkness while the Empire rests. We have the most lucid waking dreams."

"Of what do you dream, Majesty?"

"Of Albert. Of a decaying Empire, fading as the light of England fades. Of everything we have built becoming dust without a firm hand to guide it." Her eyes were glazed and she was staring away into the distance, as if seeing something else other than the shadowy interior of the audience chamber.

He stood back, inspecting his own handiwork. "Fascinating."

Victoria's head snapped around to regard him. Her eyes flashed with anger. Her tone changed seamlessly from whimsical to commanding. "We are not one of your little experiments, Fabian. You'd do well to remember that."

Fabian bristled. He felt little beads of sweat form under his hairline; it was *hot* inside the audience chamber. "Yes, Your Majesty. Of course. I merely seek to understand so that I may help—"

Victoria waved her hand dismissively as she cut him off. "Prattle and poppycock. We know how your mind works, Doctor. Do not dare to attempt to placate me with platitudes and fabrications. My body may be faltering, but my mind is not. You consider me a puzzle, a medical aberration to be solved. On occasion that perspective has proved beneficial to one's situation. But you must never forget we are also your Queen, and we demand and insist on your respect."

Fabian offered a tight-lipped smile. "You command and always will command my enduring support, devotion, and respect, Your Majesty."

Victoria almost spat at him. "More platitudes. We fear, Fabian, that your opinion of your own importance has become somewhat overblown. You are a physician. Nothing more. Remember your place."

Fabian took a deep breath and fought against the rising tide of anger that pushed at the limits of his patience. The woman was insufferable. He had saved her life! He had constructed the life-support system that had single-handedly ensured her survival. The only one who understood how to keep her breathing. The one who had given her a clockwork heart. The Victorian Empire endured because of *him*. She would do well to remember *that*.

It was within Fabian's power to end Victoria's reign with the flick of a hidden switch that he had incorporated into her life-giving chair during its construction. A safety measure, he had told himself. A means of ensuring that if it all went wrong, there was a way out. He'd initially considered this a precaution in case the surgery that had welded her to the chair had failed, but now he dreamed of the day he might trip that switch, and smiled secretly at the notion that it was he, not the Queen, who held the real power in the room.

Outwardly, however, he bowed his head and mumbled an apology, allowing the Queen to consider him admonished. Now was not the time to reveal his secrets. But there would come a point when it would prove necessary for him to assert that power. The thought galvanised him.

Victoria's breath was rasping and dry. Fabian tentatively

approached her chair and leaned in, making an adjustment to the intravenous fluid system that kept her hydrated. Close up, she smelled of stale sweat and chemicals, preservatives. He wondered whether her maids were washing her and changing her dressings as regularly as he had ordered. He would quietly check with them later.

"So? What news from the Grayling Institute?" This, then, was the real purpose of his summons.

Fabian stepped back from the chair. The bellows hissed and wheezed. He looked down at Victoria, meeting her gaze. He tried to keep the defiance out of his expression. "Things . . . progress. While the engine has proved ineffective on nearly all of our patients, on the girl it is finally beginning to work."

Victoria rubbed her hands together with something approaching delight. The grin on her face was obscene.

Fabian swallowed and continued. "Seven days. Seven days is the longest we've achieved so far. But I am hopeful the duration will increase with further testing."

"Why do they fail?"

Fabian shrugged. "The girl is frail and sickly. Her . . . special talents are a tremendous drain on her physical well-being."

"We are not interested in her physical well-being. Her talents, however, are of much interest."

"We are learning a great deal, Your Majesty. A great deal. But I have yet to identify exactly why the engine works on the girl and no one else, and whether those talents are part of the reason for our success. These are the two areas that concern me most: the long-term viability of the . . . product, and how to replicate the success with another subject. I would not want to risk causing any lasting harm to, let us say, a more significant patient. . . ."

The Queen gave a sickly laugh. "You always were of a cowardly persuasion, Doctor, too keen to keep your own neck off the block." She looked suddenly serious. "Ensure the machine is fully operational within a week. We grow weary of waiting." She laughed again, but this time it was spiked with menace. "And close your mouth, won't you? It's unbecoming."

Fabian, stunned, stammered out his reply, pushing his glasses back on the bridge of his nose. "But that's impossible, Your Majesty. Absolutely impossible. Seven days! Our success has been incredibly limited so far. We're making headway, yes. But a week! I simply can't do it. We'll need months of testing and experimentation before we're even close to being operational!"

Victoria's expression hardened. "You will do as we say, *Fabian*." She used his name as a curse. "You will go from here and you will not return until the device is in full working order." She seemed to consider her next statement carefully. "Double the amount of testing on the girl."

Even Fabian felt himself blanch at this. "But Majesty, it will kill her."

"We are not concerned with whether she lives or dies, so long as the tests prove successful. Identify the factor that separates her from the others. Discover the reason for your recent success. Go to work." With this she turned her cheek to him and waved a hand in casual dismissal.

Fabian remained still for a moment, unsure how to respond. He wanted to rage at her for the ridiculous nature of her demands, her arrogance. But he knew he could not win that particular battle. He ground his teeth, dug his nails into the palms of his hands. Victoria resolutely refused to look in his direction; as far as she was concerned, their business was over and he had ceased to exist.

Fuming, and filled with a frustrating sense of impotence, Fabian turned on his heel and stalked out of the audience chamber, leaving Victoria chuckling to herself in her chair. He would do her bidding. For now. He could do nothing else. But the time would come for him to assert his dominance. And that time was growing closer by the day.

CHAPTER

8

ackworth House, the building frequented by the members of the Bastion Society, was perhaps the most grandiose clubhouse that Veronica had ever seen. Not, she admitted to herself, that she'd seen the insides of many gentlemen's clubs in her time.

Nevertheless, this one in particular had an air of the spectacular about it, unlike most of the more austere establishments that she'd had the misfortune to frequent. Even Newbury's club, the White Friar's, with all its writers and artists and bohemian types, had nothing on this place. She looked around in barely disguised wonder. The money that must have been spent . . .

They were standing in a huge saloon, a hall that could have seated three to four hundred people. Tables were placed with unusual precision, according to some prosaic pattern that she supposed would really be discernible only from the wide baroque balcony that ran around the entire perimeter of the space, high above her head. A large marble surround, depicting characters from classical myth, enclosed a roaring fire, even this early in the day. Tall vases stood to either side of it and were filled with plumes of bright emu and peacock feathers, their multifaceted eyes watching her with unblinking interest.

Servants bustled amongst the tables, still clearing away debris from the prior evening's festivities, which—from the look of the place—had evidently been a riotous banquet of some kind. And before the little group of Crown investigators, greeting them in a haughty but polite manner, was Sir Enoch Graves, the club's premier.

The man was clearly an eccentric. She'd already been able to discern, from just the few words he had spoken, that he was possessed of both an enormous intellect and the requisite ego to accompany it. He was thin—painfully so—and in his early forties, with a pencil-thin moustache on his top lip and a shock of silvery grey hair that was parted and fell in a comma across his forehead. He was dressed in a black evening suit with a rapier strapped to his side—a dress sword— and spoke with an upper-class lisp that belied—to Veronica at least—the affected nature of his persona.

"Welcome to the Bastion Society," he said, gesturing with open arms to the room around them. He smiled, but Veronica thought it looked more like a threat. "I do apologise for the state of the place. The poor servants have their work cut out for them this morning. I think we somewhat overdid it last night."

"A special occasion?" Newbury ventured, his voice low.

Graves cocked his head to one side, as if wondering how to

respond. "A new member. We were celebrating his induction into our little club."

Bainbridge raised his eyebrow at the understatement. "Not so little," he mumbled beneath his breath.

Graves laughed. "Quite so, Sir Charles."

Newbury scratched his chin unconsciously. He was processing something, some piece of information he had gleaned from the room, or something Graves had already given away. "A new member?" he ventured. "Do you actively encourage applications?"

Graves smiled. "Are you interested in joining us, Sir Maurice? I'm sure we'd be delighted to welcome someone of your stature into our fold." He paused as if waiting for a response from Newbury, but went on when he realised none was forthcoming. "But to answer your question: No, we do not. We have a strict vetting and admissions policy, and we adhere to it with the utmost devotion." Veronica noted his hand was now resting on the hilt of his sword. "We believe in chivalry and order, in upholding the standards which have made this country great. We believe in protecting the land of our birth and setting an example for how a refined Englishman should behave. We are knights of the realm, Sir Maurice, and we act in her best interests."

His voice had gradually grown in volume and timbre as he'd delivered his carefully practised speech. Now he was grinning wolfishly at Veronica. "It is not often that we have a lady on the premises, Miss Hobbes. Please forgive me if I seem a trifle overzealous. I believe wholeheartedly in our cause."

"I can see that you do," she said, mindful to keep any judgement out of her tone. She'd already decided that she heartily disliked the man, but it clearly wouldn't do to broadcast the fact.

Bainbridge, however, was less tactful. "All laudable stuff, I'm sure—" He broke off to cough into his handkerchief, and Veronica couldn't help thinking he was disguising a laugh. "—but tell me, if all of that's true, all that stuff about chivalry and order, why would you associate yourselves with a criminal such as Edwin Sykes?"

Graves tried but failed to repress a scowl. "Direct and to the point, Sir Charles. Let me tell you something about Mr. Edwin Sykes. He's one of those newly made men, not born of good breeding stock. I'm sure you understand what I mean—" He looked pointedly at Bainbridge. "—but he's a gentleman all the same, and I understand he has been convicted of no crime. He supports and champions our cause. I have no hesitation in recommending the fellow, and whilst he may not be my first choice for a dinner companion, he is a fine and up-standing member of our society."

Bainbridge nodded. "When did you last see him here at Packwood, Sir Enoch?"

Graves looked thoughtful. "I'm not really sure, to be honest, Sir Charles. A few weeks ago, perhaps? I'm terribly sorry I can't be more specific. I've had so much on my mind. I'm running for government, you see. And what with the party last night . . . I suppose I haven't really been paying attention. Sykes moves in different circles."

"If I may, sir?" All four of them turned to see one of the butlers, an older man dressed in a smart black suit and white gloves, who had been clearing a table just to the left of their small circle. He looked incredibly nervous.

"Go on," said Bainbridge, leaning on his cane.

"I believe I saw Mr. Sykes here last night, at the party. He arrived late, after dinner had already been served. He joined some others by the fire for drinks." The man's voice wavered as he realised Graves was glaring at him. "Um, although it was only the most fleeting of glimpses. I could, of course, be wrong."

There was a warning in the delivery of Graves's response that was impossible to miss. "Thank you, Edwards, but I fear you are mistaken. Please carry on." He watched the butler scuttle away with an armful of napkin rings clutched tightly to his chest, then turned back to the others. "Edwards is getting on a bit. Not the most reliable memory, but a stalwart all the same. One of the fixtures and fittings around here, really." A moment's pause. "I can absolutely assure you that Edwin Sykes was not here at the clubhouse last night. We haven't seen him for some time."

Newbury seemed to take this in. "That would be entirely consistent with our findings, Sir Enoch. We're currently holding Edwin Sykes's body in the police morgue."

The colour seemed to drain suddenly out of Graves's face. He appeared to momentarily lose his composure. "Oh . . . oh dear . . . ," he stammered, as if unable to order his thoughts. "What . . . what happened?"

"As yet we're not entirely sure. But we suspect foul play," Newbury answered, clearly choosing to omit any details. Veronica had the impression he might be attempting to lead Graves into a trap, or at least find out if the premier knew something pertinent that he was trying to hide.

"Foul play?" Graves sounded deeply concerned by this eventuality.

"Yes. Murder." Newbury kept his voice level, calm.

"When?"

"Three days ago, or thereabouts."

"Good God." Graves looked genuinely appalled. "Good God." He glanced at Bainbridge. "Have you any notion who's responsible?"

"We're following up a number of leads." Bainbridge lied in response, and again Veronica realised her two companions were playing a clever game with Graves, trying to get him to trip himself up, circling him like hunters closing in on prey. It was fascinating to watch. "Perhaps you could help us. Do you know of anyone who might have had a quarrel with Sykes, or a reason to want him dead?"

Graves shook his head. His voice hardened. "The only quarrel I'm aware of was with you, Sir Charles. Is there any reason Scotland Yard would want him dead?"

Veronica winced. That wouldn't sit well with Bainbridge, and clearly Graves was not beyond playing his own game, trying to rile the chief inspector and lead the conversation in a different direction.

To his credit, Bainbridge allowed the comment to wash over him and continued with his questions. "Did he ever keep a room here at Packworth House?"

Graves shrugged. "We all do, on occasion. But certainly not in recent months. As I say, he moved in different circles. We hadn't seen a lot of him about. But I'm sure he was working to further our cause, whatever he was up to."

The conversation lapsed into a strained silence. The only sound was the clinking of the empty wineglasses that the waiting staff were clearing away at the other end of the room.

"Have you ever used your sword in anger, Sir Enoch?" Newbury indicated the rapier hanging from the other man's belt.

Graves seemed flustered by this sudden turn in the conversation. "I'm not sure I like the implication behind that question, Sir Maurice."

"It's a simple enough question. I'd be obliged if you'd answer it."

"Then the answer is no, I have not." Graves was clearly fuming now. His top lip quivered in anger. "Are you saying Sykes was murdered with a rapier?"

"No."

Graves looked close to exploding. "Then I fail to see the relevance . . ." He trailed off, leaving his sentence hanging.

Veronica took this as her cue to intercede. She moved a step closer to Graves, adopting a conspiratorial tone. "Sir Enoch, we do appreciate your help in this matter. We're keen not to see a scandal develop, or to cause the members of your society any concern or inconvenience. It would be particularly disheartening if the Bastion Society were to become associated with the matter, especially as you're running for government. It wouldn't look at all good in the press." She smiled sweetly. Graves shifted uneasily but didn't respond. "We're keen to bring the whole affair to a swift conclusion. You mentioned earlier that Sykes moved in 'other circles.' Perhaps you could point us at some of his associates so we could continue our investigations elsewhere?"

Graves took a sharp intake of breath. "As much as I would like to assist you further in this matter, Miss Hobbes, my hands are, alas, tied. When I spoke of other circles, I meant just that:

Sykes has friends and associates outside of the Bastion Society. If you wish to know who they are, you'll have to find some other means of obtaining the information. I'm afraid I don't know the man well enough to be privy to his life outside the clubhouse."

"Had," Newbury said firmly. "You said he 'has' friends and associates outside of the society."

"Ah, yes. A slip of the tongue. Hasn't quite sunk in yet, I'm afraid." Graves reached up and brushed his hair back from his forehead in a nervous gesture. He was clearly growing uncomfortable with the conversation. He turned to look at the waiting staff, who were still buzzing around behind him, clearing the tables in preparation for afternoon visitors. "Look, I really must be getting on. I'm dreadfully sorry to hear the news about poor Sykes. But duty calls."

Bainbridge gave a curt nod and extended his hand, which Graves accepted. "You've been most helpful, Sir Enoch. Thank you very much for your time."

Graves nodded. "Smith will show you out." He called across the saloon. "Smith!"

The young man came dashing over. He couldn't have been more than eighteen years old, and was clearly a member of the waiting staff. "These people were just leaving, Smith."

"Yes, sir. Of course, sir." He beckoned for them to follow as he led them down the hallway to the exit. Veronica glanced back at Graves as she passed through the lobby doors and saw him staring after her, his jaw set firm; his eyes hard, cold, and full of menace.

————

"Pompous, lying idiot!" Bainbridge announced brassily, almost as soon as they were out of earshot of the front door. "It's clear he knows far more about what's going on than he's prepared to reveal."

Newbury nodded his assent. "Agreed. What with the testimony of the butler and Graves's obvious shock at our news, I'd almost be prepared to wager that Edwin Sykes *was* in attendance at the party last night. Or at least someone who looked very much like him."

"But Sykes is *dead*, Newbury. We've all seen his corpse laid out on a slab across town. There's no mistaking it. So how *could* he be both in the morgue and at the party? And, if we're to believe our own eyes, he was at Flitcroft and Sons, too, emptying the jewellery cases!" Bainbridge looked utterly flummoxed. "At least two places at once!"

Newbury leaned against a nearby lamppost. He looked tired. "It's clear to me, old man, that our eyes are somehow deceiving us. Someone is playing a very clever game, and we've found ourselves right in the middle of it. And after that performance from the premier, I have no doubt whatsoever that it's somehow tied up with Enoch Graves and the strange, chivalrous world of the Bastion Society."

Bainbridge gave a hearty sigh. "The thing is, Newbury, what the devil are we going to do about it? It's not as if we can just go barging in there and start causing a scene. We don't have any grounds to search the place, even though we have reason to believe that Graves is lying to us."

Newbury grinned, a wicked, knowing grin. "There are ways and means, my dear Charles. Ways and means."

Bainbridge shook his head, but he was smiling. "Just

remember, Newbury, I'm a police inspector. I work within the law."

"And I, Charles, am an academic and a philosopher. What harm could I possibly do?"

Veronica gave him a wry look. "I think, Sir Charles, we'd be best advised to treat that as a rhetorical question."

Newbury laughed, but she saw he caught her meaning.

"Well, Newbury," Bainbridge said, "I fear I have some business to attend to. Would you mind escorting Miss Hobbes back to Kensington?"

Newbury caught her eye. He was expecting her to protest. When she didn't, he smiled graciously. "I'd be only too pleased."

"Excellent. In that case, I'll call for you tomorrow after breakfast. Let's see if we can't devise a means to shake these Bastion fellows up a little. You, too, Miss Hobbes." Bainbridge gave her a knowing look.

"Until tomorrow, then, Sir Charles," she said to his retreating back.

Veronica waited until Bainbridge was a way up the road before she crossed to Newbury and took his arm in her own. He didn't look at all well. "I suspect," she said brightly, "that Mrs. Grant will be delighted to see you. It's been a while, and she's been sitting on that stock of Earl Grey you had her buy. I think it would be best if you allowed her to make you a pot."

Newbury gave a tired chuckle. "Miss Hobbes, you do have a particular way with words."

CHAPTER

9

Newbury looked as if he were about to doze off in the armchair. If he did, Veronica decided, she would let him, then wake him after an hour or two and send him home in a hansom. It wasn't as if she were overly concerned about scandal—if she were, she might have made different choices a long time ago. Allowing Newbury to get some rest here, at her apartment, away from the temptations and the chaos of Chelsea, well, it felt . . . right. Not the entire night, but a few hours. And besides, she'd promised Bainbridge she'd keep him busy for a while.

She was sitting opposite him, perched on the edge of the chaise longue, her teacup warming her hands. She watched Newbury's chest rise and fall in a peaceful rhythm, his eyelids flutter open and closed. The only sounds were the *tick-tock* of the carriage clock on the mantelpiece and the roar of the passing ground trains on Kensington High Street below.

Veronica stood and wandered over to the window, turning back the netting and gazing out across the city. In the distance an airship, low over the horizon, was drifting smoothly across the clear blue sky. It wouldn't be long until the light began to fade.

She wondered how Bainbridge was getting on across town. Together, she knew, they could solve this. Compared to the things they had faced before—murderous automata, Revenants, rogue agents, serial killers, ghostly reincarnations—this was nothing. If they worked together, they could get Newbury back on track. It would be hard work, but they could do it.

Veronica consoled herself with the knowledge that their plan was already beginning to work—to some extent, at least, though it was clear that Newbury was beginning to suffer withdrawal symptoms: the tiredness, the sweating, the way his hand had trembled as he took his teacup from Mrs. Grant. She knew it was going to get worse. Much worse. This withdrawal was likely to cause more than the obvious physical symptoms. Newbury had come to rely on the drug, and eliminating that reliance would play havoc with his mind. Self-doubt, self-pity—all of this was to come. He honestly believed that the drug was what provided him with his insight, that without it, he'd be only a shadow of his former self. He saw it as a necessary evil, but it was time for that to stop.

Veronica turned her head and listened intently for a moment. Yes, she was right—she'd heard something clatter on the stairs. There it was again, that *tap-tap-tap*—the sound of metal repeatedly striking wood.

Intrigued, she crossed to the drawing room door. "Mrs. Grant, is that you?" she called out as she reached for the handle. She was just about to turn it when there was an almighty bang and the door shuddered in its frame. Veronica leapt back, unable to prevent herself from issuing a startled shout. Something scratched at the wooden panel.

Newbury was up and awake in seconds. He sprang out of the chair, dashing to her side, poised and ready for a fight. "Are you alright?"

"Yes, I'm alright. I just—" She stopped midsentence as the door began to shake. The shaking was accompanied by a high-pitched whining sound, the sound of blades burrowing through wood at high speed.

"Get back," Newbury warned her, and she did exactly as he said. He rushed over to the fireplace and grabbed a poker out of the grate. Then he ran back towards the door, standing ready, waiting for whatever it was on the other side to break through.

Veronica knew it must be the spider. It *had* to be. But did that mean Edwin Sykes was here, too, lurking somewhere in the background? And what had happened to Mrs. Grant?

"Here it comes!" Newbury bellowed as the wooden plug popped out of the door and a balled-up metal object came barrelling through. It hit the ground and rolled across the carpet, coming to rest upon the red Turkish rug in the centre of the room. Veronica moved swiftly to put a chair between herself and the strange mechanical monster.

Slowly, the thing unfurled, its eight spiky legs opening like a brass flower, before the leg joints inverted and raised its shining body off the ground. Four red lights glowed like multifaceted rubies at intervals around its circumference. The machine was the size of a small dog.

Veronica searched for something she could use to defend herself. There were more pokers in the grate, but the spider was now between her and the fireplace. It made a clicking sound, then scuttled away beneath the chair that Newbury had been dozing in.

"Where has it gone?" he asked as he cautiously crept farther into the room, wielding the poker like a spear.

"Careful, Maurice," she said, lapsing into the familiar address. "It's beneath that chair."

Newbury dropped to one knee, trying to get a view beneath the seat. "I can't see it there," he said.

"We can't have lost it!"

"No, it's just found a pla—" He was cut off by Veronica's panicked scream as she saw the thing appear around the top of the armchair and launch itself through the air at Newbury. He swung round just in time to raise the poker and bat it away with a resounding *clunk*. He dropped the poker and cursed in pain as the spider, bouncing off the wall, fell to the floor, curled itself into a ball, and rolled beneath the sideboard.

Veronica dashed over to Newbury. "Are you alright?"

Newbury nodded, rubbing his hands. "Yes, I'm fine. I simply jarred my hands with the impact."

"Do you think you got it?"

He shrugged. "I don't know. It hit the wall with quite a force. Where did it go?"

"Under there." She pointed towards the sideboard.

"Stay back. I'll take a look." He recovered the poker and approached the sideboard warily.

"Can you hear anything?"

"No. Can you?"

"Nothing. It's like it's stopped moving."

Newbury lowered himself to the ground, keeping the poker between himself and the sideboard at all times. He peered into the shadowy aperture. "I can see it," he said, the relief evident in his voice. "It's curled up into a ball and isn't moving. I'd say that's a good sign." He looked up at Veronica, who was standing over him. "I'll try to fish it out with the poker."

Cautiously, Newbury extended his arm and used the end of the iron poker to prod the mechanical creature.

"I think we're in the clear," he said. "The lights have gone out and it's not moving."

Veronica watched, fascinated, as he slowly withdrew the poker. Balanced on the end of it, hooked by the now-rigid legs, was the spider thing, replete in all its brass glory.

Newbury dropped it on the floor a couple of feet from him and placed the poker on the carpet beside it. "Charles's eyewitness reports don't begin to do it justice," he said with admiration. "Just look at it! What a remarkable device."

Veronica eyed the thing warily. It was grotesque. She couldn't understand why Newbury was so enamoured with it. Its bulbous body, its eight spiny legs, the bladelike protrusions embedded in its belly—it was a creature from a child's nightmare, not something to be admired and fawned over as a technological marvel. It was clever, of course, but everything about it made her skin crawl, from its purpose to its appearance.

Perhaps, also, it was the way it had moved, scurrying around on the floor and then propelling itself through the air like a pouncing cat. If one were caught unawares, it would have proved absolutely deadly. She'd been fortuitous to have Newbury there when she needed him.

"What are we going to do with it?" she said, unsure of their options.

"Bag it up and take it to Charles. This is clear evidence that Sykes is still active. Or at least someone pretending to be Sykes, with access to all of his equipment."

"Oh my God! Sykes! Mrs. Grant!" She ran to the door, flung it open, and hurtled down the stairs to the basement. "Mrs. Grant? Mrs. Grant?"

"Yes, miss? Whatever is the matter, miss?"

Veronica almost collapsed against the doorframe when she saw the elderly housekeeper standing in the kitchen, a mixing bowl and a wooden spoon in her hands, a look of concern writ large on her face.

Veronica heaved a sigh of relief. "Oh, Mrs. Grant. I thought you might have been in trouble."

Mrs. Grant's face cracked into a wide smile. "Oh, miss, why ever would you imagine such a thing?"

The question was answered by a loud bang from upstairs, the sound of something—or someone—being knocked to the floorboards. Veronica hurtled back up the stairs, two at a time. She threw herself across the small landing, catching the doorframe and swinging herself into the drawing room.

Inside, Newbury was stumbling backwards towards the window, his hands up near his face, trying desperately to hold the spider thing at bay. Its legs were clawing at his head, and the flashing blades in its belly were whirring dangerously close to his face. It was attempting to burrow into him, just as it had burrowed through the wooden door.

Veronica scanned the floor for the poker. It was still lying where Newbury had left it. She grabbed for it, rushing over to him, and lashed out at the metal beast with all her might.

The poker rebounded painfully in her hands, but the shell of the machine seemed barely marked by the impact, and the blades continued to spin and burr. Newbury was bleeding from innumerable scratches caused by the sharp tips of the spider's legs as it flayed and grappled with him, intent on finding enough purchase to pull itself in for the kill.

Newbury's breath came in short, sharp gasps. "Help . . . me . . . get . . . it . . . off!"

Veronica dropped the poker and grabbed at the spider's legs, trying to prise them away from Newbury's head. Two of them snapped back, the joints inverting so that the legs could stab at her hands and wrists. She pressed on, grabbing for more legs, ignoring the sharp pain that blossomed every time the machine managed to open up another gash in her forearms. Two more legs snapped back, directing their attacks towards her. Now she really was in trouble. She gave up on the legs and groped for the body instead, careful to keep her fingertips clear of the spinning blades. She felt the mechanisms within the machine humming, the clicking of the clockwork components inside: the mechanical brain.

She wrenched at it, tugging with all her might. To her surprise, it let go of Newbury and she stumbled backwards, tripping on the rug and sprawling onto her back. The thing squirmed in her grasp, manoeuvring itself about so that the body could pivot on the legs. She realised with horror that there was another set of blades on its back, and these were now extending towards her, spinning and howling with a startling ferocity. She tried to shout for Newbury, but she could hardly breathe.

Then she felt, more than saw, Newbury standing over her, casting her in his long shadow. He had a blanket in his hands from the chaise longue, and he threw it over the spider, bundling it up in the folds of the fabric to momentarily protect them from the blades. Then he grabbed the whole bundle and pulled it off Veronica, slamming it down hard on the floor. "Here! Grab the edge of the blanket!"

Veronica, gasping for breath, rolled onto her side and pinned the blanket to the floor. The spider was twisting and struggling in the folds of the thick fabric, its legs caught and unable to find purchase. She heard the sounds of the blades starting up again.

"It's going to try to go down through the floor!" Newbury shouted. "Hold it still!"

He fished for the poker, just off to his left, keeping his side of the blanket pinned down with his other hand. Then, on his knees, he grabbed the poker with both hands, raised it above his head, and thrust it down, point first, into the writhing mass of fabric and metal.

The sound was tremendous. The poker speared the mechanical beast right through its body, the metal rod shearing through the brass plating, smashing through the delicate mechanisms inside it, and pinning it, still twitching, to the floorboards. Sparks spat and hissed, and the blanket began to smoulder. Then the whirring blades came to an abrupt halt.

Newbury fell back, exhausted. Still on his knees, he looked over at Veronica. "Are you hurt?"

She had finally managed to regain her breath after the fall. "No. Not really. But you . . . you're bleeding."

Newbury grinned. "Isn't that always the way?" He collapsed against the arm of the chair behind him, laughing.

Newbury sat on the edge of the chaise longue while Veronica slowly and deliberately dabbed at the cuts on his face with a damp swab of cotton wool. There were scores of them, all over his forehead and cheeks, but Veronica had been relieved to find most of them superficial. One, above his right eye, was a nasty gash that continued to bleed profusely, but Newbury seemed unconcerned, preferring to focus instead on the small pile of mechanical remains on the Turkish rug.

"This rather alters things," he said, trying to swat her away as she dabbed once again at the cut above his eye.

"I suppose it does. Attempted murder is a far cry from burglary." She grabbed a fresh ball of cotton wool and dipped it in the bowl of warm water she had placed on a side table. She winced with the movement; she'd received a long gouge in her wrist during the course of the fight with the spider machine, and Newbury had already helped her to dress it.

Newbury's eyes flicked back to her face. "Indeed. It begs the question of who exactly would be out to make such an attempt on my life. Either Sykes really is still out there, somehow, and knows I'm on to him, or someone else has control of his machine and is using it for their own increasingly nefarious purposes."

Veronica stepped back, her hands on her hips. Sometimes she found it difficult to stomach the sheer arrogance of men. "I think that upon reflection, Sir Maurice, you will find the intended victim of any such assassination attempt was, in fact, me. This *is* my apartment, after all."

Newbury grimaced, and she saw her words had immediately struck home. "You're right. How truly inconsiderate of me," he said. He reached over and took her hand, giving her a most curious look that she found difficult to read. There was concern in his eyes, but there was something else, too. Realisation? Recognition? Dismay? "Of course you're right. The likelihood is that you, my dear, were the intended target of the mechanical beast. In many ways that makes my question even more of a pertinent one, and yet also profoundly more concerning."

"Do not concern yourself overly with me, Sir Maurice. I can quite ably look after myself." She tried ineffectually to stifle her wry smile. "So what now?"

"First of all, we must ensure that both you and Mrs. Grant are safe. I insist you spend the night in a hotel. Then tomorrow we shall take the remains of this device to Charles, and together we can discuss our next move."

"Very well," Veronica said, fighting back the urge to disagree. She could see the sense in his words. An attempt had been made on her life, after all. "I'm sure Mrs. Grant will be only too happy to spend the night at her sister's lodgings. I shall speak with her now. Perhaps if you could gather up the components of that . . . thing, we could take them back to Chelsea, where we know they will be secure?"

Newbury leaned over and plucked a ball of cotton wool

from the side table, using it to wipe away the trickle of blood that was threatening to run into his eye. "An excellent plan, my dear Miss Hobbes." He regarded the bloody swab in his hand. "My thanks to you. For being so . . . considerate." He dropped the swab onto the table beside the others.

Veronica smiled. They both knew there was a deeper meaning imbued in those words. "No need. No need at all. I'm only glad you were here."

Newbury nodded but didn't respond.

"Right, then," she said brightly. "I'll speak to Mrs. Grant. It won't take us long to throw some belongings in a case."

But Newbury was already staring out the window, lost in thought. She left him there, pondering whatever it was that she couldn't see, and set about making arrangements for the trip across town.

The streets stuttered by in quick succession, a series of flashing, half-seen images, turning the once-familiar city into nothing but a hazy blur. The light was failing now, and Veronica rested her head against the seat as the cab hurtled on, its steam engine roaring and hissing and spitting.

She'd seen Mrs. Grant off in a cab to her sister's rooms a short while earlier, having told her there had been an intruder and that Sir Maurice wished to ensure that everything was secure. Before she left, Mrs. Grant had packed Veronica an overnight bag for the stay in the hotel, while Newbury had scooped up the remains of the spider device in what was left of the blanket. There were large gouges in the floorboards where the mechanical beast had tried to escape through the floor, proving, if nothing else, that the thing had possessed at least some sense of self-preservation. She wondered how intelligent it had really been, and who had created it. It sat now on the seat beside Newbury, a collection of shattered clockwork and electrical components, lifeless and wrapped in a ruined blanket. She shuddered as she thought about what might have happened if Newbury hadn't been there when it attacked. If she'd been asleep . . . Well, it didn't bear thinking about. Perhaps she'd been a little hard on Newbury back at the house. She supposed that was simply a sign of her frustration with him—of his inability to see what he was doing to himself.

Veronica glanced over to see him watching her intently from across the cab, his face half lost in shadow. He smiled when he saw her looking, and for a moment she could almost believe it was the old Newbury sitting there, from the time before the opium dens and the absenteeism, the strange premonitions and the mummified hands. More than anything, she wanted that Newbury back again. She missed him terribly.

They sat in silence, regarding each other in the semi-darkness. "I miss you, too," he said softly, and she wondered if he had somehow managed to read her mind. She glanced out the window again, afraid to look into his eyes. Afraid to acknowledge the conversation.

Not now, Maurice. She almost hoped he *could* read her mind, then. *Not yet.* She didn't want to have that conversation now, not in the back of a dirty steam-powered cab, not with *this* Newbury, this drug-addled shadow of the man she loved. There would be time for that later, when he was better.

She realised she was balling her hands into fists. All she'd wanted for so long was to clear the air between them, to talk about the Queen, the secrets, the undeclared affection between the two of them. And now that that moment was here, now that Newbury was finally giving her the opening to have that conversation, all she actually felt was frustration. Because she wasn't ready. And neither, she knew, was he.

When she finally looked back at Newbury, he had shifted his position and was resting his head against the padded seat, his eyes closed, his breath shallow. They would be at Chelsea soon, back at his house on Cleveland Avenue. She breathed a sigh of relief. The moment had passed. She watched Newbury stirring fitfully as sleep tried to claim him, and she wondered what he would make of Bainbridge's little bit of interfering.

"What in the name of Hell does Charles think he's playing at!"

Newbury was storming about the drawing room, gesticulating in fury at the neat piles of papers and the clean surfaces where the stacks of dirty plates and cutlery used to be. "I mean he's . . . he's . . . he's *tidied* up!" As if in protest, he swept a stack of recent newspapers from the coffee table onto the floor, where they spread, rumpled, across the carpet.

Veronica tried not to laugh. She had warned Charles that Newbury would react like this. It wasn't so much that he liked to wallow in his clutter—more that he had a system for finding things, albeit a bizarre and disorganised one, and anybody who disrupted that system was likely to fall afoul of his temper.

Nevertheless, she'd agreed with Charles that it was the only course of action available to them, given the circumstances.

"Who is that man, anyway? Charles's bloody spy?" He glared accusingly at her. "You knew about this, didn't you?"

Veronica leaned against the back of an armchair and fixed him with her sternest look. "Really, Sir Maurice, is there any need for that sort of talk? Sir Charles assures me that Scarbright is as reliable as they come. He's been vetted by the palace, for a start. He knows all about your work. And your . . . current situation. He's here to help." She sighed. "Besides, it's only a temporary measure, until you can persuade Mrs. Bradshaw to return."

Newbury stooped and began gathering up the landslide of newspapers, his forehead creased in a heavy frown. "She's not coming back, Veronica. I'm sure of that much."

Veronica crossed the room to help him. She dropped to her knees. "Well, then. Wouldn't it be best to accept Sir Charles's gesture in the spirit in which it was intended? Let's face facts, Maurice: You're a mess." She caught herself, wondering whether she'd overstepped the mark. But Newbury seemed to be listening to her, so she continued. "See how it goes. Give it a few days. You have to admit, you could do with a hand around here, from someone who's already aware of your eccentricities."

"Eccentricities, eh?" He tried to glower at her disapprovingly but his eyes told a different story. He was amused by her sudden frankness.

"And besides," she went on, "I understand he's a most remarkable cook."

Veronica nearly jumped at the sound of someone clearing his throat behind her.

"So I'm told, Miss Hobbes, although I'll leave it to Sir Maurice to be the right and proper judge of that." Both Newbury and Veronica looked up with surprise to see that Scarbright had returned from the kitchen during their brief conversation, bearing a tray filled with teacups and saucers. He set it down on the sideboard. "Earl Grey?"

He was a smart, tall man in his mid-forties, dressed in an immaculate black suit with a bow tie and the white gloves of a professional butler. His hair was dark and swept back from his forehead, turning to mottled grey at the temples. He was wearing a moustache that curled upwards spectacularly at its tips. The result of this, Veronica thought, was that he looked as if he were permanently wearing a smile.

Newbury clambered to his feet, looking flustered. "Yes. Thank you, Scarbright. Most welcome."

"Very good, sir." He set about preparing two cups. "I thought venison for dinner, sir, prepared with creamed potatoes and greens. If that suits?"

"Um, yes, that suits very well. My thanks to you," Newbury managed to stutter out in reply. He looked like he didn't know what to do with himself.

"Excellent news, sir. I shall endeavour to have it with you shortly. Your tea." Scarbright handed the cup and saucer to Newbury before turning to Veronica. "Miss Hobbes. Shall you dine here before repairing to your hotel?"

Veronica smiled and shook her head. "I fear I must first secure myself a room in a suitable establishment."

Scarbright gave an ever-so-slight smile of satisfaction.

There was a gleam in his eye. "I took the liberty, miss, of making the arrangements on your behalf. A driver will be waiting to escort you to the Albert Hotel shortly after dinner." He offered them both a bow. "I fear I must now retreat to the kitchen. I urge you to ring if you have need of me."

"Very good, Scarbright," said Veronica, crossing the room to retrieve her tea.

Newbury watched Scarbright leave the room with a stunned look. When the door had shut behind the butler, he turned to Veronica. "Very well."

"Yes?" she ventured.

"He can stay. For now. But I'll be having words with Charles in the morning."

Veronica could hardly contain her laughter as she collapsed into one of the chesterfields to drink her tea.

CHAPTER

10

Bainbridge wasn't behind his desk when the police sergeant showed Veronica and Newbury into his office the following morning. Instead they found two foot-high stacks of paper files balanced precariously on his chair, an empty brandy glass resting on a notepad on the desk itself, and the remnants of two cigars in the ashtray.

The sergeant was only able to offer his apologies and the reassurance that Sir Charles would be back to see them shortly. If he knew the whereabouts of the chief inspector, he didn't feel at liberty to disclose them.

Newbury, whom Veronica had been surprised to find waiting for her in the hotel lobby an hour earlier, fresh-faced and chipper, dropped into the other chair beside the fireplace and grinned up at her expectantly, as if waiting for her to say something interesting or profound. Instead, she shrugged noncommittally and moved around the other side of Bainbridge's desk. She had deduced from this sudden alteration in Newbury's attitude and appearance only one thing: that, in the time between dinner and breakfast, he had once again resorted to the oriental weed. He had clearly not imbibed enough of the dreadful poison to send him into one of his fugues, but certainly enough to take the edge off his withdrawal. She could think of no other explanation.

Perhaps, she thought, this was only to be expected. At least he had chosen not to while away the morning in some sordid opium den across town. He could have resorted to the little brown bottle of laudanum he kept on the mantelpiece, taking a small draught to ease the symptoms of his withdrawal. Scarbright would know the truth. Inwardly, she smiled. Perhaps Scarbright *was* Charles's spy, after all. But if that were true, he was as much hers as the chief inspector's.

Veronica glanced over the twin stacks of files on the chair. Each one had a different name scrawled on its brown paper wrapper: *Richard Mars, Nicholas Kyme, Stuart Douglas*— the list went on. There must have been thirty or forty of them. None of the names meant anything to her, and she supposed they might be unrelated to the case at hand. Bainbridge was the chief inspector, after all. He was probably considering a plethora of other cases. Yet it was clear from the empty brandy glass and the stubs of the two cigars that he had been here most of the night, and she decided that it really wasn't much of a leap to assume he'd spent the time reading through the files.

Veronica looked at the notepad on the desk. The top page was covered in scrawl, along with a series of faint brown rings left behind by the bottom of the brandy glass. But scratched in capital letters across the centre of the page in heavy black ink were two words that jumped out at her almost immediately: FABIAN = BASTION.

She looked over at Newbury, who was still grinning. "You see it?"

Her eyes widened in surprise. "How did you—?"

"I glanced at his desk when we walked in. Force of habit. Interesting, isn't it?"

"That there's a connection between Dr. Fabian and the Bastion Society? Very. You think that's what Sir Charles has uncovered?"

Newbury nodded. "I'd wager on it." He gestured at Bainbridge's vacant chair. "I imagine they're all members of that illustrious set. He's been looking for connections, for a way in. Sometimes you can't beat good old-fashioned police work."

Veronica came round from behind the desk to take the vacant seat opposite Newbury. "I suppose this means we'll be paying a visit to the Grayling Institute?" She didn't know how to feel about that.

Newbury looked thoughtful. "Let's see what Charles has to say about it all." He looked round at the sound of footsteps from the hallway outside. "Here he comes. You can ask him now."

Bainbridge bustled into the room precisely on cue, a whirlwind of huffing and sighing and gesticulating limbs. He saw them sitting there and waved his cane pointedly at Newbury. "Ah, good. You're here. Lots to discuss." He glanced at his chair and the heaps of files, and then at Newbury and Veronica, shrugging despairingly at the lack of available places to sit. Instead, he lowered the end of his cane to the floor and leaned on it heavily, trying to catch his breath.

Newbury had a sly look on his face. "About Fabian and the Bastion Society, you mean?"

"How the devil did you know that?" Bainbridge's moustache twitched with barely concealed frustration. "Do tell me I didn't waste the entire night discovering something you already knew."

Veronica got to her feet. "Don't let him taunt you, Sir Charles. We've simply seen the note you'd written on your desk. What's the connection? Is Dr. Fabian a member of the Bastion Society?"

Bainbridge shook his head. "He used to be. Had some sort of falling out with them, by all accounts. Graves, in particular. A disagreement of some kind. I wondered if it might give us a way in."

"Good work, Charles! That's exactly the sort of angle we're looking for. I'm sure Fabian will be able to shed some light on Graves and what that lot are up to."

Bainbridge was still trying to catch his breath. "There's more. Last night. Another robbery." He looked from one to the other of them. "Same as before. But this time there's a body."

"Murder?" Newbury leapt out of his chair to join the others.

"It would seem so," Bainbridge continued, "although I'm not yet in full possession of the facts. I am led to believe that the profile is the same as the Regent Street job, however. It seems that Sykes's mechanical spider was used to force an entry."

Newbury frowned. "What time was this?"

"Late. Almost certainly in the small hours," Bainbridge replied.

Newbury gave a cackle of delight.

"What is so darn amusing, Newbury? A man is dead and we have another robbery to contend with." Bainbridge shifted uneasily. "And you have cuts all over your face. What have you been up to, man?"

Newbury grabbed for the bundled blanket he had placed on the floor by his chair. "This, Charles!" He allowed the blanket to unravel, spilling the components of the spider all over the floor in a shimmering cascade of brass. The tiny cogs and broken legs tinkled as they struck the polished floorboards, bouncing off in all directions. Veronica sighed. Newbury did like his needlessly dramatic flourishes.

Bainbridge poked at the debris with the end of his cane. "Look, is someone going to explain to me— Ah. Yes, I see. . . ." Veronica saw the realisation light up his face. He turned the remains of the machine's carcass over so that it was the right way up. He studied Newbury's face. "Is this what caused those cuts to your face?"

Newbury nodded.

"How interesting," said Bainbridge. "It's just as we'd imagined. About the size of a small terrier."

"And a darn sight more intelligent, too. Tried to escape before I got it with the poker."

"Came for you at the house, did it? Sykes must know we're on to him." Bainbridge fiddled with his moustache while he processed the information.

Veronica cleared her throat.

"Actually, Charles, it was Miss Hobbes's apartment where the attack took place. And I have every reason to believe that Miss Hobbes herself was the target of the assassination attempt." Newbury touched her arm, just for the briefest of moments. She wondered if he realised he'd done it.

"Good God! I take it you're unhurt, Miss Hobbes?" There was real concern in Bainbridge's voice.

"Just a few scratches, Sir Charles. Nothing to concern yourself with." She tried to sound dismissive, even though the large gouge in her forearm had been causing her to wince in pain all morning.

"Excellent, excellent. Wouldn't do to have you in the path of danger, Miss Hobbes. Not at all." Bainbridge straightened his back, as though signifying that was an end to the matter.

Veronica rolled her eyes.

"I gather from your outburst, Newbury, that these events occurred earlier in the evening than our robbery and suspected murder?"

Newbury was animated again. "Indeed they did, Charles. Around eight. And that can only mean—"

"—there's more than one spider," Bainbridge finished.

"Precisely!" said Newbury.

Veronica sighed. "The more pertinent point, however, is that multiple spiders suggests multiple criminals. Perhaps Sykes was just one of a number of individuals all operating with the same equipment. Could he have been part of a criminal gang? A network of jewellery thieves?"

"You make an excellent point, Miss Hobbes." Bainbridge pondered her words for a moment, and then shook his head. "And you might yet be right, but the evidence at the crime scenes was always—*is* always—the same: a man of about Sykes's height, with the same shoe size and consistent habits. It seems unlikely that a criminal gang would go to the lengths of recruiting only men of the same height and shoe size and teaching them to behave according to identical patterns, though it's not beyond the realm of possibility."

"I wonder how many of the men named in those files would match that profile," Newbury ventured.

"We may yet need to find out. But for now, I have a crime scene to attend to and another body to identify," Bainbridge replied. "I'm heading there now. Can you come?"

Veronica looked to Newbury for his answer.

"Of course we'll come. Lead on!" Newbury clapped his hand on Bainbridge's shoulder. He lowered his voice. "And don't think for a minute, old man, that I'm going to let you get away with planting your spy in my house. As soon as I can make other arrangements, I'll be sending him back."

"Quite right, too," Bainbridge replied, grinning. "Damn good cook, though, isn't he?"

"Sublime," Newbury said, pushing the chief inspector out the door.

The scene of the second robbery was a residence. A house on Cromer Street, set back from the road, nestled behind a pretty garden brimming with evergreens and late spring blooms. Veronica filled her nostrils with the heady scents as the three investigators walked the path up to the big house.

It was an imposing two-storey building, erected sometime in the preceding fifty years. It was not stately, but had a more homely appeal—clearly the dwelling of a large and well-to-do family, probably of a similar station to her own parents. The thought of them made her heart sink, so Veronica pushed the notion to one side.

No, this family was clearly different—they were interested in more than just status. She could tell from the large wooden playhouse that someone had built in the garden that whoever lived here showed an actual interest in their children. She hoped those children had been spared the horror of the corpse that Bainbridge had warned them waited at the foot of the stairs inside.

She was pleased to find, a moment later, that this was indeed the case. A bobby on the door explained that the family had been escorted from the premises first thing that morning, after one of the servants had discovered the body and alerted the police. That was a small mercy, at least.

Inspector Foulkes, who had secured the scene, was there to greet their little party when they stepped over the threshold and into the cavernous hallway inside. He looked as serious and professional as ever in his grey woollen suit and bowler hat. His full, black beard had grown since Veronica had last seen him, a few months earlier, and he was stroking it ponderously, as if trying to decide what his next move might be.

He looked up when he saw them approaching. "A fine mess we have here, I'm afraid," he said with an exasperated tone, reaching out to shake hands with the men. "I'd recommend, Miss Hobbes, that you don't come any closer, but I know from experience you'll pay me no heed." His sea green eyes flashed with amusement.

"Indeed not, Inspector," she replied, secretly bracing herself for whatever horrors she might have to face. "I rarely pay anyone any heed. I find it's the only way to form an opinion of my own." She tried to keep the sarcasm out of her voice, but Newbury nudged her gently with his elbow, as if simultaneously joining in with her ribbing of the inspector and warning her to stand down.

Veronica tried to get a measure of the situation, taking in the scene. The hallway was spacious and central to the property, with extensive wings to the left and right and a grand staircase directly opposite the main entrance. Ornate banisters curled upwards in sweeping lines of gleaming hardwood. A few uniformed policemen were milling around, and a man in a brown suit—a doctor, she supposed—was standing over the corpse on the floor. For the time being, she averted her eyes. She wouldn't look at it until she had to.

"Tell us what you've found," Bainbridge asked Foulkes with little or no ceremony.

"It's a baffling one, sir," Foulkes said, lifting his bowler and scratching his head. "It seems the perpetrator came in through the back door. There's a hole in one of the panels, about so big—" He made a gesture with his hands. "—that looks just like the hole we found up at Flitcroft and Sons over on Regent Street, and the scenes before that."

"You think the same man is responsible?" asked Newbury.

"I'm not a betting man, Sir Maurice, but I'd put my life on it." Foulkes seemed to consider this for a minute. "Only difference this time is the body. And it's not a pretty sight. It seems that whatever miraculous device the burglar has been using to cut his way in can also be used as a weapon. And a pretty damn effective one at that." He sniffed, as if demonstrating his disapproval of such visceral things. "As I see it, one of three things occurred: Either the burglar interrupted another man trying to steal the loot and finished him off, or he had a partner along with him and they fell out over the share of the proceeds. Only other explanation is that the miraculous device I was talking about suddenly turned on him, but that seems unlikely."

"Have we been able to identify him yet?" Veronica realised she was about to get a look at what might have become of her or Newbury, had the incident in her apartment not turned out as well as it did.

"Not yet. He's . . . well, let's just say that identification is not an easy matter in this instance." Foulkes screwed up his face in distaste, and Veronica gave an involuntary shudder.

Newbury was removing his jacket. He handed it to Charles. "Better take a look, then." He edged past Foulkes, heading toward the doctor in the brown coat.

"I hope you haven't had a big breakfast," Foulkes called behind him. But he was not smiling. He took a step closer to Veronica and lowered his voice to a whisper. His breath smelled of peppermint. "Seriously, Miss Hobbes. I should consider giving this one a miss. I won't think any less of you if you take my advice. If I'm truthful, I wish I hadn't seen it myself." He smiled kindly, and she knew he was only looking after her best interests—or at least what he considered to be her best interests.

She hesitated, unsure now what to do. "Well, I—"

"Charles!" Newbury's voice, raised in alarm, suddenly echoed throughout the hall. "You'd better get over here quickly."

Veronica smiled weakly at Foulkes and moved past him, heading towards Newbury and the body.

She almost baulked at what she saw. There was blood *everywhere*. Everywhere she looked: sprayed up the staircase, spattered and pooling on the floor, even dripping—drip by ponderous drip—from the glass chandelier high above them. Jewels lay scattered all around the body, in all manner of colours, shapes, and sizes; tiny flecks of beauty in the midst of utter, devastating violence.

The corpse itself—or what was left of it—was splayed out upon the tiled floor facedown, its head and right arm thrown up onto the bottom stair. And there was a hole right through the middle of it, a ragged-edged void where the spider thing had chewed through the meat and bone and cartilage, burrowing through the man's chest and bursting out through his back. Ribbons of shredded intestine hung like pink drapes from around the edges of the hole.

Newbury knelt beside the body, cradling the man's head in his hands. The face was covered in a series of ferocious gouges, and the hair was matted with dark arterial blood.

She heard Bainbridge beside her, but couldn't look away from the obscenity before her, couldn't tear her eyes away from the sheer horror of what she was seeing.

"My god!" Bainbridge exclaimed. She surmised he was experiencing a very similar response to her own.

"There's more," Newbury said, shifting the body around so they could see.

"What? What is it?" Veronica just wanted to get out of there, to get outside and away from the stink and the blood. She had no time for games.

Newbury pulled a handkerchief from his breast pocket and used it to smear the blood away from around the dead man's face. "There. Do you see it now?"

Veronica studied the man's face. The expression was one of sheer terror, the lips curled back in a frightened scream. But beneath the blood and the webwork of scratches, one thing was suddenly clear: The dead man in Newbury's arms was none other than the enigmatic Mr. Edwin Sykes.

CHAPTER

11

I t's extraordinary! They're identical!" Bainbridge exclaimed loudly. He looked terribly confused by the whole affair.

"Hmmm," said Newbury, without looking up.

Much to Veronica's unease, the three of them had returned to the police morgue. They had driven convoy across town from the house on Cromer Street, following the police wagon bearing the corpse. The journey had been arduous, conducted at a funereal pace, and now she was back at this most distasteful of establishments for the second day in a row, and starting to regret ever getting herself mixed up in the affair.

The body had been one of the most horrendous things she had ever seen, comparable to when she and Newbury had discovered the violated body of James Purefoy, the young reporter, or—perhaps worse—the shriveled, exsanguinated husks of former village folk at Huntington Manor earlier that year. It was the sheer violence of the attack, the utter disregard for life that disturbed her so. Seen like this, people became nothing but shreds of meat and bone, and she hated it. Perhaps it was also the understanding that, if not for Newbury, she might well have been discovered that morning in much the same condition. Either way, she didn't wish to spend any longer in the company of the dead than was strictly necessary.

As it was, they had been at the morgue for an hour. It had taken the police surgeon only ten minutes to complete his assessment and ready the corpse on the mortician's slab. For the rest of that time, Newbury had been examining the body in minute detail. Not only that, but he had recalled the corpse they had seen on their previous visit, which now lay uncovered on a second slab beside the new arrival.

It had been a few days since that first corpse had been found in the gutter, and the flesh had taken on a bruised, sickly hue. It had also begun to smell. Badly. As a consequence, Veronica had covered her nose and mouth with a handkerchief, which had the dual purpose of suppressing the smell and keeping her grimace hidden from the others.

Newbury was currently comparing the left hand of the new body with the identical hand of its double. He was stooped low, circling the marble slabs, a looking glass clutched in his right hand.

Veronica lowered the handkerchief. "Couldn't this be a simple matter of identical twins?" she ventured. She'd read about cases such as this, where a long-lost or previously unheard-of relative had made a sudden reappearance, capitalizing on their likeness to their more successful kin. In some cases, they'd gone so far as to attempt to assume the identity of their brother or sister, even murdering them as a means of keeping them out of the picture.

Bainbridge, however, was shaking his head. "I don't believe so, Miss Hobbes. We checked the birth records. Sykes was an only child. It was a complicated birth and his mother died during delivery. If there had been twins, the doctor would have recorded them as such at the hospital."

Newbury stepped back from the slab and looked up at them, bleary eyed. "There's far more to it than that," he said enigmatically. "There are sinister forces at work."

"Sinister forces! Whatever are you going on about, Newbury?" said Bainbridge. Veronica could tell by the way he was tapping his foot on the tiles that he was growing steadily more impatient. He'd been standing there, just as she had, for the best part of an hour. Now, it seemed, he wanted answers.

For a moment, Veronica thought that Newbury was going to ignore the question, but then he folded his arms and smiled. "One of these corpses," he said, "is a doppelgänger. A copy."

"A what?"

"A copy, Charles. It's really quite remarkable. I don't know how it was done. But the first corpse you found, this one—" He gestured towards the body on his right, the one that was beginning to putrefy. "—is not the original Edwin Sykes."

Bainbridge glowered at the body, as if willing it to disappear, or else to sit up and reveal all its secrets. "I don't understand, Newbury. A *copy*, you say?"

Newbury nodded. "I know it's hard to take in, Charles, but this isn't another case of familial secrets and long-lost twins. What we have here are two Edwin Sykeses."

Bainbridge shook his head. He looked lost, as if he simply couldn't comprehend what Newbury was telling him.

"But that's impossible," Veronica said, feeling as unsure about what she was hearing as Bainbridge looked. She covered her face with her handkerchief once again. The stench of the corpses was like rancid meat.

Newbury shrugged. "Who's to say what's possible and impossible in this world? I can only judge the evidence placed before me, what I see before my eyes. And the facts are that this—" He pointed to the eviscerated corpse they had pulled from the house on Cromer Street that morning. "—is the real Edwin Sykes. And this—" He pointed back at the other. "—is a duplicate."

"How can you tell?" she replied, trying not to sound too skeptical.

"The forensic evidence speaks for itself," he argued. "For a start, the facial structures, the sizes and shapes of the bodies—they're in every way identical. Absolutely *identical*. But this Sykes's skin has been lived in. There are laughter lines around the mouth, tiny creases and imperfections, scars. Whereas this one—" He crossed to the other slab. "—well, the skin is almost perfect. No scars, no sign that it's ever been *worn*. I mean, look at the colour of it. It's never even been exposed to the sun! It's pale, soft, and new."

"New? I'm having trouble following you, Newbury," said Bainbridge.

"Then there are the hands," Newbury pressed on, ignoring him. "Look here." He grabbed the left wrist of the first body, showing them the hand he'd been examining earlier.

He spread the fingers so they could see them. "Here. These hands are clean. Perfectly clean and unblemished." He carefully lowered the hand, placing it gently on the chest of the corpse, and then ran around to the other slab. He was bursting with energy, filled with the ebullience of the hunt. "Now, look at this. Identical in almost every way, except *here*."

Veronica gasped. "Calluses."

"Very good, Miss Hobbes!" Newbury beamed at her. "And lots of them. Look at the ingrained filth, too. These hands have seen work, and recently." Newbury looked at Bainbridge. "The evidence is compelling, Charles. I could list more: the teeth, the eyes . . . I'd wager if you sliced him open, the organs would tell a similar tale. I tell you: We're dealing with more than one Edwin Sykes."

Bainbridge was staring at him. "So you're telling me there could be an army of them out there? Any number of Edwin Sykeses? He could have set that spider device on you last night at Miss Hobbes's apartment?"

Newbury nodded slowly. "Once you accept the facts, Charles, anything is possible."

"It's unbelievable. Too outlandish, Newbury, even for you." Bainbridge tapped his cane on the floor to hammer his point home. The sound echoed out around the tiled walls. "I'm more inclined to go along with what Miss Hobbes intimated back at the Yard, about there being other men involved . . ."

"Charles. Charles! The evidence is here before your eyes! Can't you see it?" Veronica thought Newbury was about to start hopping from foot to foot with impatience.

"I don't know what to believe." Bainbridge gave a hearty

sigh. "It's a damn mess of an investigation. We can't build a case on speculation alone. I mean, how the devil would Sykes even go about *starting* to copy himself?"

Newbury moved round the slab to stand before him. "*Think,* Charles. The mechanical spiders. He didn't build them himself! He must have a sponsor, someone with the where-withal, with the right technology. Someone who trusted him to handle the spiders on their behalf. Edwin Sykes didn't master-mind the operation."

"But really, Newbury . . ."

"Charles, we've seen all sorts of bizarre things during our many cases together. Why is this any different?"

"Because we're talking about something as fundamental as the ability to copy a living person!"

"That doesn't make it any more outlandish than automata with human organs, or poltergeists, or any of the other bi-zarre things we've seen before." Newbury gesticulated at Bain-bridge, imploring him to understand.

"But who? And why?"

Newbury shrugged again. "I can think of any number of reasons. If you were a jewel thief with the ability to copy him-self, what would you do?"

"Sit and grow fat on the accumulated wealth of my dupli-cates," Bainbridge replied thoughtfully. "And pay my sponsor a hearty cut of the proceeds."

"No." Veronica shook her head. "No. We're missing some-thing. It's not that simple. If Sykes could just create copies of himself that easily, why was he at Cromer Street? The corpse with the calluses—that body has been *lived* in. Why would he still be committing a crime himself when he could have one of his duplicates do it for him? If it were me, I wouldn't risk capture."

"And there's more," Newbury said. "We still haven't explained why he was lying dead at the foot of the stairs, surrounded by the spoils of his trade. I find it highly unlikely that his mechanical beast would turn on him after all this time. Not unless someone else was controlling it."

Bainbridge leaned heavily on his cane. "This is a dark and intricate web, Newbury. And we still haven't worked out what, if anything, it has to do with Graves and the Bastion Society."

"Oh, I'm sure they're involved, Charles, somehow. There's a lot more to Enoch Graves than meets the eye."

"Sir Charles?"

Veronica turned at the sound of a man's urgent voice echoing down the passageway.

"Sir Charles?"

"Through here," Bainbridge called in reply, with a dark scowl.

Veronica heard footsteps ringing on the tiles. Someone was running. Seconds later, a young man in a police constable's uniform came hurtling out of the passageway and into the room, skidding to a halt on the slippery tiles. "Sir Charles!" he said, leaning against the wall as he attempted to catch his breath.

"Yes? What is it, man?"

"You're needed, sir," the constable said between gasping intakes of breath. "There's been an intruder at the palace. Her Majesty sent for you."

Veronica saw Bainbridge start in surprise. "An intruder at the palace?"

"Yes, sir. An attempt has been made on her life."

Veronica and Newbury turned to stare at Bainbridge, waiting to hear his response.

"Have you got a carriage waiting?" Bainbridge asked, his voice low and serious.

"Yes, sir."

"Good. I'm on my way." Bainbridge turned to Newbury. He looked as white as a sheet. "You'll have to finish things here, Newbury."

Newbury narrowed his eyes. "Charles, do you need me there? I could come along—"

"No." Bainbridge cut him off. "I'll send for you if I need you. Finish up here, then get over to the Grayling Institute and talk to Fabian. We need to find out what that fool Graves is up to, and whether he has anything to do with this doppelgänger business."

Newbury nodded. "Very well, Charles. Hurry. And give Her Majesty my regards."

Bainbridge turned and ran after the young constable, abandoning the use of his cane as he dashed headlong towards the waiting carriage.

Veronica watched him go, then turned to face Newbury, who was looking down at the two dead men with a thoughtful expression. "You want to know, don't you?"

"What?" He didn't look up.

"How he did it. How he copied himself like that."

Newbury chuckled, but didn't take his eyes off the bodies. "At this moment, Miss Hobbes, more than anything else in the world."

Veronica grinned. This was what she'd been waiting for.

All the dead bodies, all the waiting around in the morgue, the arguments, the shouting. All of it had been worth it for this. She watched him as he carefully lifted the shrouds, one after the other, and covered the corpses.

Newbury—*her* Newbury—was back.

CHAPTER

12

Amelia woke, and she knew she was dying.

She felt as if she were floating, surrounded by stark, inky blackness. Her body was numb and unmoving. Everything was still, silent.

Slowly, sensation began to return. Her head was throbbing, her heart fluttering in her chest. She was rasping for breath, dragging the air down into her lungs. And what was that? A gritty, metallic taste in her mouth. Adrenaline? Blood?

Yes, blood. She must have bitten her tongue.

Amelia tried to steady her breathing. She was on her back. Beneath her she felt the softness of her mattress and bedding. She wanted to shrink into it, to wrap herself in it like a cocoon, to be subsumed by it and retreat into unconsciousness. She longed for a place where she didn't have to think about the things she had seen, where she could escape from the world and all its horrors, from the thoughts of her own impending death and the absolute futility of fighting it.

But she could feel herself coming round, the world slowly drawing into focus. It was like surfacing from a pool of water, muffled sounds beginning to make some sort of disjointed, disordered sense.

Someone was holding her hand, speaking to her. She could make out nothing of the words: just heard the low, monotonous voice, talking ceaselessly.

She tried to open her eyes but her eyelids felt as if they were gummed shut. Her mind was suddenly filled with a cascade of stuttering images, terrifying, confusing images: fire and smoke; the whole world spinning, twirling, dancing—a constant, repeating revolution, turning again and again. Dizziness followed by screaming followed by exquisite pain. She imagined this was how most people would describe Hell.

Amelia knew she had seen her own death. She had seen the walls caving in around her, heard the deafening noise of exploding masonry, the crack of splintering stone. She had seen the world ending all around her and her own inability to get away.

And then silence. Nothing but profound, infinite silence and the smooth porcelain face of Mr. Calverton looming over her, his darting blue eyes hovering menacingly above her face.

She opened her mouth to scream, but choked on the blood that had pooled at the back of her throat. She tried to sit up, but found herself rooted to the spot. She gasped and struggled, and then felt steadying hands on her shoulders, keeping her still, keeping her safe.

It was then that she realised the voice she was hearing

belonged to Dr. Fabian, and his words slowly resolved into something meaningful. "Try to breathe, Amelia. Deep breaths." The concern was evident in his voice. "There, now." He patted her hand. "There, you're coming round."

Amelia's eyes blinked open. She searched the room in panic. No sign of Mr. Calverton, and the walls were not caving in. No fire, either. Not yet. Only the smiling, worried face of Dr. Fabian, leaning over her, studying her intently.

She took a moment to collect herself, to get her bearings. She was lying on her bed, in her room at the Grayling Institute, still wrapped in her nightdress. Her hands were trembling.

"You've had another episode, Amelia," Dr. Fabian went on. "I believe it must have been induced by the intensity of the treatment. It's the first one you've suffered in some time. Can you speak?"

Amelia swallowed. The sensation was like broken glass in her throat. "Water?" she croaked.

"Yes, my dear. Well done. Can you sit up?"

Amelia propped herself up on the pillow while Dr. Fabian reached for the jug on the nightstand and poured her a small glass of water. He handed it to her and she sipped it gratefully. "I think the worst of it has passed," she said. She felt her heart rate slowly returning to normal, but her nerves were still jangling and her head continued to pound. She felt utterly exhausted.

Dr. Fabian leaned back in his chair, causing the old wood to creak in protest. He pushed his wire-rimmed spectacles up the bridge of his nose with his index finger: that nervous gesture again. "It's my fault, Amelia. I'm sorry. I pushed you too far, too quickly. I should have been more patient. But we were making such progress—"

"No," she said. "Stop that. You're doing everything you can. We've come so far. We can't give up now."

"No, my dear. There's no chance of that. I couldn't give up on you now." Dr. Fabian folded one leg across the other. He regarded her coolly. "Do you remember your dreams, Amelia? Can you recall what you saw?"

"No," she lied. And then worried that she'd responded too quickly. She couldn't face it yet, couldn't bring herself to talk about it. Saying it out loud made it real, and all she wanted to do was forget. "That is," she continued, "nothing that makes any sense."

Dr. Fabian nodded slowly. He regarded her with interest. She wondered whether he believed her or not. "Well then, I think, my dear, you should sleep. Your body needs to recover from the trauma of the episode. The seizure was exceptionally violent." He turned his head and she saw two bloody lines on his cheek where her nails had obviously raked his flesh.

"Oh . . . I'm . . ."

"No need to apologise, Amelia. You were not in control of your faculties. Rest now for a few hours. I'll send Mr. Calverton to wake you in time to get ready for dinner."

Amelia nodded, although the idea of food was utterly nauseating. She downed the rest of her water, swilling it around her mouth to wash away the residue of the blood. Her tongue felt thick and swollen in her mouth. She handed the empty glass to Dr. Fabian, who rose from his chair and returned it to its place on the bedside table.

Amelia watched him leave the room, carefully pulling the door shut and locking it behind him. She curled up on the bed, bringing her knees up under her chin. She closed her eyes, but all she could see was fire and spinning and screaming. She felt the tears come then, a huge upwelling of emotion. She buried her face in the pillows to muffle the sound, and her body was racked with sobs.

So this was it. This was how her life would end, here, in the Grayling Institute. Even Dr. Fabian and his "engine of life" could not save her. She had seen it in her dreams. And her dreams, she knew from experience, always spoke the truth.

CHAPTER

13

The palace was a hive of activity. Bainbridge watched through the window of the police carriage as they were ushered onto the grounds by a man wearing the bright red uniform of the Queen's Guard. They came to a halt a moment later and six armed members of the guard quickly converged on the carriage, their weapons ready.

The young constable—whose name was Brown—moved to get up from his seat, but Bainbridge waved him down. "Thank you, Brown. I'll see to things from here." After peering out the window at the armed men awaiting them, Brown quickly decided to do exactly as he was told.

Bainbridge leaned on his cane as he stood, swinging the door open and hopping down from the carriage. It was cool outside, and the fresh breeze ruffled his hair. "Good day, gentlemen," he said to the guardsmen, who were each watching him warily. Their faces were stern and expressionless. They were jumpy, he realised. The attack on the Queen must have really shaken them up. Bainbridge didn't much like the idea of being surrounded by nervous men bearing rifles. "Sir Charles Bainbridge, Chief Inspector, Scotland Yard." The men lowered their guns, visibly relaxing.

"Very good, sir," the one nearest to him said. "We'll take you in."

Bainbridge fell into step with the soldiers as they marched across the palace forecourt. Whatever had gone on here, the Queen was evidently taking it very seriously indeed. This was no small matter of a thief trying his luck. Bainbridge could tell he was going to be here for a while.

Around them even more of the red-coated guardsmen—an army of them—were milling about, taking up position around the perimeter of the building. It was clear the Queen had already taken measures to increase security on the grounds. Bainbridge wouldn't have been surprised if there were more on the way. An attempt on her life, the fact that someone had managed to get so close to her: Bainbridge knew that heads were going to roll. Whoever had been responsible for the security detail that morning was going to find himself on the sharp end of the Queen's wrath.

Bainbridge looked up at the mighty edifice of the palace as they passed beneath the pillared portico. The curtains were all drawn as usual, blotting out the sunlight and keeping prying eyes at bay. He realised with a smile that this was probably the first time he had entered the building through the main entrance, rather than the more discreet doorway around the back that was the mainstay of all Her Majesty's agents.

He kept his eyes peeled, looking for any clues as to what

might have occurred there that morning. He had interrogated Brown on the journey over but the boy had known nothing of any consequence. It had soon become clear that any briefing was going to be delivered by Her Majesty herself. Nevertheless, Bainbridge liked to be prepared, and it wouldn't do to go before the monarch without at least a few observations and questions at the ready.

The six guardsmen came to a halt in a line before the doorway, stock-still, their rifles tucked beneath their arms. They turned towards him as he passed them one by one, heading towards the gaping mouth of the palace and the uncertainty that lay within. He hesitated on the threshold. "My thanks," he said to the uniformed men before ducking quickly inside.

The grand hallway on the other side of the door was cavernous and austere, like something lifted out of another era and dropped into place, right there in 1902. Bainbridge had no idea where to go. His only experience of the palace was in the secret tunnels and passageways that led him directly from the agent's entrance all the way through to the audience chamber.

He glanced around and was thankful to see Sandford, the agent's butler, waiting for him in the shadows of the immense staircase. "Sandford! Thank goodness. Can you tell me what the devil is going on?"

Sandford came forward to meet him. "Morning, Sir Charles. I imagine I know only as much as you. Somehow, someone got into the palace and made an attempt on Her Majesty's life. I understand she is quite well and that the palace has been fully secured." He lowered his voice conspiratorially. "—but I

believe she is determined to root out the incompetent responsible for the breach in security and have his head from his
shoulders."

Bainbridge grinned. "I find myself unsurprised by your
words, Sandford. Any more?"

"No, sir," the aged butler replied. "I'm afraid that's as much
as I know."

"Very well." Bainbridge removed his overcoat and handed
it to the other man. "Can you take me to her?"

Sandford smiled. "Yes. She's waiting."

Bainbridge sighed, but kept his thoughts to himself. She
was always waiting, he reflected, like the spider at the centre
of a vast and intricate web.

He followed Sandford around behind the staircase, past
rows of looming portraits and biblical scenes that adorned
the walls. There, in a hidden recess, Sandford opened a door
and ushered Bainbridge down a labyrinthine passageway in
which seemingly innumerable doors led off into unseen and
mysterious rooms elsewhere in the palace. They wound their
way deeper into the bowels of the great house until, after a
minute or so, Sandford stopped outside another unremarkable door and rapped loudly on the wooden panel.

There was no response. Sandford waited a moment longer
and then pushed the door open, holding it for Bainbridge
and gesturing for him to enter.

Bainbridge stepped into the audience chamber beyond,
unable to contain his feelings of apprehension.

"You took your time, Sir Charles." The Queen's shrill, disembodied voice echoed around the murky darkness of the
room. How did she do that? How could she see him in this

perpetual half light she lived in? He didn't know whether the lack of lighting was a result of her medical situation, or had more to do with the maintenance of her mystique: the enduring myth of the Queen, the enigmatic Empress. She had fostered that persona since the day that Dr. Fabian had installed her in the life-giving chair—unable, she said, to be seen or even portrayed in public in such a frail condition. Instead, she presented herself as the unknowable monarch, the omnipotent ruler at the heart of the British Empire, the all-powerful Queen.

Bainbridge had to hand it to her: she believed it, too. He wondered if she ever had the lights on when she wasn't receiving visitors. He supposed he'd never know. He addressed the gloom, not knowing in which direction to face. "My apologies, Your Majesty. I was attending to a matter at the morgue, with Newbury."

He heard her give a wet, rasping chuckle. "Ah, Newbury. So you managed to drag his carcass out of the opium dens."

Bainbridge swallowed. So she knew. He thought he'd managed to keep that from her. "Yes . . . well . . . I needed his assistance with a particularly baffling case."

Victoria laughed again. "Yes, we know all about your case, Sir Charles. The two identical bodies, the dead man committing crimes. No wonder you need Newbury's assistance."

Bainbridge moved towards the sound of her voice, trying to identify her location in the shadows. Victoria, wise to his movements, fell suddenly silent. Then, a second or two later, a light blinked on like a brilliant beacon in the darkness: the shutters of a paraffin lantern being opened.

Victoria was there, encapsulated in the warm globe of

light cast out by the lantern. To Bainbridge, it looked as if she were somehow contained within a bubble, floating in an unfathomable ocean of black. And there was something else, too: another person, sitting in a wooden chair opposite her. He hesitated.

"Come forward, Sir Charles."

He did as he was commanded. As he drew closer, the situation became suddenly clear. The man in the chair opposite the Queen was slumped in a death pose, the shaft of a steel bolt protruding rudely from his chest. His head was hanging loosely to one side, slack-jawed. He had been about thirty years of age, dark haired, smartly dressed in a navy blue suit. His flesh looked tanned and healthy in the orange glow of the lantern.

She looked up at Bainbridge, a wicked grin on her face. He could hear the preservative machines labouring as they fought to keep her alive.

"What happened, Your Majesty?" he said, leaning heavily on his cane.

"This man, this boy, found his way into our audience chamber uninvited. An attempt was made on our life. He tried to tamper with Dr. Fabian's machines, to disconnect the hose that feeds our body its breath." Victoria emitted a racking cough, and she spasmed momentarily before returning to normal. All the while, the machine continued to hiss and groan, her chest rising and falling in time with the bellows that operated her breathing.

"My god . . . ," said Bainbridge.

Victoria laughed. "Your concern does you credit, Sir Charles. But do not think for a moment that our confinement in this contraption is an indication of our weakness. We are quite capable of protecting ourself."

Bainbridge glanced again at the body of the intruder, the bolt in the chest. The Queen had done that?

"We are not so naïve as to believe that we do not have enemies, Sir Charles. This chair was constructed with a number of defense mechanisms and weapons that we can deploy if it becomes necessary. This man, and whomever he represents, clearly underestimated our abilities. They shall not be so foolish a second time."

"Quite," said Bainbridge, unsure exactly how to respond. He'd stood before this chair a hundred times before, and never once had he considered that it might have a purpose other than the medical one for which it was created. That the Queen was harbouring deadly weapons. He wondered absently whether she had used them before.

"We suppose you are wondering why we had him propped in the chair in such a manner?"

He was, but he had decided it would be inappropriate to ask. It was not his place to question the Queen's judgement, only to protect her and her subjects from harm.

Victoria took his silence as an affirmative. "It was so we could see his face, Sir Charles, to look upon the countenance of one who would have us dead." She chuckled again. Her tone became suddenly serious. "Do you recognise him?"

Bainbridge studied the young man's face more closely. "I fear I do not, Your Majesty."

"Then make it your business to, Sir Charles. We are intent on understanding his motivation."

Bainbridge nodded. "As you say, Your Majesty." He tugged at his moustache nervously. "Do we know how he got in?"

Victoria gave a gesture that he took to be an approximation of a shrug. "We believe that is neither here nor there. Through a window, we are told, left open by a servant to air the room. We believe he must have obtained a schematic of the palace somehow, to have navigated through the warren of passageways and hidden doors to find us here."

She looked from Bainbridge to the body in the chair. "But such matters are easily dealt with." Her tone was now dismissive, as though she considered the whole affair to be nothing but a trivial part of her day, another of the challenges of presiding over an Empire. "We have doubled the guard and sent instruction to the Royal Engineers to post their war machines in the grounds of the palace. No one will enter without us knowing of it." She paused. "We now fear, however, that whoever is responsible for the attack may escalate their offensive when they discover their initial strategy resulted in failure."

Bainbridge could see the logic in her thinking, although the idea of an outright assault on Buckingham Palace seemed unimaginable to him. Nevertheless, more sentries, more soldiers, and more police would ensure that the palace could be protected, whatever the eventualities.

The real question was from whom. "So you don't believe, Your Majesty, that he was a sole agent?" Bainbridge had heard many tales of the foolish individuals who had attempted to break into the palace over the years, usually in search of souvenirs or to try to force an audience with the Queen.

Victoria made a sound that was somewhere between a wet cough and a chuckle. "Look at him, Sir Charles. Young, handsome, wealthy. Why would a man in that position choose to break into Buckingham Palace and attempt to take the life of the monarch?" She stared up at him as though daring him to answer. "Someone got to this young man, filled his head with idealistic notions and a desire to change the world. Someone with far greater concerns than an impressionable young upstart. Someone who wants us dead."

Bainbridge nodded slowly. "Were there any signs, any warnings? Any letters of protest?"

Victoria sighed. "Every day . . . thousands of them, from all across the Empire. It seems we cannot so much as stir without causing a ripple of discontent. These are difficult days, Sir Charles."

Bainbridge had expected as much. He tried to hide his exasperation. "Are there any particular pressure groups of concern? Or perhaps one that has recently increased their activity or the frequency of their protests? Any political camps that have come to your attention?"

"Stop pussyfooting around the question!" Victoria snapped, and the sound of her voice echoed throughout the audience chamber. "If you're asking us whether we have any notion as to who is behind this attack, then the answer is no. Or rather: no one in particular. We have long lost count of the number of enemies who would see us dead. They are manifold. It is a matter that no longer concerns us." Her eyes narrowed. "It is your job, Sir Charles, to discover which of them is responsible for this insolence, so that we may smite them. Do you find that callous?"

Bainbridge had never enjoyed entering into these games with the Queen. He knew he could never win. "Not callous, Your Majesty. Just necessary."

Victoria accepted his answer with a conciliatory gesture. "We fear we have nothing to go on, Sir Charles, other than this silent corpse."

"Your Majesty has had someone go through his pockets?" Bainbridge ventured.

The monarch inclined her head. "Quite empty. Quite empty of anything useful. No papers, no wallet, no maps or instructions. No keys. Nothing. Whoever had prepared the young man prepared him well for his endeavor, and knew only too well the consequences of any mistake. We wonder if the young man himself was equally aware of his chances."

Bainbridge stared at the corpse, attempting to read it much as Newbury would have. But it was no good—he couldn't do it. He didn't work like Newbury, wasn't wired that way. Bainbridge worked on instinct, and it had seen him through twenty years of policing. He relied on his gut. And his gut was telling him Victoria was right, that the man was a messenger of some sort, a warning. This was the first wave of the attack. The Queen was sensible to fear the worst. "Whatever the case, Your Majesty, the consequences will be grave indeed when we discover who is responsible."

"Be sure of it," she replied, and Bainbridge was in no doubt as to the veracity of her words.

"I shall post a detail from Scotland Yard, Your Majesty, here at the palace. My men can work with the guard to coordinate security." Bainbridge wanted to be ready if the enemy—whoever that enemy was—decided to strike again.

"As you deem necessary," she said in a tone that suggested she thought the point of little consequence.

"And I shall have the body removed for identification purposes. I will get to the bottom of this matter, Your Majesty, I assure you."

Victoria cackled once more, and the look on her face said everything that needed to be said: that his very future depended upon it. "Leave the body for a while," she said, smoothing the front of her skirts. "We wish to look upon it some more."

Bainbridge felt a hollow sensation growing in the pit of his stomach. He shifted uneasily on the spot. He didn't even know where to begin with the investigation. If the body really was devoid of any clues, then he had almost nothing to go on. Newbury was tied up with Sykes. There was no way he'd be able to pull Newbury away from the Sykes case without the whole thing unravelling. And Newbury hadn't been quite himself for a few months now.

Bainbridge hadn't felt this lost since his early days at Scotland Yard, when he'd been hauled up before Lord Roth and berated for losing an important piece of evidence during an investigation. Little did either of them know that the Queen's agents were the ones who had stolen it, and Bainbridge spent a week on the beat for his "incompetence." Later, he discovered the truth, but by then Lord Roth had already received his comeuppance from the Queen, and Bainbridge had accepted a position as an agent himself.

He gave a short bow and the Queen shifted in her chair, dismissing him casually and returning to looking into the face of the man she had killed just a few hours earlier.

Bainbridge quit the audience chamber with a heavy heart. Newbury and Miss Hobbes would have to continue with the Sykes case without him, at least for the time being. He had no choice in the matter. An attempt on the Queen's life meant . . . well . . . Other than the outbreak of war, he could think of nothing more serious with which to occupy his time.

It was cool outside, grey clouds hanging low in the sky like oily smoke. In the courtyard a group of engineers were unloading a large structure from the back of a wagon. It looked like a huge iron cannon, but the rear end was attached to a large boxlike contraption with glass portholes on each side. The box—a generator, he assumed—contained a spinning coil that flickered with dancing blue electricity. It was clearly a weapon of some sort, but Bainbridge had no idea of its use or effect. He imagined it worked similarly to his cane—that, when triggered, it could be used to discharge massive bolts of electricity at the enemy.

Not that it mattered, of course. The palace would now be transformed into a fortress, at least until the case had been resolved, the dead intruder had been identified, and the agency behind the attack—if, indeed, the Queen was correct in her assertion—had been exposed and obliterated. Bainbridge had no doubt that the monarch would leave no stone unturned in her quest to root out the villains. She was, if nothing else, tenacious. And more than that, her desire for revenge was as boundless as her temper.

Bainbridge found the police carriage waiting for him by the main gate. He would head to Scotland Yard, gather his men, and brief them on the necessary actions. Then, if there was time, he would send a note to Newbury. It was only midmorning, and he was already feeling weary with the day.

CHAPTER

14

"Are you sure about this, Veronica?"

She looked at him blankly. "Would I be here if I weren't?"

They were sitting in a hansom cab at the foot of the long gravel driveway that curled, snakelike, across the grounds of the Grayling Institute. Veronica peered out between the window drapes. The glass was filthy with spattered grime, but she had a reasonable view of the building. She'd never seen it before, and it was completely at odds with what she'd imagined. It was a large country mansion, a former Royal residence, built in the dying days of the seventeenth century and now given over to science, converted into the laboratories and workshops of Dr. Lucien Fabian.

The house was grand and imposing, but also had an old-world charm, like somewhere she remembered visiting when she was a child. It had been a bright summer's day, and she had played on the lawn with Amelia while her parents drank pungent tea in the orangery with their hosts. Amelia had been stung by an insect, and Veronica held her hand while their mother, a cross expression on her face, pulled the stinger from her arm.

Veronica blinked away the unbidden memory. She wondered how Amelia was finding her new home. She supposed she was going to find out.

She glanced at Newbury. He was right to ask whether she was sure about what they were planning to do. Veronica *was* hesitant. Not only about their plan for her to steal into the building unannounced while Newbury was quizzing Dr. Fabian about his relationship to the Bastion Society, but also in the end result. Newbury wanted her to speak with Amelia to test the validity of his premonition, his deep-seated fear that something dreadful was going to happen.

Veronica, however, had been expressly forbidden from visiting her sister, told that it would be better to allow her to heal in isolation at the institute, without the distraction of familial concern. She did not want to disrupt Amelia's recovery. She also feared the results of her conversation with her. There was a significant part of Veronica that didn't want Amelia to confirm Newbury's assertions, because that would mean they were about to face something potentially devastating, something that had made even Newbury skittish and afraid.

On the other hand, if Newbury was wrong and Amelia had seen nothing that coincided with his predictions, then what did that say about Newbury's state of mind? That he might be putting undue stock in the supposed results of his occult experiments? That his mind was addled by months of drug abuse? Clearly, either way, Veronica would have a difficult situation on her hands. But she couldn't very well back out now, and whatever Amelia told her, she needed to know. If Amelia's dreams had revealed a looming danger, then Veronica needed to be aware so she could work to prevent it from happening.

Newbury leaned forward and took her hand. "Five minutes, Veronica. Five minutes, and then back to the cab. Do not hang around. Do not risk discovery. Get in and out of there as quickly as you can."

Veronica raised her eyebrows and fixed Newbury with an impatient stare. "Sir Maurice, I shall be in and out before anyone knows I was even here. You do not need to lecture me on taking risks."

"No," said Newbury. "I don't suppose I do." He sat back, satisfied. "You will wait here for me while I talk to Dr. Fabian?"

"Of course."

"Very well. I'm led to believe," he said, "that there are a number of possible entrances in the rear of the property, French doors that lead to the patients' rooms. If you make your way around the house beneath the cover of the trees, I'll distract the servants at the main entrance." He stood, straightening his jacket. "Good luck, Veronica."

"Good luck to you, Sir Maurice."

He swung the door open and stepped out into the bright sunlight. His feet crunched on the gravel. Taking a deep breath to prepare, Veronica followed him, keeping close to the cab. She dropped out onto the ground, circled quickly around the back of the cab, and disappeared behind the cover of the trees that lined the perimeter of the institute.

Unbeknownst to Veronica, a pair of cool blue eyes watched her progress from behind a porcelain mask as she darted from tree to tree, moving with practised ease, looking for an easy way into the building.

A balding butler in a black suit with watery, pale eyes, was waiting for Newbury in the doorway of the old manor house. Newbury smiled as he mounted the steps and the elderly man gave a brief unnecessary bow. "Good day to you, sir. My name is Carrs. Can I be of assistance?" He had a broad East End accent, although he was clearly doing his best to hide it.

Newbury tried to seem jovial, although he wasn't feeling it. His stomach was clenched and he was sweating under his collar. The dose of laudanum he'd taken that morning was already starting to wear off, and he felt his cravings returning with a vengeance. "Thank you, Carrs. I was hoping to speak with Dr. Fabian. It is an urgent matter, the Queen's business, and I seek his advice."

Carrs inclined his head. "Very good, sir. If you would care to follow me, I will show you where to wait while I attempt to locate Dr. Fabian."

Newbury realised as he ducked his head beneath the lintel of the old house how diminutive the old butler really was. He could barely have reached Newbury's shoulder, and he walked with a slight stoop. Newbury wondered if he were another of Dr. Fabian's waifs and strays, an old soldier, or

agent, or serviceman of some kind who had been rehabili-
tated at the institute and then kept on in service in recognition of the debt that was owed to him by his country.

Newbury would have liked to imagine so. But the cynic in
him wondered if it were simply that Dr. Fabian did not like
to surround himself with people who were either younger or
taller than he was. It wouldn't have surprised Newbury to
discover that was the case: Everything he knew of the good
doctor, from both hearsay and his own brief encounter with
the man, suggested Dr. Fabian had an ego large enough to
match his reputation.

Newbury followed Carrs through a number of winding
passageways that branched off from the reception hall until
they came to a chamber that had been set out in the fashion
of a drawing room. Dark oak panels lined the walls, and a
portrait of a seventeenth-century cavalier, replete with plumed
hat and close-cropped beard, hung upon the chimney breast.
His face was intent and regal, and Newbury couldn't help but
feel the painting was somehow watching him.

The room had a musty smell about it, of age and underuse.
A bookcase on the far wall was filled with leather-bound
books, their spines adorned with gilt titling in Latin, French,
and Italian.

A jug of water was set out on a small occasional table beside the fireplace, alongside two glass goblets that looked like
they might have belonged to the era of the house itself.

Carrs bade him to take a seat in an armchair, also arranged
before the fireplace. Newbury lowered himself into it cautiously, feeling the brittle leather creak beneath his weight.

Clearly, everything in the room was an antique. He wondered if it were reserved for visitors. It clearly didn't receive a great deal of regular use.

Seeing that Newbury was settled, Carrs took his leave, promising that he would return shortly with news of Dr. Fabian.

Newbury leaned back in the chair. God, he was tired. He fought to prevent his eyelids from closing. Now was not the time to let his attention drift. He had a job to do, and with Charles tied up with the situation at the palace, he'd have to deal with the Sykes case on his own. Besides, he had seen the way in which Veronica had looked at him that morning, her eyes full of hope. It broke his heart that he had let her down, and more than once. But there was still, at the back of his mind, a nagging doubt regarding her motives. He didn't doubt her affections were real, but his trust in her had been eroded by the realization that she was working secretly for the Queen.

For months now, he had observed her movements and he no longer had any doubt that she was reporting on him to the monarch. Just the thought of it was like a knife twisting in his gut. How *could* she? It was a betrayal of the worst kind. He could think of no way to justify it. He'd tried to think the best of Veronica, tried to reconcile it with himself by assuming she was doing it for the best reasons. But he could not. He could not fathom her reasons. And it hurt doubly so because he knew, deep down, that he was utterly in love with her.

Charles had told him that the Queen was worried that Newbury would be too easily drawn towards the darkness. She feared the allure of it would become too strong, that he would give in and choose the same path as his predecessor,

Aubrey Knox, losing himself to the occult. Newbury knew that was poppycock. But he presumed that was the motivation behind Veronica's betrayal.

So, unsure what else to do, he had retreated from her, hiding himself away in Johnny Chang's and other, less salubrious establishments. He had toured the seedier side of London society and lost himself to its vices. He had ignored the summons from the palace, the note cards brought by courier and then later footmen from the palace rapping loudly on the door. He had turned them all away. Even Mrs. Bradshaw had gone. But Veronica had stayed. Throughout it all, she had stayed, a constant in his life.

Newbury only wished he did not doubt her reasons.

Veronica stood in the shade of a large oak tree, close to the old manor house. She had the trunk of the gnarly old tree between herself and the building, and she was confident she had not been seen as she'd skirted the building, sticking to the flowerbeds along the perimeter wall, ducking behind evergreen bushes and trees.

From where she was hiding, she could see the extensive gardens at the rear of the property, with their impressive topiary sculptures and water features. It seemed very serene, quite unlike the previous establishments in which Veronica's parents had interred Amelia. In fact, she felt faintly ridiculous attempting to break in like this, and the thought had crossed her mind more than once that if she'd just decided to walk up to the front door and *ask* to see her sister, she could hardly be refused.

Newbury was right, though. She'd been warned to stay away—in the nicest possible way—and if she did turn up at the door, surely she would simply be reminded of this fact and asked to leave. And if she were actually lucky enough to talk her way into the institute, there was no way she would be granted any time alone with Amelia to talk candidly. She would be chaperoned by Dr. Fabian throughout her visit, with no liberty to talk frankly.

So . . . she had settled upon this. Breaking and entering. She supposed it wasn't as if she hadn't done it before, on more than one occasion. In fact, she was fairly experienced when it came to forcing an entry. Not that anyone other than the Queen was aware of it. Even Newbury only knew of a handful of occasions when she'd had to demonstrate such skills.

The thought gave her a pang of sudden anxiety. She'd been thinking for some time about telling him the truth. Ever since their recent battle with Aubrey Knox, when she'd blurted out her understanding of the case and accidentally hinted at a deeper knowledge of the situation, and therefore also at her affiliation to the Queen. But she needed to remain focused. Now was not the time for thoughts such as those.

Veronica studied the rear of the Institute. There were a number of—six, she counted—French doors, at intervals along the back of the house. She presumed that Newbury was right and each set of doors must open out from one of the patients' rooms onto the gardens. All she would have to do was find the room that contained Amelia, and then hopefully her sister would be able to let her in from the other side.

It sounded simple. But if anyone else happened to be in

any of the other rooms looking out, then her cover would be blown and she'd be out in the open when the alarm was raised. It was far too much of a risk.

Instead, Veronica had settled on obtaining entry via a window. She had spotted her target almost as soon as she emerged from the foliage to take her place behind the ancient oak: a large sash that had been propped open and left, presumably, to allow the room on the other side to air. It wouldn't be the most elegant of entrances, and from what she had been able to gather about the layout of the house, she was likely to end up in the scullery or kitchen, but it would do as well as any other. Provided, of course, there was no one waiting for her on the other side.

She was confident that, once inside, she'd be able to head in the other direction and find Amelia's room. Admittedly, she was likely to have to try a few doors, and she still ran the risk of opening one on someone who was going to bring the house down screaming, but she favoured her chances this way more than the other.

Now it was a matter of timing. She'd been observing the window for a few minutes and had seen no one pass by inside. She knew, in the end, that she was just going to have to risk it. Rather than stand around thinking about it any longer and risk missing her chance, she simply leapt out from behind the cover of the tree and bolted toward the window. Her feet slipped on the damp grass as she hurtled across the lawn, and for a moment she thought she was going to go over, but then she was at the window with her leg up over the windowsill, and then she was standing, a bit disheveled, in the kitchens.

She glanced around quickly, trying to establish whether she needed to run, hide, or tackle someone with a rolling pin in order to ensure their silence. But the path was clear. The place was deserted. She allowed herself a short sigh of relief.

The kitchen smelled of beef broth and onions. Large vats of food were simmering on the range, the lids rattling on the pans as they built up a head of steam. Veronica realised she didn't have long. Someone would be back shortly to check on the pots. That might also mean she'd have to find an alternative way out of the institute later.

There was only one other way in or out of the room, a door in the opposite wall. Veronica walked carefully around a large wooden table that was littered with kitchen implements and dusty with spilt flour, past the bubbling pans, and then hesitated on the threshold of the doorway. Someone's footsteps were coming in her direction from the corridor outside. She listened carefully to try to ascertain how much time she had. Were they actually footsteps? They sounded more like a persistent rhythm of metal striking stone, accompanied by the wheeze and sigh of firing pistons. Was it some sort of security automaton, perhaps? No matter—they were definitely getting louder, which meant they were getting closer.

She glanced back at the kitchen. Was there anywhere she could hide? She supposed she could try to scramble into the dumbwaiter in the far corner, but other than that . . .

She'd have to run. Out into the corridor, take a left, and put as much distance between herself and whatever it was that was coming from the other direction. She just had to hope they were still far enough away that they wouldn't see her.

Veronica closed her eyes, took a big gulp of air, and threw

herself out into the passageway. She glanced quickly in both directions. To the right, the path was still clear. But the sound of the mechanical footsteps was growing ever closer, a steady, ominous clanking. To the left, the passage came almost immediately to a T. She ran over to it, hopeful that the coast would be clear. It was. But which direction to take? Where would Amelia's room be located?

Thud, thud, thud. The footsteps were rounding the bend behind her. She had to commit. Right, then. She guessed that would lead her deeper into the house.

Veronica dashed along the passageway, her feet scuffing against the ancient flagstones. The walls and ceiling here were paneled in dark oak, giving everything an oppressive air. Roughly hewn wooden faces loomed down at her from above, their blank eyes judging her from their little nooks in the walls. She guessed they must have been there since the house had been built. She wondered what they must have witnessed in their time.

Another T-junction. Veronica groaned in frustration. Whichever direction she took now, she was heading farther away from the gardens and the rooms where she expected Amelia to be. But she had little choice. She couldn't very well double back, not with that thing, whatever it was, blundering around the corridors behind her. She took the passageway on the right again, listening carefully for any signs of movement or voices from up ahead.

Everything seemed to be quiet. It was a far cry from the asylum at Wandsworth, where Amelia had previously been a patient. When she visited there Veronica would regularly hear the wailing of the other inmates, the cries of the insane, the harrowing calls for help issued by people too sick to understand their own conditions. By contrast, the Grayling Institute appeared to retain the trappings of a fine country home, a manor house fit for nobility. It was an odd sort of place, and given Dr. Fabian's reputation as a master engineer, the idea of him living and working there felt entirely incongruous to Veronica. She had expected more modern surroundings: laboratories, workshops, that sort of thing. Or perhaps something clean and clinical, like a hospital. But not this.

Veronica pressed on. Soon she had lost track of the winding passageways and had given up on trying to remember how to backtrack. Instead she simply followed her instinct, delving deeper into the large house and trying any number of doors, all painted a glossy white and securely locked. It wasn't long before she had shaken off the sound of the footsteps. The whole building seemed as if it were practically deserted. She hadn't seen a living soul since her rather impressive entrance through the window: no patients, no nurses, no servants. She cursed herself, assuming that somewhere, in her haste, she had taken a wrong turn and had wandered into a disused part of the building.

She was just about to turn back and start trying to retrace her steps when she heard a noise from up ahead and started. It had sounded like a muffled scream. She felt the hairs on the nape of her neck prickle as they stood on end. The noise had seemed chillingly familiar. Had it been Amelia? Surely not.

Cautiously Veronica picked her way along the corridor. Up ahead, it turned abruptly to the right. Veronica followed it, unsure what she expected to find. Ever since arriving at the institute, she'd been filled with a growing sense of unease, and now, upon hearing that awful scream, she suspected that something was terribly amiss.

The passageway terminated in a door. She crept up to it, straining to hear any sounds from the other side. Silence. She leaned closer, wondering what use anyone could have for a room this far removed from the main part of the building. The scream couldn't have come from anywhere else. She pressed her ear against the cold wood.

Inside, she heard the muffled sounds of an animal, a low, plaintive keening, as if the creature making the sound had been in pain for some time but had now given up all hope of attention or relief.

Was Dr. Fabian involved in some sort of vivisection experiments? It wouldn't surprise her if he tested his medical machines on apes or dogs or other mammals, and it would make sense to lock them away here where the patients couldn't accidentally happen upon them. Nevertheless, Veronica couldn't suppress the nagging doubt that Dr. Fabian was up to something more nefarious. She didn't really know the man, and she had put her faith in him to heal her sister, but for some reason she had a horrible, hollow feeling in her gut, a sense of impending dread. Something about the Grayling Institute just didn't *feel* right.

Veronica tried to laugh at herself, to remind herself that her sister was the clairvoyant one, that she was probably just being paranoid. But what if Newbury were right? The dreadful thing he had predicted during his occult experiments—what could it be? Was it something to do with Amelia? She supposed there was only one way to find out.

Veronica was just about to reach for the handle when something screeched loudly on the other side of the door. She jumped back in fright with a sharp intake of breath. She felt her heart race in her chest. The sound had set her teeth on edge. What on Earth was going on behind the door? She gave herself a moment to steady her nerves before pressing on.

Tentatively, she grabbed for the brass knob and gave it a sharp twist. The door swung open. It was dark on the other side, so she couldn't see much of the room beyond, but the smell was horrendous. The air was thick with the cloying scent of faeces and perspiration, and other things she couldn't—or didn't want to—identify.

Definitely animals, then, she thought, debating whether to bother searching for her handkerchief to cover her face. Absently, she remembered leaving it at the morgue.

She stepped farther into the room, waiting for her eyes to adjust to the dim light. She could sense motion somewhere nearby. Something was turning in the darkness, something large that disturbed the air currents in the room, a machine of some sort. She could hear it whirring slowly in the darkness along with a low murmur of some sort. She walked forward and immediately got the sense that she was in a large open space, a hall or ballroom at the centre of the old manor house.

Veronica felt the wall behind her and managed to put her hand on a wall-mounted gas lamp. She felt for the knob and turned it up, spilling some light into the otherwise gloomy room. Then, turning around to see what the room contained, she emitted a scream of a sort louder than she had ever issued before.

All thoughts of secrecy or subterfuge went from her mind. She rushed forward, but then skidded to a halt, not knowing which way to look, which way to run. Tears streamed down her cheeks. She thought she was going to vomit. She realised she was whimpering with shock and anger and sheer, un-adulterated fear.

The room contained at least twenty Amelias.

Everywhere she looked, there were more of them, each identical to her sister in every way: pale skinned, painfully thin, raven dark hair. They were barely dressed, covered only in thin cotton nightgowns. Each of them was lashed up to a different machine or torture device.

Veronica stared at the contraption at the centre of the room. It was a large disc, a circular platform fixed upon a pedestal, and it was spinning, round and round and round. Upon the disc, her sister—one of the many—was strapped down, electrodes trailing from her temples. Strange occult symbols had been daubed onto the surface of the disc, and Veronica realised with horror that her sister's duplicate had been arranged in the form of a pentagram, her arms, legs, and head forming the five points of the star. She was bab-bling, too, spouting prophecies and visions of the future. They all were. Veronica realised that the murmur she heard was an incessant litany of words and phrases, snatches of things seen out of time, predictions of the horrifying things to come.

To Veronica's left, another of the duplicates was strapped into a chair, her hair lank and dripping, hanging before her wretched face. This one turned and looked up at Veronica with eyes that were sunken and bruised, imploring her to do something. Others sat on the cold tiles of the floor, rocking back and forth, scratching things into the floor with their bare fingernails, etching out the scenes they were seeing in their minds. Yet another lay dead on a table in the corner, stark white and unmoving. One of them rushed at Veronica, its hands held out before it as if to throttle her. Veronica wailed in confusion and distress and the meek creature—a shadow of her sister—fled to the back of the room, to the shadowy recesses where Veronica could hear scores of them gathered, gibbering and whispering to one another.

Weeping openly, Veronica moved towards the machine at the centre of the room. She didn't know what she was going to do. She wanted to stop the spinning. But the Amelia on the disc glared up at her, snapping its teeth like a feral animal and growling. Its eyes were full of malice and confusion. This was not her sister. This was . . . something evil. Something inhuman. Something *created*.

Whatever Dr. Fabian was doing here, she had to put an end to it. She had to save Amelia from this, get her away from this horrible place . . . if it wasn't already too late. How had she allowed this to happen? What had she done? She was the one who had pushed Newbury to talk to the Queen, to have Amelia moved here. She was the one who had put her faith in the Queen and her physician.

But there was no doubt in Veronica's mind. Dr. Fabian was the one responsible, and she would ensure he paid dearly for his crimes.

"Cracking walls and fire and pain . . . so much pain. Brass engines of destruction will tear down the world, and the man with the white face shall come out of the darkness."

Veronica looked down at the doppelgänger strapped to the machine. It had Amelia's voice, but it was raw and broken, and it was coming from inside a monster.

"The one who sits in the chair. She is the key. She is the nightmare at the eye of the storm."

Veronica realised with dawning terror that the duplicates were speaking in unison. Each and every one, chanting the words of the prophecy. It was too much. She had to get out of there, had to find Newbury, to find Amelia. The *real* Amelia.

Veronica turned to flee, but stumbled when she saw someone hovering in the doorway. The man with the white face!

Her path was blocked. The thing that was watching her had to be another of Fabian's sick creations. He was a man, of sorts, dressed in an evening jacket and white shirt, with white gloves and a featureless porcelain mask where his face should have been. From the waist down he was entirely a machine, legs driven by pistons in his mechanical thighs.

Veronica realised that this must have been the thing that had followed her here through the passageways of the old house. The strange creature cocked its head silently to one side, as if considering what to do next. Then it came lumbering towards her, its blue eyes blank and staring.

Veronica saw her opportunity. She could move faster than this strange man-machine. She backed away, drawing it farther into the room, biding her time. Then, just when it seemed as if she had nowhere else to go, she turned and bolted for the door.

She felt the thing's fingers brush her collar as she squeezed past it, but she was driven on by fear and her desire to get away, to find Amelia and get her to safety. She darted out into the passageway, flinging herself around the corner, and then on into the depths of the house. She was still weeping, tears streaming down her cheeks, blurring her vision. She didn't know what to do. She had to find Newbury. But Newbury was with Fabian.

Veronica blundered around another corner, banging her arm painfully against the wooden panels. She just needed to get out of there. Out and back to the cab. Newbury would help her after that. He would. She knew he would. Newbury wouldn't let it go on any longer.

Veronica ran on, away from the man with the white face, and away from the dreadful room. She prayed that she was right, that Newbury would help her save her sister. He was, after all, the only hope she had.

Newbury turned at the sound of footsteps in the hallway outside the door. Carrs had returned, escorting Dr. Lucien Fabian, that old master of invention, the Queen's personal physician. The man who had ensured Her Majesty's survival and, indirectly, Newbury's own.

Newbury rose to greet the doctor as he entered the room.

"Sir Maurice Newbury! Now, here's a surprise. It must be, what, four years since you last had reason to pay me a visit?"

Newbury nodded. "Yes." The date was emblazoned on his mind. He'd come to Fabian in the aftermath of the events at Fairview House and the death of his previous assistant, Templeton Black. He'd hoped Fabian would be able to help, to do something miraculous, to somehow restore the young man to life. But Newbury's actions had been motivated by his grief, and of course, Fabian had only been able to turn him away. "Yes, it's been a while."

Fabian waved Carrs away, instructing him to fetch tea, and then gestured for Newbury to return to his seat, dropping into the chair opposite him. He pushed his wire-rimmed glasses up his nose with his left index finger. "How's that shoulder, Sir Maurice? I understand the Fixer made good use of my medical machinery when he put you back together last winter. During that whole *Lady Armitage* scandal, wasn't it?"

Newbury smiled. It had not yet been a year since that first case with Veronica, but already it felt like a lifetime ago. "I'm very well, thank you, Dr. Fabian," he replied. "The Fixer did a superb job, not least because of the equipment he had at his disposal. Aside from a few scars and the occasional twinge, the shoulder is as good as new."

"Wonderful news!" Fabian clapped his hands together with a wide grin. "Most excellent news." Newbury couldn't tell if Fabian was pleased that the Fixer had successfully mended his shoulder, or because it was his machines that had made the operation possible. "It was an interesting case," the doctor continued. "I was saddened by what became of Villiers. He might have proved useful. I examined one of those 'affinity bridges' in the aftermath of the events. A quite remarkable device."

Newbury frowned. This was news to him. He'd understood the devices had all been destroyed. "Do you still have it?" Newbury asked pointedly.

Fabian shrugged. "Yes. It's in the archive. Her Majesty thought I might be able to learn something from it. I believe it was your assistant, Miss Hobbes, who helped us to obtain one."

Newbury stifled a gasp. Layers upon layers, he realised. Betrayal upon betrayal. He didn't know what to make of it all.

"So." Fabian ran a hand through his thinning hair. "I gather there must be a reason for your visit? Another case?"

Newbury attempted to order his thoughts. He was still trying to work out when Veronica could have found time to procure the affinity bridge, or had the means to do it. She was resourceful, if nothing else. "Yes, indeed. I'm hoping you can help to shed some light on it."

"I am at your disposal, Sir Maurice. I shall do what I can." Fabian smirked. Did he already know what Newbury was about to ask? That knowing look suggested that he did. Or perhaps it was simply arrogance, a sign that he was enjoying being asked for help.

"Thank you. I would be obliged if you could enlighten me as to the nature of your relationship with Sir Enoch Graves and the Bastion Society."

Fabian's jaw clenched. He visibly stiffened, then took a deep breath.

So he hadn't expected the question after all. That was an interesting fact in itself. Newbury watched him attempt to regain his composure.

It took a moment, but nevertheless, Newbury was impressed with the way in which Fabian calmed himself. He leaned back in his chair, the smile returning to his lips. "Ah, so you finally managed to catch up with Graves. How interesting. I wondered how long it would take." Fabian laughed.

Newbury gave him a confused look. "What exactly has

Graves been up to that should have brought him to my attention?"

Fabian frowned. "Well, it's your sort of thing, isn't it?" he said. "All that occult business. Secret societies, black magic, resurrection . . . an unhealthy pursuit of the supernatural. That sort of thing."

"And that's what Graves and the others are up to?" It suddenly dawned on Newbury that if what Fabian was saying were true, the case had just become a lot more serious . . . and potentially a lot more dangerous.

Fabian looked perplexed. "You tell me, Sir Maurice. Isn't that why you're here?" He seemed reluctant to elaborate all of a sudden, as if he feared he might incriminate himself if he revealed any more.

"I'm here because there's been a murder," Newbury stated. "And we have reason to believe there is a connection to the Bastion Society."

Fabian nodded. "I don't doubt it. I would imagine Graves has been connected to any number of miserable deaths over the years." He paused, eyeing Newbury, as if weighing him up. "Have you worked out what they're up to, Sir Maurice?"

Newbury chose to leave the question unanswered.

"I see not," Fabian continued. "Well, allow me to enlighten you a little. The Bastion Society is more than simply another gentleman's club. It's an ideal. A way of life."

"An ideal?" Newbury said.

"Yes. Its members must swear to uphold the glory of England. They believe it is their duty to preserve the English way of life. They believe the English race to be morally, intellectually, and physically superior."

Newbury raised his eyebrows.

"Oh yes, Sir Maurice. This is the stuff they don't publish in their charter. They're extremists, and they are highly political. They have people in the government, and they count judges, barristers, policemen, and soldiers amongst their members." Fabian smiled, folding his arms behind his back as he talked. "They have a chivalric code by which they all abide. It's like something out of the Dark Ages. A medieval code of honour. They consider themselves to be the knights of the modern world, and they go forth for the glory of England. And Graves sits at the centre of it all, dreaming of Camelot."

"And you, Dr. Fabian. You were part of all of this, too?" Newbury wondered how much of this was Fabian's bitterness talking. He'd have to dig a little further to discover the truth about why the doctor was ejected from their ranks.

Fabian waved his hands in a dismissive gesture. "Perhaps. At least, I went along with their little games for a while."

"And what was in it for you?" Newbury ventured.

Fabian grinned. "Funding," he said, "for my . . . projects. This was before I was granted the honour of serving Her Majesty. Understand that the type of experimentation and invention I am involved in, the scientific endeavours in which I engage myself, are a costly business. I needed patronage, and Enoch Graves had the means to grant it to me. The Bastion Society is very free with its wealth."

Newbury didn't like the sound of where this was heading. "Why should a society of political idealists be funding the work of a highly regarded scientific engineer such as yourself?"

"As I said, Sir Maurice, the Bastion Society is more than just a gentleman's club. Their rituals are ancient and arcane.

They believe in the permanence of the spirit and the transient nature of life, the idea that the spirit transcends the flesh and is reincarnated in a new physical form at the point of death. A very Eastern philosophy at its core. Graves could never see the irony in that." He chuckled. "To answer your question: I provided them with the means by which to carry out their more bizarre rituals. Particularly the ones pertaining to karmic debt."

"A death cult?" Newbury said.

"No, not quite," Fabian corrected. "Their belief is that each physical body is simply a vessel, a chapter in the life of a soul. They argue that an individual's life, therefore, should not be extended beyond its natural means. That it causes an imbalance if the soul remains shackled to the body for too long. Graves, for example, truly believes he is the reincarnation of an ancient chivalric warrior."

"I understand," said Newbury. He could see now why Fabian's work had put him at odds with Graves and his cronies. Fabian had saved the Queen from almost certain death by installing her in her life-giving chair. Graves would never have tolerated such an outrageous flaunting of the society's beliefs.

"I see that you do, Sir Maurice. It is an admission of my weakness that I was only ever party to their strange beliefs when it provided me with a fully stocked laboratory. I don't generally associate myself with cults of that sort."

Newbury couldn't help but wonder what sort of cults Fabian did, then, associate himself with.

"Tell me a little about this murder case, Sir Maurice. I may be able to help in some small way."

"A notorious jewel thief, Edwin Sykes, who it later transpired was a member of the Bastion Society, was found dead in the gutter a few days ago. That, in itself, wouldn't really be enough to concern me, but when Sykes then continued to commit felonies, it piqued my interest."

"Go on," Fabian said, clearly engaged.

"This morning I attended the scene of another burglary. But this time there was a body, a murder victim. And it soon became clear that the corpse was none other than Edwin Sykes. The second body was identical in almost every way to the first. Even now, we have two near-identical corpses in the police morgue."

"Fascinating," said Fabian. "How was he killed?"

"It seems as if he was attacked by his own mechanical automaton, a spiderlike machine that he used to force entry onto the premises."

Fabian laughed out loud at this and sat forward in his chair. "Ha! About the size of a small dog? That's one of mine. One of the first things I built for Graves. I was never quite sure what he wanted it for, but I tried not to ask too many questions in those days."

"How many of them did you make, Dr. Fabian?" Newbury asked.

"Of the spider? Oh, just the one." He paused to push his glasses up his nose once again. "Have you seen it? Was it still operational? It was a difficult machine to handle. It would have taken someone months, if not longer, to master."

Newbury nodded. If Fabian had created only one, who had made the others? "Yes, I've seen it. I've also seen what it can do to a man. He had a hole as large as a dinner plate through his chest."

Fabian grimaced. "Well, I can't say I ever encountered Edwin Sykes at the clubhouse. I fear that I can shed little light on your mystery. Two bodies, you say? That's quite extraordinary. Twin brothers, do you think?"

Newbury decided to keep his cards close to his chest. He still didn't know how much he could trust Fabian. Or anyone else, for that matter. "Quite possibly. The birth records suggest otherwise."

Fabian shrugged. His tone was dismissive. "You never can rely too heavily on that sort of thing."

"No, I suppose not." Newbury looked up as Carrs bustled through the door carrying a large silver tray. He realised that signified the end of their discussion on the Bastion Society. He wondered how Veronica was getting on elsewhere in the building. Hopefully she'd be out by now, back in the hansom waiting for him.

Fabian rose from his seat and took the tray from Carrs. "Ah, tea. Let me pour you a cup, Sir Maurice, and I'll give you a progress report on young Amelia Hobbes's recovery. I'm sure her sister would like to know how she's getting on."

"Thank you," said Newbury. "I'm sure you're right." But in the back of his mind he was already plotting how he could gain entrance to the Bastion Society and find out more about exactly what they were up to.

In the meantime, Veronica, distraught, had fled to the coach. She'd done so almost in a daze, knowing only that she needed to put some distance between herself and the foul things she had seen inside the building, the . . . *things* that looked and sounded in every way like her sister.

Now, however, she regretted fleeing the scene. She stood, and then sat again, squeezing her hands together in anguish as she tried to decide what to do. Should she go storming back in there and demand to see Newbury? Should she remain out here in the hansom and wait for him to return? Should she leave, taking the cab to find Sir Charles so they could return later in force?

She stood again, reached for the door, and then returned to her seat in the stillness of the cab. The horses stamped their feet on the gravel, sensitive to her nervousness. The driver had already been well tipped by Newbury to turn a blind eye to anything out of the ordinary, so she knew she wasn't going to be disturbed, no matter how much she paced around or banged her fist against the door in anguish.

Veronica stepped over to the window and drew back the curtain once again. He was still there, that bizarre, nightmarish creature with the white face, staring out at her from inside the doorway of the house. His freakish appearance had startled her in the house, and now she didn't know what to think. Was he a man or a machine? His blank, staring eyes were definitely those of a human being, but parts of his body—including both legs—were evidently mechanical. And why was he wearing the mask? Was he another patient, or one of the staff? More to the point, why hadn't he raised the alarm? And why was he watching her now from the doorway?

These and other questions were buzzing around inside her head. But she couldn't think straight. All she wanted to do was scream. She simply couldn't shake the horrifying image of Amelia's face, crying out in the darkness as she spun on that strange wheel, electrodes trailing from her temples. Or the dark, bruised eyes that stared up at her from the chair in which that other Amelia had been lashed, or the pale look of the dead one on the table.

Then there was the sound . . . the muttering, the murmuring, the garbled insights into what was yet to come. She had talked about the horrors in the darkness, the impending storm of death and destruction. She had whispered about machines that walk like men, and a siege that would bring about the end.

Veronica reached for the door. What was she doing, waiting here in the cab? She had to get back inside! She had to get Amelia out of that horrible place. Whatever Dr. Fabian was doing, it was evil, unspeakable. Somehow he was *copying* her. Duplicating her so he could torture those pitiful copies, lashing them to strange machines to induce seizures so that they might predict the future. She wondered if the Queen knew about it. Or even if the Queen was behind it.

Veronica had to find the real Amelia, who was clearly in danger. What if she were being tortured, too? Unsure what she was going to do, other than storm back inside the institute and demand to see her sister, she flung the door of the cab open—and found Newbury standing there on the gravel driveway, staring up at her in surprise.

"Veronica? Are you quite well?"

Veronica didn't know how to respond. Exhausted, confused, and incandescent with rage, she fell out of the cab and collapsed into his arms, beating her fists against his chest in barely contained rage. He held her while she wept on his shoulder, allowing the worst of it to pass.

Then, gently, he prised her away, holding her by the shoulders so that he could look into her eyes. "Was it that bad?"

Veronica could hardly speak. She wanted him to see what she had seen. She knew that words could never describe the horror of it. "Worse than you can possibly imagine."

Newbury clutched her to him once again. He stroked the back of her head. "I'm so sorry I asked you to go through with it, Veronica."

"No!" she shouted emphatically. "No. Don't you dare apologise. If it wasn't for you, I would have stayed away, just like they wanted me to."

Newbury tried to coerce her back into the hansom. "Come on. Let's get out of here, and you can tell me all about it."

Veronica stepped back from him, blocking the way into the cab. "We can't go," she implored him. "We can't leave her here. You don't understand."

Newbury put his hand on her arm. His voice was low and firm. "Veronica? Veronica. Look at me. We're being watched. We need to leave now. I promise you we will get to the bottom of this. We'll do what's best for Amelia. But right now, we have to go."

Veronica looked over his shoulder. The man-thing was still hovering in the doorway, watching them with his strange, unblinking stare. But now she saw that Dr. Fabian was also watching them intently from the window of the house. She wanted to rush over and confront him about what he had done. But instead, drained of energy and unsure what best to do, she allowed herself to be bundled back into the cab.

Newbury jumped in on the other side and slammed the door, then rapped loudly on the wooden frame to inform the cabbie they were ready to leave.

Veronica heard the crack of a whip. Then, horses neighing in protest, the hansom juddered and rocked into motion, sending a spray of gravel into the air as they shot off into the hazy afternoon.

Veronica looked back through the window, watching the Grayling Institute recede into the distance. She felt nauseated, hollow. She felt like she had abandoned Amelia to a fate worse than death.

She resolved then that she would do everything in her power to save her sister from Fabian and that horrible, porcelain-faced monster. Amelia would be free of them and the doctor would pay for his atrocities, whatever it took, whatever the consequences.

CHAPTER

15

"Tell me again what you saw."

Veronica squeezed her eyes shut. Hot tears were prickling beneath her lids. All the pent-up emotion and horror and fear and shock were now consolidating into a burning rage. Rage at Fabian for the horrendous crimes he had committed against her sister. Rage at the Queen for orchestrating and enabling such abhorrent violations. Rage at Newbury for pacing back and forth before her with his incessant questions, when all she really wanted to do was race back to the Grayling Institute as fast as humanly possible, to gather her sister up in her arms and steal her away to somewhere safe.

Veronica dug her fingernails into her palms and clenched her teeth. For all her efforts, she couldn't get the images out of her head, and all Newbury seemed to want her to do was remember them, over and over. She fought back the

urge to scream at him. It would do Amelia no good whatsoever, and in her heart, she knew that Newbury was trying to
help. But she wanted action, above all else. She wanted to *do*
something about the situation rather than simply sit there
and discuss it.

They were back in her Kensington apartment, which was
just as they had left it the previous afternoon. The deep
gouges in the floorboards and the scorch marks on the carpet
remained as stark evidence of the battle that had taken place
there. There was no sign of Mrs. Grant, of course, who Veronica had insisted remain with her sister for a few days in
the interest of safety. She only wished she could do the same
for her own sister, that she could send Amelia away to a place
of safety, away from Dr. Fabian and his sinister assistant.

Veronica took a deep breath, asserting control over the
riot of emotions she was experiencing. "There were so many
of them, whimpering in the darkness. Lashed to horrible,
mechanical implements of torture. They were barely human,
Maurice: animals in the shape and guise of Amelia, borrowing
her appearance, her voice. But they were not *her.* They had
nothing to do with *her.*" She broke off, stifling another sob.
"And they babbled. They babbled prophecies, scratching
them into the walls and the floor with their fingernails until
their fingers were nothing but blunt, bloody stubs." Her body
trembled and she let out a low, heartfelt moan at the memory. Tears streamed down her cheeks, spattering her dress
like unwelcome rain.

Newbury stopped pacing and stood before her, his face
etched with concern. "But I saw her, Veronica! I saw her with

my own eyes. Fabian explained to me how successful his treatment program was proving and then led me to her room. She looked well. Thin and tired, but well."

Veronica's confusion was like a thick London fog. She only wished she had the means by which to navigate through it. "Do you think she knows?"

Newbury shook his head. "Indeed not. I believe she is quite ignorant of the truth. I didn't speak to her for long, but what she did say made it clear that she regarded Fabian very highly indeed, and that she felt whatever restorative treatments he had been administrating were working. She said the seizures had almost completely stopped, with only a handful of reoccurrences when they had pushed the treatment too far." Newbury shook his fist at the wall in frustration. "How did he do it?"

"I don't . . . ," Veronica started, before she realised it was a rhetorical question. Newbury was thinking aloud.

He returned to his pacing, pressing his fingers nervously together to form a spire before his chest. "It could be a side effect of his treatment, an unexpected by-product." His words lacked their usual conviction. He was testing theories, running through scenarios in his mind. Veronica knew that Newbury didn't really believe it.

"No." Veronica shook her head emphatically. "This was deliberate. They're trying to harness her abilities, trying to use her to predict the future."

"They?" Newbury looked puzzled.

"Fabian and the Queen," she replied.

Newbury frowned. "You think the Queen is aware of this?"

Tired and exasperated, Veronica abandoned all pretense

of polite conduct. "Don't be so blind, Maurice. Think about it. Fabian is the Queen's personal physician, and he has her ear. Think about what he is offering her, what Amelia could do for them if they could harness and channel her abilities. A monarch who can predict the future! Of course she's aware of it. She's probably behind it!"

Newbury stared at her, agog. She could tell she was getting through to him, so she pressed on. "We have to get her out of there. This can't be allowed to go on."

Newbury turned and paced to the window. He stood with both hands on the window ledge, looking out at the street below. He was silent for a while, then he turned to face her. "Veronica, you are talking about going against the Queen."

"Yes, and I'm talking about saving my sister." She met his gaze, her eyes blazing with defiance.

"This is bigger than we know, Veronica. We must consider the implications. All of them." He turned back to the window, lost in thought.

Veronica didn't know *what* to think. Everything was spiralling through her mind, a confused mess. She had no idea what to do next. All she knew was that she had to help Amelia, and whatever Newbury said, the longer her sister stayed in that dreadful place, the more danger she was in.

"Sykes!" Newbury snapped his fingers, and Veronica gave a start. He turned to her, suddenly animated. "Edwin Sykes is the key."

"What about Edwin Sykes?" she said angrily. Now was not the time to be worrying about the case.

"Duplicates, Veronica!" he said, rushing over to her side. "There has to be a connection. Why didn't I see it before?"

It was Veronica's turn to look astonished. "Of course! You think Fabian is still connected to the Bastion Society, that Sykes was copied in the same way as Amelia."

Newbury shrugged. "I don't know. But it seems like too much of a coincidence for there to be no connection." He dropped into a chair opposite her. He looked tired, but enlivened nonetheless. "Fabian told me about their strange occult philosophies. They believe in the passing of the soul from one body to the next. Perhaps there's some explanation in that?" He shrugged. "We must tread carefully, Veronica."

Veronica nodded.

"And we must think of Amelia's health."

"Her health! He's *duplicating* her and torturing the copies! Treating them like animals!" She felt the anger beginning to swell inside her again.

"Yes. I know. And I promise you, Veronica, that we will get her out of there. We will find a way. But I saw her. I saw her in her room, and she is quite well. The *real* Amelia. The one that really matters." He paused, as if to allow the weight of his words to sink in. "We can't simply go barging in there to extract her. Not only because of the consequences with Fabian and the Queen, but for Amelia's own health as well. You saw how ill she was in that Wandsworth sanatorium. Do you think we could do any better?"

Veronica hung her head. She knew he was right. Of course he was right. What would she do with Amelia if she had the opportunity, right then and there, to get her out of the Grayling Institute? Bring her home to Kensington, where she could be attacked with killer assassin machines? Where there were no nursemaids or doctors or medical equipment that might help her? Perhaps worse, where the Queen would know she was hiding. Veronica hadn't considered that before now. Amelia had become an asset. She had a value to the Crown. Victoria wasn't likely to let that slip away without a struggle. And Veronica knew what lengths the Queen would go to in order to recover her property. She'd been charged with doing just that, on more than one occasion.

Nevertheless, Veronica could not allow Fabian to continue. What he was doing was immoral and maleficent, and she would not allow Amelia to be a part of it, whether her sister was aware of her exploitation or not.

She reached out and took Newbury's hand. It was an impulsive action, and she did not really know why she had done it, other than for the reassurance it might offer. It was cold and clammy to the touch. "So what next? How do you propose we continue?"

Newbury leaned forward in his chair, bringing his face level with hers. "We need to gain some perspective. We need to understand what's going on. Only then can we begin to formulate a plan." He squeezed her hand. "I swear to you, Veronica, we will do what is right for Amelia. You have my word."

Veronica gave a weak smile. "Thank you. I . . ."

"I know," he finished. He released her hand and stood, brushing himself down. "Tonight I shall return to Packworth House and the Bastion Society. If we can get to the bottom of their strange little club, perhaps it will help shed some light on your sister's plight. In the meantime, I will consider our options."

Veronica rose from her seat to stand before him. "*You*

shall return to the Bastion Society?" She wiped at the tears that were still trickling down her cheeks.

Newbury looked resolute. "Well, it may be dangerous. You're in no fit state for that sort of business."

She glowered at him. "With respect, Sir Maurice, I should argue that I'm presently in a better state than you." Newbury gave a sad smile, acknowledging the truth of her words. "Besides, I can't stay here. I can't sit and do nothing. Not after what I've seen today."

"Very well," said Newbury. "We shall repair to Chelsea until cover of darkness. Then, my dear Miss Hobbes, we shall practise a little breaking and entering."

CHAPTER

16

Your Majesty will be pleased to know the incident has caused no lasting damage to the equipment." Fabian stood from where he was crouching behind the Queen's life-preserving chair. He ran his fingers along the length of the air hose, testing the connections, looking for any nicks or scratches in its smooth surface. He could hear her ragged breathing as the gas was forced in and out of her lungs, causing her chest to heave and deflate, heave and deflate, a constant, rhythmic sigh. This had to be the most prolonged death in all of human history, he mused with satisfaction, a glacial descent into obliteration and decay.

"We were already well aware of that fact, Physician. Otherwise we would already be dead." Fabian winced. Victoria's sarcasm was as sharp as a knife, and it cut him deeply. His right hand moved, as if by its own volition, hovering over the small hidden trapdoor in the brass frame of the chair where the switch resided.

The switch. He could pop the housing open and flick it now, instantly stilling her clockwork heart. It would be so easy. He dared himself to do it. The ticking of the tiny meters, the turning of the cogs—one flick of that switch, and an electric current would jolt through her fat, bloated body, and the equipment would seize. It would take only seconds for her to die, but there would be time enough for her to see the face of the one who had ended her life.

His hand lingered there over the switch, as it had a hundred times before. *This time.* No one would know. He would let her die, her lungs slowly deflating, her brain silently starving of oxygen. Her clockwork heart would freeze, and he would reclaim it from her, a souvenir, a reminder of the time that she had died. He would tell them all that he had done everything in his power, that he had fought for her life, tried desperately to stop her fading, but that the intruder had somehow damaged the machine and there was nothing he could have done to save her. *So easy.*

Fabian felt an overwhelming urge to do it, to bring an end to it all, right then and there. His fingers caressed the outer casing. The brass was cold to the touch.

"Come around where I can see you, Fabian," her voice commanded.

He jumped back from the chair, startled. Did she suspect? She couldn't possibly know about his little safety mechanism. Could she? What would she do if she were to discover it? His life would be forfeit. That much was certain. She would not—could not—tolerate such a risk to her survival. Whatever the reasons—of course he would tell her he'd only wanted to provide a euthanasia device in case it all became too much for her—she would utterly destroy him if she even suspected its existence.

"Yes, Your Majesty," said Fabian. He took one last look at the air tanks. Yes, everything was in place. The intruder had barely had a chance to touch them before the Queen triggered the security measures and a bolt had shot from the chair, burying itself in his chest. He never even stood a chance.

Fabian circled around the seated monarch. He never enjoyed being this close to her. She stank. Not the subtle, sickly odour of an ageing woman, but rather the rank, wretched stench of festering decay. The chair provided the Queen with all the essentials of life, but many of her bodily functions persisted, and while nursemaids regularly attended to Victoria to sponge her down, the extent of his machinery meant that she could never truly be cleaned. Not only that, but the wounds he had opened in her chest to feed the air hoses into her collapsed lungs had never truly healed, becoming sore and pustulent beneath their wrappings.

The consequence of which—while none of her agents, visitors, or staff would ever dare react to it in her presence—was that she smelled like a pungent, rotten grapefruit.

Fabian stood before her and met her gaze, but immediately averted his eyes when he saw the admonishing glare she had fixed him with. He studied the floor by her feet.

"You seem quiet, Fabian. Tell us, what troubles you?" Her tone was mocking, patronising.

The very fact of your continued existence.

Your arrogance.

Your stench.

These were the things he longed to say, to shout into her fat, imperious face. *These are what trouble me.*

But his impulse to survive made the words stick in his throat, just as it had stilled his hand above the termination switch a matter of moments before. "Merely your health, Your Majesty. I was concerned to ensure your well-being, and whether the intruder's actions had posed a lasting threat to your continuing safety," was what he said instead.

Victoria grinned, showing her rotten teeth. "Admit it, Fabian. You are more concerned for your equipment than you are for us. We understand. We are not that different, you and we. We have a business arrangement."

Fabian contemplated her words. No. This was a test. It would not do to rise to her manipulative insinuations. "Not at all, Your Majesty. You do me a discredit."

Victoria laughed. "Perhaps," she said cryptically.

Fabian smoothed the front of his shirt nervously. He needed to change the subject. "I was paid a visit by one of your agents this morning, Your Majesty."

Victoria raised an eyebrow in interest.

"Sir Maurice Newbury," he went on. "He called upon me at the Grayling Institute."

Victoria looked immediately uncomfortable. "Did he have the Hobbes girl in tow? He usually drags her around behind him like a lapdog."

Fabian shook his head. "Not that I am aware of, Majesty. If he did, he chose not to bring her into the building with him."

Victoria gave an audible sigh of relief. "She must be kept

away at all costs. She is useful to us where she is, and if she were to discover the truth about her sister's . . . situation . . . we fear her usefulness would come to an end."

God, she was cold. Fabian swallowed. "Very good, Your Majesty."

Victoria gestured impatiently for him to continue. "So, Newbury? It seems he might be coming in from the cold."

Fabian frowned. He didn't know to what she was referring. "He's busy with a murder enquiry, I gather."

Victoria seemed animated by this development. "Yes, this Edwin Sykes matter. Duplicates, found at the scenes of two crimes. Are they yours, Fabian? Are they experiments gone awry? You said the machine had failed with every subject except the young Hobbes girl." Her tone was accusing.

"No, Your Majesty. The duplicates were not from any of my experiments. What you say is true: The engine of life has produced nothing but lifeless carcasses for anyone but the Hobbes girl."

Victoria frowned. "So tell me, Fabian, who else could be experimenting with duplication technology? We'd imagine it to be a rather small field of expertise."

Fabian smiled. "Newbury mentioned Enoch Graves, Majesty. He quizzed me about the Bastion Society."

"Ah, Sir Enoch. We should have put him down some time ago. His ceaseless dabbling in matters that do not concern him has become a most tiring distraction. We have already put a stop to his political aspirations." She gave a wet, spluttering cough that drew her last word out into a long hiss. Fabian saw flecks of dark blood spattered on her lower lip. "Newbury will deal with him now," she continued. "We have more pressing concerns." She shifted in her chair, attempting, unsuccessfully, to reposition herself. Fabian thought about trying to help her, but he knew that would only result in more biting remarks. A few moments later, she gave up. "Tell us, Fabian, what of the prophecies?"

Fabian shuffled uncomfortably. He'd been expecting this, but talk of the Hobbes girl's special talents always set him on edge. As a scientist, he was fascinated by the phenomenon, but he felt ill at ease every time he considered the facts. The girl could see into the future. He could not explain it. No matter how he tried, how hard he pushed Amelia, he could not find a rational explanation for her abilities. If he hadn't known better, he would have written it off as a hoax, but he had seen the proof with his own eyes.

Fabian had spent long nights transcribing Amelia's dreams, filling notebooks with her lucid rants, and sketching the visions she described. In time, he had witnessed those visions come to pass. It was remarkable. Truly remarkable. And it clearly had its origins in the realm of the supernatural, not the more knowable world of science. He feared he would never be able to uncover Amelia's secrets, because he could not understand where her powers came from. They were outside his experience, more the fodder of priests and holy men than of medicine.

Yet Fabian couldn't stop, couldn't prevent himself from pushing further, from testing the boundaries, from experimenting on the girl. He needed to know what made her tick, just like the clockwork heart in Victoria's chest. He needed to *understand* it. And he would not let go of the matter until he did.

Fabian realised the Queen was waiting for him to respond.

"The prophecies remain the same, Your Majesty. Each and every one of them, no matter what I do, how many of them I create . . . the same thing, over and over. They talk of destruction, the engines of war. They talk of fire and death, of the tearing down of a great house. They talk of chaos and despair. . . ." He trailed off.

Victoria nodded. "Our enemies move against us, Fabian. The intruder was just a warning. There is more to come. These prophecies—we believe they talk of the destruction of this palace, of our death. They must be prevented from coming true, at any cost."

"What shall we do, Majesty?"

"The Royal Engineers have fortified the palace. The guard has been doubled. Scotland Yard is at our beck and call. We are resolute and impenetrable. A fortress. We are England, Doctor, and we shall not fall." Victoria raised a hand to her mouth to wipe away the bloody spittle. "It has been most useful to have our suspicions confirmed by the Hobbes girl. Most useful indeed. We shall be ready for them when they come. We see great need of the girl's talents in the dark times ahead."

If she survives that long, Fabian thought. He pushed his glasses up the bridge of his nose with his index finger. He was sweating again. He didn't doubt the Queen's words—she would be ready for the upstarts, and she would smite them with all the strength of a colossus for their impudence. But who would dare to go against the Queen? Who would be so foolish as to storm the palace? And what did they hope to achieve?

Victoria gave another racking cough, and Fabian saw her

hand go to her mouth, saw blood dribbling through her fingers. He rushed forward, handing her a handkerchief to mop it away. "Majesty—you are not well. Allow me to assist you."

Victoria waved him away with a low moan. He stepped back and realised that she was laughing. "We have not been well for a very long time, Dr. Fabian. A very long time indeed." She spluttered again into the bundle of silk in her fist. "Leave us now. Go back to your little laboratory and continue with our experiments." She turned away from him, wheezing and choking as she eased her chair away into the gloom.

Fabian seethed. How dare she dismiss him in such a fashion!

He stood, watching her retreat into the darkness at the rear of the audience chamber. For a moment, he felt a flash of empathy for whoever it was who was plotting her downfall. *Let them come. Let them tear down the palace, brick by brick. Let them shatter her Empire and leave it crumbling in the dust.*

Red faced and furious, he stormed from the room.

CHAPTER

17

The hansom cab trundled along in the darkness, its wooden-rimmed wheels groaning in protest as it bounced over the uneven cobbles. A solitary lamp hung like a droplet of light from a curved brass arm at the front of the cab, and the driver hunched against the rain on his dickie box, wrapped in a thick woollen coat.

Inside, Charles Bainbridge was feeling weary and old. He'd been operating on nervous energy all day, what with launching a high-profile investigation, organizing a security detail for the palace, and liaising with the Queen's Guard. He'd barely had time to stop and think. He'd also spent another part of the afternoon at the morgue—his third visit in as many days. He was growing strangely accustomed to the place. This time, however, he'd had the unfortunate experience of standing over a police surgeon—or, more accurately, *butcher*—while he performed an autopsy on the body they had recovered from the palace.

Aside from the long steel bolt in his chest, the man had been young, fit, and perfectly healthy. As the Queen had already noted, he was clean and well kempt, and had the air of affluence about him. He had close-cropped sand-coloured hair, olive green eyes, and was wearing a fine suit from Savile Row. He wore expensive cologne and had a taste for Prussian cigarettes. Aside from these minimal facts, however, painstakingly determined from multiple examinations of the body, Bainbridge had absolutely *nothing* to go on. He didn't even know where to start.

Now Bainbridge was hurtling across town, returning to the palace for his second audience with the Queen that day. He hoped she would be satisfied with his endeavours. He suspected not.

Bainbridge slumped in the back of the cab. It looked as if it was going to be a long night, to cap a long day. He wished he could instead fall asleep with a whiskey and a fat cigar, perhaps reading his paper before the fire. It had been too long since he'd been able to enjoy a night like that.

He'd managed—just—to scratch out a quick note for Newbury, which he'd sent round to his friend's Chelsea lodgings by courier. He wondered how Newbury and Miss Hobbes had got on at the Grayling Institute with Dr. Fabian. He hoped they weren't planning any drastic measures without him; the gleam in Newbury's eye when he'd talked about agitating the Bastion Society had been full of mischief, much like the Newbury of old. While that was encouraging, and indeed the result Bainbridge and Miss Hobbes had been aiming for, the chief inspector still worried that Newbury would end up putting them all in danger.

He was still concerned for Newbury's health—and not only that, but for his mental state, too. Even with the best of motives, if he were addled by the Chinese weed, Newbury might go charging on ahead without due consideration. And Miss Hobbes, Bainbridge knew, would unthinkingly put herself at risk on Newbury's behalf, simply by virtue of the fact that she was so desperately enamoured with him. He wished he could be at their side, offering a steadying hand. But duty called.

Bainbridge thought back over the events of the day. He still couldn't quite believe the scenario the Queen had outlined for him that morning. Could she really be right? Would someone be daring enough, or foolish enough, to launch an all-out attack on the palace? Who had the means? Why should the perpetrators send a message in the form of a nameless assassin? And why was the Queen so adamant it was going to happen? What did she know that she wasn't telling him?

To Bainbridge, it all seemed somewhat unlikely. There were too many unanswered questions. He remained unconvinced that the whole incident had been anything but the ill-conceived strategy of a chancer. Perhaps the intruder had simply wanted to get his name in the history books?

No—that couldn't be it. If that were true, he would have left them some clue as to his identity. So, what, then? He sighed. There was much to consider.

Bainbridge was just about to reach for his cigar case when

he felt a dull thud against the right-hand side of the hansom. He leaned forward, reaching for his cane so that he could rap on the roof and attract the driver's attention, when the world suddenly shifted.

There was a detonation like a thunderclap. The hansom bucked and rocked dramatically onto two wheels, careening along the road for a few seconds before slamming down hard onto its side with a loud, splintering crack. The horses, startled, tried to bolt, dragging the broken carriage across the ground with a tortured screech. They neighed and whinnied in fright as they tried desperately to escape.

Amid the chaos, Bainbridge had been thrown unceremoniously to the floor, badly gashing his head above the left temple. Blood was running freely down his face. His knee had also been jarred in the fall, and he knew he'd badly bruised his right arm. He lay in a crumpled heap inside the broken frame of the cab, barely aware of what was happening, still clutching his cane.

Thud. Thud.

More explosives.

Bainbridge, still groggy, but acting under the auspices of self-preservation, sprang into action. Wrenching himself up using the seats as leverage, he stood in the shattered confines of the overturned hansom. The horses were dragging the wreckage along behind them, making it almost impossible to maintain his balance. His left eye stung where blood from his head wound was seeping into it, blurring his vision. But he knew he had to act.

Bainbridge wedged his cane between the remnants of the seats and held on to it for all he was worth, bracing himself for another explosion. All the while, he was running through possible scenarios, trying desperately to conceive a means of escape.

Woomph. The explosion came with a deafening roar. The cab juddered and shook, sliding haphazardly across the street and slamming into something solid—a building?—before finally coming to rest. Bainbridge called out as he grappled with his cane, finally losing his grip and rebounding painfully off the seat beside him, thrown back by the force of the detonation and the resulting impact. He lay there for a second while he regained his breath. Then, battered and shaken, he dragged himself back up onto his feet. His twisted knee screamed in pain as he tentatively put his weight on it.

He had to get out, and fast. The only way out of the wreckage was up, through the right-hand door of the cab, which was now doubling as the ceiling. It would leave him wide open to attack, but he was trapped where he was, and to whoever was raining the explosives down on him, he was a sitting duck. It was only a matter of time.

Bainbridge retrieved his cane, held it vertically before him with both hands and thrust it upwards with all his might, bashing at the buckled panel of the door. It rattled in its frame but didn't give. He tried again, and then again, and then finally with a third attempt the lock smashed free.

Climbing up onto the seats, Bainbridge scrambled towards the door, finding foot- and handholds wherever he could. With an almighty heave he managed to push it open, causing it to swing back on its broken hinges and clatter against the scorched side of the cab. He cautiously raised his head and peered out.

Nothing. Nothing but darkness and the patter of rain-drops against the cobbles. There was no sign of his attacker. How far had the horses dragged the carriage after the first explosion? He had no idea. He was utterly disorientated. He glanced over his shoulder. The sliding cab had ploughed into a shop front, shattering the windows and scattering fruit and vegetables haphazardly over the ground. Thick black smoke was curling into the air from the front of the hansom, where the second explosion had ripped the dickie box loose from its housing. There was no sign of the driver.

Bainbridge pushed his cane out onto the side of the cab and then, using all the strength left in his upper body, he clasped the sides of the doorframe and wrenched himself out, dragging his legs behind him. He slid off the side of the vehicle to the slick cobbles below, stifling a cry of pain as he hit the ground. He wiped the blood from his eye with the edge of his sleeve, gasping for breath.

Bainbridge didn't recognise the street he was in, but wherever it was, the area appeared deserted. Around him, everything was still and silent other than the lone creaking of the hansom's wheel, still turning languorously on its axle nearby.

The peacefulness was shattered by a shrill, piercing whistle as something came hurtling out of the sky. This was followed by the dull *thunk* of metal striking the cobbles a few feet away from where he was standing. Another explosive round.

Bainbridge didn't wait to ascertain precisely where the thing had landed. He dived for cover behind the wrecked shell of the hansom, flinging himself around the rear end of the vehicle and tumbling to the floor between the ruined cab and the shattered front end of the building. With horror, he realised that his face was only inches away from the gruesome remains of the cabbie, whose body had been nearly obliterated by the explosions. His torso had been blown open, spilling his internal organs across the stones in a red slurry, and his legs were entirely missing. His skull had fractured across his left eye orbit, and blood was still seeping out into the street, pooling beneath the cascade of spilled apples that surrounded him like a bizarre tribute. What remained of his face was filthy with blood and soot. The splayed-open carcasses of the horses were within sight as well. He could make out the rib cage of one and the haunch of another. The sight and smell of it nauseated him.

There was another almighty crack, as if the sky were splitting open. An incendiary device went up with a flash of light so bright Bainbridge wondered if he'd ever be able to see again.

He was thrown back by the impact of the cab roof slamming into him as it was shoved by the force of the explosion. He hit the floor awkwardly, jarring his elbow.

Rattled but still breathing, Bainbridge blinked desperately in an effort to regain his sight. He felt for his cane on the cobbles beside him. He found it, his fingers closing comfortingly around it. He might have use for it yet.

Stay down, he thought. *Let them think you're dead.* He tried to get his breathing under control, steadying his nerves as he waited for his vision to return.

The silence resumed. There were no sounds other than the incessant patter of raindrops and the hissing crackle of wet wood and paintwork going up in flames, as the hansom went alight in the aftermath of the explosion. It took only moments for the whole thing to be engulfed, and Bainbridge felt the ferocity of the blaze from where he was lying on the ground only a few feet away.

Then: footsteps, voices, getting closer. There were two of them. Both men. Bainbridge gripped his cane. He wasn't about to go out like this. He lay back, feigning death, his eyes open only enough to tell when his assailants were near. The footsteps grew closer, but he still couldn't see the men they belonged to.

Not yet, Charles. Don't show your hand.

He waited until he could sense the two men standing over him.

"I think he's still breathing," one of them said in a gruff voice.

"Best finish him off, then," replied the other. "Let's toss him in the wreck of the cab. The flames'll soon eat him up. It'll make it harder for the police to identify him later."

One of the men poked Bainbridge in the side with his booted foot, and then stooped closer, looking for signs of life. Bainbridge could smell his sour breath. It was pungent with gin. This was not a man of distinction; more likely a hired ruffian.

Just a moment. Just a moment longer . . .

Bainbridge suddenly whipped his cane up and around, bringing it down heavily across the man's skull, hard behind the ear.

Bainbridge rolled, using his momentum to shove the collapsing body of his attacker hard to the left. The man crumpled to the cobbles, immediately unconscious. But Bainbridge wasn't quick enough to get away from the other man's boot, which struck him in the gut. Bainbridge sputtered and tried to roll out of the way, but another blow caught him across the jaw, and his head snapped round, his mouth filling with blood.

Bainbridge kicked out, hard and low, his heel catching the other man in the knee and causing him to howl in agony and topple backwards. Bainbridge wasn't sure if he'd managed to break his leg, but he'd done enough damage to give himself a few moments to scramble to his feet and appraise the situation. He spat blood. His jaw was throbbing and he thought a tooth might be loose. No matter. He could worry about that later, he hoped.

His first attacker was still out cold, lying facedown wearing a cheap brown suit. Beside him was the bizarre weapon he had used to rain incendiary missiles down upon the hansom. It was a large brass cylinder with a padded shoulder harness and a crank on its side that was clearly the firing mechanism. There was a set of crosshairs on the side of the barrel and a second cylinder—a loading tube—fixed into the main body of the gun at a forty-five-degree angle. It was effectively a shoulder-mounted cannon, the ammunition propelled not by gunpowder but a hand-wound mechanism that flung the explosive devices through the air towards their target. It was a remarkable weapon, and Bainbridge hoped he'd never have to face one again. He considered trying to use it against the second man, now that his colleague was unconscious, but thought twice: He risked blowing himself up if he fired it incorrectly.

For now, he needed to move before the second assailant reached him. Bainbridge decided to round on him, hoping to gain the upper hand. He adopted his old boxing stance, which had served him well through so many years and so many brawls. He hoped it would serve him well now, too; he felt battered, bruised, and utterly exhausted, but he knew he couldn't outrun his opponent, so his only chance was to stand his ground.

The other man was slowly regaining his composure, flexing his leg. He was a swarthy-looking fellow, a career criminal of the type Bainbridge had learned to spot a mile off. Well built, dressed in a stained suit at least a size too big for him—probably taken off the back of a corpse—he was hired muscle, paid to do a job without asking questions. This was a contract job.

Bainbridge circled around his attacker, looking for an opening. He saw it a moment later and rushed in, jabbing at the man's face. The other man sidestepped neatly, wincing in pain as he transferred his weight to his damaged knee. "You'll pay for that, old man," he barked.

Bainbridge didn't rise to the gibe. Instead, he came on again, three punches in quick succession, this time striking the man on the jaw. Bainbridge's opponent reeled for a second, then rounded on him.

A sweeping roundhouse punch caught him fast and hard in the side of the head. He stumbled, nearly tottering into the flaming hansom just to his right.

Bainbridge tried to back away from the brute while he fought off his disorientation, but the other man was relentless, rushing forward to deliver another solid punch to the gut. Bainbridge tried to block him, but he was too slow. He doubled over, this time catching the man's good knee in his face. Blood sprayed in a wide arc as his nose burst.

"With the compliments of Sir Enoch Graves," the man said, chuckling.

Bainbridge slumped to the floor. Enoch Graves. So the Bastion Society was behind this.

Baubles of light were dancing before his eyes. He struggled against the encroaching unconsciousness that threatened to overwhelm him. Darkness limned the edges of his vision. *No! Not like this. I won't go like this.*

Bainbridge felt around him, looking for something, anything, he could use as a weapon. Nothing. His fingers scraped against the wet cobbles. Where was his cane?

The man's boot came down hard on Bainbridge's hand, and he yowled in pain as it was ground into the stone. He looked up into the face of his attacker. The man was glaring down at him with a brutal sneer, his face lit by flames from the burning carriage. Rainwater ran in trickling rivulets down his cheeks.

Every fibre of Bainbridge's body ached. He groaned as he tried to scramble away.

The man spat at him. A fat gobbet of spittle landed on Bainbridge's face, and the chief inspector flinched involuntarily as it struck home. "That's it, old-timer. You've caused me enough trouble already. It'll be easier on us both if you just lay back and accept the inevitable."

"Not likely," Bainbridge managed to croak as his foot came up, striking the other man hard between the legs. The man creased, releasing Bainbridge's crippled hand from beneath his boot.

Bainbridge rolled away, coughing and hacking. Casting around, he saw his cane lying on the ground just a few feet away. He scrambled for it, reaching it just as the man struck him hard across the back of the head with a balled fist, causing him to slump facedown upon the cold, wet ground.

Weak and in pain, Bainbridge fumbled with the cane beneath him. Holding the cane's shaft in one hand and its crest in the other, he gave it a sharp twist. The man had grabbed him by the feet and was dragging him backwards, facedown, towards the shell of the burning cab.

Bainbridge allowed his body to go limp, to give his attacker the impression that he'd given up and stopped his struggling. Beneath him, however, he felt the shaft of his cane beginning to unpack itself. Long wooden strips clicked out of their housing and slid into position, forming a spinning cage around the upper shaft of the cane. Bainbridge felt it building up momentum, the shaft humming and fizzing as the chamber generated a fierce arc of electricity, a lightning cage of deadly blue light contained in the shaft of the now-deadly weapon.

He held it tightly beneath him, allowing the charge to build as he was dragged unceremoniously across the cobbles. The heat of the flames was close and ferocious, and he knew he would have to act soon.

Bainbridge heard his attacker grunt with the effort of hauling his dead weight. The man slowed.

Now was his chance.

Using the man's grip on his ankles as a pivot, Bainbridge pushed himself up into the air, twisting his body around and thrusting down and out with the bladed tip of his cane, deep into the other man's belly.

The man wailed in shock and surprise. He immediately

released Bainbridge's feet to pull at the embedded cane that now protruded like a spear from his guts.

But it was too late. The cane discharged its electrical payload and the man shook as the electricity coursed through his body, leaping and dancing with the sheer power of the charge. He opened his mouth to scream, and blue lightning arced between his teeth. His hair rose comically, maniacally from his scalp, crackling with static energy. The air around them filled with the grotesque scent of burning meat.

Seconds later, the charge in the cane finally spent, the corpse crumpled backwards to the ground, striking the cobbles with a wet thud.

Exhausted, Bainbridge clambered to his knees. Rain lashed at his face and caused the flames to spit and hiss beside him. He wobbled, near delirium, and issued a low moan. His breath was coming in ragged gasps. He glanced over at the first man to ensure that he was still unconscious, and realised too late that the flames had spread to the shop front, and that the strange projectile weapon the men had used to bring down the cab was now lying amongst a pile of burning crates. He staggered to his feet. He had to get the ammunition away from the flames. Had to—

There was a deafening explosion, and everything went black.

CHAPTER

18

Veronica peered over the lip of the building at the twenty-foot drop and pondered, not for the first time that day, whether Newbury was utterly insane.

They'd come from Chelsea an hour earlier, after collecting an array of equipment from Newbury's home—lock picks, some small blades, an old revolver—to make a reconnaissance of Packworth House, the home of the Bastion Society. She'd never seen Newbury carry a gun, and she wondered what it was about the Bastion Society that had him spooked enough to arm himself with one now. She hoped he wouldn't find cause to use it.

Scarbright, dressed in his immaculate suit, had been waiting at the house with a note from Bainbridge. Newbury had read it swiftly in the drawing room before showing it to her. Its contents were minimal, but spoke volumes:

Newbury,

Someone is moving against the Queen. Continue with the Sykes matter without me.

Yours,
Charles

The note had been scrawled in haste; Bainbridge's handwriting was scratchy and rushed. This, then, was no small matter. It was unlike the chief inspector to be harried. Scarbright confirmed that the note had arrived by courier a little earlier in the evening, meaning that Bainbridge was too busy to call on them in person. This had sparked an hour-long debate between Veronica and Newbury regarding how to proceed. Newbury had considered calling off their plans for the evening and heading over to the palace to assist Bainbridge with whatever was going on over there, but Veronica had remained insistent. She'd argued that they needed to push forward with their pursuit of the Bastion Society. If Amelia's horrific vision of the terrible things to come—not to mention Newbury's own predictions—had anything to do with the attacks on the palace, then they needed to work out if the Bastion Society was somehow involved. Bainbridge, Veronica assured him, could handle the Queen.

Besides, by that point, Victoria would already have called in an entire armed garrison to fortify the palace. If she needed Newbury, she would already have sent for him.

All of that was true. But Veronica couldn't deny that her sister's plight had played a large part in her steering of the conversation. Amelia needed her. If storming the Bastion

Society could provide the answers as to what Dr. Fabian was doing to her, and perhaps even the key to extracting her safely from the Grayling Institute, then Veronica would not be swayed. At that point, she'd already decided that if Newbury had insisted on rushing off to help Bainbridge, she would have continued to execute their plans alone. She wasn't about to allow the matter to be swept aside—not for Newbury, not for the Queen, not for anyone.

In the end, however, Newbury had reluctantly agreed, and they caught a cab across town, stopping a few streets from Packworth House so they might approach the building more surreptitiously on foot.

Now, they were perched on the rooftop of a neighbouring building, looking down at a balcony a storey below, across the other side of an alleyway.

Newbury came over to stand beside her, putting a gentle hand on her shoulder. "Veronica. I'll ask you again: Are you sure you want to go through with this?" He sounded concerned, as if he were willing her to say no.

She nodded. She'd done worse, risked her life in more perilous endeavours. All the same, the notion of leaping across from one building to the other very much filled her with dread.

In the preceding hour, they had performed their reconnaissance of the entire building, and short of marching up to the front door and announcing their presence, they could see no better way into the premises. The balcony appeared to be unguarded, and the locks on the French doors would, Newbury assured her, be relatively easy to pick.

Veronica looked at the drop again, and her stomach

lurched. Newbury went in for this sort of thing much more than she did. In fact, he seemed to relish it, if his zeal in sizing up the void between the two buildings was any indication. It wasn't that she wasn't capable—she'd proved that time and time again, particularly during the matter of the Persian Teardrop, when she'd spent much of her time hopping about on the rooftops of Paris, trying to recover the stolen jewel. No, it was more that she'd much prefer to operate with her feet firmly planted on the ground.

Still, at least the rain had abated. The ground was still wet, but they'd been able to avoid the worst of the downpour. She only hoped the balcony itself wouldn't be too wet for a safe landing.

She was beginning to feel the chill. She turned to Newbury. "Let's get on with it, Maurice," she said, again lapsing into the familiar.

Newbury nodded. "Yes, let's." He straightened up, took three or four steps back from the lip of the building, and then dashed forward, leaping off the edge, arms cartwheeling as he hurtled through the air.

"Maurice!" Veronica exclaimed, her hands involuntarily going to her mouth. Her heart skipped a beat.

And then he was over, landing on the balcony with a thump. He skittered on the wet tiles and lost his balance, ending up on his backside. He stood, hauling himself up with support from the railings that ran around the edge of the balcony, and dusted himself off. He looked up at her ruefully. "Are you coming?" he called.

Veronica rolled her eyes. She was about to ruin a perfectly good blue dress. She reached down, kicked off her shoes, and flung them at Newbury, who, surprised, managed to throw his arms out just in time to catch them before they struck him hard in the chest. Then, hitching up her skirts, she followed Newbury's lead, pacing back four or five steps before charging forward, hopping up onto the stone lip of the building and propelling herself off the roof. She sailed through the air in a smooth arc, coming to land adroitly a couple of feet away from Newbury. He reached out to steady her as she found her balance. Her heart was thumping in her chest, but she felt exhilarated. She looked up at the building behind her. God—had she just done that?

Newbury handed her the shoes. "Let's hope we can get these doors open, or we really are stuck now," he said, with a grin.

Veronica slipped her shoes back on as Newbury fished around in his pocket, eventually producing the lock picks. They consisted of a bundle of fine metal rods, wrapped in a roll of black velvet. He dropped to his knees, carefully examining the lock on the French doors, running his fingers over the various tools as he tried to select the appropriate size and shape.

"Have you—?" Veronica began.

"Shhh!" he chided.

Ignoring him, she reached out and tried the door handle. It turned easily, and the door creaked open. "—tried the handle?"

Newbury laughed, getting to his feet. "Oh, very good, Miss Hobbes."

She shrugged. "Why would anyone lock the French doors on a second-storey balcony? Logical, really."

Newbury shrugged. "In case someone decides to jump

across from a nearby building with plans of breaking and entering?" he replied smartly.

They both grinned. Veronica peered through the opening.

The room beyond the French doors was shrouded in darkness. Veronica gestured for Newbury to remain quiet and slowly edged the door a little wider, wincing as the hinges squealed loudly in protest. She inched forward, stepping carefully over the threshold, listening intently for any sounds of movement or occupation from within. The coast appeared to be clear. She crept into the room, beckoning for Newbury to follow her.

Inside, silhouettes loomed out of the gloom, impressions of furniture and other, indiscernible shapes. Bookshelves, a desk, a tall lamp stand: everything she would expect to find in a typical gentleman's study. The place seemed relatively normal. Or so she thought until she saw the thing on the wall. She nearly cried out in fright when she caught sight of it: a stuffed lion's head mounted on a wooden plaque above the desk. It was frozen in a magnificent roar, its teeth bared, its glass eyes gleaming in the reflected starlight from the windows. A trophy, she realised, of someone's conquest in Africa. It was morbid, egotistical, and entirely unnecessary.

Newbury came up behind her. He leaned close, his voice barely above a whisper. "There's the door." He pointed over at the opposite wall, where Veronica could just make out a crack of light seeping in under the frame. "Wait here and I'll take a look."

He slipped past her, avoiding a settee in the centre of the room near the desk. Veronica watched as he slowly turned the handle, easing the door open a fraction of an inch so that he could peer out into the hallway beyond. Bright light slanted in through the crack, casting Newbury in sharp relief.

He glanced back over his shoulder. "Come on," he said. "It's all clear."

Newbury stepped through the door and Veronica followed.

Her eyes took a moment to adjust to the harsh glare of the gaslights she encountered on the other side. She found herself in a hallway, a long, carpeted corridor with five or six other doors radiating off it. A fabulous array of paintings adorned the walls, the work of romantic artists such as Waterhouse and Millais, each depicting scenes of Arthurian knights rescuing fair maidens or charging into battle, or else landscapes of a green and pleasant England, the ramparts of ancient castles in the distance. These were visions of an England that had never existed in anything other than the dreams of a few fantasists, or in myths and legends, passed down through the ages. But here they were everywhere, lining the walls, as if the members of the Bastion Society considered them windows through which to glimpse the glorious past, the secret bygone age of chivalry and magic. Veronica had to admit they did evoke a certain mood, a sense of longing for the romance of a time that never was.

She glanced down the corridor at Newbury. He was testing the doors to see if any of them were unlocked. One of them was, and without hesitation he swung it open and disappeared inside. Veronica rushed along the passageway after him on her tiptoes. Farther down the corridor she could discern the low, monotonous hubbub of many voices chattering away, accompanied by the clinking of glasses and the clatter of cutlery and china. She guessed this was from the level below, the great hall in which they had spoken to Enoch Graves during their last visit to Packworth. It was clearly far busier tonight. She wondered if it was another of their banquets.

Veronica was just about to turn into the room into which Newbury had disappeared when he reemerged, shaking his head. She shrugged, and he motioned her farther down the corridor. They tried each of the doors, finding only one other unlocked.

In here, Veronica found a bedchamber of sorts. There was a small cot in one corner, along with a gentleman's wardrobe and chest of drawers. Another painting hung on the wall—a knight, clad in shining plate armour, aiding a redheaded maiden to dismount from her steed.

Veronica gathered that the Bastion Society would see symbolism in these paintings, that their members looked to these chivalric heroes of old for their inspiration, their code. She wondered if that was really such a bad thing. Surely it was preferable to the sort of devil-worshipping cults they usually had to deal with?

They left the bedchamber and tiptoed cautiously to the end of the corridor. Here, the noise from the hall below became a dramatic cacophony. It was impossible to distinguish any of what was being said due to the sheer volume and intensity of the chatter, the number of voices talking at once.

The corridor terminated in a wide balcony that circled the entirety of the upper level. Numerous corridors branched off from this central terminus at regular intervals, and a grand, sweeping staircase joined this upper floor with the great hall below.

A waist-high stone balustrade formed a neat parapet that enclosed the balcony, enabling people on the upper level to look down upon the proceedings below. Thankfully, no one seemed to be making use of the balcony at present. Veronica supposed they were all too busy enjoying the festivities with their comrades down below.

Newbury edged towards the parapet as quietly and slowly as possible. He dropped into a crouch behind it and peered between the balusters at the hall below.

Veronica, anxious to know what was going on, dashed quickly across the open space and dropped to her knees just beside him. He looked up at her in surprise, raising one eyebrow as if to enquire what she thought she was doing, and then appeared to think better of it and returned his attention to the men below. Veronica smiled and did the same.

There must have been a hundred men in the hall, perhaps more. It was difficult to tell with so many of them moving about, bustling from table to table, conversation to conversation. They were all dressed in identical attire—dark grey suits and matching bowler hats, each with a red sash tied around their left arm. Each sash bore a different three-figure number, marked in white. She wondered what the numbers could be for. Was it some sort of pseudo-militaristic code?

The men were sitting—mostly—around large circular tables, enjoying what looked to Veronica like a mediaeval feast. Huge platters of roast meat sat in the centre of every table. The whole thing looked like an exercise in gluttony, and the manner in which the men were attacking the meal, feeding themselves with their fingers, stuffing the greasy meat into their mouths, made Veronica feel queasy.

Servants in black suits and white gloves, like the butlers and waiters they had seen during their previous visit, flitted about amongst the tables followed by bizarre eight-legged automata.

Veronica had never seen anything like them. They were waist-high, with multijointed legs and a skittering gait that reminded her of the assassin device that had attacked her and Newbury at her apartment. She fought to repress a brief shudder. These were much larger, and there were at least ten of them running about between the tables, bearing trays stacked high with empty plates and glasses. They were a kind of self-propelling trolley, she realised, each one assigned to a different waiter, who loaded the machines with the remnants of the feast and sent them scuttling back to the kitchen.

She spotted Enoch Graves standing before the fireplace, laughing and carousing with another man. Like the others, he was dressed in a grey suit with a matching bowler hat. His red sash was adorned with the number *001*—indicating his prime position within the strange society, she supposed— and he was still wearing his dress sabre strapped to his belt.

Veronica turned at a gentle tap on her shoulder. Newbury motioned for her to move away from the edge of the balcony. Veronica did so, and he shuffled along beside her.

Veronica stood, keeping her back to the wall, just out of sight—she hoped—from anyone below who might be looking up in her direction. A quick glance at the staircase told her they were still alone.

Newbury stood beside her and leaned in, so close that she could feel his warm breath on her cheek. "Let's take a look at the hallway on the other side," he whispered, pointing across the open space at a corridor across from where they stood. They'd have to work their way around the balcony to get there. Together they crept along it, keeping themselves out of view of the people below. The noise of the festivities meant that they could travel swiftly without risk of being heard, so it was only a matter of moments before they were turning down the corridor Newbury had pointed out to her.

More paintings lined the walls here. Veronica realised how much money must have gone into furnishing the house. Each painting must be worth hundreds, if not thousands of pounds. And the banquet wouldn't be cheap, either. Where were they getting their funds?

Newbury tested the handles on one side of the passageway while Veronica did the same on the other. More bedrooms, more locked doors. They were clearly in some sort of dormitory area, the place where members of the society could take rooms in times of need or inebriation. Some of these rooms appeared to have been recently inhabited, with beds that had been slept in and small piles of belongings on the bedside tables. Others were empty and disused.

The corridor terminated in another door. Veronica realised that the layout of the house must be symmetrical such that the room in front of her corresponded to the study they had used to gain entrance to the house. She tried the door. It was unlocked.

Expecting to find either another bedchamber or another desk, Veronica swung the door open and stepped inside. The sight that greeted her, however, was so grotesque that she immediately rushed back out into the corridor and retched.

She leaned both her hands against the wall, hoping to soak up some of its strength, trying her utmost not to swoon.

The room was full of bodies.

Newbury rushed to her side. "Veronica!" he whispered urgently. "Are you unwell? What's the mat . . ." He trailed off as he glanced up and saw, through the open door, the same harrowing vision of Hell that had sent her running from the room.

Naked human bodies hung from the ceiling on row after row of meat hooks, like carcasses in a butcher's shop, a forest of white, damaged hides. The bodies were once men, but they had been so brutalised, so mutilated, that they no longer resembled anything but hunks of pale, bloody flesh.

The stink emanating from the room caused her to retch again, and this time she couldn't hold back her vomit, a thin, watery stream that splashed on the maroon carpet by her feet. She wiped her mouth and looked apologetically at Newbury, but he was still staring in shock at the contents of the dimly lit room. Mustering her strength, she moved to stand beside him.

"I recognise some of them," Newbury said, his voice tremulous. He approached the door, hovered on the threshold for a second, and then went inside. Frowning, Veronica followed.

Newbury walked amongst the hanging dead, his expression switching from repulsion to fascination as he examined the corpses in more detail. Flies buzzed around the victims' heads in thick black swarms.

"These are ritual killings," Newbury said, his voice echoing. Veronica realised for the first time how big the room really was. There were probably a hundred flayed bodies in there, each of them hanging from the ceiling like fleshy stalactites. The windows had been blacked out with thick drapes, and the only light came from a bright electric strip that arced across the ceiling, humming with power. There was no furniture in the room, other than a small table bearing various implements of torture: a hammer, a saw, a whip, some tongs. The sight of them threatened to turn Veronica's stomach again.

She glanced up at the pale face of one of the corpses. The sallow, sunken eyes and the manner in which the jaw hung loosely open, clearly broken, suggested many, many hours of torture had been enacted upon the victim before he was finally killed. She noticed that the man's torso had runes and magical symbols carved on it. She examined another. This one had been tattooed with similar markings. Yet another had a large pentagram branded into his back, just below the shoulders. She could see what Newbury was getting at. Ritual killings. It seemed the Bastion Society was a lot more sinister and dangerous than either of them had imagined.

"Why?" She turned to Newbury, who was still wandering amongst the hanging bodies. "What are they hoping to gain from all this? Surely if they were only interested in murdering their enemies, they'd dispose of the bodies somewhere, rather than stringing them up like this for everyone to see?"

"I rather think that's the point of all this," Newbury replied cryptically. He swung one of the corpses around on its hook, stooping low to examine the feet. Veronica blanched at the sight of the metal hook, which had pierced the dead man's shoulder, rending his flesh around the exit wound. The blood had long ago dried and been cleared away.

Newbury was prising apart the toes of the dead man's left foot as if this were all quite normal, something he might do every day. Veronica didn't want to brush against one of them by accident, let alone touch them deliberately. The last time she'd seen death on such a scale was in the wreck of the *Lady Armitage*, the airship that had crashed in Finsbury Park last year. But it later transpired that those bodies had been victims of the Revenant plague, so in many ways they had already been dead before the crash. But this? Something monstrous was going on here.

"It's just as I thought," Newbury said as he let the body swing free again. The hook creaked on its chain, and the cadaver knocked against another with a dull slap, setting that one swinging in turn, so that its head lolled in a semblance of nodding. Veronica turned away.

"In what sense?" she managed to ask, still fighting the urge to gag. Everywhere she looked there was a putrefying eyeball, or a disembowelled belly, or worse. She settled for focusing on Newbury's face.

"Haven't you noticed? All the victims are men. There are no women in here. What does that tell you?"

Veronica sighed. Now really wasn't the time for one of his deductive games. "No. I didn't notice," she replied hotly. *I'm too busy finding this whole situation rather too appalling for words,* she thought, but didn't add that to her response.

"They're like Sykes. All of them. Clean. Unused. As if their flesh has never been *worn*." He paused, letting his words sink in. "They're copies."

"More duplicates? But the scale of it . . ." She trailed off, thinking once again of Amelia. Somehow, this whole thing was linked, but she hoped beyond hope that this wasn't what would become of those duplicates she had encountered at the Grayling Institute. That would simply be too much to bear. "You said you recognised some of them?"

Newbury nodded. "The men from downstairs. That's why there are no women. All of these corpses are members of the Bastion Society. Look here." He beckoned her over and pointed to a dangling corpse, about three feet away from where he was standing. She recognised the face immediately.

"Oh God! It's Enoch Graves!" She swallowed, but her mouth was dry. The corpse had been neutered and its chest cavity wrenched open, its heart torn out. "What on Earth are they doing here?" She was utterly appalled, uncomprehending.

Newbury put his arm around her shoulders and she fell against him, burying her face in the crook of his neck. She didn't want to look anymore.

"The occult symbolism suggests this is some sort of transference ritual," he said, lapsing into his lecturing voice. Veronica realised his only way of staying unaffected by the horrors they were facing was to turn off his emotional reaction and approach them like a scholar, without passion, like a puzzle that needed to be solved.

"Transference?"

"Yes. It's all about establishing a balance. You see, some religions and philosophies believe that every act a person commits has consequences, and that the universe finds a means to pay that person back in kind. So if you hurt someone, the likelihood is that you, in turn, would get hurt. Similarly, if you demonstrate kindness, you will be shown kindness in return. I'm sure you've heard the phrase 'treat people as you'd ask to be treated'?"

Veronica nodded. "Yes. But where does the transference come into it?"

Newbury clacked his tongue against his teeth. "Dr. Fabian mentioned karmic debt for how he'd helped to provide Graves with the means to carry out bizarre rituals. Perhaps those rituals involve inflicting pain on their doppelgängers in an effort to avoid that karmic settlement? They might think that if their duplicates suffer horribly, they won't have to." He paused, and she could feel him sighing sadly as she held on to him, still refusing to look at the dangling bodies all around her. "And if I'm right, that means they've committed some terrible atrocities indeed, if this is the result of their efforts to avoid the redressing of the balance. Either that or they're rather overcompensating."

"Or putting credit in the bank, so to speak." The voice rang out, echoing around the large room. It was a voice she recognised immediately, dripping with arrogance and affected refinement. Enoch Graves. His footsteps rang out against the tiled floor as he approached, making no effort to conceal himself from them. "You almost have it, Newbury, and I must admit I'm terribly impressed! Good show! There's just one thing you've got wrong . . ." He paused as he finally found them, brushing aside one of his dead, mutilated colleagues to clear his path. "They were never alive. We're not monsters. The machine makes copies, yes, but it never instills the spark of life. They're just dead husks that look and smell and feel like us, but they're never conscious. They never feel pain."

Graves stood before them, resplendent in his grey suit and bowler hat. He appraised them both. Veronica had turned to watch him approach, and was now eyeing him warily, wondering what he was going to do next. Was he telling the truth? If he was, what was going on at the Grayling Institute with Amelia? Those duplicates were certainly not dead husks.

"Then how could the transference ever work?" Veronica was still standing in front of Newbury. He held her firmly in front of him, and she realised that his hand was moving to his trouser pocket, out of sight of Graves. He was reaching for his revolver. "If they never feel pain, the karmic debt is never repaid. It's all for nothing."

Graves shrugged. "I suppose we'll discover which of us is right in the next life," he said, a sneer on his lips. He held his arms out as if welcoming them. "Oh, it *is* nice to have visitors. And you've saved us such trouble, coming here like this. I had intended to send someone out to kill you, Newbury, but now there's no need. It's just a shame you didn't bring Sir Charles along with you, too. We've had to deal with him separately."

Veronica felt Newbury stiffen. She prepared herself. If she could cause a distraction . . .

She rushed forwards, swinging her arm up and around to aim a blow at Graves's jaw. He saw her coming, however, and was ready for her, lashing out in self-defence and knocking her brutally to the ground with a swipe of his arm.

She'd given Newbury the distraction he needed, however, and he swung his right arm up in one easy motion, presenting Graves with the business end of his revolver. He cocked it with his thumb. "What have you done with Charles? Where is he now?"

Veronica kept her eyes on Graves as she pulled herself up from the floor. Her hands were smarting from where she'd struck the tiles in the fall.

Graves, however, had not taken his eyes off Newbury and the gun, ignoring Veronica and acting as if nothing had happened. He shook his head. "I honestly don't know, Newbury. I'd wager he's in a hundred pieces by now, blown apart on his way to the palace. But my men haven't returned, so I can't answer your question. That's the truth of the matter." That gave Veronica hope. Perhaps Charles had been able to evade them, or better still, to best them somehow. She willed that to be true.

She glanced at Newbury. His expression was hard, unforgiving. He wasn't playing along with Graves's banter. "I'm not feeling very inclined to go easy on you, Graves." He stabbed the air threateningly with the gun. His finger hovered on the trigger. Veronica wondered what he was going to do. He'd never been the sort to kill someone in cold blood, even for something as world-shattering as murdering his dearest friend. But the glint in his eye suggested otherwise. Perhaps, in this instance, Newbury felt he was the one who needed to mete out that unpaid karmic debt.

Suddenly there was a blur of motion. Newbury buckled, his face contorted in pain, and the gun clattered noisily to the tiles a few feet away. For a moment, Veronica couldn't figure out exactly what had occurred, until she saw the sabre in Graves's hand, and realised with mounting dismay that he had managed to draw it and use it to disarm Newbury, all in a matter of seconds.

Graves came forward, the tip of his sabre pressing dangerously against the front of Newbury's jacket. He looked serious now, all sense of his earlier playfulness banished. "Now, Sir Maurice," he said in a perfectly reasonable tone, "I think it's about time you and I sat down together and discussed this like gentlemen."

CHAPTER

19

"Tell me, what did Edwin Sykes do to incur your wrath? Was it the fact he stole from you? Or the matter of bringing unwanted attention to your strange little society?"

Newbury was seated opposite Enoch Graves at a large round table in a flag-stoned room on the lower level. The chamber was dressed in the manner of a mediaeval throne room, with huge tapestries covering the walls and iron candelabras bearing tall, white pillars of wax to either side of Graves's elaborate chair. The table itself was a smooth, glossy mahogany, inlaid with intricate zodiacal symbols of ebony and gold. A wreath of stylised ivy encircled an impressive goblet at the centre of the design, which Newbury took to be a depiction of the Holy Grail.

Newbury grinned. Graves really *was* attempting to re-create his ideal of Camelot right there in London. Of course, he would be at its epicentre, sitting resplendent on his golden throne.

Newbury thought he looked faintly ridiculous, dwarfed by his massive gleaming chair.

Behind Newbury two men stood guard, dressed in the matching grey suits and hats of the Bastion Society, each bearing swords and pistols. Another two had escorted Veronica to a holding cell, where Graves had assured him that she would remain unharmed, at least for the time being. Newbury supposed that would depend on how the following conversation went, and whether Graves would try to use Veronica's well-being as a bargaining tool to get what he wanted.

He was concerned for Charles, though. He knew his friend could hold his own in a tussle, but if Graves really had sent men after him with explosives, the chief inspector would have found himself badly outmatched. If it was too late, if Charles was dead—Newbury shuddered at the very thought—then Graves would pay with his life. More than that, Newbury promised himself. He would pay with his very soul.

It was clear the premier didn't yet want Newbury dead, however. If that had been his intention, he would have run the pair of them through with his sabre up in the hanging room while he'd had the chance. No, he wanted something else. Newbury wasn't yet sure what it was, but he expected it wouldn't be long before he found out.

Graves leaned forward in his throne, peering down at Newbury from across the table. "Sykes?" He laughed, waving his hand in a dismissive gesture. "Sykes? No . . . Although I probably would have executed him sooner or later for the reasons you mention. We knew all about his little crime spree. It couldn't have been anyone else–he was the expert handler of the spiders, the only one capable of using the ma-

chines for such precision work. To be honest with you, Newbury, the entire matter was beneath my concern. He'd 'borrowed'
one of our machines, but we have many more. And he made
sure that at least half of the proceeds from his late-night pursuits were added to the society's coffers. No, I wouldn't have
killed him for that."

"Then why?" Newbury ran a finger around the inside of
his collar. He was sweating, and his hands were beginning to
tremble. It had been a while since his last dose of laudanum,
and he was starting to itch again with cravings.

"Because he took it upon himself to disregard my express
orders. Because he removed one of the duplicates from the
growth chamber and employed it for his own purposes,
leaving it in a gutter on Shaftesbury Avenue to foil the police. It was a blasphemy against our beliefs, Newbury, and I
considered it a sign of his moral inferiority. He simply had
to die. So I had one of the men trail him and sabotage the
machine. Sykes might have been an expert in handling the
mechanical creatures, but he was never intelligent enough
to understand what made them work." Graves looked smug,
as if the point of his story was to highlight his own superior-
ity. "I'd have liked to have seen the expression on his face
when it turned on him. Besides, he was never truly one of
ours."

Newbury looked puzzled. "Surely though, according to
your philosophy, he'll simply be born again? So what was the
point in murdering him in such a fashion?"

"Oh, absolutely," Graves replied. "And in the next life he
will carry with him the lessons learned in this one. In truth,
all we've done by ending this stage of his existence was to

preserve the integrity of his soul. Next time he might make better choices."

Newbury laughed at the ridiculousness of it all. He couldn't quite believe what Graves was telling him: that he'd ordered a mechanical device to tear a hole through Sykes's chest for the man's own good. "That's a terribly convenient theory of existence, Sir Enoch."

Graves looked serious. "Attractive, isn't it? I can see you're enamoured by it, Newbury. We'll come to that."

Newbury ran a hand through his hair. He felt a little faint. He pressed on regardless. Graves was so egomaniacal that he seemed eager to answer Newbury's questions. Newbury decided to take advantage of the fact, gaining as much information as he could while he had the chance. He knew it might prove invaluable later, and he'd long ago learned how to manipulate the arrogance of men such as Graves. His sort, Newbury had found, were always willing to impress people with their assumed intelligence, always looking for the validation of others. "So how does the duplication process work? I understand it has something to do with Lucien Fabian?" *There,* Newbury thought, *let's see what he makes of that.*

"Fabian?" Graves almost spat the name. "That pretentious upstart? Dear me, no. The duplication technology is the work of Dr. Warrander, our Chief Engineer. Fabian was a pupil of his, a long time ago. Warrander taught him everything he knows."

Newbury suppressed his surprise. He had no reason to doubt Graves's claim. He'd always wondered where Fabian had earned his stripes. As far as many people were concerned—Newbury included—Fabian had simply emerged fully formed,

a medical man, an inventor, an engineer. He knew Fabian
had been away at war and had experimented on wounded
soldiers, finding ways to patch them up and send them back
into battle, but that was about the sum of his knowledge of
the man's history. He wondered if Graves knew about the
experiments with duplication that Fabian was conducting at
the Grayling Institute with Amelia, and whether Fabian had
also learned that from Warrander. Newbury suspected that
was probably the case. It would be too much of a coincidence otherwise. Newbury waited to see if Graves would
elaborate.

Graves smiled. "You're wondering now why Fabian parted
company with the Bastion Society. You're a clever man, Newbury. You understand so much of what's going on here."

Newbury smiled, but ignored the pandering.

Graves shrugged at his lack of response. "Fabian had always
wanted to push his work beyond the point where any of us felt
comfortable. He never really accepted our beliefs, was more
interested in the physical world than the spiritual one. When
he went to the Queen and offered to find a way to preserve her
life, he took a step too far. He was ejected from the society. By
then he didn't need us, or Warrander, anymore." Graves folded
his arms. "I must admit, Newbury, that we never even considered he might be successful. By then the Queen was already
on her deathbed. Even Warrander believed he would fail."

Inwardly, Newbury grinned. But Fabian *didn't* fail. That
must be what this whole business was all about. Fabian had
found a way to extend the Queen's existence, and Graves and
his bizarre society considered that the greatest blasphemy of
all. Fabian had offered the Queen longevity, binding her

spirit to her decrepit body beyond the course of its natural life. To Graves, this was the ultimate anathema, the gravest of crimes. The result was that the Empire was being ruled by a woman whom Graves and his men believed should have died long before, an undead monarch whose very existence undermined their core beliefs.

So was it the Bastion Society that was planning to move against the Queen? Did they want her dead? Surely they didn't have the means to storm the palace as Amelia had envisioned. Newbury needed to keep Graves talking until he found out. "I'm surprised you didn't help Fabian to the grave, just like Sykes. It sounds as if he would have benefitted from the same sort of lesson."

Graves clapped his hands together in satisfaction. "I knew you were one of us, Newbury! You're quite right. We made an error of judgement allowing Fabian to go free. But we had other considerations at the time. He'd taken a position as the Queen's personal physician. A role like that brings with it a certain level of protection, both physical and political."

Newbury nodded. "You didn't want to go up against the Queen."

Graves frowned. "We didn't have the *means* to go against the Queen. It wasn't a matter of desire."

So that was it, then. It had all been a matter of timing. They'd been preparing, and now they were almost ready to show their hand. "Surely you can't want to depose the Empress? To murder a crippled old woman in her own palace?"

Graves laughed. "Oh, Newbury, such melodrama. She'd be dead anyway if it wasn't for the machines keeping her alive. That's no life. And she's no innocent old woman, as well you know. I'm surprised to hear you rush to her defence. She'd hardly do the same for you." Graves paused, leaning forward to look Newbury directly in the eye. "The Queen doubts you, Sir Maurice. I'm sure you're already uncomfortably aware of that fact. She doubts your commitment and your integrity, to the extent that she deployed one of her best agents to spy on you, right under your very nose."

Newbury clenched his jaw. The words hit home like a knife twisting in his gut. So even this indefatigable fool knew the truth about Veronica. He bit back his retort, holding his nerve but simmering with anger. He felt a bead of sweat forming under his hairline and shivered.

"Yes. Yes! I can see by the look on your face, Newbury, that you know I speak the truth. But it matters little. Soon enough the Queen will be gone and there will be a new monarch on the throne. One who is perhaps even less tolerant of your vices. Victoria's era is ending, and with it, so will yours." Graves reached up and removed his bowler hat, tossing it on the table and running a hand through his hair. "I'm going to offer you a choice, Newbury, and you should consider it very carefully. I know all about your work and your fascination with the occult. I know your habits and how you crave the Chinese weed. I know your methods and your personal affairs. I know everything there is to know about you." He paused, giving his words time to sink in. "And still I do not doubt you like the Queen does. You are a remarkable man, Newbury. It doesn't have to end there. When she falls, there is a place for you by my side, as one of us, as a member of the Bastion Society. Unlike the Queen, we understand you, Newbury. We can offer you salvation." He smiled and held out his hand. "Will you join us?"

Newbury regarded Graves coolly. "I will not," he said, leaning back in his chair.

Graves's face fell. His extended hand curled into a fist, and he banged it angrily against the arm of his throne. "Then I fear, Sir Maurice, your time has come to its end. I will keep you alive only long enough to see the ruination of everything you hold dear. Victoria's reign will crumble, and with it, you and Miss Hobbes. I'm only disappointed that you haven't the intelligence to see what you're dismissing so casually, Newbury. You would have shined among us. Your experiments could have flourished. You would have had access to secrets you can only begin to imagine, the undisclosed history of the world. But I can see now it was not to be." He sighed. "Instead, your corpse will rot in the ground until your spirit is returned to the earth to make recompense for your inadequacies." Graves snapped his fingers, and the two guards stepped forward. He addressed them haughtily. "Throw him in the cell with the girl," he said, turning his cheek. "I do not wish to look upon him any longer."

Newbury felt the guards' hands grip his shoulders, and he stood, allowing himself to be led away. His captors led him out through a side door and along a dank passageway lit only by torches crackling in iron brackets affixed to the walls. As they walked, one guard before him, the other nudging him regularly from behind, the passageway sloped steadily down, slowly taking them beneath ground level. Other tunnels branched off at regular intervals, like rabbit warrens, and occasional wooden doors denoted access to hidden rooms.

Here, the tunnel walls were undressed and roughly hewn, as though the whole network of catacombs and tunnels had been chiselled out of the bedrock after the house above had been built. Newbury assumed this was the work of the Bastion Society, using one of Warrander's contraptions to carve out a secret haven beneath the city. He wondered how far down the tunnels went, and what else they were keeping down there.

As it transpired, he didn't have the opportunity to find out. The two guards marched him around a bend in the main tunnel before coming to an abrupt stop in front of a heavy wooden door. One of them slid open a small panel in the door and peered inside. "Stay back," he barked at the occupant, whom Newbury assumed to be Veronica. He was proved right a moment later when he was unceremoniously shoved inside with her, a sword at his back. The door slammed shut again, and he heard the key scrape in the lock.

Newbury glanced around. They were alone in near darkness, no light but what seeped in through the gap beneath the door. Newbury rushed over to Veronica, who was sitting huddled on the ground, her knees pulled up beneath her chin. "Veronica! Did they hurt you? Are you alright?"

She nodded and looked up at him. "I'm alright, Maurice. Is there any news of Sir Charles?"

"Nothing," he said. "Let's hope. He's a resourceful old fellow." He coughed.

"Did you get anywhere with Graves?"

Newbury dropped to the floor beside her, resting his back against the wall. It was uncomfortable and cold. He couldn't stop shivering. "Yes. He asked me to join them."

"He what?" Veronica was astounded. "I hope you told him you'd do no such thing!"

"Of course I did." Newbury sighed. "But there's more. They're the ones behind the attack on the Queen. They're gearing up for an assault on the palace."

"My God," Veronica said. "And have they got anything to do with what's going on at the Grayling Institute?"

Newbury shook his head. "As far as I can ascertain, they know nothing about Fabian's current . . . experiments. It seems that Fabian might have learned about the duplication technology from a man here, Warrander, and adapted it for use at the Grayling Institute. The Bastion Society isn't interested in creating living copies of themselves; that would go against everything they believe in. But Fabian has no such qualms."

Veronica bristled. "Then it's down to the Queen. It has to be. She's behind it, Newbury. I know she is."

Newbury wanted to challenge her on that, wanted to ask her how she could be so sure, but he suddenly couldn't speak. He was shaking. Sweat was trickling down his face. He ran his hands through his hair, loosened his collar. His skin was crawling, alive with sensation. "We have to get out of here," he said.

Veronica turned to face him, concern in her eyes. "What's the matter? What have they done to you?" She altered her position, kneeling before him, cupping his face in her hands. "Oh, Maurice," she said, realising.

"I'm sorry," was all he could muster. "I'm so sorry . . . the weed."

He closed his eyes. Veronica clutched him to her, holding him gently as he shook. He longed for unconsciousness. More than anything, though, he longed for the brown bottle of laudanum with the peeling label he kept in his study, for the cosy oblivion it would bring.

CHAPTER

20

B ainbridge woke slowly, consciousness returning in stuttering explosions of light
and sound: a fragment of a woman's voice,
a bright light, the scent of burning wood, the kiss
of raindrops upon his cheeks. It hurt to breathe.
In fact, simply existing seemed to be enough to
cause him pain. Every fibre of his body ached.
He was cold and wet, and he couldn't feel his
left arm.

His eyelids fluttered open. He was lying on
his back. Above him there was only the vastness
of the slate grey sky, obscured by a shimmering
cascade of raindrops that glimmered in the light
of a nearby streetlamp. To his left, a curling trail
of black, oily smoke rose in a stark column. The
cobbles were hard and cold beneath his head.

Slowly, he dragged himself up into a sitting
position. He reached for his cane. It wasn't there.
He looked around in confusion. Then the memories snapped back into place. The hansom. The

explosions. The two men who'd attacked him. He'd left his cane buried in the guts of one of them.

What had the man said to him as he'd sprawled on the ground spitting blood? "With the compliments of Enoch Graves." The Bastion Society. *Of course.* First they had made an attempt on Miss Hobbes's life, and now they'd come after him.

He had to hurry. He had to get to Newbury, to stop his friend from walking into a lion's den . . . if it wasn't already too late. He had no idea of the time, no sense of how long he'd been out cold. All he knew was that he was soaked through to the bone, and that every inch of him throbbed with pain.

Well, almost every inch. He still couldn't feel his left arm.

Bainbridge looked down. A ragged fragment of metal casing, about the size of his hand, was lodged in his upper arm, just below the shoulder. His jacket was soaked in blood around the wound, but thankfully, it no longer seemed to be bleeding. The fabric was scorched and smouldering as a result of the fiery blast. Absently he wondered how long he must have lain there in the rain.

Then his sensation returned, and Bainbridge howled as his shoulder ignited in pain. He thought he was going to swoon again, but he steadied himself with his other hand and managed to retain consciousness. He heard footsteps and voices, almost drowned out by the patter of the rain. Did the other attacker survive the explosion? Was he coming to finish him off? Bainbridge didn't have any more fight left in him.

Groggily he raised his head and looked up. A man and a woman were rushing towards him, concerned expressions on their faces. Behind them he could see the shattered remains of the hansom, still blazing, even in the pounding rain. The force of the explosion must have thrown him back at least fifteen feet, if not more. Other people were milling about, too, their faces twisted in appalled shock as they caught sight of the ruined carcasses of the horses and the exploded remnants of the three men. Bainbridge realised with a grim satisfaction that the surviving attacker must have been killed by the blast of his own weapon.

To his left he heard someone shouting and cursing. He glanced over. The shopkeeper.

Bainbridge tried to stand, but his legs were like jelly, and he collapsed back to the ground just as the two civilians arrived at his side. The man—dressed in an overcoat and wide-brimmed hat, his face mostly hidden in shadow—wrapped his arms around Bainbridge and propped him up, helping him to stand. Bainbridge leaned heavily on the man, panting for breath.

". . . the explosion and came running." Bainbridge realised the woman had been talking to him in urgent tones. He turned to look at her. She was the spitting image of Isobel. He staggered back and the man caught him, taking his weight. He looked again. It was more than just a passing similarity; she resembled his late wife so closely that Bainbridge felt his heart leap. He blinked, wondering if his mind was still addled from the explosion. No, it was true. This young, pretty woman looked just like the girl he remembered from all those years ago. Her face was framed in a bob of flaming red hair, the bridge of her nose dusted with freckles. Her eyes were the sharpest blue. Bainbridge smiled and tried to focus on what she had to say. ". . . dead. How did you get away?"

Bainbridge tried to speak but his mouth was gummed shut with blood. He swallowed and it stuck in his throat. For a minute he thought he was going to retch, but then he found his voice. "Scotland Yard," he said. His words sounded slurred and unfamiliar, even to him.

"Scotland Yard?" the man echoed. "Yes, they're on their way. We sent for them."

Bainbridge shook his head. He tried to reach into his jacket pocket for his papers, but the lancing pain in his shoulder was too much to bear, and he fumbled ineffectually. "No," he said, finally. "*I'm* from Scotland Yard. Charles . . . Bainbridge." The last word was hissed out between clenched teeth.

The woman looked shocked and fearful, as if she wanted to help but didn't know what to do. "We need to get you to the hospital," she said, glancing over her shoulder at the burning wreckage.

"No! Not the hospital," Bainbridge exclaimed. He needed to get to Newbury, to warn him about Enoch Graves. And then to the Queen, and the palace. He must get to the palace. He swooned, and the world began to spin. Everything went black.

Bainbridge staggered and came to, his eyes blinking open again. He realised he'd been unconscious for only a second or two. The man in the overcoat held him upright as he sucked the cold, damp air into his lungs and finally righted himself.

"Sir, you need to get to a hospital. You're badly hurt. Can you remember what happened?" said the woman, who was holding her trembling hands before her as if trying to keep him at bay. He realised he must have been a fearsome sight, bruised and battered from the fistfight, covered in blood and soot from the explosion.

"Of course I can remember what happened, Isobel!" he growled, swaying from side to side as his head swam. "Those damn vagabonds set upon me in my cab."

"Isobel?" The woman looked utterly perplexed. She turned to the man. "I think he must have taken a blow to the head. Let's see if we can get him out of this rain while we wait for the police. Under that awning over there." She indicated a butcher's shop across the street, the doorway of which was sheltered by a large tarpaulin.

"What? Now hang on a minute!" Bainbridge took a step forward and immediately regretted it. His shoulder exploded in pain, and lights swam before his eyes. He grimaced and relaxed into the man's supporting grip, giving himself over to the strangers.

The man heaved Bainbridge's good arm over his shoulders and supported him as they shakily walked across the street. Every step caused bursts of pain in his arm as the jagged lump of metal shifted with the motion. The rain felt cool against his face.

People had been spilling out into the street ever since the fight began, and now a significant crowd had gathered, civilians who had been dragged from their homes by the sound of the explosions, out in the pouring rain to stare in wonder at the scene of devastation in their usually quiet street. A few of them caught sight of Bainbridge, lumbering helplessly towards the shelter of the tarpaulin, and pointed him out to their neighbours, chattering and speculating about what might have occurred. Bainbridge paid them no heed.

A moment later he was slumped on the ground once again, his back to the shop door, trying to catch his breath. He willed the police carriages to hurry. His head kept nodding forward as he dipped in and out of consciousness, and the pain in his arm was a constant, sharp reminder of his predicament.

Minutes passed like hours. The man and the woman drifted away and others came. Bainbridge ignored them, hearing their tinny voices as if they were off somewhere in another room. It was all he could do to stay awake, to stay alive. He focused on Newbury, on Veronica, on the Queen. He needed to stay alive for them.

He didn't know how long it was before the men from the Yard arrived. Their carriages rolled noisily out of the night, accompanied by a hissing, steam-powered ambulance, belching black fumes into the rain-lashed night. Bainbridge watched as men swarmed from the carriages to engulf the scene. Civilians were shepherded away from the flaming wreckage; others were taken aside for questioning. Someone standing over him—a man, he thought—called for assistance, and a group of three or four uniformed men came running over.

"Blimey! It's the guv'nor!" one of them exclaimed. "Get the ambulance over here, now."

The man dropped to his knees, gazing intently at Bainbridge. "He's in a bad way." He turned, looking over his shoulder. "Come along, hurry up!"

Bainbridge lifted his head and fixed the young constable with a defiant glare. "Newbury," he croaked.

"Quite right, sir. Let's get you out of here. They'll put you right at the infirmary."

It took all the strength he had left in his body, but Bainbridge thrust out his good arm and caught the constable by the sleeve. He bunched up the fabric in his fist and pulled the man closer. His voice was a dry rasp. "Listen to me. Find Maurice Newbury. Find him, and tell him I need to speak with him."

The young bobby gave a terrified nod. "Yes, sir," he said. But it was already too late. The chief inspector had once again slipped into unconsciousness.

CHAPTER

21

For a while, Veronica had thought the world was ending.

Newbury's screams had brought the attention of the guards, who had peered in through the slit in the door, unsure what was happening inside the cell. One of them had bellowed at her to shut him up, threatening to come inside and put a bullet through his head. Veronica felt as helpless as she had ever felt, unable to quell the nightmares that were plaguing him, unsure if there was anything at all she could do to make him stop.

The poppy, it seemed, held him in a tighter, more excruciating grip than she had even dared to imagine, and now, hours without it, the weed was abandoning him, leaving him writhing in agony and confusion on the cell floor.

At first she had tried to hold him, wrapping her arms around his shoulders and whispering to him that she was there for him, that she wouldn't let him come to harm. But then he started to scream and scratch at the walls, and she'd been unable to hold him any longer.

The fever had brought with it all manner of dark hallucinations, and she had backed into a corner of the cell while he had writhed on the floor, banging his fists and fighting with demons that only he could see. He had scratched strange symbols into the dust on the ground, whispered arcane rites in languages she had never heard. And then he had screamed again, clutching at his belly as he seized, just like Amelia had seized when they were children. It had caused the memories to flood back, to overwhelm her. She'd found a piece of broken wood to wedge between his teeth and had held his head until the fitting had passed.

In his brief lucid moments he had begged her for a drop of laudanum, as if he thought she somehow had a bottle of the stuff on her person and was hiding it from him. He'd grown angry, then remorseful, and then seized again, his stomach muscles going into spasms, his fever burning through his mind as every cell in his body craved the sweet-smelling drug simultaneously.

If she'd had the laudanum, then, she would have given it to him, just to end his suffering and pain. Just to have Newbury back. But, of course, she had none, so instead she had been forced to go through it alongside him, forced to watch and listen and weep as the opium burned its way out of his system.

Finally, after five, six, seven hours—she was unable to tell, trapped in the endless night of the cell—the fever broke, and Newbury fell into a deep slumber on the cell floor.

At first, Veronica panicked that he had died. She had rushed to his side, feeling for his pulse, listening for his shallow breath. But he'd put up an admirable fight, and though weak, he was still alive.

Veronica had tried to sleep then, too, but she found she couldn't rest. Her mind was racing, full of concern for Newbury, for Amelia. Full of concern for herself and what Graves might do. Would it all be for nothing? Had Newbury gone through all of that only to face execution at the hands of the Bastion Society? Were they both going to die? She wasn't sure if she was strong enough to get them out of there alone, although if it came to it, she'd put up a damn good fight.

Finally she had fallen into a fitful sleep. When she woke, Newbury was sitting up, watching her from across the cell.

He looked dreadful. His eyes were sunken pits and his hair was matted with sweat and grime. But he smiled at her, and she knew that the worst of it was over.

"I'm sorry," he said softly, and she could sense the weight behind the words.

She nodded but didn't speak.

"What time is it?"

"I have no idea," Veronica said truthfully. "Sometime after dawn." She was huddled against the opposite wall, her knees drawn up beneath her chin. She was cold, tired, and scared.

Newbury looked bewildered by this revelation. "We've been in here that long?"

She nodded again. "And all the while, Amelia's been trapped in the Grayling Institute in terrible danger." She banged her fist against the wall in frustration.

"I'm sorry," he said again. There was nothing else he could

say. It wasn't his fault. She was grateful he didn't offer platitudes or try to reassure her that everything was going to be all right. "Have they given any indication of what they're planning for us?"

"No," she replied. "They've told me nothing. But I've been thinking about what you said, about Graves and the duplicates. About how you thought he was telling the truth that they were never actually alive." She unfolded herself as she talked, curling her legs beneath her. Newbury listened intently from the other side of the cell. She couldn't tell what he was thinking, whether he was even in any fit mental state to understand what she was saying, but she needed to talk, to get it out.

"Go on," he said, urging her to continue.

"If that's true, then what Fabian is doing with Amelia is something entirely different. His technology creates living copies. He clearly doesn't share the beliefs of the Bastion Society, so there has to be another reason, other than simply generating duplicates for ritual use." Veronica cleared her throat. Her mouth was dry. There was no water in the cell, and despite having harangued the guards a number of times, none had been forthcoming.

"I came to the same conclusion myself. I imagine it's to do with her clairvoyant abilities, that Fabian is using the duplicates to try to predict the future." Newbury coughed into his cupped hands.

"No. I don't think so." Veronica rubbed her knees to try to get some warmth back into them. "I think there's more to it than that. The Queen is obsessed with longevity. She's desperate to extend her life and her reign. I think she's tasked

Fabian with finding a way to duplicate her, to create a new, healthy body so she can continue her legacy."

Newbury sighed. "Ah, yes. The Queen. I forget, you know all about the Queen."

"Well, I . . ." Veronica was momentarily taken aback by the sarcasm in his tone.

"Why did you keep it from me, Veronica? Why am I the only one you didn't tell?" His voice was firm, controlled. There was no sign of the man who, only an hour or two earlier, had been scratching at the walls and howling in agony in the grip of opium withdrawal. He met her gaze, and she couldn't help but see the accusation in his eyes. "For God's sake, even Graves knows the truth about you!" His voice dropped, tinged with sorrow and confusion. "Why did you do it?"

Veronica's heart was pounding in her chest. She felt sick, her stomach twisted into a tight knot. Dizziness threatened to overwhelm her. It was finally here. The conversation she'd played out in her mind so many times before. The conversation she'd always hoped to avoid but knew would come one day. She was shaking. She didn't know what to say, how to explain. Why *had* she done it? Duty, she supposed. And fear.

She closed her eyes. She couldn't look at him, didn't want to see his reaction. "I did it because I thought if you knew, you'd shut me out. Because I didn't want you to believe that I doubted you. Because I didn't want to lose you, Maurice. I couldn't bear to lose you. I . . ." She sobbed, hanging her head. She couldn't say the words.

"I've known for months," he said quietly, and the words were like an arrow through her heart. "Ever since that time in the cellar with Aubrey Knox. Since I followed you to the palace and saw you go inside. You should have told me, Veronica." He paused, hanging his head. "You should have told me."

"And what then, Maurice? What if I *had* told you? What difference would it have made?" She left the questions hanging. She felt conflicted, unsure of her own emotions. On the one hand she knew that her duplicity had most likely played a part in Newbury's spiral into despondency and drug abuse, but on the other she knew that he was responsible for his own actions, and that there was little she could have done to prevent it. Part of her was furious with him, and another wanted only to gather him up in her arms and hold him. "I'm sorry," she said, and she knew it wasn't nearly enough.

For a moment Newbury didn't respond. When he did, his voice was cracked with emotion. "You could have put a stop to it, Veronica. You could have told her you weren't prepared to go on."

Veronica shook her head. "No! I had no choice! You know what she's like, Maurice. You never say no! No one ever says no to her! She would have reassigned me, and that would have been the end of it, of everything." Veronica could hear the exasperation in her own voice. "She would have prevented me from seeing you, even if it meant I'd have to face the firing squad. She would have orchestrated someone else to spy on you instead, some puppet who really would have told her everything about you. And then where would we be? Where would either of us be?"

"So it was better that you spy on me than anyone else? Is that it?"

"I didn't spy on you, Maurice! You have to believe me. I told her only as much as she needed to know. Just enough to

keep her out of our lives. I've never betrayed you, not once."
She got to her feet and crossed the cell, kneeling before him.
"I'd never betray you, Maurice." She put her hand on his
cheek. "Never."

He refused to meet her gaze.

Veronica slowly withdrew her hand. She felt like she wanted
to scream in frustration. This was everything she'd feared.
He'd discovered the truth and now he couldn't even look at
her. After all they'd been through, he wouldn't even look her
in the eye. Here, in a cell, somewhere in the bowels of the
city, waiting to die. She felt the anger welling up inside her.
"Why didn't you tell me you knew? Why did you just pull
away like that, hiding behind that damn weed instead of simply talking to me about it? You had a choice, too, and you
chose the easy way out."

He raised his head. Their eyes met. He looked scared.
"Because I didn't want to lose you, either," he said.

And then he was holding her in his arms, kissing her deeply
and passionately on the lips. She kissed him back, pulling him
closer, running her fingers through his hair. She had wanted
this for so long. But she knew she couldn't hold on to it. Not
now, not here. Not like this. Not while Amelia was still trapped
in that horrible place, and Newbury was still a slave to that
dreadful poppy.

Veronica felt numb. Slowly, she pushed him away. She was
shaking.

He stared at her, confusion in his eyes. "I thought . . ."

She shook her head. "Not here, Maurice. Not like this.
You're ill. You don't know what you're doing. And Amelia's
still out there in need of our help." She paused, fighting the

urge to reach for him again. Instead, she ran her fingers along the front of his jacket, brushing the dirt away. "When this is over. When you're better." She broke off, unable to go on.

Newbury nodded. "I will get better, Veronica. I promise you that."

They were silent for a while, both gazing at each other in the darkness of the cell. *Later,* she promised herself. There would be time then. For now she had to focus on getting out of the cell alive, on saving Amelia. She had to be strong enough for all of them. "Maurice . . . All this with Amelia and the Queen . . ." She paused, unsure quite how to go on. "I think we might be part of something dreadful."

Newbury shook his head. "No, Veronica. I can't believe that. We work for the British Empire, for the monarchy. We work for the Queen of England!"

Veronica put her hand on his sleeve. Her voice was soft. "But what if the Queen has strayed? What if Fabian's machines have turned her into a monster, unable to tell the difference between right and wrong? What if you and I and Sir Charles are working for the wrong side? What then?"

Newbury looked pained. "You can't think the Bastion Society is a better option, Veronica! Surely you can't think that?"

Veronica shook her head emphatically. "Of course not. But I'm worried there isn't a great deal of difference between them anymore. I think they're all as bad as each other: Aubrey Knox, Dr. Fabian, Enoch Graves . . . and the Queen. How could she condone what Fabian has done to Amelia? How could she encourage him?"

"I . . . ," Newbury started, but faltered.

"And look at us, Newbury!" she continued. "Look what she's done to *us*. She's poisoned us with her ridiculous games. She's had me spy on you. You! One of the best men I've ever met. *The* best man I've ever met. And look what that did to you." The tears came then, in great floods down her cheeks. She didn't even bother to try to stop them.

Newbury leaned forward, wrapping his arms around her in a warm embrace. "You might be right," he said, and she knew then that he believed it. "It'll be over soon, Veronica. One way or another."

"What do you mean?"

"The Bastion Society is moving against the Queen. They believe her to be a living blasphemy, a soul trapped in an undying body, and they intend to storm the palace to bring her reign to an end."

Veronica looked up at him, her eyes wide with shock. "It's just as Amelia predicted. Cracking walls and fire and pain. And the one who sits in the chair is key."

Newbury released her and slowly pushed himself up onto his feet. "We need to find a way out," he stated flatly. "We have to warn her. Whatever she might have done, Veronica, we can't let an army of occultists storm the palace. It'll bring the Empire to its knees."

Veronica nodded. "It may already be too late. It's been hours."

Newbury cursed under his breath. "All the same, we have to try. We have to get away from here. Graves said he would keep us alive long enough to show us the ruination of everything we hold dear. Either way, if we don't get out of here soon, we're dead."

Veronica smiled. For the first time in hours, she was starting to feel a glimmer of hope. She'd thought it was over when Newbury had been deep in the throes of the opium withdrawal. Now, he was beginning to muster his strength. He was weak and bedraggled, but he was Newbury. His instinct was kicking in. He wanted to live.

"We need to work out how to get past this lock," he said. "They took everything useful before they tossed me in here."

"The lock isn't the problem," she replied, reaching up and extracting two thin metal pins from her hair. She held them out to him. They were lock picks, taken from his collection in Chelsea and secured there as they'd prepared for their spot of breaking and entering. Experience had long since taught her to conceal a few such items upon her person, just in case. She pointed towards the door. "That's the problem."

Newbury followed the line of her finger. There, perched on the wall just beside the door, was a large mechanical spider. "Damn it!" he said. He took a few steps towards the door. Three red lights flickered to life atop the machine, a little cluster of them, like glowing eyes. The body raised up on its eight spindly legs, and it emitted a high-pitched whirring sound as the blades in its belly began to spin and hum. Newbury stopped dead in his tracks, about three feet from the door.

"It's just like the one that attacked us at my apartment," Veronica said. "It sits there quietly, powered down, until one of us approaches the door. Then it stirs. I've not dared to get too close, in case I incite it to attack."

Newbury nodded. "Graves said they had more of them." He rubbed his face.

Veronica felt her newfound hope beginning to seep away.

"I didn't know what else to do. I didn't want to provoke it. There's nothing in here we can use as a weapon. I would have had us out of here already if it hadn't been for that."

Newbury shrugged. "Bring those here. The lock picks."

Veronica got to her feet. Newbury was sizing up the mechanical beast. He took another step towards it, and the scream of the spinning blades increased in intensity.

"Maurice, don't be stupid. One wrong move and it'll tear you apart," she said.

Newbury looked back at her over his shoulder. "We're dead anyway if we don't get out of here. Might as well die trying."

Veronica didn't have any response. She knew he was right, but she could hardly condone his taking his life in his hands in such dramatic fashion. It was clear he was going to attempt to wrestle the thing out of the way.

Newbury seemed to take her silence as acquiescence. "Be ready with one of those lock picks," he said. "When I say so, I want you to jam it in the recess behind those three red lights. I think those must be its eyes."

"You *think* those are its eyes? What if they're simply lights?"

Newbury looked exasperated. He ignored her and continued. "Once it's in there, work it about a bit, try to damage the mechanisms. I want to make sure it can't see us. Confuse it."

Veronica sighed. She slid one of the lock picks into her belt and held the other in her fist like a dagger.

Newbury smiled. "Let's get out of here, Miss Hobbes." He sprang forward, surprising even her with his sudden movement. In one bound he was by the door, grabbing the spider machine from the wall by its legs, holding it at arm's length, and grunting with the exertion of keeping it at bay. The spider bucked and wriggled, its blades screaming and whining as it fought to free itself from Newbury's viselike grip.

One of the legs got free, stabbing at Newbury's hand and causing him to cry out in pain as it buried itself in flesh. But he managed to hold on, his face locked in a grimace. "Now, Veronica!" he yelled.

She rushed forward, brandishing the lock pick. The spider thing continued to writhe and squirm in Newbury's grasp. "Hurry!" he said urgently. She located the little cluster of red lights. They were less than an inch from the deadly blades. She risked losing her hand if Newbury wasn't able to hold the machine still.

"Veronica!"

So be it. She jabbed down with the lock pick, shattering one of the glass eyes and jamming the metal shaft of the pick deep into the mechanisms of the clockwork monster. She forced the pick back and forth, feeling tiny gears crack and snap inside the device.

"Good," Newbury said. "Good!"

She pulled the lock pick free and repeated the action, shattering another eye, wrenching more of the machine's delicate internal systems out of place. It continued to buck violently in Newbury's grip, but it wasn't responding to Veronica. Blood was trickling down Newbury's arm from a number of vicious cuts caused by the errant leg.

"Right, back away," said Newbury, and Veronica did as she was told, retreating into the cell until her back was against the far wall.

Still holding the now-blinded machine at arm's length, Newbury approached the door.

Oh, clever, Veronica thought, as she watched him jam the spinning blades against the door panel, aiming it carefully over the lock. Unseeing, acting purely on whatever instinct had been invested in its mechanical brain, the spider thing bit down into the wood with its saw blades.

Newbury held it there, pressing it firmly against the door as it chewed a hole in the wood. The blades screeched as they struck metal, but carved on through, cutting a large hole right through the door and taking the entire lock mechanism along with it.

Seconds later, the disc of wood fell to the ground with a loud clatter. With all his might, Newbury hefted the spider and flung it at the cell's back wall. It collided with the rock face with a crunch and fell to the ground, three of its legs hanging uselessly at its side. It scuttled for cover, banging into the wall before disappearing into the dark recesses of the cell.

Veronica stared at Newbury in wonder. Even now, he still had the capacity to surprise her.

"Come on, the guards will be here any second," Newbury called to her, reaching for her hand and dragging her towards the door. The lock was a mangled mess. She wouldn't be needing the other lock pick.

Newbury tugged at the door and it opened easily, then they were out in the corridor.

Veronica couldn't believe their luck. There were no guards. The fools must have thought after six or seven hours that the spider was enough of a deterrent to prevent them from making any attempt to escape. Instead, their inattentiveness had given Newbury and Veronica the chance they needed to get away.

"This way," Newbury said, and they set off at a run, following the incline that would take them back to the surface and Packworth House. They rounded the kink in the passage a few moments later, and Newbury ground immediately to a halt. He held his finger to his lips.

Veronica listened. There were voices up ahead. Three—no—four of them. She looked at Newbury and held up four fingers. He nodded. Releasing her other hand, he flexed his shoulder muscles and began slowly creeping towards the sound of the voices.

Veronica grabbed his arm. She shook her head, mouthing, *No!* She knew they would be armed with pistols and swords. As he was, Newbury was no match for them, even with her help. His mastery over the spider had been impressive, but this would be suicide.

Reluctantly, she pointed back the way they had come. They would have to find another way around. Newbury nodded, silently accepting the inevitable.

They turned and ran on.

CHAPTER

22

Veronica realized how big the warren beneath Packworth House really was as they walked down the seemingly endless passageway. It delved down farther and farther into the bedrock, branching off in myriad directions to form a chaotic web of tunnels and rooms. She and Newbury walked along the roughly hewn corridors, pausing every time they heard evidence of other people, sometimes doubling back to find a different way around or changing tack when they happened upon a dead end.

Veronica hoped there *was* another way out of the catacombs. There had to be. To come this far only to end up trapped down there and recaptured . . . She wouldn't even entertain the thought.

She was tired now, near exhaustion, and the emotional impact of their time in the cell was beginning to take its toll. She was operating purely on adrenaline and the need to escape, to get them both to safety. For the moment she pushed all thoughts of Charles and Amelia out of her mind—they could worry about them once they were out. She had to focus on staying alive.

Up ahead the passageway branched off into three different directions. Here, Veronica noticed that the tunnels were more ordered and uniform, finished with neat brickwork and vaulted ceilings. She guessed they were part of an older structure, long buried beneath the soil, and that the Bastion Society had somehow found a way to marry their own, newer tunnels to the existing infrastructure. She suspected they were no longer under Packworth House, but instead far beneath one of the neighbouring properties.

There were clear signs of habitation here, too. Voices chattered in the distance, and the sound of industry echoed off the barren walls: the hammering of metal panels, the grinding of gears, the splutter of steam-fired engines.

Veronica tugged on Newbury's sleeve, and he hesitated, looking back at her inquiringly. "I'll try to find a way around," he whispered.

Veronica shook her head. "No. We'll only end up running round in circles down here, heading deeper and deeper underground, further away from any chance of escape. Let's see what they're up to. If there are people here, there must be another way out."

Newbury nodded and returned to surreptitiously edging along the passageway, his back against the wall. Veronica followed him, keeping pace. When they came to the junction, they continued down the central tunnel, wary at all times of discovery.

The tunnel finally terminated in a vast chamber, a huge natural cavern, the ceiling of which was covered in a forest of dripping stalactites. The cave had been adapted to house a massive brass sphere, at least thirty feet in diameter. Its outer shell was battered and tarnished, and it sat upon a supporting pedestal surrounded by all manner of strange, bulky equipment. Funnels and tubing protruded from it like the spines of a sea urchin, and a large iron cylinder, like a chimney spout, rose from its top and disappeared into the ceiling above. It thrummed gently, vibrating through the cavern floor.

Veronica, lurking in the shadows at the cave mouth, glanced at Newbury quizzically. "What is it?" she whispered.

"I have no idea," he replied.

Cautiously, Veronica broke cover and crept into the cavernous chamber. There were no signs of life inside. Whatever the machine's purpose, it didn't currently appear to be operational.

She heard Newbury's footsteps behind her. "There's a door here," he said, approaching the vast, gleaming belly of the sphere. He pulled it open and bent low, ducking inside.

A few moments later his head reemerged from the doorway. "It looks like some sort of medical chamber. There's a chair inside, and a device hanging from the ceiling covered in banks of needles." His head disappeared inside again.

Veronica walked around the strange machine. There was a workstation wired into the sphere and covered in a plethora of buttons and levers that she assumed must affect whatever went on inside the device. Farther around the sphere she was confronted with the evidence she'd been looking for, and the nature of the device became suddenly clear.

It was the duplicating machine.

Two large glass tanks sat side by side on a raised dais, connected to the brass sphere by thick, snaking pipes. The glass panels were encased in mahogany frames, each displaying elaborate engravings and fretwork. The symbols and carved figures that intertwined in the woodwork were strange and unfamiliar, yet reminiscent of the type of ancient pagan iconography she'd encountered regularly at the museum. Both tanks were filled with a thick, viscous fluid that seemed to glow pink with its own ethereal light. One of the tanks was empty, but the other held the partially formed body of a human male. It was utterly disgusting, and Veronica blanched at the very sight of it.

The lower half of the cadaver could have belonged to any man in his mid-forties, save, perhaps, for the pinkness of the flesh and the lack of natural wear and tear. But the upper half of the torso remained horribly incomplete. The rib cage and belly were almost entirely exposed, revealing the swimming, un-living organs beneath. The right arm was still skeletal, with only the first tentative signs of muscles and flesh beginning to form around the hand and wrist.

The head, however, was perhaps the most disturbing sight of all. The left half of the face was pink and human, the eyeball staring unseeing from the socket. But the right half was a horrendous vision of exposed muscle and bone. The eye socket was an empty void, the cheekbone clearly visible below. There was no ear, and farther down she could discern part of the throat and the trailing muscle of the tongue, lolling about in the suspension fluid. Pinkish muscles were beginning to build up around the jawbone, but the back teeth were still visible beneath.

It was a vision that she knew would stay with her forever. She knew this man had never been alive, but somehow that made the whole thing worse. She shuddered to think that the body she was staring at was an incomplete copy of a man who was probably carousing in the great hall somewhere far above her. Worse was considering what he might do to it once it had been completed and transported to the hanging room.

Veronica stepped back from the tank, unable to look upon the duplicate any longer. She had no idea how the machine worked, and no desire to learn, either. It was an abomination, a travesty against nature. She found it ironic that the members of the Bastion Society could be so aggrieved by the Queen's desire to continue living, but not see the horror of their own creations.

Newbury was standing beside her. "Fascinating," he said, pressing his fingers against the glass. "The perfect marriage of science and the occult. I would never have imagined it was possible." He traced his fingers over the symbols and glyphs in the wooden frame. "Hermeticism. These are alchemical symbols." He moved around the occupied tank, examining the partially constructed corpse inside. "Edwin Sykes was one of these. The *first* Edwin Sykes, that is. The one we found in the gutter. Stolen and hot-footed away from here to foil the police."

"It's disgusting," Veronica said.

"It's remarkable," replied Newbury. "Truly remarkable. But

wrong in every sense. What they're doing here with these bodies, what Fabian is doing to Amelia . . . it has to be stopped."

Veronica looked again at the sickening face of the body in the tank. Yes, it had to be stopped. But first they had to get out of there alive. "Come on," she said, ushering Newbury back the way they had entered.

They left the strange, throbbing sphere and exited the cavern, returning to the tunnel system beyond.

Veronica selected one of the two remaining passages, but Newbury stopped her, tugging her in the other direction. "No, let's try this way," he whispered. Shrugging, she followed him towards the sound of hammering metal.

The tunnel wound for a short way before once again opening up into a large chamber, not dissimilar to the cavern from which they had just come. She realised there was probably a whole network of natural caves in the bedrock here, and that the Bastion Society had co-opted them for its nefarious use. It made a perfect hiding place, with space enough to hide an entire army.

And that, Veronica realised with awe as she looked out across the chamber, was *exactly* what they'd been doing.

The cavern was a hive of industry. She pressed herself flat against the tunnel wall, keeping back as she peered cautiously over the edge. "My god," she whispered, more to herself than to Newbury. "It's an armoury." She could hardly believe her eyes.

Row upon row upon row of gleaming brass horses, just like the ones they had seen at the demonstration in Piccadilly Circus, stood in serried ranks awaiting riders. There must have been fifty of them, if not more, shining under the electric arc lamps that filled the armoury with brilliant, dazzling light.

The horses themselves looked new and unused, fresh off the production line. They were a small army unto themselves. Unlike the ones they had seen in action, these were each adorned with deadly looking weapons. Gatling guns hung off the sides of the saddles on pivots, ready to be directed and fired by the mounted riders as they charged into battle. The multibarrelled guns were a far cry from the flaming braziers and jousts the demonstrators had been playacting with in the street.

Men in grey suits and bowler hats, but wearing leather smocks over their jackets, were bustling between the horses, tinkering with the delicate clockwork innards, refining and improving. Others were checking the Gatling guns' ammunition belts, which snaked away into the hindquarters of each mechanical animal.

Elsewhere in the chamber other men were preparing rows of projectile weapons. These took the form of long cylinders mounted on tripods, with large cranking handles that would allow the firing mechanisms inside to be wound. They were mobile cannons, she realised, light and easy to transport, and simple to fire without the need for gunpowder or other explosives. She imagined them raining fiery Hell on the palace.

Worse still was the row of ten enormous armoured suits that stood motionless against the far wall. These were more like robotic chassis than the suits of mediaeval armour they were clearly modelled to represent. They were ten feet tall and adorned with the heraldry and insignia of the Bastion Society, supported by an exoskeleton covered in shining armour plating.

The faux-mediaevalism was bizarrely at odds with the pistons and pneumatic joints that were bolted onto the frame to power it. Veronica could see where a man could climb inside the machine, inserting his arms and legs into braces so that he could use the movements of his own body to direct the corresponding movements of the exoskeleton. A large steel cowl appeared to fold down from above to protect the driver's head, echoing the visor of a knightly helmet. The things must have weighed tonnes, but the power at the disposal of the operator would be phenomenal.

It was clear the Bastion Society was readying itself to strike. Veronica was astounded by all the machinery hidden down there in those catacombs beneath the city, a secret army preparing for a personal war. This was how they were going to storm the palace, charging in on shining clockwork steeds, their weapons blazing.

They really did believe they were latter-day knights, Veronica realised, upholding the spiritual beliefs of their cause to ensure the salvation of their nation. It was utter madness, but it was real. The assault on the palace was actually going to happen. Until now it had seemed like a surreal, nebulous threat, detached from her more pressing concerns. But seeing their war machines here, ranked up and prepared for battle, the reality of the situation came crashing in.

In a strange sort of way Veronica admired their courage. She couldn't agree with their methods—of course she couldn't—but at least they were doing *something*. At least they weren't as apathetic as the rest of the population, sitting idly by as everything turned to chaos around them. They were prepared to stand up for what they believed in, even if that belief was ultimately misplaced.

Veronica could tell by the look on Newbury's face that he had come to a similar conclusion. But it didn't change anything. *We have to stop them,* he mouthed silently.

Veronica shook her head. "We need to get out and warn the palace." Two of them against a small army—they'd never be able to pull it off. They'd just end up getting themselves captured again, or worse. As it was, the guards had probably realised they were missing from the cell by now and would be mounting a search.

She surveyed the armoury chamber. There would be no use searching for an alternative exit in there. Even if there was one to be found, the sheer amount of people milling about meant they'd never be able to move around unseen. She pointed back towards the junction. "Third time lucky?"

Veronica was relieved to discover that this time the passage soon made a dogleg and began climbing towards the surface again along a gentle incline. She'd lost her bearings as they'd woven through so many tunnels, but she had the sense that they were now climbing parallel to the passage that had contained their cell.

As they climbed, it became clear that the older tunnels were in fact part of a mausoleum complex. Here, the walls were lined with macabre burial alcoves, each containing the remains of the long-ago dead. Some were elaborate coffins, tooled from blocks of glistening marble. Others had once been wooden caskets but had disintegrated over time, leaving only dusty skeletons behind.

Veronica spotted one alcove that was entirely filled with human skulls, piled up one upon another to form a wall of haunting skeletal faces, staring out at her silently from their empty sockets. She shivered with a sudden chill, and didn't know whether it was the temperature or the realisation of how many people had died to fill that single alcove. She wondered if it dated back to the plague.

There would be other, more recent mass graves all over London now for people to stumble upon in centuries to come— the victims of the Revenant plague, turned into shambling flesh-hungry monsters, rounded up by squads of soldiers, and destroyed. Many of the corpses had been ferried out to sea, dumped in vast loads over the side of the plague ships, but others had been interred in huge graves excavated by an army of steam-powered diggers. The plague continued to burn through the population of the slums, hundreds of people falling to its clutches every day. And so the diggers remained busy, carving up the landscape to find room for the ever-increasing piles of corpses.

Veronica dragged her eyes away from the heap of skulls. She realised Newbury had wandered off again, and she found him inside a small doorless room a little farther up the passage that had been converted from a tomb. She ducked her head beneath the lintel and stepped inside. She was immediately assaulted by a dry, musty smell of dust and decay. She wrinkled her nose in disgust.

The room was brightly lit by a naked electric lamp, fed by a curling power cable that snaked in through the open door from the tunnel outside. The generator must have been located somewhere else farther into the complex, probably close to the armoury.

The walls of the tomb had been pasted with schematics and maps, architectural diagrams showing the floor plan of a large building. Others were spread across a table in the centre of the space, and Newbury was studying these with interest. Veronica joined him. Arrows and boxes had been drawn on the plans in thick blue ink, accompanied by notes scrawled alongside them in red.

"The plans for their assault on the palace," she stated. So this was their hidden war room, where they had planned their offensive against the Queen.

But Newbury was shaking his head. He tapped the schematics on the table. "No. Look again."

Veronica frowned, but did as he suggested, studying the diagrams more closely. "It's not the palace!" she said, a moment later.

Newbury grinned. "Indeed not. It's the Grayling Institute."

Veronica didn't know what to make of that. "The Grayling Institute? Are you sure?" She scrutinised the plans again. He was right. "Do you think they're going to attack there as well?" She shook her head in disbelief. Were they going after more than one target? Had the Bastion Society planned a whole campaign against the Crown?

Newbury turned to her. "No. I think Enoch Graves is a considerably better tactician than he is mediaeval knight. I think they're going to storm the Grayling Institute *instead* of the palace." He smiled as he considered the implications of his words. "Oh, that's clever. . . ."

"Hold on, why would they choose the Grayling Institute over the palace?" Veronica was confused.

"Because everyone is expecting them to attack the palace. Don't you see? The intruder was a simple diversion! They set up the entire scenario to make sure the Queen wasn't—isn't—looking at what is happening elsewhere. She'll be so busy concentrating on securing the palace that she won't even consider that they might be targeting somewhere else." He was animated now, his mind making connections at a speed she couldn't even try to keep up with.

"But what will they achieve? I still don't understand. If they want to bring down the Queen, how is attacking the Grayling Institute going to help them?"

Newbury laughed. "Fabian. Fabian is the key to all of this." He paced around the table, jittery with sudden energy. "Fabian is the Queen's physician, the man responsible for keeping her alive. He's the only person who understands the machines that preserve her life, and the Bastion Society already have a bone to pick with him."

Veronica saw it then. "So if they kill Fabian and destroy his workshop, the Queen will die anyway. There'll be no one to keep her machines working."

"Precisely," said Newbury, rubbing his chin thoughtfully. "They don't want to kill the Queen themselves. That would be a step too far. Not very chivalrous, is it? But they want to put a stop to her extended life. They want her to die naturally, without intervention. By taking Fabian out of the picture they can achieve their goal indirectly and still revenge the man who betrayed them. It's ingenious."

"But the Queen will crucify them. She'll tear down their whole organisation a man at a time. It's a suicide mission."

Newbury nodded. "I suppose they think the end will justify the means. Besides"—he stooped over the table and began rolling up the plans—"they believe in the eternal rebirth of the spirit. They think they're all going to be reincarnated. Death, to them, is just the passing of a physical form." He held up the bundled plans. "We should get these to the palace—let the Queen know what they're planning."

Veronica caught his arm. "No." She was trembling, but she gripped his arm firmly, making him listen. "No. We can't tell the Queen. We have to let this happen."

Newbury's eyes widened. "What? Do you know what you're saying, Veronica? Surely you can't believe that what they're doing is right?"

Veronica glared at him. "Amelia's in there," she said.

"Then surely it's better we put a stop to it before she gets hurt?" he replied in an urgent tone.

"She's already hurt, Maurice! It's too late to stop that. But if we let this happen, we can be there, and we can get her out. We have their plans. We know how they're going to do it. We can get her away before it's too late."

"But you're talking about letting them murder the Queen!" He sounded exasperated, as if he thought she'd lost her mind.

"No, I'm not. I'm talking about letting her die a natural death. You said it yourself. And besides, after what she's done to Amelia, after what she's done to *us* . . . I . . . well . . . she can rot for all I care!" She released his arm, leaning back against the table.

Newbury ran a hand through his hair and exhaled loudly.

Veronica couldn't believe he was still defending the monarch. She'd understood his moral obligation to warn her of the attack, back when they thought it would be a direct assault on the palace, a direct attempt on her life. But this was different. This was their chance to help Amelia, to put right what Fabian and the Queen had done wrong. It would put an end to Fabian's diabolical experiments, save other people from suffering as Amelia had. If that meant the Queen had to find a new physician, or even if she faded and died without her pet engineer to keep her breathing, well . . . it was only what any of her subjects would have to face if they were in the same situation.

She turned to Newbury. "I'm going to ask you to make a choice, Maurice. I know that's not fair of me, but we're talking about my *sister*. I'm asking you to choose between the Queen and me. It's one or the other."

Newbury frowned. "How can you ask that? How dare you ask me to make that choice?"

"I can ask that because of what she's done! Because of how she's manipulated and used us for her own ends, how she's had Fabian make copies of my sister so they can be tortured and experimented upon and forced to predict the future. The Queen is a monster, sitting in her own filth at the heart of the Empire. She lost her way a long time ago, Maurice, and it's only because of you that I'm still here, still forcing myself to face her. Can't you see it? It's been staring you in the face!" She realised she'd raised her voice in frustration.

"And you're not trying to manipulate me now? Is that what that kiss was about, back in the cell? Is that it?"

"How dare you?" she retorted. "Is that what you really think?"

Veronica fought to remain calm. Couldn't he see the truth in what she was saying? Didn't he realise what the Queen was really like? She took a deep breath. She was trembling with frustration. Newbury wasn't himself. He couldn't mean what he was saying. He needed time.

Newbury glowered at her, confusion clouding his face. "I don't know *what* to think. You're being impossible, Veronica. You're asking me to knowingly allow an army of insane cultists to destroy the monarchy of England. Whatever the Queen has done—whatever—how can I allow that to happen?"

Veronica's heart sank. "*Listen* to me, Maurice," she said, her voice strained. "You're defending an ideal, not reality. The truth of the matter is that the Queen is corrupt, and she's responsible for the very mess we're in now. For Amelia . . . ." She trailed off, searching for the right words. "Would she do the same for you? If the circumstances were reversed, would she think twice?"

Newbury shook his head. "No. But you can't equate the two. She's the *Queen*, Veronica!"

"It doesn't make her any less the villain, Maurice," she said, levelly.

Newbury hung his head. The fight—and the energy—seemed to have gone out of him.

They needed to get out of there, out of that room, out of the catacombs and away from Packworth House. They could talk about it later, once they were safe and Newbury had had time to digest the truth. "Come on," she said. "We can discuss it later." She turned and ducked out of the tomb, running directly

into the path of a lumbering man wearing one of the exoskeleton suits.

Veronica screamed, and the man in the armour—his face
drawn in a vicious snarl—pounded forward, raising his arms
and bellowing as he charged at her. The limbs of the machine mirrored his actions, hissing as the pneumatic joints
brought the powerful arms up, the fingerlike claws clenching
into barrel-sized fists. He swung one of the fists at her head
and she ducked just in time, feeling the air currents sweep
past her face. The momentum carried the fist into the passage wall, where it shattered an ancient stone coffin, sending
debris sprawling across the ground. Chunks of stone and
broken bone showered over her as she tried desperately to
get away.

Veronica realised the man must have been searching for
them and that others would be on their way, too, alerted by
the noise of the fight. They'd spent too long arguing in the
map room. She had to act quickly. She had no idea how she
was going to fight a man in a ten-foot-tall suit of armour.

The man came at her again, his pounding footsteps causing the ground to shake. This time she stayed low, dodging to
the left to avoid the claw he sent hurtling towards her head.
The fist crashed into the floor, splintering the flagstones and
causing her to stumble against the opposite wall. Her hand
closed round the thighbone of a skeleton, and she yelped in
shock. Where the hell was Newbury?

The man in the exoskeleton regained his posture, servos
squealing. The steel plating around his legs clanked as he
moved. He was grinning wickedly as he lumbered across the
passageway, enjoying the pursuit of his prey. This time he threw

both his arms wide as he marched towards her, and then slammed them together in an effort to crush her between the machine's fists. The resulting impact sounded as if a bomb had been set off in the confined space.

Veronica threw herself to the floor to avoid their deadly embrace, jarring her elbows on the tunnel floor. She knew it was only a matter of time before one of the machine's fists connected with her in the confined space, and then everything would be over. She could dodge the blows for a while longer, but unless she could find a way to strike back at the encased man, all she'd be doing was tiring herself out until he finally managed to hit her, or others turned up to pin her in place.

She rolled to escape the pounding of a mechanised foot as the man made the machine stamp the ground by her head. "Newbury!" she bellowed in frustration and panic.

All she could hear in response was Newbury crying out in rage, and her hopes were dashed. He must have been fighting another machine behind them in the corridor. She couldn't see to tell.

Crying out in frustration at her impotence, she pushed herself up off the ground and almost put her head in the way of another swinging fist. She dropped backwards, catching herself on her hands and springing out of the way. There was a splintering crack as another stone coffin collapsed under the blow, plumes of dust billowing into the air.

Veronica searched desperately for anything she could use as a weapon. Aside from the heaps of old bones, there was nothing. She grabbed a shard of stone from the ground and threw it hard at the face of the man in the armoured suit, but he simply raised his arm and it rebounded from the super-structure, rolling harmlessly away.

The man was toying with her now. He jabbed at her with his right arm, causing her to dance out of the way of the machine's claws, only to do the same with the left. He repeated the action, grinning cheerfully to himself as he did it.

The grin was wiped from his face a moment later when Newbury suddenly appeared at his side, holding the sparking end of the coiling power line. The man's expression turned to one of mounting horror as he realised what was about to happen. Without ceremony, Newbury raised the end of the power line and jabbed it into the suit, pressing it between the armour plating and steel braces so that the end of it came into contact with the entombed man.

Unable to get away, or to turn the exoskeleton around quickly enough to defend himself, all the man had been able to do was watch in horror as Newbury calmly delivered the means of his death. The man's body bucked and jerked as the voltage coursed through him, causing the exoskeleton to shake and buck in time, mirroring his death throes. The passage-way filled with the scent of burning flesh.

Newbury pulled the power cable loose, careful not to touch the metal frame of the machine, and dropped it to the ground a few feet from where they were standing. The corpse slumped in the operator's pit, steam rising from the back of its head.

"You took your time," she said, smiling. She should never have doubted him.

Newbury looked focused, serious. "We need to go. Others

will be on their way." He started up the incline, stepping over the shattered remains of the stone coffins.

Veronica began to follow him, but then changed her mind and started back towards the dead man.

"What are you doing?" Newbury called, making no effort now to conceal his voice. If anyone searching for them hadn't known where they were before, they certainly did now.

"Getting us out of here," was her only reply.

Veronica approached the steaming body, grimacing as she leaned in close and began releasing the harness that held him into the machine. It was only the work of a few moments to free the body, and when she was finished, she unclipped the machine's breastplate and allowed the corpse to topple forward. Then, grabbing the dead man by his collar, she hauled him up and out, his feet banging awkwardly against the metal skeleton as she extracted him from the braces. She tried not to look at its face, which was frozen in a rictus of horror, as she dumped him heavily upon the ground.

"You're not seriously considering getting into that thing?" Newbury said from somewhere behind her.

Veronica didn't bother to acknowledge his question. Instead, she grabbed the arms of the machine and hoisted herself up, swinging herself into the operator's pit. It was uncomfortable and built for a man, but as she lowered her legs into the braces, she felt the power thrumming through the weapon. She extended her arms, sliding them into the hoops that would secure them in place, extending her fingers until the tips of them slid into the tiny thimble-like cups that would enable her to control the armour's claws.

She looked down at Newbury, who was staring at her from below with an unreadable expression. "Are you going to stand there, or are you going to finish helping me into this thing?"

Newbury blinked, and she saw the stirrings of a smile tug at the edges of his mouth. He stepped forward and took hold of the breastplate, swinging it back into place. It locked into its housing with a satisfying *click*.

"Stand back." Veronica flexed her arms, testing the movement of the device. It felt fluid and graceful, and responded to her easily. It barely felt as if she were lifting anything other than her own arms. "It's remarkable," she said.

Newbury jumped at the sound of movement in the passageway behind them. Veronica twisted around in her cradle. Another exoskeleton suit was thundering up the incline towards them.

"Get back!" she bellowed at Newbury as she lifted her leg and pivoted round, turning to face the oncoming machine. She braced herself for the impact.

The operator of the other suit began to slow as he saw what he clearly thought was one of his colleagues in the passage ahead of him, but he realised the truth when he saw her staring back at him from within the armoured enclosure, her face set hard.

He charged forward, raising his arms above his head as he stormed in, hoping to land a double-fisted blow from above. Veronica moved swiftly, however, raising her own arms and operating the claws to intercept the downward motion of the man's attack, grasping the arms of his exoskeleton in the fists of her own. She shook in her pit with the force of it, but she managed to hold him back.

The man worked to free his arms from her grip, but she held fast, straining with the force by which she had to cling to the controls.

Raising her leg, she kicked out at the other machine and connected with its right leg, just above the knee joint. The steel exoskeleton buckled with the force of the blow, collapsing in on the man's leg. Veronica heard his thighbone snap as he twisted and howled in agony, trying desperately to back away. She held on to the arms with all her might, keeping him from breaking free.

She realised that this was no fight to the death; all she had to do was find a way to disable the other machine. If she could leave it broken and stranded in the passageway, she'd be able to flee with Newbury without fear of it giving chase.

Veronica, issuing a fearsome scream, kicked out again in an effort to destroy the other machine's leg. She funnelled all her rage into the blow, all the frustration and disbelief and impotence she'd felt in recent days, all her desperation and worry and pain. To her satisfaction, the steel gave, twisting dramatically out of shape. The man's leg was utterly ruined inside the brace, and she saw blood spurt from multiple wounds, staining the ground with a spray of dark crimson. She felt a momentary pang of regret, but didn't have time to dwell on the matter.

Veronica reasserted her grip on the arms and pushed back, walking forward towards the other machine in the hope that her momentum would topple it over. The man tried to struggle, tried to hold his ground, but with his shattered leg he was unable to brace himself. A moment later the exoskeleton tipped over onto its back, taking the man down with it. He howled in pain and frustration.

Veronica backed away, watching the other machine clawing desperately at the walls, trying to find purchase enough to haul itself up. Its broken leg spasmed as the servos fizzed and popped, and the man called out in agony with every twitching movement.

Veronica didn't have it in her to finish him. She knew others would be along soon to help, and the wrecked, toppled machine would be enough to block their path while she and Newbury made good their escape.

Carefully, she turned the armour around in the passageway, unable to prevent herself from splintering another coffin in a nearby wall cavity as she scraped the sides of the tunnel with the machine's arm. Newbury was waiting for her up ahead, the bundled plans from the map room clutched in his fist.

"Run!" she shouted as she powered forward in the great machine, one foot after the other, driving herself on towards the surface. Plumes of dust and debris billowed into the air with every step. Newbury, shaking his head in disbelief, trailed behind in her wake.

CHAPTER

23

Enoch Graves sat before the fireplace at his favourite table, surveying the assembled mass of grey-suited men. They lounged about in their armchairs, sipping brandy and smoking cigars, lost in conversation, playing cards, or otherwise relaxing in each other's company. *Just like the knights of old resting before a battle.* He wondered if this was how the Knights of Jaffa had passed their time before riding into battle alongside King Richard, sacrificing their lives to bring enlightenment to the heathens. He imagined so.

Graves smiled with pride. Every man he could see formed a part of his flock. He commanded them all, and each of them was content in the knowledge that he would lead them to glory. Theirs was the noblest of causes, and he knew beyond any shadow of a doubt that they would prove themselves triumphant in the coming hours. He yearned for that time to come. His moment of glory could not arrive too quickly.

These moments sitting in the great hall amongst his men were the last calm hours before the oncoming storm. This was the eve of their sacrifice, the day they would take up arms and set in motion the chain of events that would topple the blasphemous monarchy that sat incumbent on the throne of England. Victoria's reign would end. He smiled at the thought of it. When his spirit returned to the Earth in its next life, a new time of prosperity would have settled on England.

Graves searched the crowd for Warrander, but could not see him. Most likely he was down in the armoury overseeing the eleventh-hour preparations. He'd always been conscientious—a pedant, even—unable to rest until he knew that everything was in its right place, all the preparations had been checked and checked again. Graves wanted to share a drink with him, to raise a glass in his honour, for delivering the means by which they would achieve their aims. Then he would return to the hanging room and carve out the tongue of his duplicate; a precaution against future judgement if he were to die in the forthcoming battle.

Graves reached for the bulbous brandy glass on the table and swilled it around, inhaling the heady vapours. He was just about to take a long draught of the spirit when he heard a muffled crash from somewhere across the other side of the hall. Returning his glass to the table, he stood, trying to see what the commotion was about. One of doors beside the staircase burst open, banging back on its hinges, and a man came hurtling through. He was dressed in the Society's customary grey suit and bowler hat, and he was screaming at the top of his lungs in panic, calling for everyone to clear the room, now, before it was too late.

Everyone in the hall turned to look at Graves simultaneously, waiting to see his response. The man stood there, alone at the foot of the stairs, panting and waving his arms in dismay.

Graves stepped forward and the men around him moved back to clear a path. He would publicly admonish the man for his cowardice, take him to task for attempting to jeopardise the great mission, and then order him to do penance by flagellating his duplicate in the hanging room. He was just about to speak when he heard another crash, this time considerably louder, and glanced round to the open doorway to see one of Warrander's armoured suits charging towards him from the passageway beyond. His mouth dropped open in a surprised gape. The driver must have smashed his way up through the catacombs, clearing a path through the serried rows of tombs to find its way here. He paced back until his legs encountered a table behind him. He drew his sword and held it before him, his hand shaking. The Hobbes woman, Newbury's assistant, was at the controls.

The armoured machine burst through the too-small doorway, shattering the frame and sending clouds of dust and rubble billowing into the room. Its massive steel feet pounded the tiled floor as it charged out into the hall, swinging its arms and batting his men aside as if swatting flies.

People scattered, shouting and screaming at one another, sliding under tables or fleeing up the staircase to get away from the crazed woman in the machine.

Graves saw Newbury emerge from the passageway behind

the machine, coughing and spluttering from the dust. Graves gripped the hilt of his sabre tightly in his fist and cursed. He couldn't allow the Queen's agent to get away—his escape would put their whole endeavour at risk. He would have to stop him. And when he discovered who was responsible for Newbury's release, he told himself, they would pay, very dearly indeed.

Wary to keep his distance from the rampaging Hobbes girl, Graves started out across the hall, making a beeline for the unsuspecting Newbury. The chaos would be all the cover he needed to get close to the man. He would run the agent through before the unbelieving fool even knew he was there.

Graves moved from table to table, trying to keep something—or some*one*—between himself and the armoured machine at all times. He had almost made it to Newbury when a grey-suited body, flung like a rag doll from the path of the stomping suit, collided with him, bowling him over and causing him to cry out in shock, releasing his sabre so that it skittered away across the tiled floor.

The world went into free fall, everything spinning, the chattering, screaming voices of his men growing louder, ringing in his ears. He shook his head, trying to clear the disorientation.

He was lying on the floor, a dead weight on his chest.

His head smarting from catching a table leg in the fall, Graves pounded the unconscious man with his fists for a moment before giving up and shoving him brutally to the floor. He scrambled to his feet. Too late, he realised he'd missed his chance.

The Hobbes girl reached down and snatched up Newbury

in the machine's fist, swiping him off his feet and lifting him into the air. She then charged at the far wall, bowing the suit's right shoulder and tucking her head low, preparing to smash through a tall sash window. In the machine's left hand, Newbury dangled like a child's toy, clutched between its claws and clinging on for dear life.

Seconds later, the armoured suit collided with the wall, causing the window to shatter with an explosion of glass fragments that tinkled to the floor like a shower of diamonds. Two swift kicks and the low wall had crumbled. Then the machine was through, out into the daylight and away down the street, the pounding of its feet echoing as it ran.

Graves felt the rising tide of fury engulf him. How *dare* they! How dare they do this! Not today. Not when he was so close to achieving everything he'd been working towards. He could barely believe it. He kicked the prone body of the man by his feet, so hard that he felt a rib crack beneath his foot. Then, realising he had no other options left, he clambered up onto a table and bellowed at the snivelling wretches around him to listen.

The surviving men, picking themselves up off the floor, snapped to attention, terrified to hear what he was going to say. But he would not berate them for their mistakes. Instead, he would galvanise them with a desire for revenge. "Gentlemen," he shouted at the top of his lungs, "prepare yourselves for war! We mobilise within the hour!"

A cheer went up around the hall, amidst the dust and the rubble and the spilled blood. Graves smiled. Perhaps victory was still within their reach, after all.

CHAPTER

24

"Madam, I am the Chief Inspector of Scotland Yard!" Bainbridge folded his arms indignantly and leaned back against the headrest of his hospital bed.

The young nurse, dressed in a flowing black gown with a white apron, prim white cuffs, and a matching mob cap, offered him the severest of looks. "I'm sure you're quite right, sir. But chief inspector or not, you've just had a rather large fragment of metal removed from your arm, and, if your story is to be believed"—she raised her eyebrows to indicate that she clearly thought it was not—"you've been threatened with explosives, beaten in a fistfight, and generally subjected to all manner of violent behaviour in the last few hours." She put her hands on his shoulders, gripping him firmly and trying to force him back down into the pillows. "I really do think it's best you get some rest."

"Bah!" Bainbridge muttered before finally

giving in and allowing the woman to win. He sank back into
the downy pillows and she smiled triumphantly, drawing the
sheets up over his legs. He knew she was right. He was in no
fit state for anything but rest. His arm was strapped to his
chest, and his eyes were both so swollen that he could barely
prise them open. His hair was singed from the flames, and
his legs, buttocks, and elbows smarted from all the tumbling
around in the hansom and the scrabbling around on the
cobbles. Not to mention the vicious beating he'd taken at the
hands of the ruffians. He'd been unconscious for hours and
his head was still pounding. He wanted to sink into warm
oblivion once again, to sleep away all the aches and pains
that plagued him. But he knew that wasn't really possible. He
had to get to Newbury, warn him about the Bastion Society,
and tell him to go to the Queen.

The nurse had told him he'd been babbling Newbury's
name when they brought him in. He'd been dragged across
town in the back of an uncomfortable ambulance and
dumped directly onto an operating table, still delirious from
the blows to his head and the loss of blood.

He didn't recall much of what followed, other than a bout
of excruciating pain as the surgeon pulled the shard of bomb
casing from his shoulder, and the spray of blood that accompanied it. He had swooned after that, and when he'd come
round, he'd been lying in a bed on the ward, his shoulder
strapped and his body alive with cramping muscles.

The first thing he said after the nurse had fetched water was
that he needed to speak with Sir Maurice Newbury. She told
him he'd been saying the same thing since he'd arrived, and
that they'd already sent for Newbury, and that he needed to

rest. She'd been feeding him the same lines on a rotating basis ever since, which had been over three hours ago.

Now, Bainbridge was growing impatient, and while he knew intellectually that there was little he could do other than wait at the hospital for Newbury, he hated the feeling of impotence that waiting inspired within him. He wanted to get out of there, to hail a hansom and head across town to Chelsea. He wanted to find Miss Hobbes and ensure that the reason Newbury hadn't come to find him wasn't because he was idling somewhere in an opium den, chasing the dragon and throwing his life away. Most of all, however, he wanted to feel useful, and his inability to do so was the most galling thing of all.

Bainbridge banged his fist against the side of the bed in a show of frustration, and the nurse gave a squeal of fright and ran for the door. She almost collided with another man who was entering the ward at the same time. He laughed amicably and stepped to one side to allow her to pass. "I should have realised you'd be terrorising the nurses, Charles."

Bainbridge turned his head at the sound of the familiar voice and tried to prop himself up on the bed, cursing as he struggled to support himself with only one functioning arm. "Newbury! Where the Hell have you been?"

Newbury strode quickly to Bainbridge's bedside, helping his friend to sit up. "Here, Charles, allow me."

Bainbridge gave Newbury an appraising look. He was dressed in a smart black suit with a freshly pressed white shirt, but he looked as if he'd dressed in a hurry. He hadn't buttoned his jacket and he was still wearing the previous day's stubble. He looked weary, but there was a glint in his eye that had been lacking for weeks, if not months. Perhaps he hadn't reverted to the opium dens, then?

"Thank goodness you're alright, Charles." Bainbridge saw the shock in his friend's expression, though he tried quickly to hide it.

Bainbridge coughed and tasted blood. He pulled a face. "I suppose these things are relative. I'm still alive."

Newbury laughed. "You had me worried for a while. Scarbright was waiting with your message when I returned home. What exactly happened?"

Bainbridge lowered his voice, conscious of the other occupants of the room. None of them seemed to be paying him even the least bit of attention. "The Bastion Society, that's what happened. They came after my hansom with some sort of portable cannon. Nearly blew me to Kingdom Come." He paused, drawing ragged breath. "I gave them a run for their money, though. Not bad for an old-timer." He smiled, and then immediately winced at a sharp tug of pain in his shoulder. "And you don't have to hide your dismay, Newbury. I'm quite aware of how I look."

Newbury frowned, concerned.

"You need to stay away from them, Newbury," Bainbridge continued. "The Bastion Society, that is. They mean business. I should have realised after that attack on Miss Hobbes. Whatever you were planning to do to bait them, stop now. As soon as I'm able, I'm going to send the Yard in. Graves is going to have some very serious questions to answer."

"It's a little late for that, Charles. I've just come from Packworth House, where I spent the best part of a day incarcerated and awaiting execution. Things have escalated beyond all measure of sanity. They're the ones behind the attack on the Queen, the intruder you told me about." Newbury spoke with an urgency that Bainbridge had rarely heard in him. "You're right about how serious they are. More serious than you could ever imagine. They're—" He seemed to hesitate for a moment before going on. "—they're planning to mount a full-blown assault on the palace."

"Good God!" Bainbridge exclaimed. "Good God, Newbury. So they're the ones behind it!" He sat forward, trying to ignore the pain.

Newbury nodded. "They've been secretly building an arsenal in the catacombs beneath Packworth House."

Bainbridge could barely believe it. The gall of them . . . of that upstart Enoch Graves. Still, at least the Queen was ready for them. They'd be no match for the Queen's Guard and the Royal Engineers Corps. "The Queen is preparing the palace as we speak, Newbury. Somehow, she seems to know it's coming. She's had the Royal Engineers fortify the grounds with all manner of artillery weapons, and she's tripled the guard. I've posted a security detail from the Yard."

Newbury nodded thoughtfully. "So the Queen knew about this?"

Bainbridge shrugged, and the gesture set off explosions of pain in his neck and shoulders. "She knew something was afoot. When I got to the palace yesterday, she'd already begun to make preparations. She claimed it was an obvious security measure, given the intruder, but I thought at the time that it was a little overzealous. She must have been warned, somehow. Or threatened. I'm certain she didn't know who was behind it, however." He rubbed a hand through his hair. He was so tired. "Now that we know, we can mount a preemptive attack. Get to them before they get to us, so to speak."

Newbury shook his head. "It's too late for that, Charles. They're moving as we speak. We have a couple of hours at most."

Bainbridge frowned. "A couple of hours? Then what are you doing here! Have you warned the Queen?"

Newbury gave him a curious look. "I've done my duty, Charles. But I'm no use to her there. There are others far more qualified to be at her side at a time like this. I'm an academic and a criminologist, not a military strategist."

Bainbridge nodded. He swung his legs over the side of the bed. "I'd better get over there right away."

Newbury caught his arm. "You'll do no such thing!"

"I—," Bainbridge started, but Newbury held him firm.

"Charles, listen to me. I've sent word to the Queen. If she needs us, she'll send for us. You need to stay in bed. There's nothing more either of us can do. You'll only wind up getting yourself killed."

Bainbridge gave a frustrated sigh. Newbury was right. He'd be no use to anyone in his current condition. He might even be more of a liability. He relaxed, and Newbury released his grip.

It occurred to Bainbridge that Newbury had come alone. "Where's Miss Hobbes?"

Newbury glanced absently out of the window. He seemed distracted. Perhaps the whole situation with the Bastion Society was playing more on his mind than he was letting on. "I left her at Chelsea. She has some things to take care of. She's been through a lot in the last few days, Charles. Her sister is terribly unwell."

Bainbridge tried to look sympathetic. "She's at the Grayling Institute now, isn't she? Fabian will take care of her. I know it."

"Quite," replied Newbury. "He'll most definitely do that."

Bainbridge wasn't clear what Newbury was getting at, but his head was starting to swim. He used his good arm to steady himself against the side of the bed. His eyes wanted to close. He'd been fighting to stay awake, waiting for Newbury to come, waiting to warn him about the Bastion Society. Now that he had, all the fight had drained out of him. Newbury was right. The palace was protected, and neither of them would make a blind bit of difference.

"Look, Charles, I want you to get some rest. Miss Hobbes and I will take care of everything else. You need to recuperate." Newbury leaned closer, lowering his voice to a whisper. "Have you thought about the Fixer, Charles? I could make the necessary arrangements."

Bainbridge shook his head. "No need," he said. A trip to see the Fixer, the agent's go-to man in case of medical emergencies, would be unnecessary. His wounds weren't that severe. "I'm alright, Newbury. Just tired and a bit bruised around the edges."

Newbury smiled warmly. "So be it." He glanced over his shoulder at the door. "I'd better get back to Miss Hobbes, make sure she and Scarbright aren't rearranging the furniture."

Bainbridge chuckled. "I wouldn't be surprised," he said. He reached over and grabbed Newbury by the arm. He was overcome suddenly with concern: for his old friend, for the

Queen, for everything he held dear. "It will be alright, New-bury. Tell me it'll be alright."

Newbury nodded. "It'll be alright, Charles."

"Good man."

Bainbridge allowed Newbury to help lower him back down onto the pillows. His eyelids felt extraordinarily heavy.

"I'll call tomorrow with news, Charles."

"See that you do," he managed to mumble, but uncon-sciousness was already beginning to steal over him. He lis-tened to the sound of Newbury's footsteps as his friend quit the ward, and then allowed himself to fall into a deep, wel-come slumber.

CHAPTER

25

Veronica crouched low behind a large rhododendron bush and peered out at the immense grey edifice of the Grayling Institute. Everything was eerily still. The sky was studded with brooding grey clouds, bearing the promise of rain. To Veronica they seemed like an omen, a threat of the storm still to come. It wasn't just her, either: the birds in the branches overhead weren't chirping, and the servants inside the house had appeared at the windows a number of times, looking out at the sky as if waiting impatiently for the coming rain.

Veronica realised she was holding her breath in anticipation, and reminded herself to exhale. She'd been in the same position for over half an hour and her toes were beginning to feel numb. The air was cold and damp. Close by, Newbury was kneeling in the flower bed, watching the driveway with an intense, unwavering gaze. She glanced at him and felt a surge of affection for the man.

After fleeing Packworth House they had abandoned the exoskeleton in an alleyway and hailed a steam-powered cab to take them swiftly to Chelsea. Once there, Newbury held a fleeting conference with Scarbright before changing his suit and rushing out to visit Charles. Veronica had feared he would also take measures to inform the palace about the Bastion Society. She'd been scared that he'd choose duty over any obligation he felt towards her, and scared of what that might mean for Amelia. She'd worried she might never be able to face him again if he made the wrong choice.

When he returned a short while later, he'd been pensive. He'd informed her that Bainbridge was alive and recovering in a police infirmary and that they would leave for the Grayling Institute in fifteen minutes' time. He'd told her she should gather anything she thought might prove useful, and pointed her at the hidden rack of weapons he kept in his study.

At that, Veronica breathed a sigh of relief. Newbury had clearly made his decision. There had been no discussion, no debate. At no point did he offer her any insight into his thoughts. But he had chosen *her* over the Queen, and that told her everything she needed to know. More than that, though, it meant he believed her about the Queen's duplicity. It confirmed her fear that there was something terribly amiss at the palace, because if there were not, Newbury would never have allowed the attack on the Grayling Institute to go ahead.

The consequences of such thoughts were too dreadful, too all-encompassing for her to give voice to at the time. But now, waiting in silence for the Bastion Society to make their move, it was all she could think about.

En route, Newbury had told her in hushed tones about the Queen's foreknowledge of the attack and how she'd already begun to fortify the palace. Veronica didn't see any way she could be so sure of an attack without knowing about Amelia's visions, which was the final evidence she needed that the Queen had played a part in what had happened to Amelia at the Grayling Institute. Clearly, Newbury felt the same way.

Veronica wondered what he had told Bainbridge, whether he'd disclosed any of this to his old friend. She suspected not. For all of his compassion and brilliance, Bainbridge would never have understood. He was too long in the tooth, too much in admiration of the Queen. He was a good man, and he was unwaveringly loyal. That was both his greatest strength and, on this occasion, his weakness. Whatever happened next, she hoped Bainbridge would never discover the truth that Newbury had knowingly put the Queen in danger. It would be enough to tear the two of them apart.

A shrill, high-pitched whistle, as if from an overhead missile, broke the silence. Veronica cursed softly beneath her breath for allowing herself to get distracted. The attack was starting. She couldn't see the missile, but the sound seemed to originate from somewhere just outside the grounds of the estate, beyond the gates at the end of the driveway.

Newbury glanced at her in warning. Seconds later, the lone projectile hit the roof of the building with a thunderous explosion that sent splintered roof tiles spraying into the air in all directions. Veronica ducked involuntarily. When she looked up a moment later, there was a gaping hole in the roof where the detonation had punched through to the attic space below. Yellow flames licked hungrily around the edges of the hole.

Before anyone inside the house had time to react, a dozen more bombs impacted, splashing against the building with a blinding glare. Suddenly the whole scene was a vision of perfect chaos. The sound of the explosions was like a hundred thunderclaps detonating at once, like the sky itself was being rent apart and all of Heaven and Hell was descending on the Earth. Veronica covered her ears with her hands.

A huge chunk of masonry, blown clear from the building in the fiery shower, thudded into the ground just a few feet from where Veronica and Newbury were hiding. It was all she could do not to cry out in shock as the ground trembled beneath her and she was showered with tiny fragments of stone and ash. She glanced up at the house. Part of the first floor had already collapsed, and the roof was now entirely ablaze. All the windows at the front of the property had blown out, and broken glass was spread across the courtyard as far as she could see.

She turned at the sound of a hundred mechanical hooves striking the gravel, and gasped at the dozens of men charging along the driveway on shining brass horses. Cogs and gears groaned under the strain as the clockwork beasts reared and charged, bearing their riders into battle. The men themselves were resplendent in the grey suits and bowler hats of the Bastion Society, but wore shining steel breastplates over their jackets, along with arm braces and leg guards.

The sight would almost have seemed comical, if it were not for the huge Gatling guns that hung off the sides of the mounts, burring and spitting a hail of destruction upon the house and its occupants. Many of the men also carried swords, which they held aloft as they charged, screaming bloody murder as they rode towards their target.

Behind this sea of brass and flesh, five of the armoured exoskeleton suits lumbered slowly, relentlessly, towards the house, their claws opening and closing in readiness. They planned to pound the building to dust and gravel, she realised, to leave no part of it standing. They would destroy everything in their path, ensuring all of Fabian's work—whether it was a living subject or a folio of notes detailing his treatment of his patients—was destroyed.

And all the while, bombs continued to drop from the sky likes hellish, fiery rain, creating a firestorm the likes of which she'd never seen.

Veronica saw movement in the doorway of the institute. She leapt to her feet, disregarding her cover. The figure emerging from the doorway was Amelia.

Veronica watched her sister rush out, barefoot, beneath the portico, charging headlong for the stone steps. She was dressed only in a flowing white nightgown, her hair a stark, raven black, trailing behind her as she ran. Veronica looked on in horrified slow motion as one of the mounted men yanked hard on the reins of his mechanical beast, pulling it round so that he could swing his Gatling gun around on its pivot. The weapon sang with a menacing whine as it spat hot lead at its target, and Veronica screamed as she watched her sister's white gown blossom with scores of bright, crimson petals where the bullets struck home.

Veronica tried to run, but Newbury was there, grabbing her around the waist, dragging her back beneath the cover of the trees, kicking and screaming. He forced his hand over her mouth to keep her from shouting, and she twisted and writhed in an effort to get free, all the while keeping her eyes locked on the body of her dead sister. She didn't want to believe what had happened; couldn't acknowledge it was over.

But moments later, through the veil of her tears, Veronica saw another figure burst out of the doorway, similarly attired. This was followed by another, and then another, and she realised with mounting relief that the dead woman wasn't her sister at all, but one of her duplicates—set free, she guessed, by the collapsing structure of the old house. A shattered wall or a buckled door must have allowed them to escape, and they flowed out in their multitudes like ethereal ghosts fleeing an exorcism.

Veronica relaxed in Newbury's grip, and he set her down. She watched his reaction intently as he saw swathes of the Amelia clones pour forth from the building, only to be mowed down indiscriminately by the riders and their mechanised weapons. Blood sprayed in wide arcs as the bullets shredded the defenceless girls, and Newbury's face hardened as he realised the peril the real Amelia was in. If they didn't get her out soon, she really was going to perish at the hands of a revolutionary or, perhaps worse, as the building itself came down around her shoulders.

"Come on," said Newbury, taking Veronica's hand and leading her around the back of the building under the cover of the trees, trying to stay ahead of the mounted men who were busying themselves with the hedonistic slaughter of her not-quite-sisters.

Veronica had already pointed out the location of the kitchen window. Newbury ran for it now, keeping a tight hold of her hand as they pounded across the courtyard, running through the middle of the deranged war zone towards the blazing inferno.

Gunfire rattled close by, and Veronica turned her head to see a mounted figure charging towards them, his sword held aloft, his Gatling gun spitting furiously as he swung it around on its cradle, aiming to mow them down as he galloped past.

For a moment Veronica hesitated. She didn't know which way to go. She knew she couldn't outrun the horse, and if she threw herself against the wall of the house, the man would have a clear shot at her as he rode by. But she wasn't about to allow this ridiculous man, this *pretend knight*, to end her life like that.

She turned and charged at the window, leaping into the air and burying her face in the crook of her arm as she dived at the pane of glass.

And then she was hurtling through the shattering window, colliding painfully with a butcher's trolley and sending plates, cutlery, and fragments of broken glass careening all over the floor. She skidded to a stop a few feet from the door. Behind her, Newbury fell through the opening, nursing his hand where he'd sliced it open on the jagged glass. Bullets from the Gatling gun rained into the room for a moment, and then the man and his mount were gone.

Veronica scrambled to her feet and checked herself over. Remarkably, aside from a few minor scrapes and a smarting elbow, she was unhurt.

The kitchen was already deserted. She guessed the staff must have bolted at the sound of the first explosion, probably hiding elsewhere in the house or trying to find another way out.

The kitchen behind her suddenly erupted in noise as the man who had been shooting at them outside aimed his Gatling gun through the open window and hosed the room with bullets, trying to pick out her and Newbury. Veronica kept low and wriggled towards the door on her belly, grabbing a steel tray and holding it over her head as a makeshift shield. The man's gun wouldn't pivot low enough to reach them on the floor, so he continued to hose the walls above them, meaning she had to watch for falling debris from above as she tried desperately to get to the door and away from the hail of bullets.

Seconds later the gun whirred to silence and Veronica was through the door. She glanced back to see Newbury right behind her. She helped him to his feet.

The hallway was in a atrocious state, with fallen chunks of masonry blocking a number of the corridors that stemmed from it and flames curling at the edges of the doors, spiralling plumes of thick black smoke into the air. The first floor above them had been almost entirely destroyed, and through the splintered, smouldering floorboards Veronica could see grey clouds hanging low in the sky, and the fiery trails of bombs as they streamed towards the building, causing the building to shake with every impact.

"We have to get to Amelia, now!" Newbury bellowed, and he set off down the hallway, ducking beneath a shattered beam as he led the way to her room via the route that Fabian had taken when he'd taken Newbury to see her sister during their previous visit. Veronica hoped they weren't already too late, and that she hadn't made a terrible mistake.

———

Amelia sat in her wheelchair by the fireplace and watched as the world came to an end. It was just as she'd seen in her vision, and she was prepared. She wasn't scared so much as resigned, ready to finally face the death that she'd been holding back for years.

She would have liked to see Veronica one last time. It saddened her that she'd never have a chance to share a kind word with her sister again or—perhaps more important—to thank her for everything she'd done. Veronica had sacrificed so much for her. She'd fought against their parents' prejudice at every turn, and, as a consequence she'd finally been cast out of the family home on a pittance, forced to take a job as an administrator at the museum and to spend what money she had securing an apartment of her own in Kensington. Amelia wanted her sister to know how grateful she was for that, the difference it had made. She was sure she had lived as long as she had because of that sisterly patronage.

Amelia glanced out the window. The once beautiful garden had been transformed into a blazing vision of Hell. The ancient gods, once standing proud in their evergreen vigil, had been reduced to nothing but cinders and smoke. She found it ironic that something so beautiful should be so difficult to create and yet so easy to destroy. She supposed that was true of life, too, and the fragility of it terrified her.

She had no idea why the building was under attack. She supposed she didn't really want to know. It was enough for her to know that today was the day she had foreseen in her visions. She was ready. And when Mr. Calverton came for her, as she knew he would, with his leering face and ghastly, piercing eyes, she would produce the poker she had secured in the folds of her blanket and she would defend herself. She didn't hold much hope of success, but if Veronica had taught her one thing during her short time, it was to fight. And while it wouldn't ultimately save her life, fight she would.

Amelia turned at the sound of her door creaking open. *So soon?* She had hoped for at least a little while longer. But when the man in the doorway stepped forward, she was surprised to see that it was not Mr. Calverton, as she had expected, but Dr. Fabian.

The doctor stumbled into the room, catching hold of the doorframe to prevent himself from toppling over. She saw he was badly wounded, his left thigh burned and bloody through a rent in his torn trousers. "Hello, Amelia," he said. His voice was reedy and high-pitched. He was clenching his teeth in pain, opening and closing his fists in an effort to stave off the agony of his wounds. He edged farther into the room.

Amelia was overcome with sorrow for the man. "Dr. Fabian! You shouldn't be here. Go. Get out, before it's too late. Leave me here."

Fabian used his index finger to push his glasses up the bridge of his nose. His expression was hard. He shook his head. "No, Amelia, you're coming with me." He sounded definite, commanding.

"No. I'll only slow you down," Amelia protested. "I'm dying anyway—we both know as much. You should save yourself. Your work is too important." She knew the likelihood was that they'd both die in the blaze if he attempted to rescue her, especially reduced to such an awful condition himself. At least this way one of them could survive.

Stubbornly, Fabian kept on coming towards her. "No, Amelia.

You're too important. Too . . ." He trailed off, gasping in agony as he forced himself to walk, dragging his damaged leg across the carpet. Behind him, through the open door, Amelia could see the hallway was fully ablaze. The stink of burning wood filled the air, and smoke boiled in through the opening. He must have staggered through the flames to get to her.

"Listen, I rea—" She stopped dead at the arrival of a second person, who burst in through a plume of black smoke as if emerging suddenly from the flames themselves.

The woman was wild eyed and dressed in a filthy white nightgown. She was painfully thin and her head was adorned with a spill of thick, black hair. Amelia had to look twice before she realised exactly who the newcomer was.

It was *her.*

The duplicate held its head back and screamed in wild abandon, a deep, guttural wail that bore more resemblance to the cry of an animal than that of a human being. Amelia screamed in terror at the nightmarish thing, and the strange, feral woman—who looked almost entirely like her—glared at her, drooling and swaying.

Amelia looked to Fabian, who was backing away from the duplicate with an expression of horror and surprise.

The other Amelia rushed towards her, grabbing her by the shoulders and shaking her violently in her chair. Amelia wailed as her doppelgänger gnashed its teeth only inches from her face. It smelled of faeces and soot, and its nails dug into the soft skin around her neck. She tried to push the thing away from her, but it hung on to her with surprising strength. She called out to Dr. Fabian, but he didn't respond.

Still holding on to Amelia, the doppelgänger's head lolled back, its eyes rolled up in its sockets, and it began babbling under its breath. "Cracking walls and fire and pain. Brass engines of destruction will tear down the world, and the man with the white face shall come out of the darkness. The one who sits in the chair. She is the key. She is the nightmare at the eye of the storm."

Amelia screamed. It was describing the contents of her vision. It was *impossible*. She wondered for a moment if she were already dead, if this were some sort of terrible purgatory, if she were hallucinating because of the fire, or because of her illness. She didn't know what to think. But she knew she had to get away from the creature, somehow. She couldn't bear to look at it any longer, with its dark, feral eyes; the way it screeched like an animal.

Acting purely on instinct, Amelia slapped the duplicate brutally across the face once, twice, three times, until the creature's eyes snapped back into place, its head rocked forwards, and it was once again glaring at Amelia with smouldering, animalistic menace.

Amelia raised her leg and jabbed her foot into the duplicate's abdomen. It doubled over, howling in shock, emitting a harrowing screech that chilled Amelia to the bone. It lunged at her, its nails raking her cheek as it tried urgently to scratch out her eyes. Amelia flailed her arms in an effort to defend herself, doing whatever she could to keep the crazed thing at bay.

Suddenly she remembered the poker she had hidden in the folds of her blanket. She grabbed for it, feeling its cold, hard shaft beneath the wool. With one hand she fought to extract it while using the other to fend off the mad doppelgänger as best she could. She wasn't strong enough, however. The creature batted her arm away and lurched forward, grabbing her head between its hands and squeezing, as if trying to crack open her skull with its bare hands. "Let the demons out!" it screeched. "Free the spirits! Save yo—"

The words turned into a gurgle as Amelia thrust the poker deep into the duplicate's belly. Warm blood gushed over her hands and knees. She sobbed as the creature continued its assault, still gnashing its teeth and attempting to prise open her skull. She thrust the poker deeper inside the thing, twisting it, trying anything to get it to stop. She didn't know what else she could do.

And then, as quickly as the attack had come, it stopped.

Amelia, gasping, peeled open her eyes. Dr. Fabian was there, struggling with the duplicate as he hauled it off Amelia, dragging it back towards the open door. The black shaft of the poker was still protruding from its belly, blood coursing down its legs, staining the front of its white nightdress. The duplicate kicked and snarled, gouging great scratches in Fabian's arms, but he held it fast, whimpering with pain as he fought to stay upright on his damaged leg.

With an almighty effort, Fabian pitched around and hurled the duplicate out the doorway and into the raging inferno. Amelia heard it cry out, and she caught one final glimpse of it as the hungry flames took to its hair, creating a halo of flickering fire around its head. Then it turned and bolted down the corridor to its death.

Amelia felt nauseated. Her mind was reeling, trying to process what she had just seen. She didn't know what to think, how to feel. She could hardly believe the atrocity she had just witnessed.

Amelia tried to get out of her chair, but she simply didn't have the strength to lift herself, not after the attack. Blood was streaming down her cheek in a warm trickle. She turned to Fabian. "You did this," she said, her tone accusing. "You told me you were trying to help me. You were always there for me, always by my side. I *trusted* you! And this is what you've been doing? *Copying* me! *Experimenting* on me! Turning me into a curiosity for your laboratory games." She sobbed, more out of rage than fear. "Was this why I was so important? Why you had to come here to save me? So you could continue with your disgusting experiments?" Fabian simply glared at her, his jaw fixed. "Get out. Get out of here, now!" She gestured towards the door, then wiped the dripping blood from her chin with the back of her hand. She would rather die in the fire than allow Dr. Fabian to continue to exploit her, to turn her into more perversions of nature like the one she had just encountered. That was a transgression she could never, ever forgive. A violation. An atrocity.

Fabian's face seemed to darken. His forehead creased into a harsh frown. He began creeping towards her again, but this time she knew it was not altruism that was driving him, but greed. "You ridiculous little girl," he snapped. "You ungrateful, snivelling wretch of a woman. After all I've done for you!" He limped across the carpet towards her, dragging his leg. "You're coming with me. You're my way out of all of this. You're the only one that ever worked."

Amelia knew then that she had to get away. Out of options, she flung herself out of her chair and onto the floor,

landing on her belly and jarring her elbow. She grabbed fist-
fuls of the carpet in her still-bloody fingers and began to pull
herself across the ground, trying desperately to get away
from the monster that had once been Dr. Fabian. She could
barely believe it was the same man who had been so kind to
her, who had helped her through her seizures and spent long
hours in the chair beside her bed, ensuring she was safe. *Protecting his investment,* she realised with a sense of dawning
horror. It was all pretence, every moment of it. The very
thought of it made her skin crawl.

Ahead, Amelia could see the French doors that looked out
over the garden. They were locked, as they had always been
locked, and Amelia realised that she really *had* been contained in a prison, and that Veronica had been kept away
purely to prevent her from discovering the truth. She'd been
a fool to fall for it, for Fabian's false charms. All along, the
locked doors should have told her what was going on. Nevertheless, locked or not, the French doors were her only hope
of freedom. If she could get to them, she might be able to
smash them and climb out.

Just as her fingertips encountered the glass, however, Fabian caught her by the ankles and dragged her away from the
doors, turning her forcefully over onto her back. She cried
out, and he grinned down at her from above, his face contorted into a sneer. She kicked out at him weakly, and he
raised his arm and backhanded her savagely across the face.
The pain was like an explosion in her head.

"Stay still, you little bitch!"

Amelia fought as he grabbed for her arms, trying to pin
them by her sides. She realised she was sobbing, tears of des-

peration coursing down her cheeks. "Get off me, get off me, get off me," were the only words she could find, and she repeated them over and over like a mantra. "Get off me. . . ." But Fabian had hold of her wrists now, squeezing them painfully as he forced her into submission.

"We're leaving," he said as he stooped to try to pick her up.

And that was when she saw the white-faced man over his shoulder.

Amelia screamed. Mr. Calverton was there behind Fabian, his strange, blue, unblinking eyes staring down at her, just as she'd seen in her visions. Any hope she had left dissipated at that moment, and she ceased struggling. She knew she'd never be able to fight both of them. It was over. She was about to die.

Fabian grinned.

Mr. Calverton, still unseen by the doctor, reached for her as if to help Fabian subdue her. Amelia issued a low, desperate moan. And then, through the veil of tears, she saw something she'd never even imagined in her dreams.

Mr. Calverton had his hands around Fabian's throat.

Fabian attempted to shout something, but it came out as only a strangled gurgle as Mr. Calverton wrapped his white-gloved fingers around Fabian's neck and used his thumbs to crush the doctor's windpipe.

Fabian kicked and punched and tried to prise his servant off him, but the man with the porcelain face was relentless. Amelia was chilled by the calm, detached way Mr. Calverton cocked his head to one side as he slowly squeezed the life out of the man who had made him.

She wondered what was going on behind the mask. Perhaps

the strange man-machine was seeking revenge, Amelia thought, trying not to look as Fabian's face changed hue to a bright purple and his tongue lolled out of his mouth. Or perhaps he really had come to save her. Perhaps all those times he had stood watching her, he had known the truth about what Fabian was doing. Perhaps he truly *was* more man than machine, and it was compassion that had caused him to come to her aid.

Mr. Calverton held Fabian at arm's length until the doctor's body stopped twitching and slumped in his grip. The wire-rimmed spectacles slid off Fabian's nose, tinkling as they struck the wall and smashed into a thousand shards. Then the man-machine dropped the corpse on the ground by Amelia's feet, its head banging against the skirting board with a dull thud. A second later, and Fabian was still.

Mr. Calverton turned to her and took a step forward, the pistons in his thighs sighing noisily with the effort. He held out his hand, and she reached for it just as the wall beside them ruptured with an enormous crack and a steel fist the size of a man's head came smashing through, colliding with Mr. Calverton and sending him sprawling across the floor. Amelia rolled to escape the falling debris. When she looked again, Mr. Calverton was trapped beneath a huge, jagged chunk of the wall, his mechanical legs twitching and sparking, blood pooling on the floor beneath his crushed torso.

Amelia peered through the fissure in the wall. A huge suit of shining armour was stomping away down the corridor. She heard another massive *crunch* as it struck out at another wall, causing a similar collapse, and then it was gone, disappearing through the flames. *They're trying to bring the whole house down,* she realised, taking out supporting walls as they continued to rain incendiary devices down on the building from above.

Amelia gathered as much strength as she could and crawled over to where Mr. Calverton was trapped beneath the fallen wall, careful to avoid the gruesome-looking corpse of Dr. Fabian, which was slumped nearby on the floor. Mr. Calverton's eyes were still open, staring up at the ceiling in startled surprise.

Mr. Calverton was in a bad way. Amelia couldn't even tell if he was still alive. He didn't appear to be breathing—but then, she wasn't really sure if he still needed to breathe. She kneeled before him, testing the weight of the collapsed wall. It was no use; she'd never be able to lift it. Reluctantly, she crawled over to where his head was lying on the maroon carpet.

Mr. Calverton's porcelain mask had fractured in the fall, and part of it had come away, exposing a small area of pink flesh around his mouth. She studied his eyes. Just when she was about to give up, she saw them flick around to look at her. He made a small, strange noise—the first she had ever heard him make—but its meaning was lost, muffled behind the mask and the sounds of bombing from outside.

Amelia could tell he was dying. The blood was still pooling beneath him, and she realised he must have fallen on something that had opened up his chest. She offered him a sad smile. Then, before she had time to talk herself out of it, she reached over and pulled away the broken mask fragments, revealing the true face of the man beneath.

She stifled a surprised gasp. The face was not at all what she had been expecting. Calverton had once been a handsome man, with full, pink lips and a small, slightly hooked nose. But the left half of his face was terribly scarred with a crisscross of long, puckered valleys. The flesh around the scars was drawn and pink, and they looked to her like ancient knife wounds, as if someone had tried very hard to flay his face from his skull. But what struck her most was his eyes: so sinister when seen behind the mask, but now frightened and human, and filled with sadness.

Amelia gently placed her palm against his scarred flesh. It was cool to the touch. Mr. Calverton opened his mouth and tried to speak again, but all that came out was a croak.

"It's alright," said Amelia softly. "I'm here."

He frowned, his eyes looking suddenly frantic, and he tried again to say something to her. She leaned closer, putting her ear to his lips.

"Thank you," he whispered, and then his body shook with its final breath, and he was dead.

Amelia, her heart rending, collapsed upon the body of the dead man-machine and wept.

CHAPTER

26

The house was collapsing all around Veronica and Newbury.

Veronica skidded to a halt in the hallway, glancing up frantically at the ceiling, which was groaning and buckling under the strain of the constant bombardment and the weight of the collapsed floors above. All around her, flames licked hungrily at the woodwork, and the staircase at the end of the hall was a raging inferno, the heat of which forced her back, her hands to her face. To her left, a section of the outer wall had been smashed away by the fists of an armoured exoskeleton. Through the gaping wound in the brickwork she saw mounted men still blasting away at the building with their Gatling guns, chewing up the architecture with each spray of bullets.

Veronica heard the scream of more bombs being launched, and felt the house shake with the impact of each volley. Within ten minutes, she was sure the Grayling Institute would be reduced to nothing but a pile of rubble. She looked to Newbury. "Which way?" she called over the noise of the ringing explosions. She hoped he could remember the way to Amelia's room in the midst of all the chaos.

"This way," Newbury replied, indicating a corridor that branched off from the main hallway. It was almost entirely engulfed in flames. He glanced at her, and she saw the steel in his eyes. He pulled his jacket off his back and held it over his head. "Here, like this," he said, and Veronica did the same, shrugging out of her small jacket and holding it over her head to protect her hands and face. "Are you ready?" he asked. She nodded. She was as ready as she'd ever be.

Together, they set off at a run, charging towards the flames.

The heat was incredible, and she was forced to dip her head, her eyes streaming. She charged on regardless, blinded by the smoke and the heat but running as fast as she could through the flaming tunnel, her clothes and hair beginning to singe and smoulder.

She felt someone throw their arms around her and she screamed, nearly bowling them over as she tried to get past. Her jacket fell, smoking, to the floor. She looked round, panicked, only to find herself in Newbury's arms. His face was covered in streaks of soot and he'd abandoned his jacket. "In here," he said urgently, and dragged her through an open doorway into a scene of utter devastation.

Veronica righted herself, leaning against the doorjamb as she took in the situation. The room—Amelia's room—looked like a war zone. Wreckage was strewn about haphazardly: chunks of charred brick and stone, burning fragments of splintered wood. On Veronica's left a diminutive man in a tweed jacket was crumpled on the floor, his face an obscene shade of purple, his tongue lolling rudely out of the corner of his mouth. This, she presumed, was Dr. Fabian. To her right, a large section of the wall had collapsed upon another man, crushing his legs. She realised with horror that it was the strange man-machine she'd seen in the room with the duplicates during her previous visit. Most disturbing of all was the sight of Amelia lying draped across his mangled body.

Her sister looked ragged. Her hair was awry and loose around her shoulders, and her white nightdress was covered with blood. The crimson stains looked stark against the bright white cotton. Her head was turned away from the door, and Veronica couldn't tell if she was breathing. She felt fear coil in her stomach, cold and uncomfortable.

"What have we done?" said Newbury, quietly surveying the scene.

Veronica felt panic welling up inside her. "Amelia!" she screamed, and ran to her sister's side, grabbing Amelia by the shoulders and trying to heave her off the dead man.

To her surprise, Amelia lifted her head and turned to her in shock. "Veronica?" she said, her expression one of pure disbelief. "Veronica? What are you doing here?"

Veronica laughed out loud. She pulled Amelia close, clutching her in a firm embrace. "We're here for you, to get you out."

Amelia shook her head. She was trembling. She glanced over at Newbury, then back at Veronica again. When she spoke, she sounded both relieved and anxious. "How did you know they were coming?"

Veronica tried to offer a reassuring smile. "Time for that

later." She looked down at the blood in Amelia's lap. It was all over her arms, too. "Are you hurt?" she said, suddenly panicked.

"No. It's . . . someone else's."

Veronica felt relief flooding through her. She glanced down at the dead man-machine and almost recoiled in horror. The flesh around his exposed face was a puckered mess of ropey scars. Beneath him, the carpet was thick with congealing blood. She looked at her sister quizzically.

"He saved me," Amelia said softly. "Mr. Calverton saved me from Dr. Fabian."

Veronica nodded. It was too much to process at once. Her mind was flitting from one thing to the next, trying to work out what to do. Her plan had extended only so far as getting inside the building, to finding her sister before it was too late. She hadn't yet considered how they were going to get out again.

"Can you walk?" she said to Amelia briskly.

Amelia shook her head. "No. Not very well."

They both looked up at the sound of splintering glass. Newbury was standing by the ruins of the French doors, holding an occasional table, which he then set down amongst a scattered heap of broken glass. She watched as he reached for an overturned lamp stand and began using it to bash away the remaining daggers of glass in the frame. There was their way out of the house.

Veronica looked out over the garden. Many of the bushes and trees were on fire, and the lawn was pockmarked with craters and heaps of scattered earth where incendiary bombs had overshot the house. Out there they risked being shot at by the mounted gunmen or blown apart by the torrent of bombs raining down from the sky, but it was still their best chance of escape. The house was creaking and groaning, and soon it would collapse. And even if the front entrance were still standing, they would be mown down the minute they emerged. At least this way they could dash for the cover of the trees and try to find a way out from there. It was a gamble, but it was one more gamble in a day already full of them. They had no choice. They were dead if they remained in the house.

Veronica caught sight of Amelia's wicker wheelchair. They couldn't take it—it would slow them down too much and prove too conspicuous—but it sparked an idea. She stood. "Stay here," she said to Amelia.

Newbury turned to look at her, dropping the lamp stand to the floor with a crash. "Where are you going?"

"Trust me. I'll be back in a minute." She ran for the door amidst Newbury's protests.

Out in the hallway, Veronica searched the floor for her abandoned jacket, but it had already been lost to the flames. The smoke stung her eyes and the heat was an oppressive wall that caused her to take a step back. For a moment, she considered turning back, but she steeled herself to press on. She needed to do this. She needed to protect her sister. Simply getting her away from this place was not enough. In a few days, when all of this was over, people would come picking through the wreckage of the institute, trying to ascertain what had happened. Veronica wanted them to find Amelia here in this room, dead in her wheelchair alongside Dr. Fabian. Or at least, she wanted them to find someone who they *thought* was Amelia. That way, they wouldn't come looking. It was clear the Queen knew about the clones. The monarch would no doubt arrange a cover up to ensure that that news didn't get out. But if they found a body here, with Fabian, still in situ in a wheelchair . . . well, Veronica hoped that would be enough to persuade them that the original version of her sister had also perished in the flames.

Wrapping her arms around her face, burying her eyes and nose in the crooks of her elbows, she bent low and ran for all she was worth. She cried out as the flames scorched and scalded her, licking at her ankles. Then she was through, out the other side and back in the main hallway, where the staircase had collapsed into nothing but a burning pile of timber.

Veronica coughed and spluttered, hacking on the airborne soot. *Which way?* She tried desperately to remember. It was almost impossible to get her bearings. The constant pounding was remodelling the house, collapsed walls and flames rendering entire areas of the lower floor inaccessible. Her instincts drove her left, and she ploughed on through the burning wreckage, hot ash searing her flesh where it kissed her arms and face as she ran.

Veronica threw herself around another corner, changed direction to avoid an impassable inferno, and ducked beneath a smoking beam that had fallen through the ceiling above and wedged in the passageway. Then she was outside the room where she had first found the duplicates.

The doorway had partially collapsed. The lintel and frame leaned jauntily to one side like a drunken old man, narrowing the opening. The wooden door itself had cracked under the stress and had evidently been smashed open from the inside. Splinters of it lay on the ground by her feet. What was left of it was hanging open on one hinge, swaying slowly back and forth.

Veronica approached the room and peered inside. Everything was dark. With trepidation, she crossed the threshold, sidestepping to pass through the now narrow opening. Every instinct told her to turn and run, but she knew she had no choice. She didn't have any time to waste.

Veronica's eyes slowly adjusted to the gloom. The lamps had been extinguished and the only illumination now came from the flames in the hallway, which cast everything in sharp relief. The dancing shadows gave everything a strange sense of movement. She heard breathing in the darkness towards the back of the room and realised some of the duplicates were still there. Perhaps they were afraid, preferring the comfort of darkness to the horror of the real world beyond the door. She couldn't blame them for that. All they had ever known was darkness and pain and torment. They were nothing but animals, cowering in the night.

Veronica searched the shadows but couldn't see any of them. If they remained there, they were going to die. She wondered if she should do something, try to shoo them out into the burning house, but she knew they'd die there, too, either in the flames or by the Gatling guns. There was nothing she could do. She forced herself to remember that they weren't her sister—weren't even *people,* in the truest sense—and that she couldn't save them. Amelia—the *real* Amelia—was waiting with Newbury, and that was the only thing that mattered. Besides, she didn't know if she even *wanted* to save the duplicates. She felt horribly conflicted about the fact that they even existed at all.

A pile of wreckage lay in the centre of the room. As Veronica walked towards it, she realised it marked what remained of the strange spinning machine she had seen during her last visit. Clearly, the duplicates had rebelled. Cogs, pistons, and metal brackets were scattered all over the floor, and the wheel itself, now devoid of its incumbent clone, had been broken in half, the two halves balanced in the top of the pile so that they jutted out like obscure totems. The weird occult runes that had been daubed around the edges of the wheel added to the impression, as if imbuing the sculpture with an eerie supernatural significance.

Nearby, the figure in the chair was still in situ, strapped, unmoving, as it had been a couple of days earlier. Now, however, it was clearly dead, slumped with its head resting awkwardly to one side. Its eyes were still open and they caught the reflected firelight. Its teeth were bared in a rictus snarl. Veronica shuddered and approached it, careful not to present her back to the murmuring shadows.

She tried not to look at its face as she set about releasing the cuffs. The flesh was icy cold to the touch. She had no idea how long the thing had been dead; she didn't share Newbury's ability to discern such things. Nevertheless, it would serve her purpose.

Veronica finished unbuckling the leather cuffs and slid her arms beneath the ghoulish cadaver, hefting it up into her arms. It was lighter than she'd imagined. She kept the face turned away from her, and she tried not to think about the smell.

She heard the creatures—she was still steadfastly refusing to think of them as anything else—begin shuffling about and mewling as they watched her take a few steps back with the body in her arms. "Go on, get out of here!" she shouted at them, but all she heard in response was a frightened chatter and a wail.

Veronica backed up to the doorway and then, realising she'd be unable to simply carry the cadaver through the narrow opening, dropped to her haunches, lying the body on the ground. She then sidestepped through the doorway into the corridor before dropping to her knees and dragging the corpse out behind her by its feet.

Seconds later she was running down the burning passageways again, the duplicate clutched to her, its head flopping about with her movements. All the while, explosives continued to rain down upon the building, shaking what was left of the structure to its very foundations.

She had no idea how long she'd been gone, but when she finally returned to Amelia's room, tufts of her hair smoking and streaks of soot on her face, there was no sign of Newbury or her sister. Frowning, Veronica struggled over to the empty wheelchair and slid the cadaver from her grip, lowering it unceremoniously into the chair. Once there, she propped it up as best she could and stepped back, admiring her handiwork.

She supposed it wouldn't fool someone who took the time to seriously examine the body, but anyone searching through the wreckage in a few days' time would likely find a charred corpse that looked remarkably like her sister, sitting in the remains of a wheelchair a few feet from the corpse of Dr. Fabian.

It would do. It would *have* to do.

There was a momentary lull in the intensity of the bombardment and Veronica caught the sound of a man's voice, carried in from somewhere just outside the shattered French doors. She stepped gingerly over Fabian's body and approached the doors, peering out cautiously into the garden beyond.

Newbury was standing on the patio with Amelia draped in his arms. Before them, sitting astride a gleaming clockwork warhorse, was Enoch Graves. He was dressed like the others, with a neat bowler hat atop his head, a grey suit, and a breastplate of shining steel. He held the red-crossed flag of Saint George in one hand, fluttering in the breeze atop a gilded staff, as if declaring his intent to embrace the old ways of his mother country. The other hand he used to brandish a Gatling gun in Newbury's direction. His voice was low enough that Veronica couldn't discern his words, but she could tell from the glibness of his tone and his wry smile that he was gloating at Newbury. She knew immediately that he intended to let loose with the weapon as soon as he finished his speech.

There was nothing Newbury could do about it, either. With Amelia in his arms he had no chance of even attempting to tackle Graves, and any sudden moves would certainly result in death. At this range, the Gatling gun would shred both him and Amelia apart in seconds.

Veronica stepped back from view, careful not to crunch the fragments of broken glass beneath her feet and draw attention to herself. She felt her temper flare. *How* dare *he!*

She wasn't about to let Graves ruin everything now.

Veronica hitched up her skirt, revealing her milky white thigh beneath her petticoat. There, held in a leather harness just above her right knee, was a long-bladed knife. She drew it slowly from its sheath and clutched it in her right fist, the blade pointed at the floor like a dagger.

Veronica took a deep breath and peered out again, quickly this time, trying to establish if there was anyone she'd need to deal with besides Graves. There didn't appear to be. She ran through the sequence of possible events in her mind. It was going to be risky. One false move and Graves's trigger finger would twitch and spray Newbury and Amelia with bullets. But she had to try—it was this or nothing.

Veronica ducked back into Amelia's room, treading carefully so as not to inadvertently give herself away. She stayed low as she dashed through the door and along the passageway, trying not to breathe in the thick wreaths of cloying smoke.

The door to the neighbouring room was already on fire. Standing back, she used her heel to kick it open. It shuddered and swung back in the frame, dripping sparks. The fire hadn't yet spread to the room beyond, but it was nevertheless a scene of violent devastation. The French doors had been shattered by a torrent of Gatling gun fire, which in turn had chewed up all the furniture inside the room as well as the occupant, one of Fabian's patients, an old woman who was now sprawled facedown on the hearth, an arc of dripping blood decorating the wall above her.

Veronica averted her eyes from the dead woman's back as she crept towards the garden.

As she'd anticipated, the doors here let out onto the patio behind where Graves's warhorse was standing, stamping its foot in an impatient gesture reminiscent of its real, flesh-and-blood counterparts. All she had to do now was creep out through the broken doors, sneak up on Graves unseen and unheard, and jam the blade beneath his rib cage, through the small gap in his plate armour just behind the breastplate.

Graves, thankfully, was still orating down upon Newbury, who was in turn keeping him talking, prompting him with questions and encouraging him to elaborate. She imagined Newbury was anxiously anticipating her return, hopeful she'd be enough of a distraction to give him a chance to do something. Well, she'd certainly do that.

With the utmost care, Veronica wriggled out through the shattered remains of the French doors, finding her footing on the flagstones beyond. She glanced quickly in the other direction, reassuring herself that the coast was clear. Then, clutching the knife tightly in her fist, she padded forward towards the mechanical beast and its rider.

"This, Newbury, is only the beginning. We shall build England anew, return her to her former glories. We shall placate the infidel and the Empire shall once again cover the globe!" Graves was spouting his grand rhetoric, the words of a would-be dictator. The words that would be his undoing.

Veronica appraised the situation. She was going to have to jump to strike the blow; the saddle Graves sat on was above her shoulder, meaning he was higher still. To reach him she'd need to pull herself up, her arm extended, and ensure her aim was true. If she missed and struck the breastplate or back plate instead, everything would be over.

She manoeuvred herself carefully around the side of the horse. Thankfully, Graves seemed to be lost to the vagaries of his speech and didn't appear to be paying attention to anything other than himself. As she drew closer, however, Newbury caught sight of her and his eyes involuntarily widened in surprise. Graves saw his reaction, too, and began to twist around in his saddle, breaking off from his sermon. "What—?"

But Veronica was too fast. She took two strides forward, grabbed hold of Graves's leg for purchase, and propelled herself into the air, her right hand guiding the blade in an arc. She heard Graves call out in surprise and confusion, raising his arm in an attempt at defence, and then the knife hit home, glancing off the edge of the breastplate and burying itself deep in his side.

Graves screamed in agony and Veronica twisted the handle, thrusting up with all the power she had left in her body. Graves batted at her with his fist, but she continued to drive the blade deeper, twisting it and turning it to maximise the damage, ignoring the blows that were raining down on her back and shoulders.

A second later Newbury was at her side, grappling with the flailing man, trying to pin him in place. The flagstaff fell to the floor as Graves brought his other fist around in a powerful hook, striking Newbury hard across the face, but the knife had already done its work, and Graves didn't have the strength in him to keep up the battle. Newbury, shaking his head to clear the effects of the blow, caught hold of Graves's arm and hauled with all his might, dragging the man from the saddle. Veronica rushed to help him, and, a second later, pulled down by the weight of his own plate armour, Graves slipped from the mechanical horse and fell hard against the flagstones.

Veronica heard a terrible crack as Graves hit the stones

headfirst. She looked round to see his body slumped by the horse's hooves, the neck snapped so that the head was staring up at the house from an unusual angle. Blood was trickling from the nostrils. His bowler hat had come to settle a few feet away in a brackish puddle. She felt relief course through her body and realised she was trembling.

Newbury put his arm around her shoulders. "Thank you," he said quietly. "Are you alright?"

She nodded. She had no time to think about what she had done. "Where's Amelia?"

Newbury led her around the front of the clockwork stallion, which was waiting, motionless, as if somehow lost without its rider. Her sister was sitting on the edge of the lawn, watching her with panicked eyes. She looked incredibly pale in the dull afternoon light.

"Where did you go, Veronica?" she said urgently. "You left us!"

"I had to take care of something," Veronica replied pointedly. She looked back at the Grayling Institute as the roof finally gave way, caving in on what remained of the building. Black smoke was billowing out of the windows, and hot ash filled the air like winter snow. The explosions had come to a stop. She wiped her face on her sleeve and realised the futility of the gesture when she saw how filthy her clothes were.

"We don't have much time," said Newbury, glancing nervously along the garden to where the rest of the mounted men would be waiting around the corner. "We have to find a way out of here before they find us."

Veronica glanced at the crumpled body of Enoch Graves, and then at the mechanical warhorse over Newbury's shoulder. "I think I know just the thing," she said, unable to contain her smile.

Newbury followed her gaze and caught her meaning almost immediately. He returned her grin. "Come on!" he said, rushing to collect Amelia.

Together, Veronica and Newbury hoisted Amelia up into the saddle of the bizarre steed. It stirred to life beneath her, activated by the weight of a new mount. Its glass eyes blazed a deep crimson, and its internal mechanisms began to whirr and hum.

Newbury cupped his hands to create a step for Veronica, and she leapt up behind Amelia, allowing Newbury to pull himself up at the controls. He briefly fumbled with a brass lever, and then the machine kicked into motion, lurching forward and nearly sending them all sprawling to the ground.

"Hang on!" Newbury yelled back at her, before pressing a series of buttons hidden in the crease of the beast's brass mane. Then they were off again, this time breaking into a steady gallop. Veronica held on to Amelia as Newbury guided the clockwork beast around the corner, reaching for the Gatling gun on the pivot by his left leg. He swung it up into position, depressing the trigger just as they burst out onto the driveway, showering the small army of mounted men with a vicious spray of bullets.

The projectiles pinged off their steel armour, but Veronica saw a number of them slump forward in their saddles, caught by the shower of metal cases, blood coursing from numerous impact wounds in their faces. A few of them managed to raise their weapons and return fire, but it was already too late.

Newbury, Veronica, and Amelia charged away down the driveway on their stolen mount, leaving the crumbling, smoking pile of the Grayling Institute—and the now-leaderless warriors of the Bastion Society—far behind them.

CHAPTER

27

THREE DAYS LATER

Veronica was tired of the rain.

She was tired of the vicar and his inexorable preaching, and she was tired of all the subterfuge and lies. She was tired, too, of her parents, who had done nothing but patronise her since their arrival at the church, showing nothing in the way of real compassion or grief. Their youngest daughter was dead as far as they were concerned, and all they seemed able to display was relief. To Veronica it was the most appalling show of their inhumanity. In many ways, it demonstrated to her mind that they were no better than Fabian, or Enoch Graves, or even the Queen. She felt herself welling up in frustration, and she let the tears come. It was a cathartic release, and it helped create the illusion of reality, giving the paltry crowd the impression that her sister's funeral was not the sham that she and Newbury knew it to be.

The intervening days had been trying. Veronica had been summoned to the palace to be informed by the Queen herself of her sister's apparent death. She had displayed all the appropriate shock and grief at the news, and listened in appalled fascination to the Queen's explanation of what had occurred at the Grayling Institute. But she'd barely been able to look at the monarch, and was thankful for the gloom in which the Queen lurked like a predatory spider. It kept Veronica from having to look upon the woman's face, or see the sneer she imagined Victoria to be wearing as she lied about what had happened, and how sorry she was for Veronica's loss.

Throughout the entire interview, the main thought she'd had running through her mind had been that the woman in front of her was going to die. The reign of Victoria would be coming to an end when her life-preserving machines failed without Fabian's ministrations, and, Veronica thought, she deserved it. She deserved all of it. Victoria had earned Veronica's distrust, her disrespect, and her scorn. She had played a fundamental part in Amelia's misery, and for that, Veronica could never forgive her. She only hoped the woman's death would come swiftly, and soon.

Veronica glanced over at Bainbridge, who stood by the edge of the grave, huddled against the rain and leaning on his cane, his legs wreathed in mist. She felt a pang of remorse at being unable to talk to him about what had really occurred, to tell him the truth about Amelia; at having to keep yet more secrets from someone she cared about. And that, also, was down to the Queen. But she knew Bainbridge wouldn't understand. At least, not until he had seen the Queen for what she really was.

Bainbridge had been in Her Majesty's service for nearly twenty years, through thick and thin, and Veronica simply didn't think he could accept the truth. Earlier that year he'd been confronted by the reality of the Queen's machinations when he'd discovered the truth about William Ashford, a former agent who had been rebuilt by Fabian to live a life of painful servitude to the Queen, and although it had damaged his confidence for a time, he had soon convinced himself that the Queen must have been working for the good of the country. Perhaps that's what he had to believe to stop himself from going mad. Veronica didn't think any less of him for that.

On the other hand, she found the entire matter much harder to stomach. She'd come to believe that the Queen acted only for the benefit of herself and her regime, and that she, Newbury, and Bainbridge, along with all the other agents, had been working only to forward those ends. If the Queen had a master plan, it didn't involve a great deal of altruism.

Veronica watched the six pallbearers lower the coffin into the ground. She was still weeping, and the rain was thrashing her, soaking her clothes, and plastering her hair across her face. But she didn't mind. She hoped, in some way, that the rain could wash away all the fear and tension and pain of the last few days. She wanted the rain to rinse away the doubts and the disgust she felt about killing a man, no matter who he was or what he had done. She wanted to bury all those feelings with this duplicate that everyone thought was Amelia, deep in the ground where no one would ever find it again.

She stepped forward, grabbing a handful of wet soil from the bank beside the open grave, and cast it into the hole.

"Good-bye," she said. She hoped that would be enough, but somehow she doubted it would be that easy.

Veronica caught sight of Newbury, smiling at her sadly. He looked smart in his formal black suit, even soaked through as he was. "Come on. Let's get you out of this dreadful rain, Miss Hobbes." Veronica nodded, and then Newbury stepped forward, wrapping his arms around her shoulders protectively. She folded into his embrace, putting any thoughts of scandalising her parents out of her mind. "Veronica. Come now, before you catch a chill. This place will do you no good."

Veronica rested her head on his shoulder and allowed the tears to come. She wanted to exorcise the spirits, to leave them here in this graveyard so she didn't have to carry them with her any longer when they left.

They stayed like that for a few moments, the rain pattering down against their shoulders. Then, without looking back, she allowed Newbury to lead her away to the waiting carriage. She climbed in, and Newbury stepped up and took a seat beside her, shaking out his hat and running a hand through his hair.

"Lead on, Driver," he called, and she heard the snap of the whip. The carriage rocked and the horses crashed into motion, dragging the carriage out of its muddy trench and away into the torrential downpour.

Veronica turned to Newbury, dripping all over the seats. "Thank you," she said, and then realised how horribly inadequate those words seemed for what she really wanted to say to this man. "You . . . I . . ." She didn't know how to go on.

Newbury laughed and cupped her left cheek with his hand, wiping away a tear with his thumb. He didn't have to say anything: His silence, and the look in his eyes, spoke volumes.

She leaned over and kissed him, pulling him close, the rainwater running down her face as she wrapped her arms around his neck. She wanted nothing more than to be with him, this man who had given everything for her. To be held in his arms, safe from the world and all its terrible tribulations. "What are we going to do, Maurice?" she said when they had parted.

Newbury met her gaze levelly. "I'll get well, Veronica. I promise you that."

She shook her head. "Not that. About the Queen; about Amelia and what happened."

Newbury's eyes drifted away from her face, gazing instead out of the window at the driving rain. "We can't resign our commissions. She'd never allow it." He sighed. It was clear he'd been considering this carefully. Veronica was relieved that he didn't seem likely to back out, to try to justify their position and argue that they'd made a mistake. Until now, that had been her biggest fear. "I can't see we have a great deal of choice. We have to carry on for now, at least. Until . . ." He trailed off.

Until she's dead, Veronica finished, although she didn't say the words aloud. They both knew the consequences of Fabian's death. And she knew he was right: They really didn't have a choice. The Queen was ruthless, and they would be branded traitors and hunted down if they so much as gave her the impression they doubted her motives.

"But can we ever trust her again?" she asked, genuinely unsure what she expected his response to be.

He shook his head. There was sadness and fear in his eyes. "No. I don't believe we can."

Veronica put her hand on his sleeve. "Then we'll just have to trust each other," she said, and she laid her head upon his chest, listening to the thumping of his heart as the carriage careened through the wet, cobbled streets towards Chelsea.

CHAPTER

28

So the intruder at the palace was nothing but a diversion, a red herring? A means of making us look in the other direction?" Bainbridge shook his head in disbelief. "It seems Graves was more conniving than even I gave him credit for." He tugged at his moustache thoughtfully. "But how did the Queen know about the attack? That's what puzzles me. And why was she so sure it was going to be the palace?"

Newbury shrugged. "I suppose we'll never know."

They were sitting in a quiet booth at the White-friars Club, Newbury's regular haunt, a place typically frequented by literati, poets, artists, and other associated vagabonds. The type, Bainbridge considered, who were loose with other people's money and even looser with their own morals. Or at least, that was how he saw it. Newbury seemed blind to the fact, and—as far as Bainbridge could see—actually seemed to *like* being surrounded by these people. In deference to his friend, he went along with it. And besides, the food was really rather good—and as Newbury had stated on more than one occasion—they did keep a shockingly good brandy.

Tonight, however, the place was relatively quiet, with only a few others milling about, drinking, smoking, and talking to one another in hushed tones. The general atmosphere was subdued, and Bainbridge wondered if it had something to do with the news of what had occurred in recent days. Sensationalist stories had appeared in many of the newspapers, holding forth with all manner of fabrications and lies. They were claiming that the Bastion Society had been a terrorist organisation opposed to medical progress and that they had laid siege to the Grayling Institute in protest against the new methods being pioneered there by Dr. Lucien Fabian. He supposed there was some measure of truth in that, judging by what Newbury had uncovered, but their motives had been somewhat inaccurately portrayed.

Still, he mused, at least the stories helped obscure the truth, which—to him, at least—was infinitely more distressing. That the Bastion Society had wanted to destroy the Queen, all the while claiming they were doing it for the good of the Empire, made little sense to him. The monarch was the glue that bound the Empire together. To destroy her would be to remove the very heart of the Empire itself, all that was great about England. He rather thought the whole affair had more to do with Enoch Graves and his delusions of grandeur than any sense of assumed duty or righteousness he may have laid claim to. He was as power mad as the rest of them, all the other madmen and criminals he and Newbury had come up against in their time. The difference was, he'd had money and influence. That was all.

Bainbridge took a long pull on his brandy and winced as his shoulder flared with pain. It was still strapped beneath his jacket, and he'd been grateful these last few days for the use of his cane, which he'd recovered from the police morgue after it was pulled from the belly of the dead man who'd attacked him. He still hadn't discovered the man's name, but he knew it was likely to be buried in one of the files on his desk, associated somehow with the Bastion Society.

He'd spent the last two days poring over those files again, looking for any details that might aid him in his investigation. Not that there was much left to do. The former members of the Bastion Society were all dead, to a man, hounded, caught, and executed by the Queen's agents, rooted out as terrorists and smote down. All but one: a man named Warrander, who had been found dead in his apartment, having slashed his own wrists in the bathtub. The whole thing had evidently proved too much for him.

Graves himself had been found dead at the scene, knifed in the chest, his neck broken. Bainbridge hadn't known what to make of that, but had settled on the notion that one of his own men must have turned on him in the chaos of the siege, or else one of Fabian's people had finished him off before being killed himself. He'd decided not to devote too much effort to finding out; the very fact that Graves was dead was enough for him. Whether the man's wild claims about rebirth and resurrection were true or not, he wouldn't be troubling anyone else in Bainbridge's lifetime.

Now, the chief inspector was engaged in weeding out all

the Bastion Society's connections, trying to discover who had supported them in their quest to destroy the monarchy. But he was finding their organisation had been built on smoke: every trail led to a dead end or a dead man, every address to a place that had never existed. He didn't know what to make of it all, but he knew the threat had dissipated, for now at least. There would be more like them in time. His lot, he had learned from experience, was a never-ending battle against the enemies of the Crown.

He glanced over at Newbury, who was nursing his brandy and staring vacantly at the fireplace over Bainbridge's shoulder. He looked better than he had in some time—aside from the scars on his face from where he'd fought the mechanical spider—but his eyes had taken on a haunted look. He didn't know whether it was due to his longing for the weed, or something else entirely.

"You were right about the duplicates," Bainbridge said, trying to provoke a reaction.

Newbury looked up. "What was that, Charles?" He sounded distracted.

"I said you were right about the duplicates. That business at the morgue, the things you said about Sykes. You were right. We found the room you'd told me about at Packworth House. All those corpses." Bainbridge shuddered at the very thought of it. "Dreadful business."

He'd walked into the room with Foulkes, and he knew the image of the dangling, eviscerated bodies would stay with him for the rest of his days. He couldn't understand what had driven those men to commit such atrocities. A sickness of the mind, no doubt. Nothing else could explain it.

Newbury nodded. "It's why they murdered Sykes. The real Sykes—the one you and I found at Cromer Street. He'd stolen his own duplicate and left it in a gutter on Shaftesbury Avenue, dressed in his old clothes. He was trying to trick us—to trick you—into thinking he was dead. He must have realised you were on to him."

Bainbridge sighed. "It would have worked, too, if he hadn't continued with the burglaries. I wonder why he did it."

"One last job before disappearing, perhaps? Most likely it was just an addiction, a part of his life he couldn't live without. Sometimes, Charles, a thing like that comes to define someone. They become so used to living their life in a certain way that, when the time comes for that way of life to end, they don't know who they are anymore." Newbury took a swig of his brandy. "Do you understand?"

"I think I do," said Bainbridge. "I think I do."

They were both silent for a minute.

"Do you ever doubt the Queen, Charles?" Newbury asked suddenly, before downing his brandy in one short gulp.

Bainbridge considered his answer for a long while. In the end, he nodded. "All the time, Newbury. All the time," he said, swilling his brandy round in the bottom of his glass. "But I have faith that she acts for the good of the nation, and that's enough. That keeps me sane."

Newbury frowned. "I'm not so sure anymore. All that stuff with Ashford and Knox . . . I'm beginning to think it was just the tip of an iceberg. The closer I get to the truth, the more I see things I'd rather not."

"Then stop looking," said Bainbridge. "Victoria didn't build this Empire without getting her hands dirty, Newbury. You must realise that. I've been working for her for twenty years, and I've seen enough of it in my time. I'm not as blind or as ignorant as you might think"—he offered Newbury a wry smile—"but you learn to live with it. You have to. You learn to accept that it's a necessary part of what we do. We *all* have to get our hands dirty from time to time. The Queen is no exception."

Newbury placed his empty glass on the tabletop. "I admire your ability to turn a blind eye, Charles. Really I do."

Bainbridge took a deep breath. "Don't be so bloody facetious, Newbury! You know what I mean."

Newbury nodded. "I do. I'm sorry, Charles. I'm just not sure if I can live like that."

Bainbridge sighed heavily. "Is there any other way? Do you really think there are people who don't? I mean, aren't we all part of something that, sometimes, we'd rather forget? That's just part of being alive, learning to cope with the horror of it all." He leaned forward, his hands on the table. "Better that than the alternative."

"Do you think so?" Newbury asked quietly. "Better to survive at any cost? I'm starting to think that perhaps that's the only thing that Enoch Graves got right."

Bainbridge shook his head. "Now you're just being maudlin." He could tell Newbury needed some time to mull over what had happened. Pressing him any further would simply incite an argument. He wondered how much of it was a symptom of his friend's abstention from the opiates—which, he had assured Bainbridge, he had maintained since his brutal, enforced withdrawal in the cell beneath Packworth House.

Newbury smiled. "Well, you have me there, Charles," he

said airily. He looked up, and Bainbridge twisted in his seat to see one of the wait staff making a beeline for their table. "Can I tempt you with something to eat, Charles?"

Bainbridge shook his head. "No, not tonight. I have an appointment with the Home Secretary for dinner."

Newbury raised his hand to wave the waiter away. He turned back to Bainbridge. He was smiling, interested now. "The Home Secretary?"

Bainbridge smiled. "Yes. Something about a bureau he's setting up. He's asked for my advice."

Newbury laughed. "Did you tell him how you felt about politics?"

Bainbridge chuckled. "I told him he could talk while I eat, and we'd see where that led us." They both laughed heartily.

"Have you any notion of what it's about, this bureau?"

"None at all," Bainbridge replied. "Although I'd hazard a guess it has something to do with this Bastion business. No doubt the government have got the fear of God in them now, having seen the damage a small bunch of upstarts like Graves and his friends could wreak. They're probably planning to send some sorry beggars on a wild goose chase, hunting down similar outfits all across the Empire. A fool's errand, in my opinion. I'll tell him as much over dinner."

Newbury raised an eyebrow. "Interesting," he said, but didn't elaborate.

"I've been meaning to ask after Miss Hobbes. How is she holding up after the business with her sister?" Bainbridge tugged on his moustache. He'd seen Newbury leave with the poor girl after the funeral, and hadn't heard anything of her since.

"As you'd expect," Newbury said rather cryptically. "It'll take her some time to get over the blow, Charles. She cared deeply for her sister, and the shock of what has happened . . . Well, she'll need some time."

Bainbridge nodded. "Absolutely right," he said, glancing at his pocket watch. It was close to seven o'clock. "Good heavens!" he pronounced suddenly, standing up and nearly sending the table flying. "I'm supposed to be in Whitehall." He bustled around, looking for his cane. "Lost all track of the time," he muttered under his breath.

Newbury fell back in his chair, laughing.

"Yes, that's right, you enjoy yourself at my expense, Newbury. You're not the one who's keeping the Home Secretary waiting!" He tried to sound scornful, but he couldn't keep the laughter out of his voice. It was good to see Newbury smile.

"Dinner tomorrow at Chelsea? Scarbright's promised to cook his famous venison again."

Bainbridge grinned. "How could I resist?" Then he offered Newbury a scornful look. "You're not keeping him, you know. A temporary arrangement, that was all."

Newbury laughed. "Whatever you say, Charles. Whatever you say." He rose and took Bainbridge by the hand. "Now go on, go and find out what the Home Secretary is up to. I'm dying to know."

Bainbridge gave a heartfelt "Bah!" before dashing for the exit, his coat still flapping over his arm. For the first time in a few months, he had the feeling that Newbury was going to be just fine without him.

CHAPTER
29

The rain was still pelting against the roof of the hansom, a constant, distracting patter that seemed to drown out the sound of Veronica's thoughts as much as the creaking and groaning of the vehicle. It had been raining for days now, a relentless downpour that caused everything to take on a drab, grey appearance. Or perhaps, she mused, that was more a reflection of her mood than the effects of the weather.

Veronica stared out the window as they trundled down the narrow lane, bouncing and jolting over the uneven road, little more than a dirt track potted and rutted by years of use. The rain was like a veil drawn across the world. Through it she caught only glimpses of the village, as they passed by rows of squat terraced cottages, the central green, the public house. Veronica was now a few miles south of London in a small village called Malbury Cross, which she had first visited three or four months earlier while investigating the affair of a clockwork scarecrow that had taken to hunting the local people through the usually quiet streets.

When the time had come to find a bolt-hole for Amelia, it seemed as good a place as any. It was out of the way, and—clockwork scarecrows aside—seemed quiet and tranquil, just the sort of place for someone to repair to while they convalesced, away from prying eyes.

Veronica heard a bird squawk loudly nearby and looked out the window, but could see nothing beyond the blur of raindrops striking the pane. The hansom ploughed on across the slick, waterlogged ground, and Veronica sighed and rocked back in her seat, feeling drained.

It had been a gruelling week, culminating in Amelia's counterfeit funeral, and the consequences of all that had happened were only now beginning to dawn on her. Fabian was dead, the Bastion Society was in tatters, and the Queen . . . Well, she supposed Victoria's days were coming to an end.

Most important, however, was the fact that she still had Amelia, and the burden of her sister's care was now Veronica's to carry alone. Newbury would help—of course he would—but it was unfair of her to expect any more than that of him. He'd already done so much, given up so much of himself to come to her aid. Now, it was down to her.

The hansom drew to an abrupt halt before a small thatched cottage. It was a pretty, picturesque little building, detached and at the far end of the village. It sat squat in the centre of an extensive, mature garden. Rose and holly bushes bordered an uneven flagstone path up to the front door, and smoke curled like grey ghosts from twin chimney pots. It looked inviting, even in the pouring rain.

Veronica grabbed her umbrella from the seat beside her and climbed out of the cab, dipping her head against the pounding rain while she struggled to put her umbrella up. It offered little protection against the onslaught, and within moments her skirt was plastered to her legs, soaked through to the skin. She felt sorry for the driver, who was hunkered down on the dickie box beneath a thick woollen overcoat and a black cap. He looked like a drowned rat. She paid him his fare, plus a few extra coins in an effort to compensate him for the long drive and the inclement weather. He nodded in gratitude, water dripping from his chin, and took the reins, cajoling the horses into action. The beasts' breath made steaming clouds in the air.

Veronica turned and fumbled with the latch on the front gate, eventually having to balance the umbrella under one arm as she simultaneously opened the latch and hefted the gate itself to force it open. The hinges squealed, and the rain stung her eyes as she ran up the path towards the cottage, leaving the gate hanging open behind her.

Veronica rapped on the door and then tried the handle. It was bolted from the inside. She waited on the step, pressing herself as close to the building as possible in search of any semblance of shelter the overhanging thatch might offer.

A few moments later she heard footsteps and the sound of the bolt scraping in its brackets. She heaved a sigh of relief in anticipation of the coming reprieve from the downpour. Hot tea and a towel were, at that moment, the two things she desired most in the world.

The door cracked open and a suspicious-looking face peered out at her through the gap. When the woman saw it was Veronica, she flung the door wide open and beckoned her quickly inside.

The housekeeper, Mrs. Leeson, was a short, rotund lady in her late forties, with a kindly manner and a prim and proper accent that suggested she had once seen better days. She wore her platinum grey hair scraped back in a bun so severe that the resulting facial expression was one of permanent shock. She had an authoritarian air about her that gave Veronica the impression that she may once have been employed as a governess or schoolmistress.

Today, however, Mrs. Leeson looked heartily relieved to see Veronica at the door. "Oh, do come in, Miss Veronica, out of that rain." She took Veronica's umbrella and busied herself shaking it out before helping Veronica off with her coat. Veronica stood in the hall, trying not to drip on the sea green carpet.

"I'll pop the kettle on, miss, while you make yourself comfortable. Miss Amelia is in the drawing room." Her face grew momentarily more serious and she leaned in conspiratorially. "I fear the seizures have been growing steadily worse, Miss Veronica. Very frequent and very violent. I know you warned me in advance, Miss Veronica, but I didn't expect anything like this."

Veronica smiled. "I understand, Mrs. Leeson. I'm speaking with a doctor tomorrow. Someone who will be able to help. He'll prescribe some medication and I'm sure that will make all the difference." She'd made an appointment to see Dr. Mason at the hospital in Wandsworth. She hadn't yet decided how she was going to broach the subject with him, but she knew he'd find a way to help. She was considering telling him she needed the medicine for herself, that she'd begun to have seizures similar to those suffered by her late sister, but the thought of lying to such a good man tied knots in her stomach.

Either way, her words seemed to appease the housekeeper, who smiled and nodded appreciatively. "Excellent news indeed, Miss Veronica. I knew you'd have the situation in hand." She clapped her hands together. "Right. I'll fetch the tea. And a towel, too, I'd imagine, judging by the amount by which you're dripping on the carpet!"

Veronica smiled, and Mrs. Leeson bustled off down the hallway towards the small kitchen at the rear of the cottage. Veronica tried to shake the worst of the water from her skirt, and then followed her down the hallway as far as the drawing room door. Pausing there for a moment, she peered inside.

Amelia sat in a wheelchair by the window, which looked out across the farmer's fields to the rear of the property. She looked pale and thin, but there was a glow about her Veronica hadn't seen in years. Perhaps it was the fact that, for the first time in as long as either of them could remember, she felt like she had a home. For years, Amelia had been bounced from sanatorium to hospital, gradually losing not just her strength of body, but her strength of spirit, too. Now, Veronica thought, it seemed like she might finally be regaining some of that lost strength of heart.

Veronica rapped on the door and stepped into the room. Amelia turned and saw her there, and her face cracked into a beaming grin. "Veronica! You're all wet!"

Veronica couldn't help but laugh. "Have you *seen* the weather? Of course I'm wet!"

"But you still came," Amelia replied, and Veronica walked over to stand before her, stooping low to kiss her gently on the cheek. "Is it done?" Amelia asked, her voice suddenly anxious.

"It's done. Everyone believes you're dead."

Amelia stared out the window at the rain-lashed fields and the dark smear of clouds beyond. But Veronica knew she was seeing something else entirely. "Even Mother and Father?" she said.

"Yes. Even them."

"How were they?" Her voice sounded strained, as if she feared whatever answer Veronica might give. All of the brightness Veronica had seen in her just a moment before seemed to have suddenly drained away.

Veronica felt a pang of guilt. She couldn't bring herself to tell Amelia the truth, of the look of relief on their mother's face as the pallbearers lowered the coffin into the ground. "Distraught. Sorrowful . . ." She didn't know what else to say.

Amelia turned to her, her eyes wide. "Perhaps we should tell them the truth, Veronica? Perhaps if they knew? . . ."

Veronica shook her head. "No," she said softly. And then more firmly: "No." She squeezed Amelia's shoulder affectionately. "You know we can't do that, Amelia."

Amelia sighed. "Well, I suppose being dead isn't such a disappointment." She looked up at Veronica and smiled, changing the subject. "How is Sir Maurice?"

Veronica raised her eyebrows at the question. "He's well enough. I think the whole affair has rather exhausted him. Being incarcerated beneath Packworth House put a terrible strain on him." That, she thought, coupled with the fact he hadn't yet reconciled himself to the notion that the Queen— the monarch he had supported and admired for so long— was likely to die soon as a direct result of his actions. Worse than that, though, was the despondency that had stolen over him as he'd grappled with the truth about the Queen's motives. That she'd been so fundamentally involved in Amelia's plight was a betrayal of everything he had held dear, and he was struggling to understand his allegiances and the new world order that resulted from them. Veronica was concerned that, if left unchecked, that despondency might draw him back to the Chinese weed. She couldn't allow that to happen, not under any circumstance whatsoever.

Amelia frowned. "Veronica, I know about the laudanum."

"You do?" said Veronica. She met Amelia's steady gaze. *Of course you do,* she thought. *You've seen it in your dreams.*

Amelia nodded. "How is he?"

Veronica sighed. "He's . . . he's bearing up. It's difficult. He doesn't seem to want to talk about it."

Amelia smiled. "He's a man! Of course he doesn't want to talk about it."

Veronica laughed, and Amelia joined her.

"He knew, you know. That's why we came to the Grayling Institute in the first place. He wanted me to talk to you, to see if you'd seen something in your visions. He'd been experimenting, dabbling with things he shouldn't have been. A mummified hand, laudanum . . . whatever." She waved her hand in a dismissive gesture. "He said that something dreadful was coming. And it was."

The blood drained suddenly out of Amelia's face. She went deathly white, paler than Veronica had ever seen her. She looked frightened. Truly petrified.

"My God, Amelia, what's wrong?" Veronica glanced over her shoulder, panicked that Amelia had seen something behind her that she'd failed to notice. But there was nothing there.

Veronica dropped to her knees before her sister. She put her hand to Amelia's face. Her skin felt cold to the touch. "Tell me what's wrong!"

"He saw it, too?" Amelia asked quietly, as if scared of the implication of her own words.

"What? Amelia, what's the matter? Are you talking about Newbury? What do you think he saw?" Veronica was growing concerned. Something was very wrong.

Amelia's eyes flicked round to look at Veronica, and what Veronica saw in them filled her with dread. She'd never seen anyone look so scared in all her life. She didn't know what to do, how to help.

When Amelia spoke, she could barely stammer out the words. "Veronica . . . it's not what you think. Whatever happened, however bad it was . . . it's going to get worse. Newbury was right. Something dreadful is coming."

"But what about the Grayling Institute? What about the Bastion Society and the duplicates, what Fabian was doing to you? Surely that's what he meant?"

Amelia shook her head. "No. That's not it. I've seen it, too, lurking at the edges of my dreams, always just out of focus.

Something horrible is looming. The future is already taking shape, Veronica, and I'm frightened."

Veronica clutched Amelia to her, hugging her tightly. "It'll be alright, Amelia. I know it will."

"No, Veronica. It won't." Amelia sobbed, and Veronica stroked the back of her head affectionately. "If Newbury has seen it, too . . ." She trailed off.

"Seen what? What is it?" Veronica frowned in confusion. "I don't understand, Amelia. What is it you've seen?"

"I don't know!" The frustration in Amelia's voice was evident, as if she were desperate to explain but didn't know how, couldn't find the words. "All I have is a single word, a word that's still there when I wake: 'executioner.' That's it. That's all there is. That and a feeling of utter dread." She was weeping now, tears streaming down her cheeks.

"An executioner?" Veronica tried to wipe Amelia's tears with the back of her hand but her sister batted her away. She wouldn't meet Veronica's eyes.

There was a rap on the door and Mrs. Leeson burst in, carrying a tray bearing teacups, a teapot, and a neatly folded towel. When she saw Amelia she hesitated, unsure whether she'd interrupted something she shouldn't have.

Veronica stood, beckoning her in. "Come in, please, Mrs. Leeson. I'm sorry if we startled you. Amelia's not feeling terribly well. If you wouldn't mind popping the tray on the table there, I'll look after things from here."

"Of course, Miss Veronica," Mrs. Leeson said, clearly thankful for the reprieve. She did as Veronica had requested, setting the tray down carefully and then beating a hasty retreat from the room, pulling the door shut behind her.

Amelia hung her head. "I'd hoped it wasn't real. I'd hoped my mind was playing tricks on me, after everything that Dr. Fabian had done. I wanted so much to ignore it, Veronica. But it's true. And it's awful. Whatever it is, it's truly awful."

Veronica slumped into an armchair opposite her sister. *An executioner?* For a horrible moment she wondered if it wasn't all to do with the Queen, if Victoria had discovered the truth about what had happened at the Grayling Institute and was planning to seek retribution. Would the Queen send someone after them? Could that be the executioner Amelia had referred to? She had no way of knowing. But she'd learned to trust Amelia's instincts, and the thought filled her with trepidation. *Something dreadful is coming. . . .* She shivered, suddenly cold. After all they'd been through. Hadn't that been dreadful enough?

Veronica watched Amelia as her thin body convulsed with tears and she curled up in the wheelchair, her face buried in the crook of her arms. Whatever, or whoever, this "executioner" was, Veronica resolved to fight it. Despite what Amelia had said, the future was still malleable, and if Amelia had seen something in it . . . well, that was only one likely outcome. It could still be altered. The vision was a warning, nothing more. Everything would depend on what they did next.

Outside, the rain continued to hammer against the windows. Veronica rose from her seat and reached for the towel Mrs. Leeson had left for her, dabbing her face.

She needed to talk to Newbury. His experiments might have to continue. And that, she realised, was a sacrifice they would both have to make.

CHAPTER

30

The audience chamber was shrouded in a blanket of impenetrable gloom, so dark that he had no real way of discerning the true size of the place. It might have been as small as his own drawing room or as large as a dance hall, but without a point of reference, without a light source to anchor himself, he had no way to be sure.

He supposed that was precisely the point. The Queen, he had been told, had a flair for the theatrical. He supposed she did it to unnerve her callers, to remind them of their insignificance, their place in the grand pecking order of the Court.

He peered into the stygian depths. There might have been a hundred other men in the room with them, or there might have been none at all. Not that it really mattered to him. He was here to see the Queen.

He had been there only once before, a meet-

ing that—as far as any official records were concerned—had
never actually occurred. He supposed he would have to get
used to that. It had been dark then, too. He'd hardly even
seen the Queen during the course of his interview. But it had
most definitely been her. That sharp, acidic voice, the sound
of Fabian's labouring machine: they were unmistakable.

The man could hear the machine now, wheezing noisily as
it inhaled and exhaled on behalf of the monarch, accompanied by the creak of the wheels as the Queen herself slowly
rolled the life-giving chair towards him.

He remained still and silent, partly to avoid a transgression of etiquette, partly in an effort to discern how well she
could see him in the darkness.

The mechanical chair drew closer and then came to an
abrupt stop. Still, he waited for the Queen to be the one to
break the silence. He sensed her close by, heard her chuckling softly under her breath. Then, a moment later, she spoke.
"Good day to you, Physician. We hope you bring us pleasing
news. It has been a . . . trying week."

"So I understand, Your Majesty." He hesitated, unsure of
the best way to deliver his news. In the end, he decided simply to spit it out. "It is done. It worked."

Victoria clapped her hands together in obvious glee. He
imagined her fat, pink face grinning evilly in the darkness.
"Is she here?"

"Yes, Your Majesty. She's here. I thought you might like to
meet her." He swallowed. His mouth was dry.

"Most excellent, Physician. Show her in!" He could hear the
anticipation in her voice.

"She is already here, Majesty. She is standing beside me."

So she couldn't see him in the dark, after all. He made a mental note of that.

Victoria laughed again. He heard the grating of a metal hood being lifted from a lantern, and then suddenly a bright globe of light bloomed into existence, stinging his eyes. They took a moment to adjust to the yellow glare.

When they did, he found himself looking upon the seated Empress. He didn't know whether to feel revulsion, admiration, or fear. She was everything he had been told to expect: Fabian had turned her into some sort of bizarre marriage between woman and machine. She was inexorably welded to the life-giving chair, large tubes jutting out from her chest, pumping air into her failing lungs. Bags of fluid hung on overhead frames, feeding her veins with whatever preservatives stopped her body from rotting. He would need to find out. He would take a sample of the fluids away for analysis.

"Where is she, Physician? We cannot see her."

He realised that the child, scared, was hiding behind his legs. He coaxed her out, leading her forward towards the light—and, he thought, toward the monster waiting at the heart of it.

He watched the little girl as she approached the monarch. She was pretty, if a little undernourished, with long dark hair and big, frightened eyes. If he hadn't known better, he would have said she looked around six or seven years old. But this girl had not been born of natural means, and had not lived for more than a week.

"She's a pretty little thing," said the Queen, making it sound as much like a threat as like a compliment.

"She has your eyes, Majesty."

The Queen emitted a wet, rasping chuckle. "You have done well, Physician. You shall be rewarded for your loyalty."

Victoria turned to the girl, holding the lantern high so that the child squealed and covered her face from the sudden glare. "Do not be afraid, girl. You must learn never to be afraid. Fear will be an emotion you inspire in others, a tool for achieving your aims. It will not form part of your own emotional vocabulary."

The man frowned at her words, and wondered, not for the first time, whether he had done something calamitous in aiding her in her machinations.

Victoria regarded the child coolly. "You shall be named Alberta. We shall teach you many things. You shall know glory and power, and you shall understand the importance of Empire. You shall refrain from knowing men, for you shall be married only to your country. One day, Alberta, you shall be Queen."

The child nodded, but remained silent.

"We have arranged a nanny for you, Alberta, and she will show you to your room. There will be time later to discuss your education." The Queen turned to look at him. "Take her to Sandford, Physician. He will make the necessary arrangements."

"Of course, Your Majesty." He turned to leave, putting a hand on the girl's shoulder as if to shepherd her towards the door.

"Oh, and Warrander?"

"Yes, Majesty?"

"There is a switch embedded in this chair that we require you to disable—a legacy of the unfortunate Dr. Fabian."

"Yes, Your Majesty. Of course," Warrander replied. "I'll attend to it directly."

He led the girl away from the seated Queen and into the darkness of the audience chamber. He felt a smile twitch at the corners of his mouth. A new era was dawning, and when the time eventually came, he'd have no need of a switch. Unlike Fabian, Warrander had never minded getting his hands dirty.

ACKNOWLEDGMENTS

My thanks go out to Stuart Douglas, Paul Magrs, Mark Wright, Cavan Scott, Nick Kyme, Mark Charan Newton, Lou Anders, Michael Rowley, Mark Hodder, Mike Moorcock, Scott Mann, Emma Barnes, Liz Gorinsky, Charlotte Robertson, and the many, many others who showed me support during the writing of this book. Most important, heartfelt thanks to my wife, Fiona, and to my children, James and Emily, for putting up with an absentee father and bringing me cups of tea and hugs when I needed them.